Swamp Angel

Colleen Boyd

SPENCER
HILL
PRESS

Spencer Hill Press

Contact: Spencer Hill Press, PO Box 247, Contoocook, NH 03229,
USA
Please visit our website at www.spencerhillpress.com

First Edition: December 2013.

Colleen Boyd
Swamp Angel : a novel / by Colleen Boyd – 1st ed.
p. cm.

Summary:
A teenage boy is saved from death by a swamp angel, and their
blossoming friendship teaches him the true meanings of courage and
sacrifice.

The author acknowledges the copyrighted or trademarked status and
trademark owners of the following wordmarks mentioned in this
fiction: 1984, Band-Aid, Barbie, Barnes & Noble, Chicken Soup for
the Soul, Coke, Converse, Daytona 500, Dollar General, Ford Taurus,
Forrest Gump, Gatorade, GameStop, Good Morning America, Google,
Hershey, Hulk, iPod, Jell-O, Mario/Super Mario Brothers, Pac Sun,
PlayStation 2, PowerPoint, Puffs Plus, Red Sun, Sharpie, Jeep, Story
of the Year, Styrofoam, Super Glue, The Godfather, The Hitchhiker's
Guide to the Galaxy, The Road, Vaseline, Velcro

Cover design by Lisa Amowitz
Interior layout by Marie Romero

ISBN 978-1-937053-77-2 (paperback)
ISBN 978-1-937053-76-5 (e-book)

Printed in the United States of America

For my grandparents, Tom and Karlyn Walsh.
Thanks for always being there.

"In all things of nature there is something of the marvelous." — Aristotle

Chapter 1

It's never fun to wake up in the middle of the night. Take me, for example.

I flip the light switch in the bathroom, flinching when the harsh lights flash on. With the gleam bouncing off all the shiny surfaces, I have to squint as I stumble over to the sink. I'm surprised that the mirror doesn't crack in horror when I look into it. My black hair is messier than usual, and another zit has popped up on my chin. Good job looking like a troll, Rylan.

Shivering, I turn the faucets on. I stick cupped hands under the running water and splash the liquid onto my face. In the mirror I watch little droplets snake down my cheeks. This was supposed to wake me up, but it isn't working. I still feel like bricks are dragging my eyelids down. My mind screams for sleep.

Gripping the sink, I stare my reflection dead in the eye. "Dude, it was just a dream," I tell myself. "It's not real, and it won't ever happen. Don't let it affect you. It'll go away eventually."

But that's the problem. I've told myself the same thing every time that stupid dream has woken me up in the middle of the night.

When would this horror show quit bothering me? I thought by now I would've moved on to having more normal dreams. You know, the type teenage guys like me are supposed to have. Like about girls. Even one dream about Melanie Sweet, the hottest girl ever to live in the dinky town of Roland, Florida, would've been perfect.

But no. For almost a month, the same dream has been crawling into my head every time I hit the sack. At first it was something I just shrugged off. Everyone has crazy dreams once in a while. But when it wouldn't go away and I began losing sleep, it got annoying. I tried everything to make the dream go away, from not sleeping to sneaking sleep meds behind my dad's and Grandma Babette's backs. However, nothing's worked, and I know it's only going be a matter of time before someone notices I can barely stay awake.

Shaking my head, I release the sink, turn both the faucet and lights off, and stagger back to my room. Like always, it looks like a hurricane has torn through it. Babette's life mission is to nag me about it until I clean it up, but as long as I keep my door shut I can get away with it.

I navigate around mounds of crushed laundry as I head back to my bed, a single futon mattress placed on the floor. Picking up the blanket I'd flung aside minutes before, I lie down. On the ceiling a bunch of cracks bend to form some odd, lopsided flower. I stare at it for a few minutes as I try to work up the nerve to go to sleep. But what if I have that dream again?

I look at my alarm clock. 1:27. I frown. Screw it. I'm wasting sleep over something that won't even happen.

"I'm NOT going to have that dream," I tell both the flower and me. Before what I've said can sink in, I roll over and close my eyes.

I'm standing at the edge of the dock. Behind me creaky wooden planks lead to the swamp bank. From there, the dirt path winds its way up to the house. For years I've walked it, traveling down to the edge of the swamp whenever I needed a place to think. But what am I doing here right now?

Confused, I glance around, but I don't see anything out of the ordinary. Then again, when you live with a large portion of swampland in your backyard, you begin to think anything extraordinary *is* ordinary. Giant cypress and tupelo trees grow straight out of the water, casting reflections on the murky surface. Sunlight peeks through leafy tree branches, dappling whatever it touches. Bright orchids and bromeliads add pops of color to tree trunks, accompanied by twisting vines and ivy. It can smell funny sometimes, but the swamp is one of my favorite places.

If I wanted to, I could sneak the boat out and explore. But a glance over at the berth reminds me it's not there. The boat hasn't been there for two weeks, ever since the old engine died.

Since I can't remember why I came here, I turn and walk down the dock. Just as I'm at the end, I hear a loud splash. I don't need to look back to get an idea of the source— frogs, waterfowl, or even gators. They're all animals I've seen before, so it's nothing new. But my gut tells me to check what's going on anyway. So I do.

Standing some distance behind me is the most beautiful girl I've ever seen. She's definitely ten times prettier than Melanie. Only an inch shorter than me—and I'm a friggin' giant—she has long, white-blonde hair with a slightly green

tint and pale skin. She wears a short sleeveless green dress that demands that I stare at her legs.

But it's not her figure that gets my attention. It's her eyes. Calm, pale green orbs, set into a doll's face, look right at me. I don't know what it is, but something about them makes me wanna gawk.

"Um…hi," I say, my throat dry from the appearance of this goddess.

She doesn't speak.

I try a different approach. "What's your name?"

Still nothing.

"If you want a tour, the boat's in the repair shop. You're going to have to wait," I explain, pointing over at the empty dock spot.

Once again she stays silent. Now I'm concerned.

"Are you okay?" I walk over until I'm standing right in front of her. Slowly, so I don't spook her, I gingerly touch her forearm. "Is something wrong?"

She finally moves as she wraps me in her arms, hugging me. What the—I don't know her! Hasn't she heard of stranger danger? I mean, I'm not gonna hurt her, but who does this? At first I don't know what to do other than to push her off. But then I realize—a hot girl's hugging me. She feels cozy and soft, like sunlight. She's also shaking, like she's upset or something. Did she hug me to feel better? I don't want to let the feeling go, and I don't want her to feel bad, so I return the favor, wrapping my arms around her.

But then her warmth is gone. Her skin bubbles feverishly as it turns a light shade of green. The pupils of her eyes thin to slits, like those of a cat, and her elongating nails dig into my skin. Horrified, I want to let go and run. But I can't. I literally can't move. I'm frozen in a hug with a monster.

The monster leans back and stares at me. Her new, dark-green hair hangs in her face and bunches around her sharp horns. But despite the hair curtain, I can still see where her mouth is. Or, at least, where it should be. Large leaves cover her lower face like a surgeon's mask. I shake with fear. The last thing I'll ever see is her removing that mask to eat my face.

No. Instead the complete opposite happens. Cool lips brush against my cheek as she kisses me through the leaves. Moving her mouth next to my ear, she finally speaks. Her voice is like the wind: it's loud at one moment, barely audible the next. What she murmurs with that voice, however, strikes me to the core.

"I am…forever watching…"

And then she collapses, turning into strings of ivy that wrap around my body, trapping me, choking me…

Suddenly I'm flying up in my bed. My blanket is twisted around me like a pretzel. Liquid ice sweat covers my body, and I can't stop panting as my heart races like a car going around the Daytona 500. I look around to find that I'm still in my room, and it's still dark outside. Snatching my alarm clock off the shoebox that's my bedside table, I read the numbers.

1:36.

I swear under my breath. Not even ten minutes have passed and I've already had that damn dream again. Chucking the clock at the wall, I turn over and cover my head with a pillow.

I really need to get better sleep meds.

Chapter 2

"Rylan? Dude, you look like shit."

You can always count on Aidan Marce to tell the truth, no matter how harsh it'll sound. Opening one eye, I glare at him from where I'm lying down on the porch. I was hoping to catch some sleep before Aidan came over, but apparently that's not happening.

I managed to get through the night after the second wake-up call, but like every time after reliving the dream, I couldn't go back to sleep. I finally gave up around six and decided to get up and prepare for school. Avoiding questions from Dad and Babette was easy, since Dad leaves for work before I wake up and Babette hates getting up before nine. But there's no fooling Aidan.

"Wow, really? I didn't notice," I grumble. Sitting up, I grab the backpack that I was using as a pillow and stomp down the steps. It's then I notice someone's missing. "Where's Nadia?"

"She had to go in early for math help. Pre-calc's killing her," Aidan reports. Leaning against the handlebars of his bike, he watches me as I unlock my ten-speed from the porch railing. I have a driver's license, but because Roland's so small, there's really no point in having a car, so I usually just ride my bike wherever I have to go. It's been our routine for a long time for Aidan and his twin sister, Nadia, to bike over to my house so we can all ride to school together.

All of us have been friends since third grade when the Marces moved here. Our little group had been a foursome then. Besides Aidan, Nadia, and me, there had also been Dunstan Lebelle, my best friend since kindergarten. That ended in the eighth grade, when Dunstan's dad got elected Roland's mayor. When we started high school, all ties of friendship were severed, and he instantly became high-school royalty because of his dad's position, leaving us stuck somewhere between geekiness and popularity. That hurt all of us, but the twins were especially devastated; they'd never lost an important person before. Of course, that didn't stop us from trying to talk to him, but he just flat-out ignored us, glaring like we were crap under his shoes until we finally gave up.

We'd never meant anything to him, apparently.

I pull the chain out of the spokes of the front wheel. Straddling the seat, I start riding down the driveway with Aidan next to me.

"She's having trouble in math?" I ask, confused. "But that's her best subject."

Aidan shrugs as he pedals. "I know. But she said Mr. Astor doesn't explain enough and barely gives out any examples."

"Do you think she's exaggerating?"

"When have we known my sister to exaggerate?"

He's got a point there. Nadia is as much a straight shooter as her brother. "I guess never."

We reach the main road that winds its way through Roland before merging with the main highway, and I fall behind Aidan as we ride. Cypress trees stretch up to the sky

on either side of us, not as green as they could be because of the drought we're in the middle of.

My home's on the very edge of town, but it doesn't take long to reach the town center. After puffing our way up Zoomer's Hill, we fly down into Roland. Whatever image you get when you hear the word "town" is probably what Roland looks like: one major street lined with all the important buildings like a town hall, a post office, a supermarket, and a firehouse, with smaller streets split away from the main one, little twigs off of bigger branches. Those are bordered with more houses and measly shops that sell who knows what.

We weave around the few cars parked against the curb and watch the town wake up as we pass. Shop owners, familiar with our daily trek, wave at us through their windows.

Soon we're out of the downtown area and pedaling along Main Street. Up ahead is Roland Roux High, named after the town founder. It's nothing more than an old, oversized brick box with a narrow parking lot in the front and a forest of trees in the back, like you'd see in a lot of small towns. Some cars are squeezed into parking spaces, and numerous students are lounging on the lawn.

As we pull up to the bike rack, I see Nadia sitting at the top of the entry steps with her nose in a book.

"Nadia!"

She glances up and smiles. Bending the corner to mark her place, she grabs her backpack and practically jumps down the stairs to us.

"Morning, guys," chirps Nadia.

"Morning."

Aidan looks up as we lock our bikes in. "Did you get that homework help from Mr. Astor?"

Nadia nods. "Yeah. But I swear he needs to retire soon, the poor guy. He thought I was you."

Deep down, I can't blame Mr. Astor. Despite the fact that they're fraternal twins, Aidan and Nadia look and act incredibly alike. Both are a head shorter than me, and they share the same short, reddish-brown hair and hazel eyes. The only way you can tell them apart is with Nadia's pierced ears, the little makeup she wears, and her curvy waist. She may be flat as a board up top, but Nadia's behind is the stuff of dreams according to the guys in the locker room.

We go inside, and already I can tell it's going to be a normal day. Tim Powers and his girlfriend Ellie Holen are having their daily fight. Vivian Reese is sucking face with some random guy. School geek Junior Small—his real name, I'm not lying—is being hassled by some members of our pathetic football team.

"It's good to be back in reality," I tell myself, shaking my head as we work our way down the hall towards my locker.

"Huh?" asks Aidan, confused. "What'd you mean?"

I shake my head. "It's nothing."

Reaching my locker, I dial in the combination, open the door, and catch my literature textbook as it falls out.

"Are you sure?" says Nadia with concern as I rummage through the mess of papers, notebooks, and a lunch from last week. "Because you look horrible, Rylan."

"I just had a rough night," I mumble. I find my first-hour history textbook and stuff it into my backpack.

"What happened? Did Rylan have a little nightmare?" Aidan teases.

"Cut the crap," I growl. "I'm serious. I—"

"Dunstan!"

Back down the hall, the football players have stopped beating up Junior to flock around Dunstan like he's king of the school, which he is. Even the seniors know it.

Many pairs of eyes follow him as he struts down the hall with his arm around his girlfriend, who is none other than Melanie Sweet. He knows everyone's staring, and so he puffs out his chest and raises his chin like a proud peacock. I roll my eyes. He thinks he looks all powerful and mighty. But he's wrong. He looks like a jerk.

But as he passes us, I can't help but feel a little jealous that he scored Melanie. Not that it was hard with his looks; he has what girls would probably call the "Greek god" appearance with the blue eyes and blond hair and whatever. Then again, if you stuck dark-haired, skinny-ass me next to him and asked a random girl who she'd rather go on a date with, I think we all know who she'd choose.

Melanie cuddles Dunstan closer. Her long, honey-colored hair frames her blue eyes and heart-shaped face. Her wildflower perfume drifts over in a fragrant cloud. All it takes is one sniff, and I'm instantly infatuated. Aidan's no exception either.

"Lucky bastard," Aidan mutters when the couple is out of earshot. "Scoring Melanie like that? I'd do anything to have her."

"Please. You're bad enough without her. You don't need her influence," Nadia mutters. For some reason, she hates Melanie, always insisting she's nothing more than a blonde bimbo with a head full of air. Aidan says she just hates the fact Melanie has every guy in school wrapped around her finger.

"Not funny," Aidan grunts as I slam my locker shut. "Jealousy doesn't suit you, sister."

"And your taste in girls needs improvement, *baby* brother."

Aidan scowls. He hates it when Nadia reminds him she's the older twin.

"If you say I have bad taste in women, you're saying Rylan has bad taste in women, too."

"*Please* don't bring me into this," I beg. I learned long ago that it's best to stay out of the twins' way when they argue.

Nadia doesn't back down. "I never said Rylan had bad taste!"

"You know, Rylan also thinks she's the hottest thing ever." He turns to me for support. "Right?"

I open my mouth to agree, but remnants of last night's dream float into my head. Before the girl had changed, *she* was the most beautiful person I'd ever seen, even if she was only in a dream.

I surprise myself and say, "I've seen prettier." Aidan gapes at me while Nadia looks both pleased and, strangely, hopeful.

"What?" Aidan croaks. "How? Who could be hotter?"

I stare down at my feet as I stick my hands into my jeans pockets. When I was eating breakfast and sneaking a cup of Babette's coffee this morning, I decided to try telling someone about the dream. I hadn't so far because I didn't want to get others involved, but maybe this would somehow get them to stop and I'd be free once and for all. There's no telling if it'll work; however, at this point I'm willing to try anything.

So I go for broke. "Well, you see—"

The bell interrupts me, announcing that class starts in one minute. Only a few other students still loiter in the hall.

"Crap!" Aidan and Nadia swear at the same time. They still have to get their first-class stuff out of their lockers, and they're up on the second floor. Ignoring the rule about running in the school, they dash down the hall and out of sight.

I sigh as I head off to history class. I guess I'll have to tell them later. Outside a nearby window, a tree shakes its

leafy branches as if agreeing with my choice. Because it's been so dry, the leaves are patchy, and I can see the sharp wood underneath as it reaches out for something to hold onto.

Her nails are sharp as knives. I can feel them cut through my shirt and dig into my skin.

Once again, the beauty-turned-beast holds me in her grasp. I wait as she leans back, knowing what's going to happen. She'll look me right in the eye and say…

"MR. FORESTER!"

I jerk away, breaking out of the hug. She's never done that before, shrieking in a voice that shouldn't belong to her. I'm terrified of what other things she'll do differently—scary things. I bring my arms to my face, close my eyes, and brace for any blows.

"Mr. Forester!"

Lowering my arms, I open my eyes. Instead of snake eyes, I stare into the cold steel of Ms. Stern's glare. It finally comes to me that I'm not at the swamp. I'm actually in Biology II, being woken up by the one teacher in the whole school who hates people dozing off in class more than anything. Crap.

"Mind telling me what's making my lesson so boring that you're napping through it?" Ms. Stern crows.

"Well…um…er," I stutter. Everyone except Aidan and Nadia snickers, amused to see someone in trouble.

Ms. Stern stops me before I can explain. "I don't want excuses, Mr. Forester. But since you're one of my best students, I'll let this slide. Now can you please pay attention?"

"Yes, ma'am," I mumble.

Ms. Stern marches back to the front of the room. She shoots out one more disapproving look, which shuts everyone up immediately. If seasons needed leaders, she'd be the Winter Queen. She'd be perfect for the job, not just because of her icy stare and attitude, but also her graying hair, pale skin, and colorless wardrobe.

"As I was saying I'm assigning y'all a project."

Everyone groans, myself included.

Ms. Stern ignores the moaning and continues. "It'll be an individual project on the life forms of the local swamps. I want you, in a research paper and PowerPoint presentation, to tell me all about the flora and fauna of a typical swamp, along with the type of ecosystem that composes swamps."

Ms. Stern starts passing out a stack of papers. "Here's the rubric, along with all the details about what I am expecting you to include. If you have any other questions, ask me now."

"How long does this have to be?" someone asks from the back.

"Long enough to include everything needed. At minimum, your paper should be at least three pages and your PowerPoint should be at least eight slides with a ten-minute presentation."

Nadia raises her hand. "When's this due?"

"In about two weeks—the date's on the handout," Ms. Stern declares. "And Nadia? Do me a favor and make sure your brother doesn't copy off your assignment *again*."

She stares evilly at Aidan, who slinks down in his seat like he's melting into a puddle. A couple times before, Aidan tried to pass off Nadia's assignments as his own work, disguising them by changing words around and putting his name on them. This worked with some of the more gullible teachers, but it didn't fool Ms. Stern. She saw the similarities right away, and Aidan almost ended up getting suspended.

13

The bell rings. "Class dismissed," Ms. Stern calls out. We all rise from our seats and charge out the door.

"Look at this," I complain as I read the rubric. "Did you see how many requirements Ms. Stern has for this?"

I look over at my friends to see them staring at me.

"What? Do I still have something on my face from lunch?" I wipe my chin with my hand.

"No." Aidan shakes his head. "It's...you fell asleep in class."

"So? You do too, sometimes."

"Rylan, you *never* fall asleep in class," states Nadia. "It's not like you."

I sigh as I quickly admit defeat. "I know. I haven't been getting enough sleep at night. I can't help it."

"Not sleeping?" asks Nadia, concerned. "What's wrong?"

I try to tell them about the dreams again, but the bell rudely interrupts me. They really need to lengthen the passing periods around here.

"I'll tell you after school," I tell them over my shoulder as I walk off in the direction of my next class.

"All right, what's up?"

Aidan, Nadia, and I are back to our perch on the front steps of school. Gold afternoon sunlight peeks through the trees, reflecting off the few cars remaining in the parking lot. A lot of other students have already gone home, but some are still hanging around campus for after-school clubs.

I look at Aidan. "I know what I'm about to tell you will make me sound crazy..."

"Rylan, we've known you're crazy for a long time. It's nothing new."

Nadia elbows her brother in the side. "Ignore the idiot. Continue."

"Long story short, I've been having this weird dream."

"Just a dream?" Aidan chuckles. He leans back on the step and places his hands behind his head. "I have dreams too, dude, but they don't cause me to sleep in class."

"This dream isn't normal."

"You mean only one particular dream has been bugging you? For how long?" asks Nadia.

"A little over a month. It happens about every time I try to sleep. It wasn't bad at first, when they didn't wake me up. But lately it's been getting so intense that I do."

"What's this dream about?"

I look up at the sky as I remember. "It starts out with me down at the dock. I don't know why I'm there, so I turn around to go back to the house. But then I hear a splash, so I look back. And this beautiful girl is standing there."

"Hold on," interrupts Aidan. "When you say 'beautiful girl,' is that what you meant this morning when you said you've seen girls prettier than Melanie?"

I blush, embarrassed. "Yeah."

"She's a dream girl, dude. She's not real; she doesn't count!"

"Aidan, quit interrupting," scolds Nadia, "or Rylan will never finish."

Aidan shuts up.

"I greet her and ask what she's doing here. She doesn't reply. I get worried, so I go over to her and ask if she's okay. She suddenly hugs me. But when I return the hug, she turns into this green, snake-eyed monster. I'm terrified, but I can't run. It finally ends when the monster leans back, *kisses* me on the cheek, and whispers, 'I am forever watching.' Then she turns into a bunch of ivy and I wake up."

Both my friends gape at me.

"Shit," Aidan swears, speaking first. "That's one weird dream. You've been having it every night for a month?"

"Yeah."

"Have you told anyone else?" asks Nadia.

"No. Just you two."

"Why no one else?"

"Because I thought I could make it go away myself. Nothing's worked."

"No wonder you look so trashed," says Aidan.

"Today I decided maybe telling someone would make it leave. That's why I'm telling you guys."

"We shouldn't be the only ones to know about this," Nadia declares. "You have to tell someone else. This could be some bad medical condition or something."

"I guess. Who else is there to tell, though?"

"Your dad?"

I give her a sad look as I shake my head. "Not him. He'd only tell me they'll go away eventually."

"What about your grandma?"

"It's worth a shot," Aidan persists. "Isn't she into translating dreams and woo-woo stuff like that? Maybe that's the key."

"All she'd do is fuss over me like some little kid and take me to Doc Norm's office."

However, Aidan has a point, now that I think about it. Babette has a lot of weird but interesting hobbies, and one of them is interpreting dreams. She has many books about the subject lying around the house, and every once in a while she asks me if I've had any dreams she could look into.

"Point taken," I agree. "I guess it wouldn't hurt to tell her. But I'm not using my name. I'll tell her it's one of you guys so she doesn't fuss as much."

"Then can it be Nadia?" urges Aidan. "'Cause I'd rather not have her hassling me with whatever nasty medicine she'll come up with."

This earns Aidan a hit on the head, courtesy of me.

Chapter 3

I walk into the front hall of the house "I'm home!"

"Rylan? That you?" Babette's voice floats in from the kitchen.

"Yeah, it's me."

"Come here. Your snack's waiting."

Some people may think it's dorky that your sixty-seven-year-old grandma makes an after-school snack for you. To me, it just makes her cool.

Gripping my backpack by the strap, I make my way to the kitchen. Like the rest of the house, it's all inlaid wood. The scrubbed cabinets and counters dully shine. Tonight's dinner is cooking on the stove. Babette sits at the kitchen table reading a book. In front of her is a plate of cheese, crackers, and assorted fruit.

"How was school, hon?" she asks with a smile. Babette has curly black hair with some gray streaks and sky-blue eyes. When people first meet her, many find it hard to believe she's really her age, with the passionate personality she has. Other than Aidan and Nadia, she's my best friend.

"Decent," I reply. I grab some sliced apple.

"Have any homework?"

"Of course. Algebra II, Spanish, American history…" I tick assignments off on my fingers.

"That sounds fun."

I snort. "Yeah. But what can you do?"

I watch Babette as she nibbles on a cracker. Unless I want to discuss the dream with Dad around, I have to ask her now. But how to do it? I can't just randomly bring it up. She'll suspect something. She's quick like that.

As I prepare some elaborate lie in my head, Babette asks, "How're Aidan and Nadia?"

And there's the perfect opening. "They're fine. But Aidan's been having weird dreams lately and it's starting to affect his sleep."

This instantly catches her attention. "Weird dreams?"

"Yeah. He just told me about it today."

"Really."

"Yeah. Aidan thought he could make it go away by himself. But nothing he's tried has worked."

"Not even sleep medication? Some strong substances can put a person out like a light."

"Nope. The dream still gets through."

Babette sighs. "What type is it? Is it a nightmare or a fantasy?"

"It's really like both. And he's been having it every night for the past month."

"He's been having only one dream for a whole month?"

"Yep. Every time he hits the sack. He told me to tell you because he thinks maybe knowing the interpretation of his dream could make it go away."

"That's good reasoning." Babette nods. "Of course I'll help Aidan out. What's his dream like?"

I rehash the dream to Babette. With each word, she looks more enthralled and more serious. My stomach starts to sink a little. Is the dream bad news?

"That sounds like quite a dream," says Babette after I finish. "Seems like he told you everything about it." She eyes me suspiciously, because Babette knows my friends well enough that Aidan and long descriptions don't really mix.

"He told it in a lot of detail," I lie on the spot. I hope my face isn't turning red like it sometimes does when I fudge the truth.

Babette narrows her eyes as she stares some more, but thankfully she soon changes the subject. "Hmm. From what you told me, it sounds like Aidan's had a brush with the supernatural."

"What do you mean?"

"I mean that Aidan's dream isn't normal."

"No offense, but I kinda already knew that."

Babette smiles. "I know. You're a bright boy, Rylan. But the dream monster? It isn't just a random, made-up monster. It's actually something I've heard of before."

"Huh?"

Babette rubs her forehead like she does when she starts explaining something to me. "From the description, the monster that Aidan is seeing in his dream is a *Palus Angelus*, otherwise known as a swamp angel."

"Swamp angel? What's that?"

Babette holds up a finger. "Wait here." She stands and leaves the kitchen. A few minutes later she returns with a thick book that she hands to me as she sits down. Examining the cover, I read the title stamped across the front: *Marshes, Swamps, and Bayous.*

Babette takes it back, opens it, and flips through it until she stops at a certain chapter.

"'Swamp Lore and Legends,'" she reads aloud. Her finger trails down the page until it points to a picture. "Is this what Aidan described?"

I study the picture. It's a black and white inking of… something. It has long hair, pointed ears, and curved horns. Skinless batlike wings, dripping with vines and covered with moss, grow out of its back. Clawed and webbed hands dig into the tree it's standing by while its hooded snake eyes stare into me.

"It's her," I whisper.

Babette crosses her arms. "That's what I thought."

I skim the paragraph underneath. "It's written here that stories about these things go as far back as the fifteenth century. That's when the first 'recorded' sighting happened over in England somewhere. There have been sightings in swamps all over the world ever since, but its actual existence has yet to be proven." I look up. "This still doesn't explain why Aidan's randomly having dreams about this."

"Keep reading." Babette nods towards the book.

I peruse the pages again. "'Swamp angels are said to exist to be the protectors of swamps and marshlands. They keep an eye on the plants and animals living there and keep the ecosystem in a healthy balance. If something goes wrong in the swamp—something they can't stop alone, like human destruction and deforesting—they use their brand of magic to step into people's dreams to warn them…'"

My voice dies as I pause. Does this mean what I think it does?

"If Aidan's been having dreams with her kind in them, something must be wrong with the swamp," Babette declares. She sounds worried.

"Don't tell me you believe this," I groan with disbelief. I sound harsher than I mean to be, so I add in a gentler tone, "This is just some made-up thing to explain something. This isn't real."

"So you don't believe it?"

"Of course I don't." I close the book with a snap. "Believing in swamp angels is like believing in unicorns and elves. They don't exist."

"But the dreams—"

"Logical explanation. Probably something he ate."

Babette sighs. "If you insist." Slowly she rises and heads for the back door. "But I'm going to go check to see if someone's been dumping trash in the swamp again."

It happens every once in a while. Loaded trash bags somehow end up in certain parts of the swamp. There usually aren't that many, but they always contain this toxic chemical and trash waste that's bad news for the ecosystem if left alone for a long time. Periodically, Babette checks everything over so this doesn't happen.

"How are you going to do that without the boat?" I ask. "And what about the ivy in the dream?"

Babette shrugs. "I don't know how that fits in. Perhaps his mind just added it in for special effects."

She's halfway out the door when she turns back to me, suddenly looking a little upset. "I'll manage without the boat; however, Mr. Harold called today about it. He can't fix the old motor, so he ordered a new one. It should be backon the water by the end of the week."

"That's good. I was assigned a project in science to study swamp wildlife. I want to take it out and get some pictures."

"Good plan." Babette glances at her watch. "I'll be back before dinner. Can you watch the house while I'm gone?"

"Sure."

The back door squeaks as Babette leaves, and I watch her through the screen as she disappears. When I can't see her anymore I finish the rest of my snack. Picking up my backpack, I place the swamp book in it—it's good research material—and head up to my room. Instead of starting my homework, I call Aidan. He picks up on the third ring.

"Hello?"

"It's me."

"Hey dude. What's up?"

"Put your sister on speaker. I've got something to tell you both."

He does, and soon we're tying up the phone line.

"What do you need to tell us?" asks Nadia.

I tell them everything my grandma told me about the dream.

"Aw, man. Did you have to tell her it was me?" Aidan whines when I tell them I used his name.

I ignore him. "From what Babette said, having a swamp angel in your dreams means the swamp's in danger."

"Do you think someone put cleaning chemicals in the swamp again?" asks Nadia.

"I don't know if it's even that, since it's never really the same thing," I tell her the truth. "Babette's down at the banks checking it out right now."

"I bet my life savings it's Mr. Lebelle," Aidan says with disgust. "That guy's been trying to buy your property forever."

Mr. Lebelle is Dunstan's dad, the mayor of Roland, the richest guy around, and the town's biggest asshole. He's been hassling Babette to sell the swamp ever since I was six years old. The plan, it seems, is for him to build some fancy shopping center to increase tourist revenue and get more people to move here. But Babette tells him no every time because the conservation of the plants and animals is ten times more important. I completely agree with her.

Sometimes I think it was Mr. Lebelle's fault that my friendship with Dunstan completely tanked. I mean, it had to be hard being friends when your parental units were always butting heads. Granted, Mr. Lebelle never threw me out of the house when I came to play, but he rarely tried

to talk to me or take his son and me out somewhere fun. With a dad like that, it had to pressure Dunstan somehow to please him, and maybe abandoning me was the only way to do so.

"I know. Babette suspects him, too. But there's no proof. And even if it were him, he wouldn't do it himself. He'd have some hired thugs do it so he would look innocent if they got caught."

"Thugs? Since when did Lebelle become the Godfather?" Aidan jokes.

"Probably the same day the town chose him to be mayor."

We talk some more, and soon it's time to hang up. Before I do, Nadia asks if we'll be getting the boat back soon.

"It'll be back by Saturday."

"Excellent. I was hoping we could take it into the swamp and get some pictures for Ms. Stern's project."

"Genius!" exclaims Aidan. "Why didn't I think of that?"

As I hang up, I hear Nadia. "Because you're stupid."

I finally start on my math homework when Dad walks into my room without knocking. He tends to do that, despite all the times I've told him not to.

"Sorry!" he apologizes when I glare at him. His eyes fall to look at my shoulder. "Just wanted to make sure you were here and everything."

I look down at my Algebra II worksheet. "Did you just get home?" It's a stupid question to ask—he still has his tie on, so the answer's yes—but it's the only thing I can think to say.

"Yes. But I can't find your grandmother anywhere."

"She's checking the swamp to see if anyone's been dumping trash in it again."

Dad pales, making him look a lot older than he is. Even without the pasty complexion, he still looks aged. Unlike me, he's got dull brown hair, with wire-frame glasses that sit on the bridge of his nose. The only thing we have in common is our eyes, which are bright green with gold flecks. Babette calls them "money eyes."

"If she had to go down there, shouldn't she have taken you along?" Dad asks my collarbone.

"She told me to stay here and do my homework." I gesture to my backpack. "She's fine on her own, anyway. It's not like she can get too far without the boat."

"I know, but at her age—"

"—she's as healthy as ever. That's what Doc Norm said at her last checkup," I remind him with an all-suffering groan. "Are you just worried about her being attacked?"

Dad doesn't even try to deny it. "Yes. Aren't you?"

"Nothing's going to happen," I tell him, trying to ease his fears. "It was a freak accident before. You need to move on—like the rest of us."

It's the wrong thing to say, for his eyes narrow angrily as he goes on the defensive. "I *have* moved on," he states through gritted teeth. He turns to leave but barks before he goes, "I'll call you down for dinner as soon as Babette returns."

I try to get back to my homework, but I can't. The numbers are plastered across the page in some unreadable code I can't decipher. I give up, rise, shuffle over to my bed, and fall flat on it, burying my face in my pillow.

I'm suddenly very tired, yet I don't feel like sleeping. Too many thoughts are swirling around in my head. I just lie there and think, attempting to sort them out.

"He didn't look at me again," I mumble to myself. When I was younger, I used to think he did it because I was ugly. Now that I'm older I know the real reason.

I look too much like her.

Dinner goes like usual. Babette talks about her day and the swamp patrol. She says she didn't find anything, but she's still keeping an eye out. Dad goes on about his day in the office where he works as a lawyer in Roland's only law firm. I tell them both about school and the project. I don't bring up the dream, and neither does Babette. She knows as well as I do what Dad's reaction would be. He'll think it's "complete nonsense", as he thinks most of Babette's hobbies are. Not that he tells her that. Because then that would create confrontation, which he avoids like the plague—weird given his job—and make him more upset than he already is all the time.

Once the table's cleared, I go back upstairs to tackle my homework again. This time I actually get into it, and by 9:30 I'm all done.

I'm putting my stuff away when there's a quiet knock on my door. I already know who it is.

"Come in, Babette."

"Hey, hon," she says as she enters. "How are you?"

"I'm fine. Why?"

Babette shrugs. "You seemed tense at dinner. And you didn't look up from your plate the whole time. Was it my cooking?"

I immediately shake my head. "No! No, Babette. It wasn't that. It never will be your cooking." I run my hand through my hair as I look off at nothing in particular. "It's just…Dad got nervous when he came home and I told him where you were."

"Is that all?"

"No. He wouldn't look me in the eyes again. If anything, that's the real problem."

Babette gives me a hug. She knows how I feel as well. There are days, although not too many, when Dad won't look at her, either. I stand there, accepting her embrace, as I lean my forehead against her shoulder.

"I hate when he does that," I sigh, both bitter and exhausted. "It's like what happened was my fault and he's punishing me for it."

"It wasn't your fault and you know it," Babette scolds me as she steps back. "No one saw it coming. These things just happen, right?"

"Right," I mutter. I don't sound convincing, even to myself.

However, Babette ignores my tone. "Good. Now don't stay up late, or you'll be snoozing on your desk tomorrow."

If only she knew…

"All right. 'Night, Babette."

"Good night, Rylan."

The minute she leaves, I collapse on my bed for the second time today. All my energy has seeped away, leaving me completely tired. But this isn't new. I always end up feeling this drained when *that* subject's brought up.

Babette has told me many times that it's not my fault. Deep down, I know she's right. No one asked for what happened to happen. But with the way Dad avoids me, sometimes I end up feeling guilty. I can't hate him for that, after what he's been through, knowing I serve as a constant reminder of what he can't ever have again. Even so, does he have to go through the grieving process forever?

I exhale and turn to look at the picture on my bedside table. I'm in it, but younger, wearing a huge smile full of crooked teeth. Hugging me is a beautiful woman. She has long, wavy black hair and bright blue eyes. We're sitting on the porch steps during a sunny day, beaming at the camera.

"If only we knew, Mom," I murmur to the picture. "Maybe we could've done something to stop it."

I shake my head. I'm not going to let tonight end in a pity party. Rolling over, I yank my comforter over me and fall asleep in my clothes. And as I close my eyes, I take comfort in knowing that, since I got my dream dissected by Babette, I'll be able to actually sleep tonight.

Chapter 4

I'm an idiot.

Did I honestly think the dream would go away if I told someone? Where do I get these crazy ideas? I only had it once last night, but it was so bad, so vivid and almost sinister, I ended up rolling off my mattress and hitting my face on my bedside table.

Hours later, here I am, trying to stomach my lunch and wincing from the giant aching bruise coloring my cheek. All around me teenagers sit at nearby tables, talking loudly and chewing food. The noises mix together into one long drone.

"Rylan!" Out of nowhere comes Aidan, carrying a tray laden with enough stuff to prepare a bear for hibernation.

I turn in my seat. "Hey."

He flinches when he sees my face. "Ouch. What happened? Get in a fight?"

I roll my eyes. "Yeah, with my bedside table. I already told you and Nadia about it on the way here, remember?"

"Huh?"

Again I retell last night's events, remembering to leave out the confrontation with my dad. I don't want to share that with him.

"Whoa," Aidan drawls. He stuffs some French fries into his mouth. "Tab's massad op, yude."

"Don't talk with your mouth full. It's disgusting," Nadia chastizes him as she approaches the table. As I brush Aidan's crumbs off me, she looks at my injury. "Feeling any better?"

Thank God Nadia doesn't have her brother's memory. "No," I mutter. "It hurts like hell *and* I'm still sleepy."

Nadia picks at her slightly wilted salad. "I'm sorry the dream didn't go away."

"It's not your fault."

"But look what happened. Who knows how much worse this could get?"

"You could start sleep-walking," Aidan suggests as he sips his Gatorade.

"Thank you for that," I tell him. "Nadia's right, though. What happens now?"

"I don't know," replies Nadia. She bites her lip as she fiddles with her fork, obviously thinking about something.

Somehow, Aidan pulls one of those mind-reading tricks twins sometimes do. "Thinking about the monster?"

Nadia nods. "This is the first time I've even heard of this creature. A swamp angel…it must be terrifying."

"It is," I confirm. "You should've seen the picture. It was scary, yet pretty at the same time."

She smiles at me. "I'd like to see it sometime."

My stomach does a flip-flop as my mouth dries. That grin of hers is giving me that feeling again. Way before the dream even started happening, I've been getting these hunches that Nadia might be flirting with me every time she gives me the look she's giving me right now. It makes me nervous as hell. I mean, Nadia's pretty and nice and all, but she's only a friend. If she does like me, I don't want to hurt her.

30

Fortunately, Aidan interrupts before anything becomes too awkward. "I wanna see it, too."

My eyebrows arch. "You care enough about my dream to want to see the picture in the book?"

"No way! I need the book for research for that stupid biology project. There was hardly anything on Google about swamps and their plant life and crap."

Nadia snorts. "That's because you didn't even look yesterday."

Aidan scowls as we chuckle, but the twitch of his lips tells me he's not as angry as he looks. It's impossible for him to stay mad at either of us for long.

The area around me suddenly darkens. At first I think one of the light bulbs overhead burnt out, but that changes once I see the harsh faces of my friends. Someone's standing behind me, and from their glares I can easily guess who it might be.

I peek over my shoulder to see none other than my ex-best friend, Dunstan Lebelle. People around the cafeteria crane their necks to see what he's doing with someone like me.

My eyes narrow suspiciously. "What?"

"When's your swamp boat going to get fixed?" he asks. His words come out quickly like he can't stand talking to me any longer than he has to, and his shifty eyes confirm it. "It's been said around town that your boat got busted and sent in for repairs."

"So?"

"So I want to know when it's back 'cause I want a ride on it. Everyone in Biology II got that project, and you're the only swamp tour in town."

"Technically we're not a tour," I clarify for him. "We don't provide much information. We just take people out—"

"Don't care," Dunstan interrupts. "So when's the boat gonna be fixed?"

I feel my hands clench, but I mentally tell myself to relax. "It'll be back by Saturday. You can come then."

"When on Saturday? I've got a date with Melanie that day."

I turn back to my lunch, silently dismissing him. I've had enough of this conversation. If I talk to him any longer, unresolved issues from our shared past may surface, and I don't want to deal with those. I guess I am Dad's son after all.

"I asked a question, Forester."

"Whatever time fits your busy schedule," I mumble. I can't see his face, but I know he's glaring at me. "And one other thing, Lebelle," I add, giving him a backwards glance. "Tell your dad to quit using the swamp as his personal dump site."

Dunstan's eyes go angry and his hands curl like he wants to hit me. "You'll get in trouble for spreading lies like that, Forester. You have no proof."

"No, but he has a reason to. Your dad's been trying to buy our land for years. What better way to get it than to poison it and convince everyone it's unsafe?"

Dunstan's fists clench even tighter. "It's not us!" he insists with a growl. Before I speak again, he stomps back to the popular table. The caf is quiet for a couple seconds, but once everyone realizes the action's over, people quit staring and resume eating and chatting.

"That was awesome," Aidan praises me. Nadia nods with approval.

"He had it coming, the liar," I grumble.

I don't believe Dunstan for a second. He's smart enough to know that, if Mr. Lebelle gets caught poisoning the swamp, he'll be thrown out of office, and Dunstan's popularity will go right along with it. So, like his old man, he denies it every time he's confronted with the issue. The worst part is almost everyone in town believes him and his dad. No doubt he's somehow got the council wrapped around his finger.

"Do you have to give the enemy a boat ride?" inquires Aidan, looking unhappy. He's been calling Dunstan "the enemy" and other villainous nicknames ever since he kicked us to the curb.

I shrug. "It's not like we can turn him down."

"And if he goes on a tour, everyone else will follow. The whole 'popular bandwagon' thing." Nadia's fingers make air quotes. "Besides, the money isn't bad."

"Exactly."

Aidan goes back to devouring his food. "Even if it's good business sense, I'd never let that guy on your property. Dunstan's nothing but trouble."

"I know. His whole family is."

The rest of the week passes not too quickly, but not agonizingly slow, either. All in all, an average week—until Friday afternoon. I ride up the driveway. School's over, and Aidan and Nadia have gone home. Reaching the porch, I hop off my bike and chain it to the railing. As I'm about to climb the steps, I notice a black Lexus in the driveway. It looks familiar, but it doesn't belong to us. The only car we have is Babette's beat-up truck, and Dad takes that to work every day.

I'm about to peek through the mystery car's windows when I hear something. It sounds like people shouting, and it's coming from the dock. My curiosity piqed, I walk over

and descend the path towards the swamp banks. As I get closer, the voices become more clear.

"Why won't you sell?"

"I've already told you why a million times, Jules."

When I finally reach the dock I see two people arguing. One person is Babette. The other person is Mr. Lebelle. His pale hair flashes in the patches of sun. Neither of them notices my arrival.

"Why can't you see selling the swamp would be in the town's best interest?" Mr. Lebelle's face is turning red in the attempt to control his famous temper. He's so the stereotypical villain type, it's almost clichéd.

"And why can't you see selling the land would be the worst mistake I could ever make?" Babette retorts. She looks calm, and frankly is doing a lot better hiding her frustration than he is. "If I sell the swamp, what would happen to the plants and animals living here? If their habitat is destroyed, they'll have nowhere to go. They'll end up *dying*, Jules. Swamp land is disappearing around the world, and it's our job as good human beings to preserve what's left."

"The animals will find another place to live, Ms. Daniau. Don't you care about the town? Roland would be better off if we had more shops. More people would start moving here!"

Babette crosses her arms and shakes her head. "My final answer is no, Jules. Now if you don't mind, I have work to finish and a grandson to greet."

Babette turns to leave and finally realizes I'm standing there. Her face cracks into the type of smile you put on when you've been caught at an inconvenient time.

"Rylan! When did you get home?" Babette asks *way* too friendly. She really didn't want me to see this.

I shift my backpack on my shoulders and reply, "About five minutes ago." I don't take my eyes off Mr. Lebelle. He doesn't look very happy to see me.

I know what's happening, but I ask anyway. "What's going on?"

Babette clears her throat. "Mr. Lebelle came over for…a chat," she says in the same overly sweet tone.

Chat, my ass. He was harassing her again.

Before I can add my own two cents, Mr. Lebelle gives his watch an overdramatic glance. "Would you look at the time!" he states. "I do believe I have to go back to my office." He gives Babette one last look. "Please, Ms. Daniau. Think the offer over. When you reach a decision, please call me." He gives her a smarmy wink and strolls down the dock towards me. If he thinks he can have the last laugh, he's got another think coming.

"You do realize she's never going to call you," I mutter as he walks by. He gives me that "this isn't your business" look adults give kids, but I keep talking. "I hope it doesn't take the rest of your life to realize this swamp is never going be yours. Babette will see to that."

"Keep out of business that doesn't involve you, kid," Mr. Lebelle snarls.

"If it involves the swamp, it is my business," I growl back.

Mr. Lebelle's eyes narrow dangerously and scowls, but he doesn't talk again. Grumbling to himself, he stomps up the path and disappears. Seconds later there's the slam of a car door, the sputter of an engine, and the furious roar of wheels squealing down the driveway. Gradually the sound of the car fades into the distance.

Heaving a sigh, I turn to a tired-looking Babette. "You okay?"

She gives me a hug. "I've been better. Then again, I always wind up feeling like this after *he* pays us a visit."

"What did Mr. Lebelle want this time?"

Babette rubs her temple. "The same thing. I was down here preparing the dock for the boat's return after checking the swamp, and he swaggers down here like he thinks I'm selling."

I pat her back. "Ignore him, Babette. He's a jerk." Calling him a jerk is putting it mildly, but I know better than to swear in front of my grandma.

"I know. He'll leave us alone eventually. We just have to wait it out." We head back to the house.

"If he doesn't, you could get a restraining order filed," I joke, trying to make her laugh. "Dad would be happy to do that."

Babette chuckles. "I'm sure he would. But I don't want to turn this into a bigger problem than it already is."

"It's already a big problem. The guy wants the swamp so bad, he's practically stalking you. What if he resorts to something worse?"

"He wouldn't dare, lest he draw attention to himself," Babette points out. "As long as I live, that man will never lay his hands on this swamp."

"What happens when…?"

"When my dying day comes it'll be up to you men." Babette gives me a reassuring smile. "But between your father's law experience and the iron will you just showed, I think everything will be fine."

I gently nudge Babette. "I have you to thank for that."

She nudges back with a playful smirk. "You're welcome."

We lapse into small talk as we reach the front yard and head inside the house. As I close the door behind me, there's a loud snap. My head whips around and I scan the front yard. I don't see anything but trees with their branches moving in the slight breeze. I finally decide nothing's there, and I go inside.

But even inside four walls, I can't shake the feeling I was being watched.

Chapter 5

The smell of coffee and badly burnt toast wakes me up. When I peel my eyes open, I stare at the bright sunlight streaming through the blinds. It's going to be a good day.

My clock reads 8:59. I figure that Aidan and Nadia won't be over for at least another hour, which gives me plenty of time to help get the boat back to the dock. Getting up, I grab my worn blue bathrobe and slip it on as I shuffle downstairs with a yawn.

I blink as I enter the kitchen. Am I seeing things? I blink again.

"Hi, Rylan!"

I jump a foot in the air when I realize my friends are, in fact, sitting at the kitchen table, nibbling on toast and drinking coffee. Feeling myself blush, I yank at my robe to make sure everything's covered. Thank God I chose to wear pajama bottoms last night instead of just boxers.

"Wh-what are you guys doing here!?" I stutter.

"Waiting for you, you goon. You promised to take us out today. Remember?" Aidan replies with a noisy sip of orange juice.

"Yes, I remember. But I didn't expect to come downstairs and find my friends raiding my fridge." I roll my eyes.

"How'd you get in here anyway? Don't tell me you invited yourselves in."

"We didn't," admits a red-faced Nadia. She's staring off to the side and doing her best not to look at me. "Your grandma let us in half an hour ago. She said to let you sleep and that we could make something to eat if we got hungry."

Aidan holds out a plate stacked with toast. "*Bon appetit*, dude. Breakfast time."

I come forward and grab a piece of toast. I take a bite, ignoring the fact Aidan was the one who cooked and the bread's all hard and black.

"Where's Babette?" I ask while pouring myself some coffee to wash down the shards of toast.

"She's putting the boat back in the swamp," mumbles Aidan as he happily chews on his breakfast.

I take a sip and make a face at the coffee's bitterness, then open the fridge to look for the cream. "She told me we were going to do that together."

"She told us to tell you not to wait up. According to her, you looked very tired and she wanted you to rest." Nadia scoops soggy cornflakes into her mouth, ignoring her plate of toast. She's always been wise enough to avoid her twin's cooking.

I violently shake the practically empty cream bottle until a couple of drops squeeze out. "She's right about the tired thing. I should thank her."

"Are you still having that dream?"

"Yeah but that's only half the reason why I didn't get any sleep last night." I tell them about Mr. Lebelle's latest visit.

"What an asshole," mutters Aidan. "How dare he bully your grandma like that."

"He isn't very smart with returning to the scene of his crime," Nadia adds.

"Babette hasn't found any trash in the swamp all week," I confess. "There's no crime. I think it was a false alarm."

"But, Rylan, what about your dream? Didn't the book say that thing only show up when the swamp's in danger?"

"Yeah. But it's probably all a mistake." I down the last of my coffee and start clearing the dirty dishes. Nadia hops up to help, dragging a complaining Aidan out of his chair to do the same. When Babette comes through the back door a couple of minutes later, she finds the three of us loading plates into the dishwasher.

"Good morning, Rylan. How are you?" Babette asks.

"I'm fine," I tell her as I stick the silverware in. "Thanks for letting me sleep in. Did you manage to get the boat back in safely?"

Babette nods. "Yes. Your father dropped me off at Mr. Harold's repair shop. I drove back with him and he helped me put the boat in the water."

"Oh. Okay."

"Why don't you go upstairs and get dressed? I'll finish loading the dishwasher for you and we'll all meet down at the dock."

I nod, then race up the stairs two steps at a time. I'm ecstatic about getting the boat back, and I can't wait to get on the water.

I yank my sweatshirt on as I jog along the path. Since I've been down here too many times to count, I could walk this way with my eyes closed.

I finally pull my sweatshirt down just as the dock slips into view. Nadia, Aidan, and Babette sit in our boat, the *Dahlia*. It's old, beat-up, and we've had it longer than I've lived. With the new motor on the back, the *Dahlia* now looks like two odd ends fused together. But even with the old motor dying, it's going to be a long time before Babette feels the need to replace it.

"Come on, Rylan! Let's get this show on the road!" Aidan shouts.

"'Show on the road?' More like show on the river," Nadia teases.

"Right. Hold it steady."

Aidan and Nadia lean over and grab the side of the dock while I carefully step in. I move on tiptoes to the stern and take my place next to Babette.

"Everyone in?" asks Babette. We nod like a group of bobble-heads. "All right. Aidan and Nadia, you've been out before, but I still have to go over the rules. Okay?"

"That's fine," they agree at the same time.

"First off, always keep your hands, feet, and assorted limbs inside the boat. Second, stay in your seat at all times, and don't stand up or move around the boat until we've returned to the dock and the motor is off. Third, don't disturb the wildlife while taking pictures. And finally—"

"Don't leave your clients behind."

I can't help but groan; I know that voice too well. With resentment I turn in my seat to see Dunstan standing at the edge of the dock, his arms crossed. To my surprise, Melanie's also with him, hanging off his arm like a Christmas tree ornament. My friends hiss angrily, not pleased to see their sworn enemies.

"Dunstan Lebelle. I haven't seen you in a long time!" Babette gives him a small smile. "How are you?" It sickens me, watching my grandma be so pleasant to the son of the guy trying to kick her off her land. I know why she does it; she doesn't want to give Mr. Lebelle another reason to hate her, and I don't blame her. But it's disgusting how the whole town trips over each other trying to please the guy.

"I'm fine." Dunstan uses a softer version of the brusque tone he uses around me. "I'm just here for a boat tour as research for my Biology II project."

"Me, too," giggles Melanie.

"That's wonderful. Of course you and Melanie can join us." It's like Babette is talking to an old friend. Gag me.

Dunstan grunts a "thank you" and climbs into the boat. As Melanie gets in, Babette goes over the rules again. Her words go over my head, turning into one long buzz. I glance over at my friends. Both look like they either want to jump ship or yell at me for inviting the Golden Couple down here, although Aidan does look a little pleased to be in the same boat with his not-so-secret crush. Not so much for Nadia.

"—and that's it! Please enjoy yourselves."

She starts the motor with a pull of the cord. The blades churn in the water, and we pull away. The dock grows smaller and smaller until we finally turn and I lose sight of it.

Nothing but water, trees, and the occasional bank of mossy land now surrounds us, a little dry looking because of the drought. Bird song floats in from wherever birds are hiding. Green, opaque swamp water laps the boat's side, lower than it normally should be. I take a deep breath of swamp air. It smells woody and fresh, like new life.

The peace is soon gone as Dunstan starts acting up. It's little stuff, like dragging his hand in the water and shifting around and snorting at whatever anyone but Melanie says, but it's all adding up to the point when I just wanna smack the guy. Instead, I opt for taking my camera out and take photo after photo of the swamp like the twins are doing.

"Limit your flashes, please," Babette orders as she steers the motor. "Too much light will scare all the animals away."

"Sorry, Ms. Daniau," Aidan apologizes.

"Aidan, you're practically a family member, so you should realize 'Ms. Daniau' was my mother. Call me Babette."

Aidan gives her one of his good-boy smiles he uses when he's in trouble and nods quickly. Babette kills the engine, and the boat drifts along with the current until we reach a big open section of water encircled with mossy banks. The camera flashes quiet. Every now and then Babette tells us some fun fact about the swamp:

"Swamps provide a reliable water source for a variety of birds and mammals.

"The plant community within a swamp depends on the swamp type and climatic temperatures.

"Despite the high ecologic and economic values of swamps, they still remain threatened by human activities."

That last fact seems to be directed partly at Dunstan as a warning to his dad. He, however, doesn't catch the hidden warning, since he's both taking pictures *and* cuddling with a giggling Melanie. I feel familiar jealousy at the sight, and I sigh.

"Rylan? You okay?"

"I'm fine," I lie to Babette. "I'm just glad to be back out on the boat."

"Really?" This comes from Dunstan, of all people. He glances at me impassively. "I'd thought you would hate to be out here. You must be pretty brave."

I look over at Dunstan, wary of his tone. Something isn't right with it. "What do you mean?"

"I mean that after the little accident with your mom, you'd think you'd never come out here again."

My heart stops. I'm not exaggerating. I swear, for a pure second, my chest seizes and all the blood flowing in my veins pauses. I can't believe he would say something

like that. From the looks on everyone's faces, they can't believe it either.

Aidan's the first to react as he growls, "Shut up! You jerk…how can you say something like that?"

Dunstan ignores Aidan's outburst as he keeps his eyes trained on me. His face is indifferent, but I know he's smirking on the inside. Why's he doing this? What does he want me to do? React? I would, if I could get any movement back in my freakin' legs. However, they seem to be paralyzed at the moment. I settle for glaring at him.

"Don't tell me you haven't gotten over it. It's been, what? Ten years since?"

"He said shut up!" Nadia snarls. She bares her teeth in primal fury and seems almost ready to pounce on him.

But if he catches on, Dunstan doesn't show it. "I just think it's amazing you'd still come out here. I know I wouldn't."

"Mr. Lebelle, it is in my power to turn this boat around and end this tour early. So I suggest that you stop this conversation at once," Babette threatens him. She doesn't shout, but her iron tone is just as—if not more—frightening as any yelling could be.

Melanie tugs on Dunstan's arm.

"I don't wanna go back yet. I need to take more pictures for my project," she whines. Nadia rolls her eyes.

"Fine," Dunstan growls, turning away from me. I finally think he's going to shut up, when he has to mutter to himself: "Christ. You freak. You used to be so chill. You never used to be this big a hardass with your mom around."

I hear all of that, and I can't believe it. I can't believe he said that. I can't believe he brought the whole subject up. He knows how much it hurts. He knows how much I cried about it to him and *only* him since the twins hadn't moved here at the time. He was the one who let me decide what we played when I was sad, whether it was some ball game or swamp pirates or PlayStation 2. He was the one to hug me on a daily basis when Dad wouldn't even look at me. He was the one who said everything was going to be okay with a toothy smile, despite his own parental problems with his mom and dad fighting so loudly you could hear it from the street. And who *is* he to talk about mother problems? His lives off in Miami and last time we actually talked, they didn't keep in contact. He shrugged it off like it was nothing, but I know it stung. I know that more than anything.

And he's the one who uses this knowledge to stab me in the back.

My temper finally snaps and all reason flies from my head. I shoot straight out of my seat, not completely registering the rocking boat, my terrified friends clinging to the sides, or my grandma's shouts to sit back down.

"I'm a hardass? I'm a hardass? You're an asshole!" I roar. "Of all the crap you had to do, why did you have to bring that up?"

I regret shouting this when, not a moment later, I feel them coming. My hands fly up and my fingers dig into my hair. Gritting my teeth, I try to suppress them, but the preceding shakes come anyway. A second later, the dreaded flashbacks begin to play.

A high-pitched scream—a splash—
"Mommy's got you, Rylan!"
"Look out!"
She looks behind her—

"You're one to talk about talking crap, Forester." Dunstan's voice interrupts the memory, and I can't help but feel a little grateful. "Accusing my dad of poisoning the swamp? What a bunch of bull."

"It's not bull," I snarl. "Your dad's dumping trash into the swamp and you know it!"

Dunstan finally loses it and stands up. The boat tilts dangerously. Melanie and the twins shriek, grasping the sides like they're glued to them.

"You two sit down this minute!" Babette bellows. She's holding onto the motor for dear life. Neither of us listens.

"You wanna run that by me again?" Dunstan growls. His fingers curl into fists.

"Your. Dad. Is. Poisoning. The. Swamp." I let each word out slowly like Dunstan's a dumb little kid who needs help understanding. "He'll do anything to get his hands on this land. He's nothing but a bully and a dou—"

I don't see it coming until it's too late. Pain shoots through my face as Dunstan smashes his fist into my jawbone. He hits so hard I'm surprised to feel nothing break. The momentum from the blow makes me stumble back, causing my heels to catch the side of the boat. Balance lost, I fling my arms about to steady myself, but it's too late. With a splash, I fall into the swamp.

Murky greenness surrounds me, lukewarm and dark. Plants that look like they belong on a different planet grow up from the swamp floor, moving in motion with the water. Some leafy mess tangles around my leg, wanting to keep me in. I kick it off, swim to the surface, and take in a lungful of muggy swamp air.

"Rylan! Are you all right?" I squint up at my grandma. She looks very scared, her eyes wide and her mouth open. Aidan and Nadia are petrified, completely frozen except for their roaming eyes that flicker over the entire swamp. Even Melanie is pale-faced. Other than sporting a furrowed brow, Dunstan looks impassive.

"I'm okay," I manage to admit, coughing up swamp water.

Babette spins on Dunstan like an angry bear. "What were you thinking!? I told you to sit down, but did you listen? Instead, you hurt my grandson and throw him into the swamp!" She pronounces the word "swamp" with such emphasis her body shakes. *"The swamp!"*

Dunstan stares at my grandma like she's lost her mind. He clearly doesn't understand why she's freaking out, even though the reason's perfectly obvious. He would know. I guess he's dumber than I thought.

Babette heaves a massive sigh, reining in her temper before ordering the twins with a tired huff, "You two, help Rylan get back in. I'm turning this boat around; this tour's over. And the next time I see your father, Dunstan, he'll hear about this. Mark my words he will."

Shaking her head and muttering to herself, she starts the engine. I swim over and start climbing in.

"You okay?" asks Nadia. She still looks a little freaked, but she sounds like she's calming down.

I nod. With a loud grunt, the twins try to pull me into the boat. It ends up being harder than it looks, since there's nothing my feet can push off of and my legs kick around stupidly. Even when Aidan and Nadia grab my hands, their combined strength can't completely get me in.

Eventually we start making some headway, and just as I get my arms over the side, I hear it: a creak of trees and an almost silent splatter of water, like a hand cutting through the surface. I wearily glance around. I've a feeling I've heard this before. But where…?

One small splash…then one giant one—
Midnight hair getting sucked under the surface—
"Mommy! MOMMY!"

My heart starts skipping every other beat as bile creeps up my throat and adrenaline rushes through my body. With newfound vigor I try to climb into the boat as fast as I can.

"Whoa! Why the rush?" asks a baffled Aidan.

"Get me in here. Get me in here now!" I order. I have to get out of the swamp before it happens again.

But it does.

I feel it before I see it. Dozens of thick, razor-sharp needles pierce my right leg, sinking into my skin. It hurts like nothing I've felt before, and a strangled scream of pain escapes me.

Babette whips her head around, the motor forgotten. "Rylan! What is it!?"

"Get me out! GET ME OUT!" I scream. Fearfully, I look over my shoulder, but seconds later I wish I hadn't as the attacker comes to the surface. It has a scaly body, sharp claws, feral eyes, and a long, ugly, sneering snout that's clamped around my leg.

Melanie identifies it with a shriek. "GATOR!"

Knowing he's been discovered, the gator sinks under the water, disappearing from view. In that same instant, Babette flies forward, seizes one of my arms, and begins pulling on it like a madwoman.

"Pull!" Babette yells, terror in her voice. She doesn't need to repeat herself as Nadia and Aidan yank on my other arm as if their lives depend on it. Dunstan and Melanie stay in their seats, too horrified to do anything but watch.

"Hang on, dude! We'll save you!" Aidan shouts. He sounds the most scared I've ever heard him. He tugs so hard, my arm feels about ready to pop out of its socket. With my free leg I fiercely kick at the water, trying to land one on the gator. But it's a futile effort, with the gator's mouth stuck shut like a steel trap.

The alligator starts jerking on my leg even harder. Its teeth dig in deeper, cutting flesh and bone like Styrofoam. I bite my tongue as I try not to scream in pain, but it's near impossible to stay silent. Between the gator bite and all the pulling, I feel like some tug-of-war rope.

"Let go of me!" I shout. The sole of my sneaker finally connects with some part of him—I'm not sure which—and I feel his hold loosen. Soon he lets go completely.

"I kicked him! He let go!"

"Keep pulling!" yells Babette. With one more heave, they pull me out of the water. I flop onto the *Dahlia's* floor. My lowers legs still hang over the side, but I'm too out of breath to really do anything other than sink my nails into the grubby carpet. Panting heavily, Babette and the twins release my arms.

"Rylan?" Babette whispers.

I take in big gulps of air, trying to slow my out-of-control heart. "It's...over," I pant. A hysterical laugh flows from my mouth. "Thank God it's over."

I speak too soon.

A second later, I feel the alligator's jaws on my lower leg again. A second horrible pain shoots through my body. And I'm completely pulled from the boat into the water.

"RYLAN!" Nadia screams. Everyone makes wild attempts to grab me, but all they snatch is air. The last I see of them are their horrified faces. And then there's nothing but green.

I look at my enemy. He's a big guy, a little bit longer than the boat, and his snout is completely around my blood-gushing leg. I try kicking at him again, but this guy's learned his lesson. Every time I aim at him, he dodges it, his body writhing from side to side.

My hand brushes against something leafy underneath me, and a stream of bubbles escapes my mouth. The gator's already pulled me down to the bottom. Seeing that renews my will to live and I keep fighting back. But this guy's determined not to let go.

I'm losing air. My lungs are crying out for it. My vision's going blurry. All the energy I'm using isn't helping. I try paddling to the surface.

And then he hits me. The alligator somehow maneuvers his tail around and smacks me hard.

Time slows as I fall back. All air has been knocked out of me. There's nothing left to live on. Strangely, nothing hurts. My body feels peaceful and floaty, like a balloon. Reality finally sinks in; there's no escape.

Is this what it's like to die? All your functions slowly shutting down, one by one? Your brain telling you to stop struggling because everything will be okay? Your vision growing dark as you stare at the last thing on earth you'll ever see?

Is this what Mom felt?

Everyone says that when you're truly ready to go on, you have some sort of vision. Most say that you see "the light." Others think your released soul hangs above, watching the tragedy unfold below. I'm no exception, because as my sight finally starts to fade I have my vision, too.

But it's no golden light.

With unnatural speed, something big suddenly shoots towards us out of the murkiness, ramming into the alligator with tremendous strength. The gator writhes and shrieks in pain, loud enough I can hear it underwater, and immediately releases me. As I drift away with the current, I use the last of my strength to look back. I see two shadows fighting. One is the gator, claws slashing and jaw snapping. And the other…it looks like a human. Long hair flies away from it, tangling in the odd shapes on its back…

I can't think anymore. My mind's going black…

Crickets are singing. Birds are crying shrilly. A soft wind blows, lapping my face as I hear water flow somewhere nearby. All these noises are so comforting.

Why does being dead sound like the swamp?

I crack my eyes open. Up above me, leafy tree branches crisscross each other in a fine pattern of lace. My hand feels the ground. It's soggy, clay-like soil, half dirt and half water. This is the real swamp. Babatte's swamp. And that means...

"I'm alive."

Like a fool, I grin. But I don't smile for long. As I slowly pull myself up to a sitting position, a throbbing pain charges through my body. The strange euphoria I felt when I was dying has evaporated, leaving behind the dregs of what really starts death: severely excruciating torture.

I grunt, wincing at the raw hurt. It feels like the entire Roland Roux football team has pummeled me into the ground. As I shift my feet, an even worse pain suddenly gnaws at my right leg. I cry out as my eyes slam shut. I'd completely forgotten about the bite.

Gritting my teeth so hard that they probably crack, I hold back tears as my fingers dig into the ground on instinct. When the ache becomes more bearable, I open my eyes and look at my injury. My breath catches in my throat.

I can't see the wound.

My right jean leg has been cut away at the knee for the makeshift bandage that's now on my leg. Layers of clean leaves—pond apple leaves, by the looks of it—are neatly bound over the bite with some type of thin vine. The vivid green is mottled with the dark brown of absorbed blood. Skinny rivulets have escaped the bandage and run down my leg in little red rivers, but other than that it's clean.

How in the world did that get there? I rack my brain for possible explanations. Could I, unconsciously, have done all this? Looking down at my leg, I shake my head. No. It couldn't have been me. My jeans were cut cleanly, like with a knife or other sharp object, and I don't have one. I don't see any pond apple trees growing around the clearing I'm in either.

Then who?

My mind starts to rewind, going over every moment up to now. It stops at the moment before I had blacked out, the moment I had my death vision. *Someone* had hit the alligator and made him let go. Had Babette or someone jumped in to save me? Were my friends the people who did all this?

But wouldn't they have stayed with me after the rescue? Sure, someone would have to run back to the house to call 911. You can't get any cell phone service out here. But wouldn't at least one person still have been here to make sure I didn't die?

"Guys? Are you there?" My question echoes in the silence.

My savior floats into my head again. Because I was passing out and the water was so unclear, I didn't get a good look. All I can remember is a lot of long hair. And some funny-looking things on its back...

My thoughts are interrupted by a sudden crack. It's nothing big, just a small sound like something has stepped on a twig, but after all this, I'm not taking any chances. I glance around the clearing.

"Hello? Anybody there?"

No reply. I don't see anything.

But I still feel like something's watching me, like on the day Mr. Lebelle came. It's unnerving, feeling like someone can see everything about me. The life I've lived so far is an open book for them to read and learn from.

I shake my head. I'm getting paranoid. Besides, it was probably just an animal. I glance at my leg. Since I can't move it without screaming, I guess I have to wait until someone finds me.

Sighing, I look out over the water, preparing myself for what could be a long wait. But I don't have to wait long. Again I hear the same crack from before, but now it's sharper, more direct. Is it someone who can help me? The crack sounds a third time, and this time I can pinpoint its location.

It came from above.

I look up over the swamp to the trees on the other side of the water.

That's when I see the person.

The branches of the tree they're standing in hide them well, so I can't exactly see them. But I know I'm not making things up, because those eyes can't be imaginary. Large, glass green, and split in half by the thinnest pupils, they're the eyes of a monster.

The monster of my dreams. They're an exact copy.

My breath escapes as I stare into them. They stare right back, unafraid and unflinching. Unintentionally, we get into a staring contest. Nothing's said, and there's no silent communication between our eyes. It's like when two cars are waiting at a red light and the drivers happen to look over at each other. They're strangers, but they still acknowledge the other person being there and existing on the road of life so they don't run into each other.

I find that I don't want this to end.

"RYLAN!"

The yell comes out of nowhere and nearly gives me a heart attack. Tearing my eyes away, I watch as Babette

comes crashing through the undergrowth. With no regard that I might be severely injured, she bounds over and grabs me in a bear hug.

"Rylan! Oh my God, Rylan," Babette whimpers. She gently rocks me like I'm five years old again. There are some more footsteps, and Aidan and Nadia soon appear. Relief fills both their faces, with Nadia crying happily on Aidan's shoulder.

Just as I think she's going to crush me, Babette finally pulls back, her face shiny with tears. "Rylan, I thought I'd lost you. I thought I was never going to see you again. I—"

I hold up a hand. "Babette, it's okay. I'm alive. Not perfect, but I'm alive." I gesture to my leg.

"Holy crap!" the twins say together, staring at my leg with horror and disgust. It only takes one glance for Nadia to really start sobbing.

"Nadia! Nadia…don't cry," I murmur in an attempt to comfort her. Since she's such a happy person most of the time it hurts to see her like this. "It'll heal up. It's fine."

"B—but it—it's horrible! You near—nearly drowned an—and now you're hurt!" Aidan pulls her into an awkward hug, trying to calm her down.

Babette examines my leg, impressed by its tidiness and cleanness. "You bandaged your wound? Very resourceful, Rylan."

I open my mouth to tell them it wasn't me, but nothing comes out. I know the person in the tree did this. They saved me, bandaged the bite, and stayed behind to see if I'd be found.

But those eyes weren't human. They weren't made up either. What I saw in the water, with that long hair and those things on its back…

My brain paralyzes as one last chunk of memory clears up. Those things were wings.

"Rylan?"

"Huh?" I look over at Babette.

"You were staring out into space. Everything okay?"

I nod, both to answer her and confirm my decision. It's better if I don't tell them. I still can't believe it myself.

"I'm fine," I mumble. "The bite just really hurts."

"Can you stand?"

"Probably not. It even hurts to move my toes."

"We'll have to carry you," Babette concludes. She motions at Aidan and points to my left side. "Aidan, help me walk Rylan back to the house. Nadia, stay by me in case I need help."

Squatting down, Aidan and Babette pull my arms onto their shoulders and grip them firmly.

Babette looks over at Aidan. "Ready?"

"Yeah."

"Okay, on three. One, two…"

With a huff Aidan and Babette pull me up. I stand on my good leg, the damaged one slightly bent to avoid brushing the ground.

"You okay?" Babette asks me.

"I'm fine," I mumble, not really hearing her question. I'm too busy looking back at the trees across from us. The eyes are gone, faded into the foliage that was surrounding them. Whoever—or whatever—it was must've been scared off by Babette's not-so-subtle arrival.

As Babette and Aidan lead me away with Nadia at their side, my eyes still remain on the branch where I saw the person standing. They risked their life to save me. It's thanks to them I'm alive. But I never got to thank them. I never got to see my hero's face.

All I can see is blackness rushing towards me…

Chapter 6

Beep…Beep…Beep…

My senses slowly come back to me one at a time. First I hear a series of beeps, one following the other in a line of continuous noise and thus ruining any chance of going back to sleep. Then the smell hits me. It's not pleasant: a mixture of sanitizers, hurried people, and stale air, all covering up the hint of one other smell.

Blood.

My eyes open. I'm staring at an off-white ceiling. Looking to my side, I see white fabric room dividers, IV bags, a mess of wires and cords, and beeping monitors.

I'm in a hospital.

"Dude, I think he's waking up."

"Rylan? Are you awake?"

With an audible crack of my neck, I bend my head up. Across the room are Babette, Aidan, Nadia, and Dad. All of them, looking bone-weary tired, sit at the round table pushed into the corner.

I attempt a smile. "Hey, everybody."

Everyone sighs, relieved that I'm still here. Always one to get things done, Dad immediately walks over to my bedside and asks my hair, "How are you, son?"

It's not the smartest question, but he means well. "I'm a little sore, but otherwise I'm fine."

"And your leg?"

The aforementioned body part is in a plain white cast hanging from a ceiling sling. "Can't feel a thing."

"Good. That means the doctor actually did his job right."

Everyone crowds around my bed. Babette pats my shoulder. "Do you need anything? We can page your nurse if you need to eat."

"No thanks, Babette." I plop my head back on the soft pillow. "But I got a ton of questions."

"I figured as much. What do you want to know?"

"How long have I been out?"

"Five or six hours, maybe more? We didn't keep track."

"Where am I?"

"St. Amabilis General Hospital. The ambulance got here as fast as possible."

"As in St. Amabilis in Harraway?"

"Yep."

Harraway is the town closest to Roland, about twenty-five minutes of driving. It's a swamp town like ours, but five times bigger and with less swamp. Those who can drive usually go there every weekend to hang out at the outlet mall.

"What happened? I remember that you guys found me and were carrying me back. Then everything went black. How'd you even find me in the first place?"

"Whoa. Slow down." Aidan raises his hands. "Can't give you answers if you keep asking questions."

"Sorry."

"Yeah. Well, everyone was freakin' out when you got pulled underwater. I was all scared and thinking I was never gonna see you again. Nadia was bawling her eyes out. Melanie was about to faint, and even Dunstan looked

worried. Your grandma was almost ready to dive in after you.

"Just as we were thinking you were a goner, there was this really loud screech like a dinosaur getting attacked by bagpipes." Everyone in the room rolls their eyes at his description, but he keeps going. "The next thing we know, there's a dead gator bobbing on the surface."

I gag on air. My winged hero killed the alligator?

"It's disgusting, isn't it? I practically barfed, it was gross. With its tongue hanging out and blood comin' out of its head and its eyes all glassy and—"

"I don't need an image, thank you."

"Sorry dude. Anyway, the gator came up and everyone was all grossed out. But your grandma told us all to calm down because a dead gator was a good sign because you managed to defend yourself and were gonna swim up to the surface soon. But you didn't come up. By now we thought you were dead and everyone was crying. I even think I saw a tear go down Dunstan's face."

I snort. "I'd be surprised."

Nadia joins in. "We took the boat back to the dock and when we got there, we started looking around, running down the banks and calling your name. But suddenly Melanie said she heard something. We all stopped and listened, and we heard it, too! It was someone shouting in pain. Babette told Dunstan and Melanie to go up to the house and call the police, and then she ran off while Aidan and me followed. Jackass and Ditzy must have taken off after they called, 'cause we haven't seen 'em since."

"At first we couldn't find anything while wading through all those plants, but then Aidan spotted something through the trees. We all ran towards it. And there you were. You probably know what happened from there," Babette concludes.

58

"I'm guessing that after I passed out, you guys carried me back to the house where Dad and the entire Roland police force were waiting? And as soon as everyone saw I was alive, everybody left except you four and an ambulance, which basically took me here with you in tow?"

Babette chuckles. "That pretty much sums it up." It's so good to hear her laugh. I'd thought I'd never hear it again.

I exhale, exhausted. "What a day," I mutter, rubbing my head with a tubing-free hand. "And all I wanted was to work on my Biology project."

"Well, you're not going down to the swamp anytime soon. You're going to be in here for a little bit, according to the doctors," Dad reports.

"How long is a little bit?" I ask.

"A week and a half."

I groan. "That long? I can't stay in the hospital for a week and a half! What about school?" I almost add "And what about her?" but I shut my mouth.

"Nadia and I can bring you your homework and stuff," Aidan offers.

"And the doctor thinks you might get out early," Nadia adds. "He said the bite's healing well and you won't get stuck with any permanent damage."

"Speaking of the doctor, I should go get him," says Dad. He goes to leave, but stops at the doorframe before turning back. "Did anyone see where Dr. Felix went after his last visit?"

"I think I saw him go to the right." Babette points down the hall. "I'll help you find him."

"Thanks, Babette." He glances at the space next to my head. Even now he can't look at me. "Remember to page if something goes wrong."

I swallow my disappointment and nod. "Will do."

As soon as they leave, Aidan closes the door.

Nadia raises an eyebrow. "What was that for?"

"I don't want anyone to hear us," Aidan replies. He comes over and plops down on the edge of the bed, narrowly missing my uninjured leg. He leans forward, staring at me intently while completely invading my personal space.

"What are you talking about?" I ask, weirded out by his behavior more than usual.

"You had a chance to ask questions. Now it's my turn. I wanna know what happened."

My stomach flips. If I talk, I might spill about my hero. For that and some other reason I can't pin down, I want to keep quiet. "Your turn? But nothing happened. I killed the gator and saved myself. End of story."

"No it's not!"

"Yes it is."

"Don't give us that, dude. You're not telling us everything."

"Nothing happened. Really. I don't want to talk about it."

He just keeps looking at me. It's one of those looks that could make a wall crack open and spill out whatever's behind it. The longer this continues, the more unnerved I get.

I'm just about to cave when Nadia asks, "Is it because of your mom?"

Her simple question breaks Aidan's spell as we both gawk at her. She knows too well I don't like talking about anything having to do with my mother. Otherwise, I wouldn't have gotten so angry when Dunstan brought the subject up.

"Why do you ask?"

Nadia suddenly gets nervous and looks down at her fingers, which wriggle like little fishes. "Well, um, I mean, I…thought that you'd be, er, feeling a little traumatized since you survived when your mother…" Her voice flickers and dies, unable to complete the sentence.

The reality sinks in, cold and mind-numbing. Now that I think about it, here I am, lying on a hospital bed with enough wiring to make a power line, while Mom didn't even reach the ambulance. For her, no sirens, no hospital smell. No doctors and nurses wearing white coats, no continuously beeping monitors, and no lifeline.

Just one lost, abandoned boy crying over a bloody shell.

I fall back on my pillow in a daze. "My God."

"I'm so sorry, Rylan. I didn't mean to make you upset. I…I don't know what I was thinking," blubbers Nadia.

"Nadia, it's okay. You're right."

"Really?" Aidan asks.

I sigh, exhausted. This isn't my favorite subject to talk about, but they won't leave me alone until I do.

"I didn't remember it until now. I didn't know why I didn't want to talk about this until now," I admit. My cheeks burn with shame. How could I forget it? "But now…I'm resting on a gurney in a hospital where she should've been ten years ago." I feel my spine rattle as flashes swoop through me.

The drip of water from soaked clothes…

Tiny hands paddling at the emerald, opaque stream—

"Mommy?"

Something creeping toward the surface…

"If she could've gotten here, she'd be alive."

Nadia slowly shakes her head. "She was dead even before Doc Norm and everyone else arrived, Rylan. Nothing could have been done for her."

"They didn't even bother taking her to the hospital, Nadia. She didn't get all of this." I gesture with both arms at the equipment surrounding me. "There had to be something they could've done."

"The doctors said—"

"You can't believe all doctors," I almost snap. "Especially the ones who say everything's going to be okay. That's the biggest lie a doctor can ever tell you."

Everything's going to be okay, sonny.

No one talks when I'm done. With each look we give each other, we try to will someone to speak and shatter the gloom that's suddenly entered the room. It ends up being me.

"Didn't you have questions for me?" I asked Aidan.

Thanks to a short attention span, he doesn't remember. "Huh?"

"The reason why you closed the door?"

"Oh. You sure you want to talk?"

I shrug. "Yeah. Whatever. It's not going to go away otherwise."

"Ok." He looks around the room to make sure no one's there—no one is—before turning to me. "What happened?"

"What do you mean what happened? You were there. You saw the whole thing."

Aidan shakes his head furiously. "Not like that. I want to know what it was like for you, with getting pulled under, fighting the gator, and rescuing yourself."

"Why do you want to know about that? It was horrifying and scary, and I thought I was going to die."

"Please? I'll be your best friend."

I roll my eyes with a groan. "Fine. You guys saw the gator yank me under, right?"

Aidan nods.

"After I got pulled in, I tried to kick him, but he dodged it every time. By then he had me down on the swamp bottom and I was freaking out."

"And?"

I swallow to wet my throat before continuing. It's time now for reality to step down and for fantasy to take over.

"Thankfully, there was a rock lying nearby. I managed to grab it, but my vision was going blurry by then, so all I could do was swing it around and try to hit him with it. It took a couple tries, but I finally got him. He shrieked, let go of my leg, and I swam away."

"But why away and not back to the boat?" Nadia asks, at a loss to understand why I didn't do the most obvious thing.

I quickly think up another lie. "I didn't know that I'd actually killed that alligator. I just thought I might've stunned him or something, and once he shook off the surprise he was gonna come after me again. So I just kept swimming, not looking back and not looking where I was going."

"And then?"

"I finally realized my lungs were burning up, so I broke the surface to breathe. I didn't see you guys anywhere. I did see the shore and crawled out of the water. Seeing how bad the bite was, I tried bandaging it with some leaves. I think I passed out as soon as I was finished."

"How long where you out?"

"I don't know. But when I did wake up, I heard you guys shouting and running around. Then you all came bursting into the clearing. 'You know what happened from there,'" I quote my grandma.

"Yeah, we do." Aidan runs his hand through his hair. "God…I can't believe this happened to you. I didn't think it was going to happen again after…"

"History has a habit of repeating itself," Nadia states. "Only this was something we could've done without."

"We would've been fine without the first time, too," I mutter. Avoiding my friend's pity-filled gazes, I look over at the window across the room. Outside, there's nothing but bright blue and bits of cotton cloud. What I wouldn't give right now to be up there, like a bird, unaffected by any trouble.

"Rylan?" Nadia asks.

"Yeah?"

"You okay?"

I shake my head, tossing away any more daydreams lurking in my head. "Yeah. Just wishing I could get out of here."

Nadia starts to speak, but before she can there's a knock at the door.

"Come in!"

Dad, Babette, and some doctor in mint-green scrubs and horn-rimmed glasses—stereotypical much?—comes in. He has a manila envelope under his arm and looks relieved to see I'm awake. This has to be Dr. Felix.

"Hello, Rylan. How's the leg?" asks Dr. Felix.

"It's fine, Dr. Felix." I carefully hide a snort. Of course my leg isn't okay. That's a stupid question for a doctor to ask when he knows perfectly well that I'm injured.

"You know my name?"

"That's what Dad said your name was."

"Ah. Yes, I'm Dr. Felix, and I'm the guy who fixed your leg. You got a real number done on it."

"Yeah. Gators can really do that."

Dr. Felix laughs. "Making jokes, huh? That's a sure sign that you're getting better already."

Dr. Felix takes a large X-ray out of the envelope and holds it up to the ceiling so the fluorescent light illuminates it. "All right, here's what Rylan's leg looked like when he was brought in."

"That had to hurt," Aidan announces. Nadia winces.

I have to agree, it's pretty bad. The bones in my lower leg have multiple fractures, some wide and hulking, and others that are so hair-thin that you can't see but you know they're there.

"Believe it or not, the bite is a whole lot better than we thought it would be," Dr. Felix informs us. "When we started doing X-rays, we thought that the bone had completely snapped—an alligator's bite can do that—and intensive surgery would be required. But then we saw the pictures and we were shocked with the discovery."

"What discovery?" asked Babette.

"That it was already healing."

"Hmm?"

"You see, a bone starts healing when it and the surrounding tissue start to bleed. When we take X-rays of patients with broken bones, that's usually what we end up seeing. But in your case, it looks like the process was, shall we say, 'sped up.' Some of your matrix is already mineralizing and turning into bone."

Dad looks amazed. "My son's leg is already halfway repaired?"

"Not halfway, but definitely on the road to recovery. It usually takes up to six weeks for a bone to completely heal, yet it seems that Rylan's healing time has been cut down."

"Whoa," Aidan gasps, looking as astonished as everyone else.

"How's that possible?" I ask. "I would think it'd take some type of miracle for a bone to heal that fast."

"We looked over your medical records," explains Dr. Felix as he puts my X-ray away. "And they're pretty good. Despite a few cases of influenza, the common cold, and chicken pox when you were five, you've been quite healthy for most of your life. It's most likely because of how fit your body is."

The doctor's reasoning sounds...well, reasonable. But what of my winged hero? Is he or she the real reason my leg is healing ahead of schedule? Did it cast some magic healing spell or something?

Dr. Felix looks up from the folder. "Interesting cast you made yourself by the way, Rylan. What were those leaves?"

I'd forgotten about that. "Uh, pond apple leaves. There was a tree growing on the bank I landed on and I just acted."

"How could you, though? Even with the cast on you could barely walk, so how could you even stand on that leg, let alone get the leaves? And no bone can heal that fast, can it?"

Curse Nadia and her awareness. Why did she have to ask that?

"I didn't stand. There was a branch low enough that I could lean up and grab some. There was also a lot of crawling involved. And for healing fast…I don't know what to tell you." I shrug. "I'm not a doctor."

Dr. Felix interrupts. "Other than Rylan's overall good health, it's most likely the alligator didn't bite his leg as hard as he could have, and therefore it didn't break too badly. That's what seems most likely."

Nadia eyes my leg. She still looks unsure, but the only thing that comes out of her mouth is, "How long do you think Rylan's going to have that cast?"

"My guess is a little over two weeks. Perhaps more," Dr. Felix informs us. "But we still want Rylan to stay here for at least a couple more days, in case there's infection."

"Very well. Thank you, Dr. Felix," Babette thanks him. I don't feel as grateful. The last thing I want to do is stay immobile in a place with gross food and background music consisting of beeping IVs.

Dr. Felix smiles. "No problem. I'll send Nurse Vandale by shortly with some food and a new IV bag; that one's almost out. If you need anything else, just page me." He opens the door and leaves.

Dad glances at his watch. "As much as I know everyone is enjoying the visit, it's time to go."

As my friends groan, I ask, "When will I see you guys again?"

Dad turns his face towards the door, totally avoiding me. "We'll try to come in tomorrow. Babette will bring some more things down so you won't be bored."

"Bye, dude." Aidan and Nadia wave goodbye. Babette gives me a gentle hug, and they leave. I watch their silhouettes pass the drawn blinds at the window.

I sigh tiredly, resting my head on my pillow. Sleep would be good, but too much is happening to me and I know I won't be able to settle in. It's more than a single sane person can handle. And I'm stuck here, with nothing to look forward to except getting out. Because once I do, I'm finding that swamp angel.

That is, if it even exists at all.

I'll just have to see.

Chapter 7

"Turn that radio down, you hooligan! I can't watch my show with that junk blaring."

I shoot Mr. Polanski a frustrated glare. That's the fifth time today he's said that. "It's not that loud, sir. I can barely hear it myself."

He doesn't look at me as he keeps his beady eyes glued to the tiny television screen in the corner. "Well it's no wonder! Kids these days keep the volume up so loud, they'll be deaf by the time they're twenty! That's why you can't hear it! When I was your age…"

As the TV show blares its tinny, high-pitched noises, I bury my face in my hands and again wish I wasn't here.

It's been two days since I was admitted into the hospital. And let me just confess that if I was suddenly given the choice to stay here or go to Hell, the latter would definitely win out, especially considering the torture I've been going through.

How people think hospitals are quiet places is beyond me. Wouldn't you think the patients might want some quiet time while they heal up or wait for operations or whatever? Apparently no one's come up with that idea, because it's never quiet. Gurneys roll by, people who've lost someone wail in the night, and doctors and nurses yell orders at each other. The worst is the stupid IV machine, which is constantly beeping and waking me up in the middle of the night when the dreams—yes, I'm still having them—aren't. I've been making do with the room's radio, but if I don't get my iPod and headphones soon, I'll go crazy. The one thing Babette forget to bring me...

Then there's my psycho nurse, Ms. Vandale. She's this giant woman with bulging biceps straining against her scrubs, feathery brown hair, and thick Coke-bottle glasses perched on her stub of a nose. Her whole appearance reminds me of a rather muscular owl. She never lets me leave my hospital room, mutters random things under her breath, and has practically numbed my right arm with too many shots to count. If I can't hold anything when I go home, it's her fault completely.

Suddenly, there's a metallic crash in the hallway right by our door so deafening I jump in my bed, sending my strung-up leg swinging. It even draws Mr. Polanski's attention away from the TV screen. Following the clatter is the sound of rolling wheels and things sliding on the floor, all topped off with a stream of unflattering curses.

"How are we supposed to heal and relax with all those gibbering idiots out there!?" Mr. Polanski rants as he turns back to the TV. "This is a hospital, for land's sake, not some orchestra pit!"

Did I forget to mention my demonic roommate? Mr. Charles Leroy Polanski is probably the grumpiest, grayest old man ever to walk the planet—or roll, since he sits in a wheelchair. The hospital staff was *so* kind to make me share my room with him while he waits for some type of operation. It hasn't even been a full day since he came in and already he's criticized my taste in music, reduced one of the nurses to tears, and told me so many "when I was

your age" stories I want to scream and beat myself into unconsciousness.

The door springs open and hits the wall with a loud crack. It's Vandale, balancing my dinner tray in one hand while herding in a stressed-looking Aidan and Nadia, fresh out of school. Aidan holds my backpack, so Vandale hands Nadia the tray and instructs her to make sure I eat everything before leaving.

Mr. Polanski scowls. "Yippee. Just what this hospital needs—more noisy kids mucking about. Do me a favor and see if you can actually stay quiet while you chit chat." He reaches over with his long arms and pulls at the divider curtain, obscuring himself from view.

"Damn. Who stuck a stick up your roommate's ass?" Aidan growls.

I frown at the divider curtain. "Who knows? Perhaps he was born with a stick already there."

"Maybe that's why he's here. He's having an operation to get his ass stick removed," suggests Nadia.

I wiggle around under the sheets as well as I can since my leg is up. "So how's life back in the real world?"

"Boring as ever." Aidan sits on my bed. "Nothing interesting."

"How's everything at school?"

"Nothing new there," Nadia says. Coming over, she gives me my dinner tray. Spaghetti with mystery meatballs, wilted salad, milk, and lime Jell-O. Yum.

"Although you're now considered a celebrity," Aidan adds. "Everyone's talking about the whole thing. There are these crazy rumors flying around about how everything happened."

"Dunstan works fast."

"Who else? It's thanks to him you've got sudden status—he couldn't keep his big yap shut."

"Asshole," I grumble. I look over at the hallway window while twirling noodles around my fork. Slowly a little ball begins to form. "What happened out there? I heard something crash."

"Some orderly tried to wheel an instrument cart and a gurney together, but the hallway was really narrow so he ended up going against the wall and the cart tipped over," Aidan answers.

I shake my head in disbelief. "What a freaking mess."

"Yep."

"Didn't I tell you kids to keep it down!?" snaps Mr. Polanski from behind the curtain. "I can't hear my show with you all hee-hawing like that!"

That instantly shuts us up as we all wrinkle our noses. Hee-hawing?

Aidan shakes his head over the word choice. "Who in their right mind says that?"

Nadia makes a face. "Uh, no one?"

"Right." I point at my backpack. "Can I have that?"

Aidan hands it to me.

"So what do you think everything's going be like when I go back home?" I ask as I unzip it.

"Everyone's gonna act either all weird, treat you like some kind of hero, or just check to make sure that you're okay and then move on with their lives," Aidan predicts.

I raise an eyebrow. "You only said the last one because that's where you and Nadia fall."

"Well, it's true. I mean, you're okay, so that's all that matters. This isn't something any of us are ever gonna forget, but everything's fine now."

"I guess…" Finding nothing important in my backpack besides homework, I ask, "Is this all you had?"

"That reminds me." Nadia pulls a little paper bag out of her own backpack. "Your grandma told us to give you these."

"When did you see Babette?" I ask as I open the bag. My headphones and iPod are right on top, and underneath are some paperback books and candy.

"When school let out, we stopped by your house to see if your family wanted to come," Nadia explains. "Your dad wasn't there, and Babette was all about cleaning the house for your return. She gave us all this and told us to give them to you."

"And here we are," Aidan concludes.

I quietly open a Hershey bar and break some squares off. "That's cool of her, cleaning the house. I wish her the best of luck when she takes on my room."

I pass the chocolate out. Both stick their pieces straight into their mouths as I nibble on mine.

"How's your leg?" asks Nadia after swallowing her chocolate.

I look up at my leg. "It's fine. Dr. Felix said it's healing well and we can take it out of the sling soon. He said it might be a couple more days before I'm released."

"And not a moment too soon. Imagine if you had to stay any longer."

"If that happened, you'd never see me again, 'cause I'd be committed to some crazy asylum for the rest of my life."

Aidan chuckles. "Life would be very boring if you went. Who else would I play video games with, get homework help from, and check out Melanie with?"

Nadia instantly frowns. She crosses her arms and looks away, refusing to be part of the subject.

"How is Melanie? Did the attack traumatize her?"

"She's fine," Aidan reports, ignoring his sister's eye-roll. "The attack didn't affect her at all. Happy as ever."

"And still with Dunstan," Nadia adds. She seems pleased with this piece of news.

This is surprising. "I thought she might break up with him after seeing what a bastard he was. It's his fault I was nearly alligator food."

Aidan shrugs. "Who knows? It's not like—"

A knock at the door cuts Aidan off. "Mr. Forester? Is your food fine?"

"I'm done." I hold up my still-full tray as Vandale enters the room.

She eyes all the food left. "Already? You didn't eat much."

"I'm not really hungry."

She heaves an exaggerated sigh as she picks up my tray, muttering something about teenagers and their appetites before she orders, "Remember to push the buzzer when you need me to escort your friends out. It's almost the end of visiting hours."

"Actually, we were just leaving right now," Aidan tells her, rising from my bed. "Lots of homework to do, ya see."

Nadia leans over and hugs me carefully. "Bye, Rylan. See you soon."

I pat her back. "Right back at you."

I watch until I can't see them anymore, then lean back with a contented smile. The visit made me feel much better. Maybe the rest of my stay won't be so bad after all.

Mr. Polanski suddenly throws back the curtains. "Finally. I'd thought that noisy bunch of yours would never leave. All they did was talk. Now when I was your age…"

And any good feeling I had is now out the window. I groan as Mr. Polanski starts another story. I hope to God I can survive this.

Miraculously, I do. Slowly but surely, each day somehow passes. I eat my crappy hospital food, find ways to entertain myself, do my homework, and try to survive Vandale's and Mr. Polanski's craziness. Thanks to the daily visits of Aidan, Nadia, and occasionally Babette—Dad never comes back— I'm able to live through the madness that is St. Amabilis.

I'm next to Babette as she finishes all the paperwork. We're in the front lobby, all ready to go. It's three in the afternoon, and it's a beautiful Saturday outside. Perfect weather for swamp angel-hunting when I get home.

"That's it!" Babette concludes as she signs her last signature. She neatly stacks the papers, hands them to the lady at the front desk, and we leave, me limping and stumbling all the way. These crutches are going to take some getting used to.

Babette helps me up into the truck and we're soon on the road home.

"The swamp hasn't been the same without you, you know," Babette tells me.

"What do you mean?"

"A lot of people have been taking tours ever since your accident. But it's not the same without my first mate sitting next to me. Even the swamp seems upset you were gone."

"Seriously?"

"Seriously."

"You're pulling my leg."

"I'm not. You can see it for yourself tomorrow."

"I have to wait until tomorrow?"

"You heard what Dr. Felix said. He wants you to rest today, and I intend to make you follow his advice."

"But, Babette, I really want to go down to the swamp." I can't wait anymore. I need to solve this swamp angel/hero mystery.

"No buts. And why would you want to go down there anyway? You just got out of the hospital after being attacked by an alligator, for goodness sakes! I'd think you'd avoid even *thinking* of going down there after what happened."

"I'm not scared of the swamp; it *didn't* attack me. It was the gator. Those I'm afraid of, not some piece of land we look after."

Babette wearily nods. She knows I have a point. "I guess I'm just overreacting. I'm sorry."

"It's okay. I know you mean well."

A moment of silence passes before I try again.

"Can I go down to the swamp?"

"No, and stop asking."

I do. It's pointless to argue with Babette any longer. I really am going to have to wait until tomorrow.

Some hours later I'm in my now-clean room, courtesy of Babette. I'm lying in bed, typing on my laptop and sipping the water Babette brought up. As soon as I got home, Babette immediately put me to bed, telling me to stay and rest unless I have to use the can. It's so boring, I feel like I'm back in the hospital, just without the crazy roommate and overbearing nurse. I feel antsy and want to do nothing more than limp down to the swamp. But I can't, because Babette's probably one second away from establishing a guard post outside my room.

Someone knocks at my door.

"Come in," I say, my eyes not leaving the screen.

To my surprise, it's Dad, still in his suit. "Hello, Rylan." He speaks to my nose. He's actually looking at my face, so this makes me feel a little better.

I close my laptop as I reply with, "Hi Dad."

"How's the leg?"

I shrug. "It's fine. Practically feels like normal, but Babette won't believe otherwise. She's made me stay in bed since I got home, and I'm bored."

"The day's nearly over." Dad pushes his glasses up his nose. "Just go to sleep and it'll be tomorrow before you know it."

I look out my window. The sun's starting to set behind the black outline of the trees, setting the sky on fire.

"I guess," I mumble. When I don't keep speaking, Dad takes it as a sign to leave and he turns to go.

"I never saw you in the hospital after your first visit."

Dad stops, not turning around to face me.

"My friends visited every day, and Babette every other day, but you never showed up."

I see his shoulders slump.

"How come, Dad?"

Dad still faces the door as he gives his reply. "I know you wanted to see me, and I'm sorry I couldn't make it. But I couldn't get away from work, Rylan. I'm stuck in that office all day, and it's hard to leave."

"That's not the real reason."

Dad doesn't talk.

"It's Mom, isn't it? You stayed away because this whole incident brought up old memories."

Dad still says nothing.

"It's been ten years, Dad. Even after all this, I'm trying to move on. Maybe it's time you did, too."

That's the last straw for Dad. He storms out of my room, slamming the door behind him. I keep an eye on it, hoping Dad will come back in and we can talk everything out, but I soon give up. It's pointless. Dad's not coming back and I bet I've just earned a whole week of silent treatment. That's what usually happens when we fight about Mom.

I toss my head back and close my eyes. This isn't the homecoming I was hoping for.

"I am...forever watching..."

The remnants of those words echo in my mind as I wake. My clock reads midnight, and everything around me is black. It's like darkness has come to life and taken over my room, to turn it into part of its somber realm. I look around, staring at everything and wondering to myself what creatures live in a shadow world. Night demons, vampires, werewolves...

Swamp angels...

I can't wait anymore. I have to get down to the swamp. I need to find her.

I grab my crutches leaning against the wall. With their help, I pull myself upright and make it over to the window. It's too risky going out the front door; someone could catch me, that someone being Babette, who has to be the world's lightest sleeper. In my current state, she'd be out of bed the moment I trip over myself. So time for Plan B. Fiddling with the lock, I slowly open the window. Cool night air blows in and hits my bare chest, making me shiver. I limp over to my dresser and pull out a sweatshirt, then snatch the sneaker for my non-broken foot off the floor. Finally, I pull open my desk drawer and after some digging find a ball of string.

I sit on the windowsill, tug my sweatshirt on, and stick my shoe on my foot. Carefully, slowly, I swivel my legs around—first one, then the other—until I'm outside, sitting on the roof. Silently, I congratulate myself for making it this far without waking anyone up.

But here comes the tricky part.

I pull my crutches through the window and tie them together with the string. Quietly as possible, I scoot to the roof's edge until my legs are dangling freely over the edge. Like lowering a bucket into a well, I carefully lower my crutches off the roof. They hit the ground with a soft *clack*. I drop the rest of the string. Watching it fall only emphasizes the distance between me and the ground, and for a second I think of how I'll end up back in the hospital again if I fall and how stupidly dangerous it all is.

But it's worth it to get the answer. Scooting away from the brim, I start moving towards the left, where the top of the trellis is. It's nothing spectacular; just your basic trellis of crisscrossing white pieces of wood with vines growing on it. I don't even know if it will hold me up, but until my leg heals, it's the only way.

My butt hurts from going over the shingles in my cotton pajama pants, but I reach the lattice. In a feat worthy of a trapeze artist, I twist my body around and begin to descend. It's real hard for someone with a broken leg, but before long I'm on the ground.

I hop over to my crutches quickly, my arms flapping like bird wings until I can tuck them under my arms. Then I'm off like a shot, limping quickly towards the swamp—and my answer.

The swamp's incredible at night. Most people think it's creepy, with the trees and water turning into unidentifiable forms that give the impression of hiding monsters. But it's not scary at all, as long as you avoid the water and whatever could be lurking in it. The darkness works with the swamp by softening it, turning trees into sculptures of black velvet streaked with silver moonbeams. Throw in millions of diamond stars glittering above, and a chorus of crickets and bullfrogs, and you probably have the most beautiful landscape ever.

But that's not my focus as I stand at the end of the dock. I'm on a mission to see if she does exist. I need to know if I'm going crazy.

I need to know if fantasy is real.

"Hello? Anyone out there?" I call out. I'm far enough from the house I don't have to worry about waking anyone.

"If you're here, you know who you are. I…want to thank you," I continue.

There's no reply, but I keep talking.

"I don't know…if you're real or not. I mean, if you are, that's okay. Weirder things have happened, I guess."

Nothing's said back. I shift awkwardly on my crutches, feeling stupid. Why did I do this again?

"I may be insane for doing this, but…yeah. Just wanted to say thanks," I conclude. Turning around I limp down the dock.

However, I suddenly get the feeling I'm not alone. You know the feeling; you can't see anyone, but you know someone's there behind you.

I spin around. "He-hello?" I croak.

There isn't anything at first. But then something moves. Something big shifts in the shadows. There's a creak of boards.

And she steps out into the moonlight.

Chapter 8

All my breath escapes me in one awe-filled gasp.

She's here. She's real, standing right in front of me.

She's beautiful.

It's like the picture in Babette's book has stepped off the page. She's tall and elegant, wearing a long dress made from woven grass and cinched at the waist with vines. The moonlight illuminates her otherworldly features— pale green skin, long, dark green hair, small curved horns growing out of her forehead, pointed ears, four-fingered hands with claws and webbing, narrow gills on her slender neck, a leaf mask that covers her mouth, and bony, skinless, ivy-covered wings on her back.

And the eyes...those emerald, kindly snake eyes that right now stare at me very intently, waiting for me to speak.

"Um...he-hello."

I mentally curse myself for stuttering, but she doesn't notice as she keeps staring at me.

"I, er, guess you must've heard my little speech," I continue. "Well, I, um, meant all of it. You saved me from that alligator, so thank you."

She stays silent, but she does take a step forward. What's she going to do? Attack me? Kill me? Eat my flesh and spit out the bones?

She smiles with her eyes.

I know that sounds impossible, but it happens. Her eyes suddenly lighten, burning with life, and I feel this…aura of happiness and pleasure pulsing from them. If her mouth was uncovered, I bet I'd see a grin.

She finally speaks in the voice from my dreams.

"You…are welcome."

I smile slowly. It's amazing to hear that voice for real.

There's a moment of silence before she speaks again, like she's building up her strength to talk.

"Thank you…for coming. I was…hoping you would…with the dreams…I sent you."

"So you *are* behind those dreams. I thought it was just something I ate."

She shakes her head. *"It is not. For if…we are in…a dream, it is a…dream we send. It means…the swamp is…in trouble."*

"Yeah. I told my grandma about it. She's been patrolling the swamp since."

She nods. *"I…have seen her. She always…checks to see…that everything is…fine. She is…a good friend…to this swamp. And always…has been."*

"But she hasn't found anything," I tell her. Perhaps it's a stupid move, but I take a few steps forward. She stands her ground. "Babette's looked all over, but she hasn't found anything harming the swamp."

"She hasn't…found it…because it is right…under her nose."

"Huh?"

The swamp angel steps towards the edge of the dock and motions at me to join her. At first I hesitate, but when she does nothing else, I curiously hobble over. I notice the

smell coming off her. It's like cut grass and fresh leaves and surprisingly not too swampy.

She points into the water. *"There. It is…there."*

Squinting, I try to see whatever she's looking at, but all I see is rippling black. "What's there?"

"The…poison. The…trash."

"It's under the water?"

"Yes…right there. I have seen…the man put it…there. As he has…other times before."

"Man? What man?

"A pale man…with moonlight hair, eyes…of ice, and…a voice of…death."

My hands clench around the grips of my crutches as my temper simmers. Mr. Lebelle. It has to be him from her description. That bastard.

"I know him," I grumble. The swamp angel winces at my sudden change in tone, but she doesn't speak. "Don't worry. I promise you that man will never bother the swamp again. I'll tell my grandma to look here, and she'll take the trash out. But why he would hide it here, I have no clue."

"The man…would hide it…here because he…knows you… would not look…here because…it is obvious. He knows…you would look in…other spots…like before, but not this…one." She tilts her head like a questioning puppy. *"Do you…understand…what I say?"*

"I do. But how do you know how to talk, and why do you pause?"

That question totally changes the subject, but I have to know why. Ever since her first words I've noticed her talking pattern and I wonder if she's noticed it herself.

She looks taken aback and confused. *"What do…you mean?"*

"I've read about you in books. You never show yourself to humans, so how do you know how to talk like one? And when you do, there's this break in the sentence…like this. It's not a bad thing!" I add when she starts to apologize. "I just want to know why."

"Like you, I…learned from a book, left…behind by a man… long, long ago. And…my speaking is most…likely," she begins, *"because I…have never…spoken until now."*

This surprises me. "Don't you talk to the animals or something? How can you deal with all the quiet?"

"The swamp…is never quiet." She pauses, realizing she broke the sentence, but continues. *"The songs…of the animals…are always here. We talk to each…other through our…minds. So yes…I do talk to them."*

"But can't you use your voice for that?"

"It is unfair…to the animals. They can't speak…like us. So I try…to make them…comfortable…by speaking like…them."

"How does it feel to really talk?"

Her face lights up with joy. *"It is…wonderful. Even though… my voice…is not used…to this."*

"Practice a bit and you'll get better. Practice makes perfect," I suggest. She smiles at me with her eyes again as we lapse into silence. But it's not an awkward silence. It's filled, comforting. It's a moment when, for once, everything feels right in the world.

I yawn. Loudly. Even with all the excitement of tonight's discoveries, my need for sleep's finally caught up with me.

"You look…tired. I think…you should go…to bed. Since you have…received the message…I shall no longer…haunt your dreams. Sorry…to have kept…you awake." She hangs her head, her fingers tapping together nervously.

I want to pat her arm, give her a hug—just do something to cheer up this innocent and childlike creature. Since she hasn't been anything but polite to me, I know I can trust her. But I have no idea what she would do if I touched her, even in a friendly way. I fear I could break her with a single

brush of my fingers, shattering her delicate skin like a glass figurine.

"It's okay, really," I tell her instead. "You were doing it for the good of the swamp. And losing some sleep never killed anyone. Although that doesn't seem to go for alligators." I look down at my cast.

She giggles. It's a magical, beautiful sound.

"I want to see you again."

This quickly quiets her as she stares at me in nervous shock. *"W—why?"* she stutters.

"Because you're interesting. You're a swamp angel, for God's sake. People don't know you exist or they think you're made up. But here you are, standing right in front of me," I exclaim. I'm getting more excited thinking about it. "I want to know everything about you."

"Are you…sure?" she asks. *"There are things…about my species…that you could not…begin to comprehend…"*

"Try me."

She stares at me for a minute, then nods her head. *"All right. You can…come see me…again. But tell…no one."*

"Trust me, I won't," I promise her. "Can I come tomorrow night?"

"Yes. Night is…good. I shall meet…you here." She holds up a hand and wiggles her fingers like she's waving. *"Good night."*

"You, too." I turn around and start down the dock. I'm at the end when one final thought pops into my head.

"Wait." I glance back to see if she's still there. She is. "I never introduced myself."

"You don't…have to. I know…your name."

I raise a suspicious eyebrow. "How did you know my name?"

"I have heard…people call your…name before," she answers as if this doesn't sound weird at all. *"As I said…in the dreams I…sent you, I…am forever watching…, Rylan."*

Any normal person would probably freak out learning that, for their whole life, some magical being's been observing them who knows when. But I'm not scared. It's not like she's a stalker. Maybe it's because she said my name. She said it as if it was a sacred word, all soft and sweet like it was a newly found treasure.

"Yeah. That's my name. What's yours?"

She stares off at nothing in particular. *"I...have no...true name."*

"Don't the animals call you something?"

"The animals...sometimes call me...their mistress. Other times...they call me...their guardian." She lifts and lowers her shoulders in what I recognize as a shrug. *"But I...do not think those...count as names."*

"Do you know what we...humans call you?" It's strange to refer to myself as that.

"Yes. It is Palus Angelus...otherwise meaning...swamp angel. You may...call me that."

I shake my head. "Nah. You need a true name, not some scientific description."

"Then...can you please...choose a name...for me?"

I bite my lip. "You sure you want me to name you? I don't want to give you a bad name you're going to hate."

"I trust...your judgment."

"Okay... Um..." My eyes wander around as I think of possible names. Dahlia instantly comes up, but I squash the idea just as quickly. No need to burden her with my family's problematic past and equally painful present.

Random names all having to do with nature begin to surface and swim through my head, but none of them are any good. Flower? No, she's not an animated skunk. River? That's not even a name! Forest? Might as well add Gump to the end of it.

I'm close to giving up when I glance at a nearby tree. Silvery green ivy wraps around the trunk in a giant hug, its heart-shaped leaves swaying lightly in the barely-there breeze. I look back at the swamp angel, and see the same plant woven along her bony wings, fresh and pretty as the plant on the tree. The same plant I held in my arms in the dream…

"Ivy."

"Pardon?"

"I said Ivy," I repeat. While I say it again, something clicks as I feel the word roll out of my mouth. *Ivy*. It's perfect.

"That should be your name. Ivy," I tell her.

"Ivy." She pronounces the name as if she's tasting it. Her eyes fill with a happy light and she giggles. *"My name…is Ivy."*

"Okay, Ivy. I'll see you tomorrow."

"Yes…tomorrow."

Giving her one last smile, I start limping up the path. When I look back again, she's gone, merging into the swamp she loves so much.

"Under the dock?"

It's Sunday morning and I'm in my bathrobe eating pancakes down in the kitchen. Babette looks at me oddly from by the stove, where she's frying bacon. Dad's off somewhere, probably in his study.

"You mean you never checked there?" I ask with false innocence. I just told Babette everything that the swamp angel—*Ivy*—told me about the trash.

"I don't think whoever's messing with the swamp's ecosystem would put trash in such an obvious place."

Babette pokes the sizzling meat with the spatula. She doesn't say his name, but I know she's referring to Mr. Lebelle.

I drizzle more syrup on my pancakes. "Yeah, but that's the point. Whoever it is would stash it under or near the dock because he'd know we'd suspect nothing would be hiding there."

"That makes sense," Babette agrees. She tosses in some sausage patties, which join in the loud crackling. "I guess it wouldn't hurt to check."

"Good." Cramming the last bit of fluffiness in my mouth, I set my silverware down and grab my crutches. "I'll come with you."

"Oh, no you don't. You're not going down to that dock, young man," Babette declares as she clears my plate.

"But Babette, Dr. Felix said I only had to rest yesterday!"

"Yes he did, and I won't make you stay in bed today. But you're going to stay here while I go. I don't think your crutches are able to make it down the path. It's too rough. You'll end up tripping over something."

I scoff. She doesn't know that I'm the guy who not only made it down to the dock, but also did it in the dark WITHOUT falling flat on his back.

"But Babette—"

"No buts, Rylan. You're staying here and that's final."

"Fine," I grumble. I exit the kitchen with a scowl on my face like some grouchy toddler. Plopping down onto the couch, I turn the TV on and bitterly watch the morning news.

I hear the back door creak open and closed as Babette exits the house, and I huff. Why does she insist on treating me like a baby whenever I get hurt? This always happens, no matter the injury. Like when I broke my arm on the twins' trampoline when I was twelve. I could move around and do everything just fine, but Babette still made me rest

while she did everything, and I hated that forced inability. I'm feeling like that right now, sitting on the couch watching today's weather forecast.

Some time later, I'm watching the perky faces of those "Good Morning America!" people talk when I hear the screen door swing open. I spring up and hobble back into the kitchen. Babette's grabbing a cup of coffee, and she looks frazzled and tired.

"So? Did you find anything?" I ask.

She takes a big sip before she answers. Her eyes look so exhausted. They're missing the brightness they usually hold, which means things aren't good.

"Yes," she answers, rotating her mug in her hands. "I found something real interesting, all right."

My heart skips so many beats, I might go into cardiac arrest. So Ivy was right.

"What is it?" My throat is dry, cracking my voice.

Babette sighs before she begins.

"I had my rubber slickers on and was wading into the water with my pitchfork. I probably had the head in about five feet from the end of the dock when it hit something big and sort of soft. So I stabbed it and pulled it out, and do you know what it was?"

"No. What was it?"

"An open trash bag full of crap. I can't begin to tell you what I suspect the stuff in it to be, but whatever it is it's stronger than ever. I felt around and under the dock and there have to be at least twenty of them, maybe more." She sips her coffee.

"How long do you think they've been under there?"

"Don't know, but I'm guessing a month, maybe longer."

It was a month ago that Ivy started sending me the dreams.

"It's bad, Rylan. The garbage is really starting to take its toll. The effects finally started showing when you were gone—plants yellowing and dying rapidly, and numerous dead fish and even some birds floating in the water. And at this rate it's only a matter of time before it's absorbed into the soil and the entire swamp's infected."

Babette sets her mug on the counter, her tiredness replaced with fierce determination as she reaches for the telephone. "I need to call the town hall immediately. This needs to be reported."

"The town council isn't gonna do anything, Babette. Mr. Lebelle's just going to use this against you. He'll claim the swamp is 'too dangerous' and some strip mall would be better. No one on the board will disagree with him. He has too much influence over them. They're all scared shitless."

"Don't swear, Rylan. Gentlemen don't do that," Babette scolds me as she presses buttons. "And I'm sure there's at least one town council member who isn't corrupt and will help us out."

She brings the phone to her ear and listens to it ring. Seconds later, someone must've picked up because Babette starts talking. "Yes, this is Babette Daniau, and I've found trash in my swamp."

Leaving Babette to report her findings, I make my way over to the stairs and go to my room. Pulling the charger cord out of my cellphone, I dial Aidan.

He picks up on the last ring. "Hullo?" he answers, heaving a big yawn.

"It's me."

"Rylan? What are you doing?" I hear scuffling in the background and the squeak of a mattress. "It's like nine thirty, dude. You know I don't wake up until at least ten on the weekend unless it's something important."

I resist the urge to roll my eyes. "I know, but I've got important news I have to tell you and Nadia and it can't wait."

"What—*yawn*—type of news?"

"Put your sister on and I'll tell you."

"Fine. I'll go get her."

Seconds later I hear a door slamming open, treading feet, muffled yelling—I can make out the word "Rylan"— and then the beep of the speaker phone mode turning on.

"Hey, Nadia?"

"Hi Rylan." Unlike her brother, she doesn't sound tired at all. "Aidan said you had something to tell us?"

"Yeah, dude. I got Nadia. What's going on?" Aidan asks, rejoining the conversation.

I breathe deeply. "You guys are never going to believe this, but Babette found trash in the swamp."

The reaction's immediate.

"What! Again?" They both shout at the same time. They always seem to be surprised despite it happening before.

"Yeah. Babette told me it's really bad."

"Where'd she find it all?" Aidan asks.

"Under the dock."

"Under the dock? Seriously?"

"It's actually not a bad hiding spot, bro," Nadia pipes up. "Mr. Lebelle *would* stash all the trash under the dock because he knew no one would look there."

"Oh."

"Babette thought the same thing when I told her. But she went along with it and now we have twenty-something garbage bags floating in the swamp, spilling God knows what into the water."

"Shit. That *is* bad. What are you going to do?"

"Babette just phoned the town hall to report it. She says they'll help, but I doubt they will."

"Yeah, since Mr. Lebelle has all of them under his thumb," Nadia grumbles. "He'll just use this little discovery to get what he wants."

"That's what I told her. The more proof Mr. Lebelle has of the swamp being 'unstable,' the more likely he's going to persuade everyone his mall idea is better."

"Yet your grandma calls them, giving Mr. Lebelle exactly what he wants."

I shrug as I take a seat on my bed. "Yeah, but Babette has faith there'll be one brave council member who'll help us."

"Let's assume there is such a person," Aidan suggests. "How exactly would the dude be helping out? He isn't gonna come over there himself and pull out the trash bag by bag."

"They'll do what they always do. They're going to call some professional clean-up crew who'll come out and properly clean the trash for us. It's what happened last time we found crap in the swamp," I tell them.

"I remember that! Wasn't it, like, toxic goo hidden inside a hollow log or something?"

Nadia snorts. "It was never toxic waste, you goon."

There's a sudden knock at my door.

Placing my hand over the mouthpiece, I yell, "Just a minute!" at the door. Into the phone I whisper, "Got to go, guys. Someone just knocked, and it's probably Babette and her phone report."

"Okay. Call us back sometime soon and tell us what she said," Nadia demands. "We want to help in any way we can."

"Yeah. Call us," Aidan chimes in.

"Will do. See ya."

"Bye, Rylan."

"Bye, dude."

I press the END button just as Babette knocks again.

"Come in."

Babette slowly enters. I can already tell her conversation with the town hall hasn't been successful. In those few minutes, it seems her hair has gone whiter and more wrinkles have appeared.

"I'm guessing it didn't go so well?" I ask.

"It didn't," Babette mutters. "All they did was call some clean-up crews for me. They didn't speak about investigating. You were right. They're too scared of Mr. Lebelle."

"When are they coming?"

"The cleaners? They'll come by today. No doubt Mr. Lebelle will accompany them." She rubs her forehead and sighs. "This is *not* what I need right now, with you getting out of the hospital and whatnot."

"I want to say something comforting, but I think nothing will work right now," I confess, giving Babette an apologetic smile. "Sorry."

"Your sorry is appreciated. Thank you." Babette returns the grin, but it's small and exhausted. It's the type of smile you see people wearing when they're not okay, but they lie so they don't make everyone worry. It never fools anyone. In fact, it ends up making people more nervous than before.

I rise from my bed and stumble over to Babette. "Everything's going to be fine," I tell her. "Trust me. This is going to blow over soon. Mr. Lebelle will come over, you'll fight, and he'll leave all mad like always. Everything will be back to normal."

Except for my new friend, but I digress.

Babette hugs me, careful not to crush my crutches into my rib cage. "Thanks for that, Rylan. You're right, again. Who knows? Maybe Mr. Lebelle won't show up today."

He does.

The clean-up crew's sanitizing the dock within an inch of its life and doing whatever they do to get rid of all the crap. Men in rubber armor carry weird contraptions back and forth between their white truck and the dock. From the foyer, I can hear the powerful roaring of slurping vacuums.

However, the blast of the machines pales in comparison to the thunder on the front porch.

"This is the last straw, Ms. Daniau! Do you know what would've happened if all this had been found too late?"

"It wasn't, Jules. The trash was found and the crew told me there's no lasting damage."

"But what if there had been? The whole town could've been in danger; this feeds out into the swamp surrounding the town, and it could have gotten into our water supply or local farmland and everyone would leave!"

I really, *really* want to slam the door open and tell Mr. Lebelle he's an asshole and to stop poisoning the swamp because he's never going to win. But I can't. Babette's forbidden Dad and me from coming outside, stating she could handle Mr. Lebelle on her own and he could use my injury as another reason why the swamp should be his. So Dad's off somewhere like always and I'm stuck inside, sitting on the stairs and listening to the two bicker.

I drum my fingers against my cast as I doodle on it with a Sharpie. How much longer is this going to go on before Mr. Lebelle storms off again? I zone in on the argument. Hearing him talk, it's hard to believe I used to go to this man's house on a regular basis to actually try and prove to him I could be a good friend to Dunstan.

"I make my offer again, Ms. Daniau. Let me buy your swamp!"

"And I repeat, Mr. Lebelle, the answer is no! Now I'm kindly asking, please leave us alone."

I think he's about to go when Mr. Lebelle pulls out the big guns. "What about your grandson?"

The Sharpie falls from my hand. It hits the floor and begins to roll away, but I don't know where it ends up.

Babette doesn't seem too shocked he brought me up because she stays as calm as ever. "What do you mean about my grandson?"

"It's come to everyone's attention—Rylan, is it?—recently got attacked by an alligator. I don't know about you, Ms. Daniau, but I would want the swamp destroyed if the same thing happened to my son."

"It wasn't the swamp itself that crushed Rylan's leg, Jules. It was an alligator attack that wouldn't have happened if your son hadn't pushed him in."

"From what Dunstan told me, he tripped over his own feet and *fell* in. Do you honestly think I won't believe my own child?"

"No, I *think* you should examine both sides of the story before you draw conclusions."

Mr. Lebelle sighs. "Then if you wish, I'll ask Dunstan about it again, but even if he did do it, nothing bad would have happened if the gator and the swamp weren't there. You wouldn't have even been in that situation."

"It is *not* the swamp's fault. Why should it be destroyed for something it didn't do?"

"It played the part of habitat. Take away the habitat and you take away the danger in it and the danger it could be if truly poisoned."

"You also take away valuable land the plants and animals need."

"They can all find a new home, Ms. Daniau. They're meant for adaptation. They'll be perfectly fine."

"No they won't be, Jules. Now I'm asking again. Please go. I'm not selling."

But he can't keep his big mouth shut. "So are you asking for another death like your daughter's?"

That tears it.

Before I can know it, I'm slamming the porch door open and furiously hobbling out. If the situation wasn't so serious, their identical expressions of surprise would be hilarious. But I'm too angry to find anything funny right now.

Babette gets over her shock quickly and starts scolding me as the sound of working machinery dies. "Rylan! I thought I told you to stay inside the house."

"Get out," I growl at Mr. Lebelle, ignoring Babette. "Get off our land and leave my family alone."

Mr. Lebelle smirks. "Eavesdropping, eh? Someone should have done a better job at teaching you manners, kid."

"You mean like my mother? Sorry, but she's not here, as you well know. You were at her funeral with your son." I point to the driveway with my crutch, trying my best to look menacing. "Now get in your car, go away, and never come back."

His oily smirk falls from his face and is replaced by his trademark scowl. He stomps off the porch, down the driveway, gets to his car, and drives away.

"Why didn't you stay in the house like I said?" Babette asks.

"Because I couldn't let him continue. Dunstan bringing her up was one thing, but Mr. Lebelle totally crossed the line!" I stare at Babette, my breath coming out in short angry puffs. "Don't tell me you're not mad. You have to be."

Babette frowns. "I am, but showing it won't change anything. Rude as it was, he still said it and it can't be taken back. No point wasting anger over something that can't be changed. But hey," she comes over and pats my shoulder,

"thanks for coming out here and telling him off. It's highly appreciated."

Despite myself, I crack a tiny smile. "You're welcome."

"Now I know you were sitting on the stairs listening in, but what about your father?"

"I think he's still hiding out in his study."

"Should I go tell him World War III is over for now?"

"Probably."

Babette steps into the house as I prop my head against the wall. Seconds later, mechanical roars and squeals make me jump. Realizing I should go inside unless I want to go deaf, I grab my crutches and hobble back inside, but not before I send a glance over my shoulder toward the swamp, thinking of Ivy. She must be terrified with all the noise down there. Something tells me she hasn't seen any machines other than the boat. I bet she's never even seen the world beyond the swamp. How long has she lived there?

More questions are surfacing. Guess I have to wait until I see her tonight to get my answers.

Have you ever wanted something to come fast? You spend your day pacing around the house, looking at the clock every five minutes, grumbling to yourself why time had to slow down today of all days, and you eventually feel like exploding with impatience. Ever felt like that?

That's what I'm feeling as I wait for night to fall.

When the clean-up crew finally leaves, we have dinner. I swallow my food like I'm a starving man. Dad and Babette take notice, but I lie that I'm really hungry and have homework to do. After clearing the table, I hang out in my room doing random stuff while waiting for the adults to fall asleep. When Babette pops her head in to wish goodnight, I make a show of lying on my bed and pretending to sleep.

When I hear the last light turn off, I get off my bed, still fully clothed, and proceed to escape the house the same way I did last night. Because of my impatience, I'm not as careful and end up making some noise as I scurry around. But no one comes after me, so I'm safe.

Once outside, I haul ass down the path. My armpits hurt from swinging my crutches so much, but I ignore it as I emerge from the trees. The dock looks like it did last night, as if a haz-mat team had never scrutinized it.

Pulling back my sleeve, I check my watch in the light of the half-moon. 11:46. I stand there and wait for Ivy to come. As minutes pass I go over questions in my head. How old is she, what other magic can she do, are there really more of her kind, what do the animals she talks to talk about? The list goes on. My curiosity's overflowing.

Behind me, the dock creaks and claws clack against wood. I turn and look. It's Ivy, standing about two yards away from me. She looks as enchanting as she did last night.

"Hey, Ivy."

Her eyes instantly light up. *"You called me…by my name."*

"Of course. That's your name now."

"My apologies. I am…still getting used…to it."

"It's fine. How are you?"

"I am fine. But…my ears hurt…horribly. Many people in odd… dress came down with…strange contraptions. They made much… ruckus, and scared the animals…and me. But they took…all the poison with them."

I chuckle. "Yeah. That was the cleaning crew the town sent over when Babette called in."

"I saw her, too. She…came down early in…the day and…poked around the dock…with a sharp stick. She found it. Did you tell… her?"

I nod. "Yeah. She didn't believe me at first, but I convinced her."

"Yes, you did. Thank you…very much." Ivy bows regally, her hands together. *"The swamp…shall soon be back…to normal…because of you."*

"No problem."

Ivy takes a step forward as if she's scared I'll be like a rabbit and dart off. When I make no movement she walks closer until she's right in front of me, staring deeply into my eyes. Being this close, I can pick up the details of her beautiful face. Her skin is actually made of little scales and her eyes have splotches of every shade of green sprinkled around the black slits. My own eyes fall on the mask over her mouth. I wonder why she wears that.

"Why…are you looking at me…like that?"

"N-nothing," I stutter, looking away. "Sorry. I was just spacing out."

Ivy tilts her head, looking confused and, therefore, utterly cute. *"'Spacing…out?' What is that?"*

"It's when you don't pay attention to what's in front of you because you're thinking of something else."

"What were…you thinking about?"

"Er…how lovely it is that the swamp's cleaned up." Damn. I can feel my face flushing.

"Yes…it is nice the swamp…is clean." She doesn't notice the raging red taking over my cheeks. *"And as thanks, I…wish to give…you something."*

"You don't have to give me anything."

"But I do…wish to. As a token…of appreciation. And possibly…friendship."

I smile as I nod. "Okay. How could I possibly refuse?"

Ivy beams and offers me a hand. Its webbing is nearly translucent in the moonlight. *"Take…my hand."*

"Why?" I stare at it. It's not like I'm scared of her, but this will be the first time we've ever touched.

"I need to take...you to where your...reward lies. I shall not harm...you, so please...trust me."

She doesn't have to tell me twice. I know I can from those unguarded, innocent eyes.

"Okay," I answer. I drop one of my crutches. And stepping forward, I take her hand in mine.

Chapter 9

The common misconception concerning snakeskin is that it's either slimy or dry. Subconsciously, I'd had the same thought about Ivy's skin, but as I hold her hand now I learn otherwise. Her hand's delicate, her skin soft like some down pillow, and the webbing's like lace. A powerful, unknown energy courses from her hand, traveling to every limb and spreading this amazing feeling throughout my body.

Ivy glances down at our hands serenely. *"Your hand is... strong."* She looks back at me. *"And yet also...very kind. These are...kind hands."*

The telltale blush is back. Not wanting her to notice, I say, "Can we go?"

Ivy takes no offense as she nods. *"Yes."*

Gently pulling my hand, she walks to the end of the dock, me limping behind her. We stop at the edge. I look down, watching my shifting reflection on the water below. "Er...what now?"

Still holding my hand, Ivy steps off the dock and walks on water.

My jaw literally drops to the floor as I stare at where her feet are. She isn't sinking, but floating on the surface.

"Holy crap," I whisper. "Oh my—how'd you—"

Ivy giggles at my babbling. *"It is…something I can do. The place where we…go is not…far. Just never let go…of my hand, and you will…float, too."*

I stare back down at the water. What if I sink? I'm not exactly prepared for a midnight dip, especially with a cast that can't get wet. But I've promised myself to trust Ivy. After all, she saved my life.

I nod. "Okay." Ivy gives my hand a reassuring squeeze. I drop my second crutch. Closing my eyes and holding my breath, I take a leap of faith and step off the dock.

Nothing happens.

I open one eye. The other soon follows.

I'm walking on swamp water. It feels so weird under my feet. I can feel the liquid under my soles, and it seems both solid and breakable at the same time.

Ivy gently tugs my hand, amused at my amazement. "Come."

Like a mother leading her child, we walk away from the dock. We take a left and go down the middle of a watery passageway.

Trees bend over us like wicked hands about to snatch us up. Owls hoot in the darkness. Diamond stars are scattered irregularly across a velvet-black sky. Their pinpoint light shines on the rippling water.

"This is incredible," I glance around to take in everything as fast as I can. "I can't believe I'm doing this. This is… wow."

"I am glad to see…you like it."

"I do. I just hope my cast doesn't get too wet."

"Is that…what the thing on…your leg is?"

"Yeah. Didn't you already know that?"

"I…have never left this swamp." She gestures at the surrounding plants with her free hand as if they'll nod in agreement. *"I do, however, know…a little of…human culture."*

"How?"

"For ages, many…types of people have…come to this swamp. The early people called Indians…the settlers…the ones of today. I…have seen many…come and go. I have learned…from them."

Indians? Pioneers? Holy crap, how old is she?

I'm about to ask when Ivy suddenly halts. Turning to the right, she points into the trees.

"There."

"What's there? I don't see anything."

"Follow me."

Pulling me with her, we step off the water and back onto solid land. She doesn't let go of my hand, so the magic supporting my busted leg still flows into me. Weaving through the trees, I squint, trying to see where we are. I've stayed on the boat the majority of the times I've come down here, because I've rarely tried walking along the swamp banks for fear I'll mistake water for land and end up taking a swim.

I stare at the overhanging branches that grow thicker and thicker. "I've never seen this part of the swamp before."

"Really?"

"Yeah. I stay in our boat whenever I come down here."

"That was how…it was for…all the others. They too stayed in… their floating crafts for…fear of the water. That is why this…has never been found."

"What do you mean?"

For an answer she pushes some low-hanging branches ahead of us to the side. A giant clearing is revealed. It's like God had taken a razor blade and shaved away a patch of trees. With the moon above like a light bulb, I see everything perfectly. Long, thick grass carpets the entire ground, spotted with swamp fern. Shadows of surrounding trees dye chunks of the land dark gray.

The most stunning, however, is the black gum tree. Centered right in the middle, its long limbs reach right for the sky. A couple of ghost orchids, pale and delicate, mix in with the leaves.

"Wow."

"This is my...secret place," says Ivy. *"When I am not out... traveling around the swamp...I come here."*

"So it's like a house for you." I glance around. "Who knew that a clearing could be here?"

"No one. No one has...ever found this place...like I said."

We walk up to the tree. Scraps of dark blue dance between silvery black branches and dark green fronds.

"My tree." Ivy introduces it to me like an old friend. *"It has been...with me for a long...time. It provides much...for me."*

"Like what?"

"A place to...sleep. I sleep in...the branches with...leaf blankets. Food to eat, with...its black stone fruit. And," she kneels at the base of the trunk, *"a place for...my treasures."*

Carefully I kneel down next to her. I soon spot what she means. Near the ground is a hole, about medium size but hidden well by a clump of weeds. Silently, Ivy reaches behind the plant and inside the hollow trunk.

"It is in here...somewhere," she murmurs under her breath, feeling around for whatever she's looking for, concentration written on her face. There's a thunk, a scraping sound, and she nods to herself. *"There it is."*

"What is it?" I ask. I'm nervous, but I can't help it. There are a million and one possibilities of what she could pull out, and most of them aren't pleasant. But she doesn't pull out a skeleton or a decaying body.

Out of the hole comes a roughly carved box. It's the size of a loaf of bread and it looks old: the wood's well worn with scratches all along the outside.

Ivy reaches back into the hollow and pulls out more boxes. There's four in total, all different sizes and all crudely carved from wood. The last item brought out is a gunnysack, the bottom crusted with dirt.

"Please, sit," she requests.

I carefully turn and sit down, my legs spread out and my back against the trunk. Ivy sits to the side, surrounded by her containers.

"Where'd you get all these?" I ask. "Did you make them?"

Ivy shakes her head, her green hair moving like willow leaves in the wind. *"No. They were left…behind."*

"By who?"

"The natives. They…believed that powerful spirits…lived in the swamp. So they would…leave presents to…appease them."

"But there were no spirits. It was just you."

Ivy gives me a surprisingly saucy smirk. At least, I think she's smirking from the way her eyes crinkle. *"Are you so sure…about that?"* The smirk dies down to another eye smile. *"Yes. Most of the presents they left…were food I ate long ago. But some…were boxes filled with…beautiful things."*

Ivy picks up a box and removes the lid. Inside is jewelry. All of it looks ancient. There are strips of leather strung with clay beads and strips of rawhide braided together with feathers. Wooden and cloth symbols with meanings lost in time hang from more leather thongs. It's a mass of bracelets and necklaces, all mixed together.

"They gave you all this?" I lean forward for a closer look.

"Yes. But…there is more."

She grabs another box and takes the lid off. There's more jewelry inside, but it's all made from plants. Long grasses and thin vines are woven together to form some type of string, and bits of nature are used for decorating: slivers of wood, dried flowers, pointy reptile teeth—I shudder when I look at those—and tiny stones.

"These are ones…I made."

"Whoa. You made these?"

"Yes. I was inspired…by the pretty things…in the box. I tried making one, and another one, and soon it…became a pastime." Sticking her hand in, Ivy digs through the tangle. *"I wish to give you…one of these."*

"Why? I should be giving you something after you saved my sorry butt."

"But you are the one…who trusted me, even…though I am not… normal."

I shrug. "Being normal's overrated. It doesn't exist anyway."

I swear I see her pale green cheeks get a little darker. *"I still want…to give you something. Here."*

Ivy pulls a bracelet out of the knot. It's a braid of dried grass with little pebble beads.

She holds it out to me. *"This is a favorite…of mine. Your wrist…please."*

Taking the ends, Ivy snugly ties the bracelet around my right wrist. Her hands brush lightly against my arm, and her silken skin raises goosebumps on the back of my neck. I pull my wrist close, inspecting the brownish-gray pebbles closely. They almost seem to glow in the dark.

"This is so cool."

"Do you…like it?" she asks, sounding nervous.

I give her a reassuring grin. "I like it a lot. Probably one of the best presents I've ever gotten."

"That is good. That is very…good."

"Hey. You're getting better at talking."

"Really?"

"Yeah. There was only one break in that sentence."

Joyful rays practically bounce off her as Ivy claps her hands together. *"That is good! I thought it…would take a while… to speak well after all…the years of true…silence."*

Years of silence? My eyebrows furrow together.

"How long has it been since you last spoke?"

Her face becomes blank as she thinks.

I dare myself to pry further. "How long have you even been alive?"

Ivy's silent for a time as she stares up into the sky. The numerous stars wink down at her, like they're giving her the okay to spill. And she does.

"I have been here…since the stars were first…in the sky."

That's totally unexpected.

"You mean…you're like a billion years old?" I ask. My brain's overloading again, feeling both heavy and light as it buzzes like a radio full of static.

She nods slowly. *"More or less. I…cannot remember. It was so long…ago."* Ivy sighs deeply, leaning her head against the tree trunk as she studies me. *"Time becomes nonexistent for someone…like me, who can live forever. It is just an empty word with…no true meaning."*

"You're *immortal?*" The buzzing is getting louder.

One of her eyebrows arches. *"Yes. How else could…I have lived so long?"* Ivy doesn't ask rudely, but more like she's befuddled at how such simple logic could escape me.

Feeling stupid, I make myself look across the clearing. "I don't know. I mean…wow." I glance back at her. "Are you sure you're a billion years old?"

Ivy laughs with that magical laugh of hers. *"Yes. Either that…or just a really long time."*

I chuckle at her witty comeback. She *is* getting good at talking.

"So…what is your own age?"

"Me? I'm sixteen. A pretty small number compared to your age."

"But a rather large…number for you. You are close to being…one fifth of your proposed lifespan."

"Yeah." I drift off, not knowing where this conversation's heading. It's not that I don't like what we're talking about. I've just never had anyone I could discuss the deep stuff with, not even my own friends. Now that I do, I don't know what to say next.

Fortunately, Ivy speaks before I have to.

"I am sorry if…this is something odd for you…to talk about."

"Nah, it's fine," I reply. "To be honest, it's really refreshing. I don't get to talk about deep stuff a lot."

"Deep?"

"It means talking about insightful things, like the reason we're here or the mysteries behind every living thing."

"Ah. I understand." Ivy nods her head to show comprehension. *"But how come you have…no one to converse with like this?"*

"I do. They're just not the right type of people. My friend Nadia is serious enough. But her brother Aidan, my other friend, is always with her, and he's the world's biggest goofball, so that ruins any chance of serious discussion."

"What of your family?"

"Babette gives me plenty of good advice, but sometimes she has a habit of fussing over me so much it's annoying. And Dad…"

My voice dies in my throat. I don't want Ivy to know about the situation with him so soon. If I tell her about Dad, I have to tell her about Mom.

"Your father?" Ivy prompts, waiting for an answer.

"Dad's no good like that," I mumble. "He's bad with words. I've never really liked talking to him, anyway."

107

Ivy tilts her head again, staring intently as if she senses something more. My hands start to sweat. I fear she'll catch on.

But she doesn't probe. *"So I guess…I am the only one…you can talk to deeply."*

I nod, fingering my new bracelet. "Yeah. But that's okay, so don't worry about it too much."

"All right."

That comfortable silence we've experienced before descends on us, making both of us relax. Leaning against the tree as if we're merging with the bark, we look up at the sky again. The millions of stars hang there like frozen snowflakes.

"The sky is gorgeous tonight…is it not?"

"Yeah," I answer, not looking away from the speckled black.

"Do you know…of constellations?"

"Yeah, but I can only find one of them." I point up. "Like, there's the Big Dipper. And that's about it."

Ivy giggles. She points up at where the Big Dipper is. *"If you add some…stars on, you have Ursa Major."*

Squinting hard, I see the emerging shapes stand out amongst billions of dots.

"I think I see it."

"Above that is Ursa Minor." Leaning over to the left, her arm falls across my chest as she gestures to another star formation. *"It is also known … as the Little Dipper."*

"How do you know so much about stars?" I ask. Her explanation sounds like something out of an astronomy book.

"I learned from…listening," Ivy answers.

She hugs her legs, her chin resting on her knees. It's such a human thing to do; it's amazing to think she's never interacted with human beings before, but has so many mannerisms memorized.

"For years before you...people would camp along the shore...at any hour," Ivy continues. *"I would study them...for their behavior was so amazing...and foreign. They would look up and observe the sky...like we are now...and name the heavenly bodies out loud. I heard them...and I memorized them so they would...be in my mind forever. And I also received help...from that."* She motions to the sack.

"How did a sack help you?" I ask.

She laughs again. *"Not the sack itself. What is...in it."*

I feel like face-palming myself. No duh. Of course it wouldn't be the sack. Rylan, you moron.

Ivy doesn't notice my embarrassment as she drags the bag over. She drops it in between us, reaches inside, and pulls out a book. It's really damaged, with a peeling, water-stained cover, curling pages, and the embossed title about rubbed off. But there's enough I can make it out.

"The Heavenly Bodies," I read aloud. "This helped you out? How'd you even get this in the first place?"

"Yes. I taught myself...how to read, and learned from it. As to... how I got it, the man who was reading it...accidentally forgot to take it with him. The same as with...all my not gifts. They were forgotten, left behind accidently...so I gave them a home."

"Is this the only book you have?"

"I have a couple...of others. They are stored in my sack...with the clothing."

"People forgot to take their clothes with them?"

"Yes. They must...have been quite forgetful if that is...what they forgot."

I guess she's never heard of skinny dipping. "Yeah. I guess they were."

I hand the book back to Ivy, but instead of sticking it back into the sack she opens it up, turns to a page, and begins to read.

"The planet is a very small stage…in a vast cosmic universe."'

For someone who pauses while speaking, Ivy reads pretty well. Her soothing voice tells me the history of space, and I relax as the words wash over me. My eyelids get heavy and start to fall. Maybe it wouldn't hurt to close my eyes for a few seconds….

"Rylan? Rylan?"

My eyes flutter open to see Ivy peering down at me. She's shifted over and is sitting so close, our hips are brushing. This is the closest we've ever been.

"Ivy? What's going on?" I ask, blinking groggily.

"Nothing. I was reading and looked over…to see you had…fallen asleep."

I sit up. "Sorry about that. Must've been from your wonderful reading."

Ivy smiles, but it's a fleeting smile. *"I have truly enjoyed this…but I believe it is time for you…to go."*

I see what she means. The horizon has turned a dark blue. Dawn's coming.

"Yeah. I better get home before anyone finds I'm missing."

With Ivy's help I stand up, and she takes my hand. Her power flows through me once more. We walk across the clearing and through the trees until we're back at the bank. Stepping onto the water, we silently make our way to the dock.

On the way, she speaks again. *"I think we should have our meetings...at my tree from now on. We will be safe there. There...will be no risk of being found...unlike if we stay at the dock."*

I nod in agreement as we reach said destination. "Sounds good. I like that place anyway."

Ivy helps me off the water. Once she knows I'm fine, she lets go. The strength her power gives me stays with me long enough that I can grab my crutches without falling over.

"Tonight was the most enjoyable night...of my life." Ivy gives a little bow. *"Thank you."*

"You're welcome," I reply. "I'll come back tomorrow at the same time."

"I will be...waiting." Her eyes grin as she gives me her little finger wave. *"Goodbye...Rylan."*

"Bye, Ivy,"

Turning around, I head back to land, feeling her gaze the whole way. It's when I reach the end that the feeling disappears. I don't bother looking back.

I already know she's gone.

Chapter 10

"Good morning, Florida! This is your host Frankie McGee with—"

With a loud *whap*, I shut off my alarm before Frankie finishes whatever he's yelling. Bed springs squeak as I sit up, rubbing leftover sleepiness from my eyes. I gaze around my sunlit room as I try to make sense of last night.

Did everything really happen? The whole thing feels so dreamlike, I can't decide if it was. There were stars, trees, things, magic…and her. There was a swamp angel named Ivy, elegantly beautiful with enchanting eyes. Did I really meet her? Did I really talk to her? Did I really hold her hand?

Yawning, I stretch up towards the ceiling, enjoying the sensation of flexing muscles in my back. As I drop my arms a flash of light green catches my eye. A braid of dried grass strung with stone beads circles my wrist. The corners of my lips curve upwards.

Last night was no dream.

Because I can't ride my bike, Aidan and Nadia drive over in their secondhand Jeep. I climb into the back seat and Nadia carefully drives us to school. We get there right on time and go our separate ways to our lockers. No one seems to notice the cast at first.

But any hope of going under the radar is destroyed when I limp into first period English. Everyone falls silent as they hear the click of crutches on the floor. I feel them watching me as I go to the teacher's desk.

"Here's my homework, Mrs. Karcy," I mumble, handing it over.

"Thank you, Rylan." Mrs. Karcy smiles kindly. "I hope it wasn't too hard."

"It wasn't. Thanks, ma'am."

I hobble down the rows, making sure to stare at my seat and nothing else. I don't want to meet anyone's eyes. I hate unnecessary pity.

"All right, let's get started," Mrs. Karcy calls out. As she does roll call, I hear the whispers of the curious crowd.

"I can't believe he survived."

"I was so scared when I heard about it."

"Do you think his leg hurts? I didn't think he'd be back so early."

Give me a break. Is the whole day going to be like this?

It's in the cafeteria where I snap.

"I can't take it anymore!"

Aidan looks up from his bowl of soup. "Huh?"

"I said I can't take this anymore. The whispering and staring is driving me crazy. I want it all to stop."

"But you're a celebrity now!" exclaims Aidan, waving his spoon around.

"For all the wrong reasons," I complain. "No one wants to be famous for surviving an alligator attack and finding twenty-three bags of crap on your land."

"There were that many?" Nadia asks.

"That's what the haz-mat guys said. Not many people know it, but it's only going to be a matter of time until everyone in Roland finds out."

"What was the time estimate for those things?"

"Guys said they'd been there one month tops."

Nadia shakes her head. "Wow. One whole month." Then she frowns, befuddles. "But that's weird. Hasn't the swamp angel dream been haunting you for a month, too?"

"*Was* haunting me," I correct her. "I actually haven't had one since Babette found the garbage."

"They stopped just like that?"

"Yeah."

Aidan takes a giant sip of soup. "That's weird. If I didn't know better, I'd say this swamp angel was real."

Oh the irony.

"I know."

"Dunstan!"

I hear his name, but I don't bother turning around. I'm still mad at him for knocking me into the water, and ever since the garbage was found, the fury has doubled.

"Has that asshat even talked to you at all?" Aidan asks, staring coldly at wherever Dunstan is behind me.

"No. We're both avoiding each other, which is easy considering we don't have any classes together. Thank God."

"He needs to apologize," Nadia growls. "It's his fault that alligator nearly killed you."

"I don't want his stupid apology. I got more important things to deal with, anyway."

Aidan shrugs. "I guess that makes sense, with the swamp and the project and—"

"Project?"

"Yeah, dude. Don't tell me you forgot about Ms. Stern's project?"

I slap my forehead. "I did. Crap, I'm so behind on my research!"

"Don't worry about it," says Aidan, drowning saltines in his soup. "You got loads of books on swamps lying around your house and you got your grandma to talk to. You'll have your research done in no time."

"If you want, we can share our research," Nadia offers, almost flirting as she does.

"No thanks, Nadia," I smile. "I have plenty of material to use. After all, I have the entire subject growing in my backyard."

For the rest of the day, classes plod along like a bunch of turtles. Each consists of the same things: teacher's fake sympathy, classmates whispering, and me trying to ignore it all.

I do pretty well until I run into Dunstan.

It's before the last class of the day, Spanish, and I'm at my locker trying to pull my Spanish book out. Aidan stands nearby and waits since he's in the same class.

"Need help?" Aidan asks as I pull on the stuck textbook.

"I got it." I grunt as I tug on the binding. "Damn. Whose idea was it to make our lockers this—"

Suddenly I yank the book free. It goes flying as I fall back, my balance lost. Aidan catches me before I hit the ground. The textbook slides along the floor, making people step back to avoid it. Eventually it stops at someone's feet.

Dunstan's feet.

There's a western-style stare-down as we glare at each other. Curious classmates watch us, wondering if this will end with a fistfight. As I stare at him, I see his eyes shining like ice chips. They're his father's eyes in every way, from the obvious simmering anger to the formidable sense of privilege, and that's not a compliment.

Eyes...of ice...

Out of nowhere, Ivy's words resurface. Before I can process them correctly, the bell rings for the one-minute warning. Students file away until it's only Aidan, Dunstan, and me out in the hall. With one last sneer, Dunstan finally leaves, too.

Aidan steps forward and grabs my book off the floor.

"Thanks, man." He nods, and we both head to class, completely silent. We can't think of anything to talk about that could terminate the weirdness of my confrontation with Dunstan.

Thank God the day's almost over.

When school lets out, the twins drive me back home, where I hang around the rest of the day. Before long, night falls, and it's time to go. I grab not only my sweatshirt and shoe, but also my backpack. Since Ivy shared her stuff with me, I'll return the favor.

Climbing off the roof is awkward because of the extra load. With my backpack slung over my shoulder, my balance is thrown off and I come close to falling off the roof. But I safely make it to the ground and limp down to the dock. I move so fast that my leg, even in its cast, shouldn't be able to take it without starting to ache. But there's no pain. There hasn't been any for a couple of days, actually. Is that Ivy's doing? I wonder.

I arrive to see her standing at the dock's end, looking out over the water. The boards creak under my feet, and she turns around. Her eyes smile.

"Hey, Ivy."

"Hello, Rylan. How…are you?"

"I'm fine. How about you?"

"I am always fine…when the swamp is fine." She sticks her hand out to me. *"Come."*

I drop my crutches and take her hand. The power I first felt comes back, and I step onto the water. We slowly walk away.

Ten minutes later, we're sitting under the tree in Ivy's clearing facing each other.

"What is in…the bag?"

"Some stuff of mine," I tell her, unzipping my backpack. "You shared some of your possessions with me, so I figured I'd do the same."

Ivy stares at the items sticking out of my bag with happy curiosity. *"You did that…for me?"*

"Of course. Why wouldn't I?"

I reach in and grab some paperbacks. "Here's some more books. These are some of my favorites."

Ivy leans forward to look at them, but she doesn't take them. She wants to, though; her fingers won't stop twiddling.

"You can touch them. It's not like they're going to explode if you do."

"Explode?" Ivy shrinks back, her eyes widening until they're like giant green plates.

"No! No, that's not what I meant," I correct myself before I scare her even more. "It's just a figure of speech. These won't explode, I promise."

Hesitantly, Ivy reaches out towards them and strokes the cover. Seeing nothing has burst into flames, Ivy's cheerfulness returns, her concern erased away like words on a blackboard. She reads the titles gleefully.

"The Hitchhiker's Guide to the Galaxy. Red…Sun. 1984."

With each new book I hand her, Ivy becomes happier.

"I never knew so…many books existed," Ivy whispers. examining the cover of *The Road* with fascination.

"There's a lot of them out there. So much so that they build buildings to store them all," I tell her.

"Really?"

"Yeah. They're called libraries, and they let you borrow as many books as you want as long as you remember to take them back eventually."

"Amazing." She drifts off as she stares back at my bag, eyebrows raised. *"I see something white…sticking out of your sack."*

"Oh. That's my laptop." I pull it out and hand it over.

"What does it do?"

"Open it and you'll see."

Ivy runs her thumb along the edge and cautiously opens it. She jumps a little when the screen lights up, but soon Ivy's staring at it eagerly, the light from the screen making her face aglow.

"What does this…marvelous thing do?" she quietly asks.

"A whole bunch of stuff. You can write papers, play games, chat with friends…"

"How so?"

"With all those little keys and the track pad."

Ivy lightly drags her fingers along the keys. When she touches the track pad, she gives a yelp of surprise as she watches the arrow dart about.

"It moves!"

"It's supposed to do that." I chuckle at her childlike wonder as she makes the cursor move in a flurry of circles. I pull out another thing from my bag.

"This is called an iPod."

Ivy puts my laptop aside as she takes the music player. As with the laptop, she runs her fingers along it, admiring the smooth surface.

"i…Pod." She tests the unfamiliar word, the letters rolling out of her mouth. *"It is so small. What does such a… small thing do?"*

"It holds music," I explain. "You connect it with a computer, which you can store music on, and transfer it onto this. After that, all you have to do is turn it on, plug in some headphones, press the button, and you've got music."

Ivy winds the headphone's cord around her fingers. *"What does human…music sound like?"*

"It sounds like anything—you can find music that sounds like whatever you want to hear."

I take my iPod back from her and turn it on. Sticking one earbud in my ear, I scroll through my library until I find some songs that Ivy might enjoy. I press the play button, then check the volume to make sure it isn't too loud.

"Stick this in your ear," I instruct her, handing her the other earbud. Ivy takes it, gives it a curious look, decides it won't attack her, and pushes her hair back, uncovering her long, pointed ears. She sticks it in, and at first, there's no reaction. But seconds later her head begins to bob in time with the beat. She stays quiet throughout the song, only speaking when the song ends.

"That was beautiful," she says with a big eye-smile as she removes the ear bud. *"It is like nothing...I have heard before."*

"You've heard music before?" Now that I mention it, she never did ask me what music was.

"Oh yes, I have heard...music before. This whole swamp is... made of music."

Quietly Ivy stands up and takes a few steps away from her tree. Facing the surrounding woods, she opens her arms wide as if trying to hug everything.

"Music is as old as time. It...has always been there, waiting for... anyone to listen. Trees sway, water gushes, and animals live. All... these things and more enhance its quality...making the purest notes imaginable."

She turns back and faces me, arms still raised. *"And if all humans...would rest for only a minute...they could hear it with me. Do you...not hear it? It is the sound of the world singing."*

Ivy tilts her head back and closes her eyes. From her peaceful face, I can see she's listening to this song, letting the majesty of everything wash over her. I close my eyes. At first I don't hear anything.

But like the rising tide, it eventually washes over me.

I can hear it. The wind weaving in and out of the trees. The swamp water swimming along its course. The call of insects, birds, and mammals seeking their friends. It's all mixing together, each beat and tempo, making a melody of complete beauty.

I open my eyes to find Ivy watching me, a graceful calmness on her face. I smile, showing her that I heard it, too.

"Was it beautiful?" Ivy asks as she sits down again.

"It was." My own voice sounds ugly after hearing it. "You're lucky to listen to that every day."

"You can hear it every day...too. Just close your eyes and reach out...and you will find it. The earth's hymn hides from no one."

120

We're silent for a minute before I hand her a book.

"Read aloud again. Hearing you is like hearing the earth sing; it's pretty."

A dark green flush taints her cheeks.

"A-all right," she stutters. She takes Babette's copy of *Chicken Soup for the Soul* from my hands, opens it to a random story, and starts to read. Time passes slowly as she recites, stopping every so often to ask me questions about items and words she doesn't know about. I reply the best I can, and with each answer Ivy learns more about the real world.

It's when we get to a story about kids surviving a fire that Ivy falters. She stops reading and stares at the page like it's going to come alive and attack her.

"Ivy?" I ask.

She doesn't respond but I can see her hands quivering, making the book visibly wobble.

"You're shaking, Ivy. Tell me what's wrong." I reach over and rub her shoulder.

Ivy slowly closes the book with a deep breath and sets it aside. *"There was a fire…in there."*

I don't know what she's getting at, but I go along. "Yeah. There was."

"They lost everything. Nothing…was left. Even their pet perished…in the flames." She shudders. *"What it must have been like…to watch their entire life…turn into smoke and ashes."*

"But they all survived. That's what matters."

"But what if they…did not?" She shivers again. *"I can think…of nothing more gruesome than dying…like that."*

"Ivy? Are you…are you afraid of fire?"

Ivy freezes at the question. Her body goes rigid, but she manages to nod. *"Yes…I am,"* she admits, almost shamefully.

"There's nothing wrong with that. Everyone's scared of something." I point to myself. "Like me. I'm going to be scared of alligators for the rest of my life."

Ivy laughs, but it's a scared laugh. *"But do you let your fear consume you...until even merely thinking about it...brings pain to your heart?"*

"Well, no. I usually have more important things to think about."

"That is not the same for me. I have let my fear...soak me to the bone. Even the word...fire...chills my heart."

"Why *are* you so scared of fire?"

She looks off into the swamp as if hoping her answer will come running out of the trees and she won't have to confess anything. Of course, it doesn't, and eventually she tells me.

"Because...it is one of the few things...that can kill me."

Talk about an about-face.

"But...you said you were immortal," I say, remembering last night's conversation.

"Immortality is a lie," Ivy states, still looking out over the clearing. She's so quiet I nearly miss when she starts talking again. *"Humans think it exists, but...it does not. No one can live forever. Not...a single one."*

"But you've lived so long..."

"Only because nothing has...come close to killing me."

"What can kill you?"

She finally looks at me. Her eyes are stony and her voice deadly serious.

"Fire is deadly. If even...a single spark touches me...all of me will burn to ash. Knives and sharp things, human weapons...I am weak against those, too."

"How do you know that?"

"There have been plenty of times...when I have accidentally cut myself on sharp rocks and sticks. If...if they can cause me to bleed, they can also cause...my death. But other than that," she concludes, *"nothing can hurt me."*

"Wow." I shake my head. "I so wasn't expecting that."

"I hope you are all right…with this." Ivy's grimness is instantly replaced with worry that, with each thing she tells me about herself, I'll want to run away and never come back.

"Of course. I'm not going anywhere," I console her. Then I do something that surprises the both of us.

I take her hand in mine. And as the usual energy flows into me, my thumb slowly rubs across her knuckles.

What the hell! I can't do this! I've only known her three days, and now it's like I'm flirting with Ivy. Which I can't, because I don't know if we even qualify as friends, and she isn't even human to boot. She's going to get the wrong idea, then I'm going to be in hot water, and then…

"This is pleasant."

"Huh?"

Ivy smiles. *"Holding hands…it is pleasant."*

I slowly release the breath I didn't realize I was holding. She thinks this is something everybody does, and doesn't see the romantic connotations behind it. I guess my butt is safe for now.

"Yeah…it is," I agree, managing to relax. And for the rest of the night that's how we sit.

Just the two of us, hand in hand.

Chapter 11

"Babette?"

It's a few days later. School's over and I'm looking for my grandmother. I've got something to ask her.

"Babette? Where are you?"

"I'm in your father's study."

My stomach instantly takes a nosedive. Crap. The study? Dad's territory? The one room of the house I try to avoid? I hate that room!

"Rylan? Dear?"

"Yeah, I'm coming."

With a deep sigh I cross the foyer and go up the stairs, making a quick stop at my room to deposit my backpack. Then I head down the hall until I'm standing in front of it.

The door.

To the study.

I sigh again and open it.

Sunlight hits my face. The shades are pulled up, lighting up the flawlessly neat room. Papers are neatly stacked on the dust-free oak desk and all the books on the bookshelf are alphabetized. The home computer's hibernating, purring like a sleeping cat.

Sounds cozy? Well, it's not. Especially if your mom's staring at you from every angle.

Ever since Mom died, Dad's kept practically all of the pictures of Mom in his study. Stuck in all different types of frames, they dot the room wherever he put them. All those smiles and eyes are too much. It isn't helping him get over Mom, but he gets stubborn and defensive whenever I try to move them.

Babette's gazing at the big family portrait. That picture is the newest—and last—of them, taken only a week before the accident. Mom had wanted a "refined" picture of the family, so we drove to Harraway and got our photo taken by a professional. Dressed in our best, Babette sits in a cushy chair flanked by Mom and Dad. Six-year-old me sits on Babette's lap. We're all looking at the camera with grins on our faces.

Those smiles wouldn't be there by the end of the week.

"I remember this as if it was yesterday."

I glance at Babette as I come to stand next to her.

"You were such a ball of energy back then. By the time we could get you to stay still, the poor photographer wanted to pull his hair out." She quietly chuckles at the memory. "But look at the reward for all our patience."

She falls silent, and for a couple of minutes we quietly look at it. My eyes lock with Mom's, and I can't break away. It's hard to want to stop staring at her eyes. Ocean blue, they seem to cast a spell every time I look at them.

Just like Ivy's.

"Rylan! Your leg."

Babette's outburst reminds me why I came here in the first place.

"Oh, yeah. Remember that appointment with Doc Norm on Saturday? I was going to ask if we could get something

earlier. Because as you can see, I don't need my crutches anymore."

I honestly don't. I've walked all around the house without the damn things, and my leg didn't hurt at all.

It's probably Ivy's doing, but who am I to complain?

An hour and a half later I'm lying on a cot, staring up at the ceiling. Over in the corner, Babette patiently waits in a chair. Doc Norm stands over me, running his fingers along my cast as he examines it.

"Tell me when you first noticed you could put weight on your leg, Rylan," Doc Norm asks me, his graying handlebar mustache twitching.

"It was earlier today at school. It wasn't aching as much as it used to, so that was pretty weird. But the actual discovery was in the cafeteria. I'd sat down to eat when I realized I'd forgotten to get a drink."

"And?"

"And the thing about RR High's cafeteria, Doc Norm, is when hungry students are concerned, that place gets packed. It's like walking through a hedge maze just to get to the bathroom. With my crutches, it took all of lunch period to get to where I was going. But I was just fed up with wasting my time, so I basically said 'Screw it' and walked over to the drink fridge without my crutches."

"A rather risky move, Mr. Forester." Doc Norm clicks his tongue with disapproval. "Putting weight on your leg before it heals completely can make the fractures crack open again, and you'd have to wear your cast even longer."

I give him a good-humored grin, already knowing what's coming next. "But I don't, do I?"

Like the fine doctor he is, he smirks. "Not completely, no." Removing his hands, he picks up his clipboard and starts writing.

"So what's the diagnosis?" asks Babette.

"The cast stays," declares Doc Norm, not looking up from what he's writing. "Even though his leg's healing fast, it's still too early to remove it. However, at this rate, you can come in for removal in a week and a half."

"For now?"

"I'll give him a walking heel to make it easier to move around and put weight on his leg. Otherwise, the rules stay the same. No sticking objects in here to scratch an itch, keep it somewhat elevated, and don't get it wet. I noticed the base of the foot has come in contact with water."

"I must've forgot to cover it in the shower one time," I lie, my face reddening. The truth is I haven't forgotten. It's wet from walking on water with Ivy.

Fortunately, Doc Norm thinks I'm blushing out of embarrassment and not because I'm lying. "Be more careful, Rylan. The cast can't do its job if it's just a soggy piece of fiberglass."

"Yes, sir. I will."

Or not.

Hours later, I find myself breaking the rules when I visit Ivy.

She takes notice of the missing crutches as we sit under her tree. *"Your metal instruments...are gone."*

"I had an appointment with the doctor today. You know what a doctor is, right? Anyway, he said I didn't need them anymore."

"That is wonderful."

127

"Yep. Instead of crutches, I got this walking heel I'll use until the cast comes off, which should be soon."

Ivy eye-smiles, clapping her hands together. *"That is very good news! Now I am even more…happy for you."*

I give Ivy the same knowing smirk I gave Doc Norm in his office. "And it's all thanks to you, Ivy."

Her cheeks flush green as she looks down at her nervously tapping fingers. *"I did not do…anything."*

"But you did. You used your magic to heal my leg."

Ivy's head snaps up so fast it's surprising it didn't go flying off her neck. *"H-how did you…find o-out?"*

"It was kinda obvious. When I was I in the hospital— the place where doctors work—they told me the damage to my leg wasn't as bad as it was supposed to be. Back then I wasn't sure if you were real or not, but the report they gave made me think that something magical had happened. Meeting you face-to-face pretty much confirmed it."

Ivy looks at me a few more seconds before she visibly relaxes, the surprise fading away. *"You are quite the…detective, I believe the term is."* An amused smile plays on her lips. *"Because you are right. I can perform…magic."*

"What kind of magic is it?"

"It is the type…when you just envision what you want to happen… and it happens."

"Awesome." I'm astonished. "In the books I've read, people who did magic needed wands and magic words."

"Really? How interesting. But that is…not the way with us. We are beings of pure magic, so much so the power comes off of us in waves, affecting all around us. So we must find ways…to 'burn it off,' as you would say." She eye-frowns at the word "burn."

"You say *we.* I'm probably asking a stupid question, but are there more of you? Your kind, I mean."

Her reaction isn't what I expected it to be. Her eyes dim in sad wistfulness and her ears droop.

"It is not a bad question. And yes…there are more of my kind. We are a completely female race. We live in swamps all around this world. But over the centuries, that number…has dropped. There are few of us now."

"How do you know?"

"We are connected. I…feel it." Her hand drifts over her chest to where her heart must be. *"Every time a sister dies…there is this pain in my heart. I just know that…there is one less of us."*

Ivy looks unhappy, and I feel bad about bringing something up that pains her. Time for a distraction.

"Can you show me some magic?"

Ivy glances at me the same way she did when I first told her I knew she could practice it. *"Pardon?"*

"I was asking if I could watch you perform some magic," I repeat. "The whole walking-on-water thing's cool, but I want to see what else you can do."

She stares at me, disbelieving, but then she nods. *"Yes."*

Getting up from her seat, Ivy steps away from the tree. She looks around the clearing, trying to find something in the dark. Spotting something—I don't know what, since I can't see—Ivy lifts one of her hands forwards, her fingers sticking outwards. For a minute, nothing happens.

But then there's a loud woody creak like the type the dock makes if you step in a certain spot. Ivy's hand starts shaking a little.

Out of the darkness comes a flying log.

It's not going fast, and it isn't like Ivy's going to let me get hit by it. But the fact that a log is floating without any help fills me with pure disbelief. As in the oh-my-God-I-can't-believe-this-is-happening kind of disbelief.

Carefully Ivy sets the log down. It's all the proof I need to know what she's capable of, but she doesn't stop there. Leaning over, she rests a hand on the mossy log. It glows white where she touches it. She moves it away, and I gasp.

There's a ghost orchid growing from where her hand was. Its whiteness is perfectly contrasted by the dark wood.

Ivy looks at my gaping face, wearing fear and hope on her own. *"Do you…like it?"* she asks, hoping my answer will be good.

"Wow."

That's all I can say. Wow.

"Wow?" Ivy doesn't know if that's a good thing.

"Yeah." I smile to show her it's okay. "Wow."

She gets the hint, and Ivy eye-smiles as well.

Magic can do that to a person.

"Dude! Your leg!"

Next morning the twins pull up in their car. I completely forgot to call and tell them about my leg yesterday, so it's a complete surprise for them.

"Good morning to you, too," I tell Aidan as I climb into the car. Story Of The Year blares from the stereo, singing about girls in pain and something never ending.

"Sorry, man. Just didn't expect you to have your cast off so soon. Why didn't you tell us?"

"I forgot. And it's not off yet," I correct him, pulling up my jean leg for a demonstration. "I still have it. The only difference is the walking heel Doc Norm gave me."

"So that's what that is." Nadia glances at me in the rearview mirror as she shifts the car into drive. "I didn't know you had an appointment with the doctor."

"I didn't. But yesterday during school, I realized my leg really didn't hurt when I went to get a drink—don't give me that look, Aidan, you know what I'm talking about— so I told Babette about it. Next thing I know, I'm in Doc

Norm's office being told my leg's healing so well I can walk with this."

"Yay for you, Rylan!" Nadia congratulates me as we pull out on the main road.

"Thanks. What's even better is that Doc Norm is sure this thing can be taken off in a week and a half."

"Even better, dude!" cheers Aidan. "Now we can go back to riding our bikes instead of being chaperoned by Grandma Nadia!"

"Don't call me a grandma, Aidan!" Nadia growls, trying to keep her eyes on the road and ignore the urge to hit her brother at the same time.

"Why not? You drive like one."

"I'd rather drive like an old lady than some complete psycho who's still on parental probation because he likes crashing into trees for fun."

"Hey! That only happened once! And I clipped it, not crashed it!"

I try my best not to laugh. Hurtful as Aidan's comment is, Nadia *is* the type who drives ten miles under the limit. Aidan, on the other hand, is the type who goes—or went, at least—ten or more miles over the speed limit. It's a good thing Mr. and Mrs. Marce won't let either of them on the highway yet. Otherwise there'd be the worst pile-up Florida has ever seen.

My second day back is better than the first one. Sure, practically everyone who talks to me can't keep their eyes from falling onto my leg. But at least no one's whispering behind my back anymore. Even better, I don't run into Dunstan.

But I do run into someone quite different.

"Rylan! Omigod!"

Out of nowhere, Melanie pops by the water fountain as I bend down to take a drink. Surprised, I nearly drop my backpack on my broken foot.

"Melanie! Er, hi." I quickly scan the hallway for Dunstan, who wouldn't give a second thought to using me as a punching bag if he saw me talking to his girlfriend. Other than a couple of Dunstan's senior jock friends currently glaring at us, everyone else is minding their own business.

"Hi yourself." She giggles at my awkwardness. "And don't worry. Dunstan's all the way over in the gym. I have his schedule memorized."

"Oh. I never said I was looking for him."

"But you were checking out to see if he was coming. If he was, though, I'd make sure he wouldn't do anything stupid like beat you up."

"Thanks. That's…reassuring."

"Anyway, I just wanted to see if you were okay," says Melanie, tossing her mane of spun gold over her shoulders. "I mean, when I heard you survived, I never went to see you in the hospital. And now you're here with that nasty cast on your leg. By the way, where's your crutches?"

"Don't need them anymore. Got this walking heel now."

"Oh really? That's so cool." She doesn't even look at it as she goes on. "But are you feeling okay?"

"I'm fine," I tell her. "I'm still here, right?"

"Yes, you are," Melanie teases, batting her eyelashes effortlessly as she stares at me with those big blue doe eyes. I swallow, my throat suddenly dry as the Sahara. What's going on? Why can't I speak to the girl of every boy's fantasy without feeling like it's wrong? I open my mouth to try and talk, but the warning bell rings.

"Oh! Looks like we need to go." Melanie pats my arm and gives me a huge glowing smile. "I'd walk you to class, but it seems like that's your friend's job."

She gestures with her head behind me, and I look back. Aidan and Nadia stand at the end of the hall, leaning against the giant glass window. Aidan's beaming proudly, happy that his best friend is talking to the cutest girl in school. Nadia, however, has her arms crossed and this sneer on her face like she wouldn't mind seeing Melanie drop dead where she stands.

"Yeah, it is," I confess. Carefully I inch my way around Melanie. "Well, I gotta get to class. Don't want to be late."

"Totally! I should get going, too." Melanie gives me a flirty little wave goodbye. "Bye, Rylan. I hope we talk again real soon." Her heels click against the linoleum as she heads off to her next class.

As soon as Melanie turns the corner, Aidan's all over me.

"Dude! Tell me that you were just totally flirting with Melanie Sweet." He's so loud, I wonder why teachers don't stick their heads out of their classrooms to see what the fuss is about. "Tell me you were flirting with the hottest girl in school!"

"I was," I admit, feeling completely awkward; I'm still not sure it actually happened.

Aidan claps me hard on the back. "You are my hero, man! Melanie was so into you. Maybe she'll break up with Dunstan and go after you!"

"Yeah, like that'll happen in a million years. And if it did, Dunstan would cave my face in," I note as we start down the hall. "All she did was ask me if I was okay. I wasn't flirting back."

"When Dunstan hears about this he isn't going to be happy," Nadia finally mutters. "Then you won't be laughing."

"Ah, but that's the beauty of it, sis." Aidan turns around and walks backwards, facing us as he continues. "The bastard can't touch Rylan because of his leg. If he tried,

he'd get in big trouble with the teachers. He's smart enough to know that."

"You have a point. But he'd wait until my leg was all better and *then* beat me up."

Aidan snorts as we reach the stairs, not turning around as we descend. "Not with his one-track mind. By the time your cast is gone, the whole thing will've completely slipped his brain, especially since he doesn't have much of one in the first place. If he does remember, Melanie will tell him it was nothing."

"And he'll go along with it, and we can all go back to our normal lives," Nadia states, her voice firm and her face icy. If she tried to smile, no doubt her skin would crack and fall off in pieces.

"Yeah, as normal as it is to have a friend who survived a gator attack," Aidan as we reach the bottom of the stairs.

And who's also friends with a swamp angel, I want to add, but I don't.

"Mr. Forester, please stay back. I want to talk to you."

Bracing myself, I turn around and approach Ms. Stern's desk. Biology II just wrapped up, and it's time for me to rush to my locker and grab the books I need for next class. But now I can't.

"Yes, Ms. Stern?" I ask with caution. I don't think I did anything wrong, but for all I know I might have offended her in the worst way possible. That's how Aidan usually gets in trouble, and I feel like blurting out his famous "Whatever it was, I didn't do it!" line.

Ms. Stern sits at her desk, her steel eyes watching me very carefully. "First off, relax. You're not in trouble."

My hands unclench and my shoulders sag.

"Unless you don't turn your information in on time."

I seize back up again.

"Information?"

"Yes. Your friends may not have told you, but while you were in the hospital I did an information check to see if anybody was procrastinating or using faulty research. Everyone brought in the data and pictures they were using, and everyone checked out well. Except, of course, Mr. Marce and a few other students."

Figures Aidan would procrastinate. Also figures my friends would forget to tell me about something this important. Dammit.

"I'm guessing you're telling me that being in the hospital's no exception and I need to bring all my research in before the end of the week."

"I was thinking more along the lines of tomorrow at the end of class," says Ms. Stern with a toothy smile. It's a crocodile smile, all white and pointed, and it reminds me too much of the reason I have a cast.

"Bring me all the photos and research you're using for your report tomorrow," Ms. Stern demands. "If not, I'm going to have to deduct points from your overall grade. The rubric is very clear that there are no extensions on this project." She gives me the look she gives students like she's daring them to defy her. "Understood?"

"Yes, ma'am."

"Good. Dismissed."

I lurch out of Biology II, angry thoughts buzzing in my head like bees in a hive. I knew I was behind on my research for this, but the last thing I'd expected was an information check. Shit. I'm really gonna need to work tonight if I'm going to get it all done.

But maybe Ivy can help.

I can't help but jump at the noise from the squeaky spot when I reach the dock. That very board has been noisy for years, so I should be used to it. But throw in a black night sky with a sliver of moon, twisted shadows, and unidentified animal sounds coming from all directions, and I'm ready to jump at anything that pops out at me.

I glance down at my watch. This wasn't nearly as nerve-racking when Ivy was here to greet me, but it is now since I'm the first one to arrive. I hope everything's okay with her. I hope nothing bad happens to *me* while I'm waiting. With this creepy atmosphere I could believe a some serial killer is hiding among the trees.

Someone grabs my shoulder.

"Gaaah!" I jump like ten feet in the air, twisting around with my fists ready to punch any hockey-mask-wearing creep in the gut. But it's no psychopath. It's only Ivy, staring at me like *I'm* the crazy person.

"It's you," I murmur, my hands dropping to my side. "Hey."

"You screamed. Are you all right? Did I do…something wrong?"

"No. You didn't." I cast a look around, taking in all the blackness. "It's just creepy to be down here alone in the dark. It makes you feel like some crazy person's watching you."

"I hope…I am not this crazy person."

"You're not. No way could you ever be that."

"I am sorry I was…not here to greet you. I had something…to take care of."

"What was it? Are you okay?"

"Yes, I am fine."

I breathe a sigh of relief. With her immortality, it figures she wouldn't be hurt, but it's concerning all the same.

"Then what happened?"

"A swamp bird had broken his wing. He came to me…knowing I could help him. So I used my healing magic…and came here as soon as I was done." Ivy chuckles softly. *"He is probably still waiting back at the tree…to thank me since I rushed off so quickly."*

"Why'd you leave him?"

"I sensed you were waiting for me," says Ivy. *"And I did not want to…keep you waiting too long."*

"Oh. Thanks." I reach over and grasp her hand. "Shall we?"

Ivy looks down at our intertwined hands with sweet happiness. *"Yes."*

This time we step off the dock and onto the water together. I'm confident enough to do this by myself without her pulling me behind her. But I feel the imprint of the camera through my messenger bag, and I wonder if Ivy will let me take pictures.

That I'm not as confident about.

"So where's the little guy?"

We've entered Ivy's clearing and I'm looking around for the bird. I'm curious to see what type it is.

"He is resting under the tree. I shall tell him not…to be scared of you."

"Can you also tell him that I want to take his picture?" I ask Ivy while I stick a hand in my bag, digging around for my digital camera.

"Picture?" Ivy asks, baffled. *"What is this 'picture' you speak of?"*

"Pictures are taken with cameras," I say. "And this is a camera." I hold it up like a trophy.

Ivy leans in for a closer look. *"I think I have seen these before."*

"You have?"

"Yes. When you would take people out on the boat...I would see little flashing boxes in people's hands. I think these are the same things." She blinks. *"They always made me...nervous for some reason. I always avoided...them whenever I saw them."* Ivy looks at me, curious. *"What do the pictures they take look like?"*

"Whatever you want it to be." I turn it on. "Think of it as something to capture time with. All you do is aim, push this button, and you have a photo."

"Does it hurt?"

"It's perfectly harmless. I'll show you."

Holding the camera out and turned towards me, I give it a goofy grin and push the button. It flashes, lighting up the dark swamp behind me like a strobe light.

"See? Doesn't hurt at all. And," I press some buttons until my face pops up on the built-in screen, "there! There's the picture."

Ivy takes the camera back and stares at the screen with fascination. *"It is you! This really does...capture moments in time."* She turns it back around so that the lens faces her. *"How does it work again?"*

"Just push the button on top."

Ivy fingers the button and presses it. She gives a slightly pained yelp when the camera flashes, and she almost drops it.

"The light is bright." Ivy hands the camera back to me.

"Yeah. Sorry about that. I should've told you how bright it can be," I apologize while I search for Ivy's picture. A half-pint laugh escapes me.

"What is so humorous?" Ivy asks in the middle of rubbing her eyes.

"You got your eyes closed," I chuckle, showing her. She laughs when she sees herself. It looks like she'd been sucking a lemon.

Suddenly, something joins in our laughter with a harsh croak. Ivy instantly looks over to the tree.

"Oh! I forgot about him."

Ivy makes her way over with me right behind. She bends down like she's looking for something. Stepping back, she turns and looks at me.

"I have calmed him down. He was worried I had…forgotten him. I also told him about you…and your picture box. He is fine with it."

Ivy steps to the side, and the bird comes into view.

It's a great blue heron. His blue-gray feathers blend in with the dark ground around him, but at the same time they manage to stick out, shining like they've been coated with Vaseline. Sitting atop his legs, he turns his rusty-gray neck until he's looking at me with his white and black face and little yellow eyes. The yellowish beak, sharply tapered and elongated, points at me as if picking me out of a crowd. That, or he's ready to stab me to death with it.

"You sure I can take a picture? He's looking at me like he's debating whether or not to skewer me with that beak of his."

I feel a reassuring hand on my shoulder and Ivy's voice in my ear, which sends shivers down my spine. *"It is fine. He told me himself…he would not hurt you. Besides, he knows if he did…he would face my unyielding displeasure."*

The heron nods his head as if agreeing.

"Okay then."

I crouch down until I'm facing the bird eye to eye. Turning the camera back on, I move it around until I see the

perfect snapshot in the viewfinder. Before I lose my nerve, I press down the button.

With a whirl, the camera flashes. The heron doesn't look away, nor does he close his eyes in the picture.

"He wants to know...if it came out well," says Ivy behind me.

I look at the screen and smile. The picture's perfect. Real professional looking, if I do say so myself.

"It's excellent, Ivy," I tell her. To the heron, I say, "Thanks."

He nods his head like he understands, then starts shifting around in his seat. He wants to get up. I quickly back away as the heron raises himself up on his long, skinny legs. I feel my eyes widen. I've always known herons are big birds, but this guy's enormous; his head comes up to my waist and his neck isn't even extended.

The heron turns to Ivy, and for a minute he stands there looking at her before he spreads his wings and sinks into what's unmistakably a bow.

I detect motion behind me. Ivy's bowing also, her bone wings spread out and her hands to her side. Seeing the two like that, I recognize how awesome a picture it would be. My hands go for the camera button. The flash lights up the night.

Hours later I'm back up in my room, sitting at my desk. Outside my window I see the faint colors of sunrise dyeing the horizon. This is the first time I've ever stayed up all night. But I can't sleep when there are photos needing to be downloaded.

Somehow in the time I was out there, my simple mission to take pictures of swamp life turned into taking a bunch of pictures with Ivy and me. I smile as I scroll through them on my laptop. There's us sitting, standing, making silly faces—or maybe that's just me—and all around being a teenager with his otherworldly friend. About half of them are bad because Ivy had trouble keeping her eyes open, but there are a couple that stand out.

The first is the two of us sitting against the black gum tree trunk. We're both smiling at the camera, our heads almost touching.

I find my second favorite and my grin gets even bigger. In it, Ivy stands against the trees. She's looking at the camera, her head tilted cutely and her eyes smiling. It's a full-body shot, so I can see all of her magical, mystical glory. Ivy looks like a model in a well-made costume. She's so beautiful…I can't stop staring at her face.

It's a face that puts Melanie's to shame. Is this why I couldn't talk to her today? Am I losing any sense of attraction to her because of Ivy?

I shake my head furiously. No. That's not the reason why. And it *can't* be the reason why.

I know the truth. And I refuse to risk that again.

Chapter 12

"Rylan, you don't look so good."

Exactly four hours later I'm in the car with the twins, just about to nod off on Aidan's shoulder.

"Sorry," I mumble, rubbing my eyes as I yawn like a lion.

"It's okay. But honestly, man," Aidan smiles really big, "you know I don't swing that way."

It takes me five seconds to realize what he's implying.

"Screw you!" I punch Aidan in the shoulder as he cackles.

Nadia rolls her eyes. "Excuse the moron, Rylan. But he's right. You look pretty bad."

"How bad?"

"Here, look."

Keeping one hand on the steering wheel, Nadia reaches into her backpack pocket, digs around, and tosses something back to me. I catch it, feeling the flat circular shape of a compact mirror.

"Since when have you worn makeup?" Aidan asks as I snap it open.

"What are you talking about? I've always worn makeup."

"Yeah, but nothing too noticeable. I mean, you hogged the bathroom this morning putting on that stick stuff."

I don't hear Nadia's reply because I'm focused on my reflection. Other than the inch-thick, grayish-purple bags under my eyes, I look fine.

"It's just bags under my eyes. Nothing fatal."

"But it looks like you've haven't been sleeping again." Nadia peeks at me in the rearview mirror. "Did those dreams come back?"

"No, they haven't." I let out another yawn. "I had to stay up late to get all the information I needed for Ms. Stern's info check today."

Aidan's jaw flaps open. "Dude, you were in the hospital! Doesn't she have any sympathy?"

"Nope."

"Then it's official," declares Aidan with finality, falling back in his seat. "Ms. Stern is the Devil incarnate."

"Speaking of devils, that new horror movie I want to see came out a couple of days ago," Nadia pipes up. "Why don't we go see it today?" Ahead of us Roland Roux High appears, popping up like from out of a toaster.

"Sounds good to me," Aidan replies. "Let's go when it's really dark, so we end up driving home thinking some bad guy's behind us."

"I don't know," I say as Nadia pulls into the school parking lot. "Babette might not let me go to a movie on a school night."

But it's more than it being a school night. What if I miss my meeting with Ivy? She'll probably think she did something wrong and I'm never coming to see her again.

"But you have to come," Aidan whines. "You've haven't done anything fun since you came home."

"Try telling that to my folks."

"Why don't you tell them yourself?" Nadia asks. "Try calling them."

"I can't. My cell died, so I had to let it charge."

"Use mine." Nadia leans back with her crimson cell phone in her outstretched hand. "Here. If you call now, you can probably reach your grandma."

Hesitantly, I take the phone and flip it open. I enter my home phone number, but my finger pauses over the Call button, not wanting to push it.

"Well, dude, are you going to do it or not?"

I mentally facepalm. This is ridiculous. Ivy would be okay with me missing one night, right? I have a life, which does include other friends I like spending time with. I could always leave a note for her. I press Call and bring the phone to my ear. Babette picks up on the third ring.

"Hello?"

"Uh...Babette?"

"Oh, Rylan. Hello!"

"Er, hello."

"Where are you, sweetie?"

"I'm in the school parking lot. And, um, I was hoping I could ask you something..."

"Of course, hon."

"I was just wondering if...I could go see a movie tonight with Aidan and Nadia."

There's silence on the other end before Babette speaks again. "It's a school night."

I start picking at a hole in my ripped jeans. "I know. But as Aidan put it, I haven't done anything fun since I got home."

"Rylan, it's hard to do anything 'fun' with a broken leg."

"But a movie? Please, Babette, can I go?"

"I don't know..."

"Here, Rylan." Nadia reaches for my phone. "Let me talk to her."

"Hold on, Babette. Nadia wants to talk to you." I hand it off. She opens the door and gets out, talking all the way.

"Hi, Babette! Yes, it's me…I know it's a school night, but Rylan…I actually have to agree with my brother on that one….You do, too? That's good to know. Yes, I promise we won't get in trouble….Okay, thank you. Bye!"

Nadia ends the call with a victory grin. "Your grandma said you can go."

"Yes!" Aidan fist-pumps the air and ends up hitting the car ceiling. "Ow!"

"How did you convince her?" I want to know, since it's an impossible feat to persuade her to do anything when her mind's made up.

"I gave her simple reasoning she couldn't argue with," Nadia tells us. "I also promised we'd go to the earliest showing possible."

I shrug. "Works for me."

"Me, too," Aidan agrees, waving his hands around like the pain will fly off.

"Let's just hope Ms. Stern doesn't give me a detention for sloppy research," I mumble as I climb out of the car after Aidan. But with the stuff I've found and the pictures I've taken, that shouldn't be a problem. Slasher movie, here I come!

Or not.

Some time later, school ends. I don't have detention because Ms. Stern found all my pictures and research acceptable, and the three of us are sitting along the front steps. Well, more like Aidan and me. Nadia's pacing around as she talks to her mom, telling her about tonight's plans. From the little snippets I hear, they're trying to organize the time to go.

"Figures my sister would forget to call the parents." Aidan leans back on the staircase.

I play with my backpack zipper. "She didn't forget. Nadia never got the chance to call them until now 'cause the bell rang by the time she remembered. You know the rules."

"Yeah, yeah. No cell phones at school unless you want them taken away and never want to see them again." Aidan stretches his arms over his head with a groan. "I can't wait until I get my phone back so I can stop using the house phone."

"You got it taken away *again*?"

"Yeah. I get caught with it five times on school grounds in three days and they think they can take it away until I learn how to be more 'responsible.'" He throws his hands up in frustration. "I'm plenty responsible!"

"Coming from the guy who drove the Jeep into a tree going fifty," Nadia mutters as she comes over to the steps, her conversation with her mother finished.

"How long are you going to hold that against me? For the umpteenth time, I was distracted!"

"Changing the radio station doesn't qualify as a distraction."

"Whatever."

"Anyway," Nadia looks over at me, "Mom's okay with us going, but only when our homework's done."

"*All* our homework? That's going to take forever!" complains Aidan. "I got a load of crap to do, on top of that satire piece I have to write for Karcy."

"That's what happens when you procrastinate," sniffs Nadia without a hint of sympathy.

We all head over to the Jeep.

"Don't worry. I'll help you with the satire. I've been done with mine for a while," I tell Aidan. "But can we stop at my house first? I left my laptop charger at home."

146

"Yeah. Of course." Aidan gives me a thankful grin. "Thanks, man. Where would I be without you?"

"Probably in summer school until you're thirty," Nadia mutters as she starts the engine. I can't help but laugh as Aidan's face collapses into a scowl.

At home, I jot a quick note for Ivy and pin it to the dock where she'll find it and it won't get wet. When Nadia asks me why I went down there, I lie and say that Babette had asked me to check the boat before leaving.

Thanks to the mountain that is Aidan's unfinished homework, we don't leave until eight forty-five. We would've left sooner, but both Mrs. Marce and my growling stomach insisted we stay for dinner.

Afterwards, we drive to Harraway and get there in time to see the nine-fifteen showing. Buying our tickets, we drag Aidan past the concession stand and find our seats. The theater's dark, smelling like butter and salt. The only sounds you can hear besides the previews are people slurping sodas and munching on popcorn. If I close my eyes, the noises distort and turn into something familiar…

Damn. No matter where I go, it seems the swamp is always going to follow me. Or maybe this is guilt because I'm here instead of meeting Ivy. But I shouldn't feel guilty about this. It's not criminal to go out with your friends, for God's sake.

I manage to make it through the movie. I don't really remember the whole thing, except nearly everyone died and the ending was the crappy type that leaves you wondering if an equally bad sequel will come out.

"If there's a sequel coming out, I want to see it," Aidan announces on the way home.

"But what else could they use for a sequel? There's nothing left they could use for a plot line." Nadia pulls into my driveway.

"What they do with all horror series, sis—bring the bad guy back from the dead and make him chase after the girl who got away."

"You'd think Hollywood would realize by now that trick is as stale as year-old bread." Nadia parks and looks back at me. "Thanks for coming, Rylan. I had a wonderful time."

"Thanks," I reply, trying not to feel awkward. This feels like we're saying goodbye after a date.

"Bye, dude." Aidan waves while I climb out of the car. I wave back and watch the Jeep drive off until it reaches the main road and disappears.

Sighing, I pull back my sleeve and check my watch. 10:53. Dad and Babette have gone to sleep, trusting I'll get home on time and in one piece. I glance over at the swamp pathway. I could go down to the swamp and see Ivy…

I'm interrupted by a giant yawn. I'm too tired. Staying up late these past days is finally catching up with me. I trudge up the stairs and let myself in.

Hopefully, Ivy will understand.

Around me, darkness swirls, coloring everything black. There's little light to be found because of the new moon. For once there's no sound: no cries, no chirps, no roars, nothing. It's like the swamp has gone to sleep.

Wait. What?

Looking around, I see I'm standing on the dock. How did I get here? Didn't I decide to go to bed?

A breeze dances across my torso, making me shiver. I about swallow my tongue when I see I'm only in my pajama

bottoms and nothing else, with not even a shoe for my good foot. What the hell...

"Rylan? Ryyyylan?"

My heart speeds up at the sound of my name. I look around, but I don't see anyone. "Hello?" I call out.

"Rylan?"

I relax when I recognize the voice. It's Ivy.

"Ivy, it's me. It's Rylan. I'm right here."

"Rylan? Where are you?"

I stagger down the dock. "I'm coming, Ivy. Just stay where you are."

By the time I come to the end, I realize I can't go anywhere. I can't walk on water. And though no one would know if I took the boat out, I don't want to disobey Babette on principle.

Now what do I do? I gaze down at the water and see that, by luck, a long log has gotten itself wedged between the dock and the opposite bank. Floating branches are really common, but none of them have been big enough to get stuck before.

"Rylan?"

Carefully I cross the log, half-crawling most of the time while ignoring the warm water lapping at my cast. Reaching the other side, I stand and follow Ivy's voice.

When I find her, she's standing by some boulders near the rim of her clearing. Ivy's holding a rock up as she looks under it, as if she'll find me under there.

"Ivy? I'm right here."

She doesn't answer. She doesn't even turn around. She just sets the rock down and moves on to the next one, calling out my name. *"Rylan?"*

"Ivy, I'm right behind you." Why won't she look at me?

"I cannot find you...Rylan." Ivy talks to herself as she lifts up each rock. *"Where did you go? Why are you...not here?"*

"But I am, Ivy. I'm right here."

Ivy finishes searching under the rocks and for a moment gazes out into the dense trees. *"Where are you, Rylan? Why am I…alone?"*

"You're not!" I cry out in frustration. "I'm right behind you! Just turn around and look!"

She does. Ivy turns around and walks towards me until we're only a foot apart. But she isn't looking at me. She's looking over my shoulder, just like Dad.

"Do you see me now?" I furiously wave my hand in front of her face. "I'm right here."

When Ivy speaks again, she's talking to herself.

"Rylan? Where are you?"

She stretches out her hand and touches me with it. It goes right through me. Like I'm mist. Like I'm a ghost.

Like I wasn't even here to begin with.

"IVY!"

With the speed to rival a rocket launch, I shoot out of sleep and into the real world. I look around my room, cold sweat running into my eyes. It's still dark. I reach for my clock.

2:57.

Throwing my bed sheets to the side, I grab my sweatshirt as I throw the window open. I don't care if I've forgotten my shoes. I don't care if I wake up every person in Roland.

I have to see Ivy.

I scale down the trellis and limp as quickly as I can to the swamp. Carefully, I avoid anything my bum leg could hit and make it to the dock in record time.

She isn't there.

"Ivy?" I swivel my head around, but she's nowhere.

"Ivy! I'm here. I'm right here."

No reply. Nothing but the night sounds of the swamp. It sounds almost like they're scolding me for leaving her.

I lean over, catching my breath. "Come…find me," I pant.

"Rylan?"

My heart skips a beat, hearing her voice behind me.

"Ivy?"

The boards creak. *"Yes, Rylan. It is me."*

We're both quiet, neither of us talking. The swamp's fallen silent, its inhabitants' attention now focused on the conversation between their queen and the human.

I speak first. "Are you okay, Ivy?"

"I am fine, Rylan. What about yourself?"

"I'm fine. Did you get my note?"

"Yes. And it is good…for you to spend time…with your human friends."

So she did read the note, and she was okay with my plans. "Then why…"

"Why what?"

I scratch the back of my head. "I…I had a weird dream."

"I know. I did…send the dream."

I look out over the glittering black water. "Why, Ivy?"

"I did it by accident. I…I did not mean to."

She looks incredibly guilty, so I don't think she's lying. "Accidently?"

"The more time we spend…together, the more connected…we are. Sometimes my worries will…transmute over into you. You see my… feelings through your dreams."

The book said nothing about that. "Really?"

"Yes. It has happened before with…the swamp animals. They tell me when I do…it is usually when something bothers me. My powers… go a little haywire."

"Then you were sad, weren't you? The dream was sad. You were looking for me and couldn't find me even though I was right there. It was like I'd abandoned you."

"I…see. And I was. I…missed you."

"I went to a movie with my friends and felt too tired to come down here," I say. "I'm never going to 'not come' because of you. You're my friend."

I finally turn around so I can reassure her some more, but I freeze. Guilt stabs at me deeply.

She's crying.

It's not full-out bawling, but in the little light available I see two wet trails slowly dripping from sorrowful eyes.

"Ivy?"

Her wet eyes close as she slumps forward, her shoulders shuddering.

"I am sorry," she whispers. *"I promised I would never send… another dream, but I did… I broke my promise. I made you worry. I made…you guilty. I am so…sorry."*

If guilt can cause heartache, then I've definitely experienced it. Seeing Ivy hunched over and crying for probably the first time in her really long life is making me feel like the worst person in the world. With her tear-streaked face in her hands, she looks so fragile, vulnerable, and human.

I come forward and give her a hug.

Ivy goes still as I wrap my arms around her. It's amazing. We're the same height, but Ivy feels so small and skinny compared to me. My hands brush her wings, feeling the smooth ivory bone humming beneath my fingers. A hand goes up to the back of her head and tangles in her satin hair as her head rests on my shoulder.

"Shhh," I murmur in Ivy's ear, beginning to delicately stroke her neck. "It's okay, Ivy. It's all going to be okay."

"I am so sorry," Ivy whispers into my shirt. I can feel her tears leaking through the fabric.

"There's nothing to be sorry for," I murmur. "I'm not mad. You were just sad, right?"

Ivy nods against my chest.

"So that's it," I continue. "You just had an accident, and those happen to everyone. Okay?"

Ivy pulls away slightly, meeting my gaze. Her eyes shine with unshed tears, but she's starting to look a little better.

"Friend," Ivy pronounces the word as though it's new to her. *"You called me 'friend.' Am I…a friend?"*

"Of course," I chuckle. "Of course you're my friend."

Ivy's eyes give off the clearest, brightest, happiest light I've seen from her, and I swear I see the corners of her mouth curve above her mask. I pull her back to me and she returns the hug, encasing me in steady arms.

"Rylan?"

"Yeah?"

"What is the water…coming out of my eyes?"

I secretly smile at her simple question. "Those are tears."

"And this? This…holding each other?"

"It's a hug. It's a way to show you care," I rest my chin on her shoulder. "I'm sorry I didn't come to see you and made you worry. But I'm never going to abandon you, okay?"

Ivy nods.

"Good. And I'm gonna make this up to you. I will. I promise."

And I seal it with a squeeze.

Chapter 13

My day falls into a schedule: I wake up, go to school while listening to Aidan complain about Nadia's driving, have my classes, avoid Dunstan, go home, do my homework, eat, wait for the household to fall asleep, and meet up with Ivy. Over and over again it happens.

It's the nightly meetings that are enjoyably irregular. It's because of them I'm losing track of time.

There's never a clue what will happen, but it's always amazing. Sometimes Ivy shows me around the swamp. Floating over water, I see the land in brand new ways. Trees are taller and leafier and flowers are more powerful-smelling. The animals are almost tame; she tells me that keeping the swamp in balance means keeping the animals in order and taking care of them when they don't. Water fowl, otters, deer, and others—but no alligators—come to greet us on our walks. Ivy mind-talks to them and tells me what they say back. Who knew animals could be so wordy?

Other times we stay in Ivy's clearing. Sitting under her tree, I spend whole nights teaching Ivy about the things I stuff in my backpack to bring along. One of the most memorable items was the hairbrush.

"What is that?" Ivy had asked when I pulled the brush out.

I held it up. "It's a hairbrush. Humans use it to keep our hair neat. I don't think that word applies to my mop, though."

Ivy laughed as she took it from me and turned it over in her hands. With the lightest touch she ran her fingers over the prickly bristles. *"May I use it?"*

"Go ahead."

On her first attempt, Ivy tried to brush her hair with the handle. Once I corrected her, she still couldn't reach because her wings got in the way. Instead of giving up, she asked *me* to do it for her. I blushed, and my face got even redder when I agreed. However, it wasn't weird at all. Ivy only moved a little when I accidentally pulled on the knots too hard. We talked like we normally did, except I had trouble paying attention when I kept feeling how smooth Ivy's hair was.

Sometimes all we do is lie under the tree and talk until our voices are hoarse. Ivy shares secrets of the swamp and little snippets of memories from long ago, yellowed with age but still comprehensible. In return, I tell Ivy all about the human world. She loves hearing about civilization and all the things humans do. The subject matter doesn't even have to be exciting; a simple play-by-play of my day enthralls her. Then again, when you live in partial isolation and can never really leave, I guess you'd be into learning everything from anything.

Even the stuff that's hard to explain.

"How can humans be?" Ivy asked me that one night when I was explaining the idea of countries and nationalities.

"How can humans be what? I don't understand."

"You told me…about the human race," Ivy explained. *"You told me how your people…live in a place of clashing cultures and*

beliefs where people…always fight and think they are right. I have to wonder…is that what it means to be human?"

Rubbing the back of my head, wondering how I was going to explain this, I started rambling.

"Not really. To be human…means living a life worth living. So you can look back on your memories and be proud about them when you're old, gray, and sitting in some retirement home."

"And such a life entails?"

"For me, living a good life means being a good person. You have to respect everyone, even bad people. It means being ready to die for what you believe in and for the people you care about. You have to be fair when it comes to other's beliefs. Accept people's differences, but at the same time stand by your own beliefs and be your own person."

"But from what you told me…this creates conflict."

"It does. But what can you do? People have a right to their opinions, and they're always going to have different ideas. It's learning how to live with them all that we need to find out."

"And when you do?"

"When we do, the world may finally be at peace. 'Cause that's a big part of living your life well: not causing other people strife and living in some sort of harmony."

"Have you yourself reached that yet?"

I shook my head, feeling like the world's biggest hypocrite. "No. I probably won't for a long time."

Ivy stared at me deeply. "But it is not impossible. Someday… will you reach the time you can do that?"

I leaned back until my head rested on the tree trunk. "Some people think what I've said just now is a bunch of crap. At one point in my life, I would've called it crap, too." Turning to look at Ivy, I smiled slightly. "But yes. I believe with some time, I can mostly be what a human is supposed to be."

I'd be lying if I say I remember the rest of what we talked about that night. After that conversation, it seemed everything else that followed was pointless and mediocre. I guess that's how you feel after having an enlightening discussion. Everything else loses the power behind it.

But in all the times we've talked, there are still some questions I haven't asked yet. I haven't asked about her actual birth. Where did she and her race come from? Were they made along with everything else four billion years ago? For some reason, I'm holding back. I can't figure out why. But maybe I'm scared: scared of offending her, scared of asking something she can't answer. It's stupid to be nervous of your best friend.

But she's not like anyone else.

I think she's holding back on me, too. There are these moments when I just know she wants to ask about something I haven't told her, like my mom. I've gone into detail about everyone in my life, but Ivy's smart enough to see half of a supposed couple is missing. It's like, along with sensing I don't want to talk about it, she can distinguish I'm still hurting because of it. She couldn't be more right. I want to tell her, but I don't want to get hurt.

Will this ever stop haunting me?

"That's awesome!" Aidan shouts.

It's Saturday, a little more than a week and a half after the movie fiasco. I'm lying on my bed with my phone to my ear, my laptop sitting on my stomach and acting like an electric blanket through my thin T-shirt.

"Yep." I watch the cursor move around the screen. "When I go in today, there's a very high chance I'll be walking out on two feet."

"When's the appointment?"

My eyes fall on the laptop clock. "In half an hour. Babette's driving me up there."

"What about your dad?"

I hesitate for a second as I hit my pointer finger against the plastic casing. "Dad…hasn't said anything yet. I bet he won't once this thing's gone."

"You sure?"

"Aidan, you're making him sound like a jerk." I can practically hear the frown on Nadia's face.

"He's not as bad as you make him out to be," I mutter. With a click I shut my laptop.

"All right." Aidan backs down. "But hey! No more cast means we can ride our bikes again! I can't wait to feel the wind through my helmet, the pavement under my wheels, the rush of pure speed!"

"The honking of drivers telling you to get out of the way before they turn you into road pizza," Nadia deadpans.

"Oh, my dear sister. You make me sound like I'm as bad a driver on my bike as I am with the car."

"Well, there was that time with the side of the house…"

"I was seven! It was the first time without training wheels!"

"Admit it! You're a natural disaster when it comes to transportation."

"No! Never!"

"Anyway," I interrupt before things get nasty, "do you guys wanna come with us to the doc's office?"

Aidan smiles. "'Course, dude. I'll come. Anything to support my best buddy."

"Awesome. Nadia?"

"As much as I want to, I can't." She sounds apologetic. "I have a…meeting with a friend."

My eyebrows shoot up, and I imagine Aidan's do the same. Another friend? I thought *we* were Nadia's friends. I mean, sometimes she talks to other girls at school, but she mainly sticks with her brother and me.

"Really?" I try hard to not sound surprised. "Anyone we know?"

I hear Nadia's breath hitch before she gives a name. "Lizzie Wendell."

I feel my eyebrows rocket off my forehead as Aidan audibly gasps. Lizzie Wendell? Why would Nadia hang out with Lizzie Wendell? Lizzie's perky and cute and all, but in the Roland Roux High social pyramid, Lizzie ranks near the top. She's the type of girl who hangs out with Melanie.

"What!?" Aidan's voice sounds distant and off. He's not yelling into the phone, but at Nadia herself.

"Aidan! How many times have I told you not to yell at me!?" Now Nadia's yelling at her brother.

"About as many times as you've commented on my driving skills!"

"Guys!" I shout. "I'm still here, you know."

"Sorry, Rylan," they both apologize.

We're all quiet for a moment before I ask the question needing to be asked.

"Lizzie Wendell? That's, um, interesting. When are you meeting her?"

"At the Harraway mall in forty-five minutes."

Aidan takes a blunter approach. "Since when have you been friends with Lizzie? You know she hangs out with Melanie sometimes."

Nadia sighs. "I know. But I've talked to Lizzie a couple of times. She's actually really down-to-earth and interesting. Yesterday I decided to try and have friends that are girls, so

I met her in the hallway and she was more than happy to make plans with me."

"Er...good for you, Nadia."

"Thanks, Rylan. Sorry I can't come to Doc Norm's office with you. Aidan, I'm taking the Jeep so you'll have to bike over to Doc Norm's."

"Fine."

"So you'll come?"

"'Course, dude. I wanna watch the big hulking thing come off."

"Thanks, man."

"Rylan?" I hear Babette's voice boom up the stairs. "It's time to go."

"Coming."

Grabbing my other sneaker, I head downstairs, speaking into my phone. "I gotta go. Babette's got errands, so she's making us leave right now."

"We should get going, too," Aidan tells me. "See ya soon."

"Bye, Rylan," says Nadia.

"Bye."

I end the call just as I reach Babette and the front door.

"Ready to go?" she asks.

I nod. "Yep. Can't wait to get this stupid thing off me."

"Be grateful that it was only this long. You could've needed to wear it a lot longer."

"But I didn't," I mutter to myself as we cross the porch. And it's thanks to Ivy.

"Did I make it?"

Like a human tornado, Aidan bursts into the doctor's office like a massive gust of wind. The secretary gives him

160

a harsh glare, but Aidan either ignores it or doesn't see it as he comes over to my seat.

I shake my head. "Nope. You made good time."

"Sweet! Oh, hey Babette." Aidan waves at my grandma.

"Hello, Aidan." Babette smiles. "I'm guessing Rylan told you the cast was coming off today?"

"Uh huh. Rylan tells me and my sister everything." He gives me a chummy pat on the shoulder, but I barely feel it as a twinge of guilt goes through me. He's lying. Or, more like it, I'm lying. I don't tell him everything.

"Rylan?"

I look up to see Doc Norm standing in the doorway. "Yes?"

"Hello again." He gestures to my leg. "Ready to get your cast off?"

I stand. "Yeah. You mind if Babette and Aidan come?"

Doc Norm doesn't speak as he turns away, but he signals them to follow.

Half an hour later, I'm out.

"Be free, little bird!" Aidan proclaims once we're outside the office. Babette shakes her head, but I grin as I bend my fixed leg. Man, does it feel good to have that cast off.

"Want to go to Wally's and celebrate?" Aidan asks.

"Yeah." Going to the truck bed, I pull my bike out; I convinced Babette to bring it along in case something like this happened. She was skeptical about bringing it—"Who rides a bike right after getting a cast off?"—but Doc Norm said my leg had healed so well, it's like it wasn't broken in the first place.

"What time will you be home?" Babette asks.

"Before dinner." I wave goodbye as I pedal after Aidan. "Bye!"

"Don't get into any trouble! I'm too young to have a jailbird for a grandson!"

I laugh. As I follow Aidan, I test out my leg. It's working wonderfully. The wind on my face, the sound of rubber scraping against cement, my legs pushing away at the pedals and the strength going into them. Oh, yeah. This is what I've been missing.

"Enjoying yourself?"

I catch up to Aidan and give him a smile that's just as wide as the one he's giving me.

"Yeah. I've really missed this. Can't wait to ride to school."

"Me, too," he agrees.

"But for a totally different reason."

"Come on, man! Don't start ragging on me, as well."

"Calm down, dude. I'm kidding."

We lapse into a comfortable silence. The streets of Roland fall behind as we ride on. Before we know it, our destination is coming up on the right corner.

When you first glance at Wally's, you have to wonder if you're in the right time period. The little diner looks like something straight from the 1950s, thanks to the metal siding, the bright-red and sea-foam green paint job, and the curvy neon sign. The inside only adds to the time warp. You got worn, blood-red booth seats, round silver-trimmed tables, a soda fountain counter, and enough memorabilia plastered on the red and white walls that you could turn the place into a museum if you wanted to. But it's a museum that serves the best burgers in town, and it'll suck if it ever closes down.

We stick our bikes in the bike rack and head inside. Not bothering to look at the menus, the two of us grab a booth near the left corner. Since there's no school, the place is full of classmates eating and joking. Dunstan and Melanie aren't among them.

"Hey, boys." Wanda the waitress comes over with two glasses of water and her paper pad and pen at the ready. "What can I get you today?"

"Two of the biggest hot fudge sundaes you can get," Aidan orders for us.

"Comin' right up." Wanda leaves to place our order.

Aidan stretches and places his hands behind his head as he looks around with happy contentment. "Man, we haven't been here in ages!"

I nod. "Yeah. It's been a while."

"I wonder what kept us away?"

"Probably the mountains of homework teachers give us because they think we have nothing else to do, *and* my recently-healed leg."

"Here, here." Aidan raises his glass. I do as well, and we tap them together with a loud *clink*.

Taking a long sip, Aidan asks, "So how does it feel to be a free man?"

I set my glass down. "Pretty good, now that I know my grandma won't be fussing over me practically every freaking second."

Aidan starts playing with the saltshaker. "She honestly did that?"

"Okay, no, but that's what it felt like. Watching my every move, thinking I'll collapse if she turns away for one second; it's just like when Mom…" I trail off, just realizing what I'm about to go into.

Fortunately, Aidan's smart enough to swiftly change the subject. "So what's up with my sister?"

I spin the straw in my glass and watch the slowly melting ice cubes dance. "How am I supposed to know? You're her brother. You live with her; therefore, you should have more of a clue than I do."

"Yeah, but it's just weird. Nadia doesn't do stuff like this." Aidan glances over at the kitchen to see if our order's coming. It's not, so he looks back at me with a rare flash of genuine freaking-out on his face. "I mean, first with the makeup, and now she's off at the mall with Lizzie Wendell. *Lizzie Wendell.* If she wanted to make friends with other girls, I thought she would start with someone else, like Gwen Deena. You know, the sporty, act-like-a-guy types." Aidan moans with exasperation and leans back in his booth seat. "Girls are so confusing."

"Tell me about it."

"Do you know what happened after our phone call this morning? I went to Nadia and asked for more of an explanation of what's going on, and she doesn't say anything! I point out that she was perfectly fine with telling *you* everything, and she goes all red and says I don't know what I'm talking about and that she only told you to explain why she couldn't come to the doctor's office." Aidan shakes his head. "Jeez. If I didn't know any better, my sister likes you!"

He laughs. I don't, as my mouth goes dry and my mind blanks. I've had my suspicions. But makeup? Hanging out with girls who are her complete opposite? It sounds like Nadia's trying to impress someone. I have the feeling that person is me.

Crap! What do I do now?

"Rylan? Dude?"

"Huh?"

"Come on, dude. Weren't you listening? I asked if—"

Before Aidan can finish, Wanda's back. She's balancing a tray with two steaming hot fudge sundaes in giant bowls.

"Here ya go. Two big sundaes." She hands us our spoons. "Enjoy."

Swamp Angel

As soon as Wanda's gone, Aidan starts inhaling his ice cream.

"Ah! Sweet fudgy goodness!" Aidan purrs around his spoon. "I haven't had one of these in such a long time. I forgot how good they are."

I swallow a big spoonful. "Same here. This was much needed."

Pleasant silence falls on us as we both focus on consuming our desserts. Aidan gobbles his up, having to stop more than once to get rid of his brain freeze. I crack up at the priceless faces he makes every time he gets one.

Aidan's almost done when he asks, "So, remember the thing I asked you before our sundaes came?"

Crap. Of all the times Aidan had to recall a question. I quickly hide my nervousness before it surfaces. "Um, no. What was it?"

"I asked you how your project for Ms. Stern was coming."

Phew. It's not about Nadia. I can breathe again.

"I'm almost done. But let me guess." I smirk when I see the look on Aidan's face. "You're not even close to halfway done on your own, are you?"

"Dude! Why do you have to be such a freaking overachiever?" Aidan doesn't answer my question, but he doesn't deny it either.

"I'm not an overachiever—"

"Rylan!"

I come one millimeter away from hitting my knee on the underside of the table as I jump in my seat. Melanie's suddenly standing in front of our booth as if by magic, dressed in shorts and a tank top. She's blinding us with her pearly white smile.

"Aw, Rylan. Did I scare you?" Melanie playfully pouts as she leans on the table.

165

"Hi, Melanie!" Aidan greets her, obviously delighted that's she here talking to us.

"Er, hi, Melanie," I greet her, slowly sliding back into my seat. "Yeah. You did kinda scare me."

"I'm so sorry!" She points to the door with her perfectly manicured fingernails. "I just came by to see if anyone I knew was here and when I looked in the window, what do I see? You and your friend Adrian!"

"Aidan," he corrects her. He's not bothered that she got his name wrong as he looks back and forth between the two of us.

"So I thought I might hang with you for a while." Melanie straightens up and tosses her hair over her shoulder. "Mind if I sit here?"

If Dunstan finds out about this, I'll be dead before the weekend is over.

"Well, actually—"

"Really? Thanks." Melanie slides into the booth seat. As she does, I feel her bare leg rub up against my own. It takes all my willpower not to blush.

"So what's going on?" Melanie says, never looking away from me.

"Uh, well, we were just finishing some sundaes." I gesture to the bowls. Melting ice cream floats around in cooling chocolate.

"Omigod, that looks so good. Too bad I'm on a diet." Half standing in her seat, Melanie shouts, "Waitress!"

Crap. If she's ordering food, that means she's staying. Aidan looks beside himself as she orders a salad.

"So what else is going on?" I swear if Melanie had laser vision, my face would be melted, she's staring so intensely.

"Well, um, I—"

"Rylan got his cast off!" Aidan shares the happy news.

Melanie lights up faster than a light bulb as she finally notices Aidan. "Really!? When?"

"Just half an hour ago. Doc Norm took his cast off and we rode here on our bikes to celebrate." Aidan's so absorbed in telling Melanie everything that he doesn't pick up the "shut up" glare I'm giving him. "Omigod! Rylan, I'm so happy for you!"

I suddenly find myself in something resembling a hug. Melanie's arms feel like steel cables as they go around my neck and squeeze the life outta me. Her perfectly groomed nails are shovels digging into my shoulder blades. My head is pushed into the crook of her neck where the perfume I once found so enticing is now overpowering.

This is no hug. It's nothing like Babette, who's squashy and warm. It's nothing like Nadia, who's firm and friendly. And it's sure as hell nothing like Ivy.

"What the hell is this?"

I turn and look over my shoulder, and the number-one reason why I didn't want Melanie around is glowering at the end of the table. Dunstan.

"What the hell is this?" Dunstan asks, or more like snarls, again. Facing a pissed-off lion sounds more inviting right now. He was always possessive with what he considered his, from the last pudding pop to his toy cars back when we were kids.

Melanie's the first to react. "Dunstan!" she squeals. Letting go of her vice grip on me, she climbs out of the booth and prepares to hug Dunstan. But instead of accepting it, he pushes her to the side.

"What are you doing with my girl?" Dunstan growls, practically baring his teeth.

"Oh, Dusty, calm down." Melanie puts a hand on his shoulder. "I was just talking to them. No need to get

jealous." She bats her eyelashes quickly. "You know my eyes are only on you."

Dunstan doesn't listen. He doesn't even look at her as he continues scowling at me.

"I'm not doing anything," I tell him, trying to keep calm. "Aidan and I were sitting here eating when Melanie came up to us and started talking. I was just being polite."

"Wouldn't the polite thing to do be not to hit on someone's girlfriend?"

"I wasn't hitting on her. I swear!" I look at Aidan desperately for help.

He quickly responds. "Yeah! Rylan wasn't doing anything wrong. I saw the whole thing. They were just talking about how Rylan has his cast off and—" Aidan slaps his hand over his mouth, realizing he's said too much. But judging by Dunstan's twisted look of glee, he was too late.

"Really? I guess I can finally do this!"

With speed I didn't know he had, he grabs my shirt collar and yanks me out of my seat. He pushes me into the table edge, causing the tabletop to shake and calling the attention of everyone in the diner. I feel them staring at us, and it's like my first day back to school after the accident all over again.

"Let me go!" I try to pull out of his grip but it's a futile effort.

"I don't think so." Dunstan's voice is deadly calm. "I think a lesson's in order, Forester. Maybe this'll teach you not to flirt with my girl from now on."

I know what he's referring to. He's talking about the first incident in the hallway.

"You said he wouldn't remember anything!" I accuse Aidan. He can only shrug apologetically as he looks from me to Dunstan and back again.

"Guess I'm not as stupid as you thought I was." Dunstan pushes me against the table even harder. My hand knocks against something. A quick glance tells me it's one of the ice cream bowls.

"Hold still, Forester," Dunstan snarls, pulling a fist back. "This'll only hurt a little!"

As his fist flies, I snatch the bowl and shove it into Dunstan's stupid face. Vanilla soup and chocolate chowder go everywhere. He falls back as he shouts in shock, and he raises his hands to wipe his eyes.

I'm gone as soon as he lets go.

"Run, Rylan!" Aidan shouts. He doesn't need to tell me twice. I sprint out of Wally's, scamper to the bike rack, yank my bike out with the strength of the freaking Hulk, and pedal away like Death's on my heels. I hear Dunstan's infuriated roar from behind me.

"I'll call you later, dude!" I hear Aidan shout out. I hope Dunstan doesn't take his anger out on him. That's something he would do. Even when we were friends, he always smack around whoever gave him trouble. He got chewed out for that a lot, but at the time I thought it was amazing how he didn't let anyone get away with hurting him.

I think differently now.

I don't stop until I'm safely home. Not bothering to lock my bike to the porch, I hurry up the steps, throw open the front door—and run right into my dad.

"Rylan?" Dad eyes my flushed face and the sweat on my forehead. "What happened?"

"Nothing, sir," I mutter, staring at the floorboards. I try to walk around him but he cuts my escape off.

"Rylan, your face is bright red and you're puffing up a storm. It's obvious something's wrong."

"So now you're finally paying attention to something other than yourself for once?"

His face hardens, but he doesn't say anything other than, "You know I'm down in the office most of the time. And whenever I do come home, you're off with your friends or hiding in your room, or—"

"I don't hide in my room. And if you know I'm in there, how come you never knock to say hello? Huh?"

"I have my own work to do in the study and that takes up all my time until dinner," explains Dad, like that'll clarify everything.

"Figures you would pull that excuse out," I snap as I again try to go around Dad again. This time he lets me. "Too busy...just admit you can't talk to me because I look exactly like her! It's been ten years, Dad!"

Dad doesn't blow up and start shouting his voice hoarse. He face becomes stonier, his eyes slit, and his frown increases. I'm actually impressed to see emotion on his otherwise expressionless face.

"Go to your room," he growls at me. "Now!"

"Fine." I stomp up the stairs to show his anger is well felt. "I'll happily be punished for telling the truth that needed to be told a long time ago."

"Go."

I clomp off down the hallway, into my room, slam the door closed, and fling myself on to my bed. Closing my eyes when my face hits my pillow, I lic there, my breathing slowly returning to normal. Egging Dad on wiped me out like I'd finished a marathon. I should probably feel guilty over fracturing his feelings like that, but I don't. He's been unemotional for so long, I think he needed this. It proved something he won't admit: he's still alive while his wife is long gone.

Suddenly my jean pocket starts buzzing, and I pull out my cell phone. The screen reads *Aidan*, and the number is his house phone number.

"Hey."

"Hey, dude." Aidan sounds rushed and winded.

"You okay? You're out of breath. Please tell me Dunstan didn't use you as his personal punching bag."

"What? No!"

I sigh with relief. "Thank God. I was scared he'd go after you since he couldn't pile-drive me into the ground. What happened after I left?"

"Dunstan ran after you as soon as he got that gunk out of his eyes, but by then you were long gone. So he roared in frustration and stormed back inside to the bathroom. Melanie went to offer him support, and I decided it was time to leave. So I paid the waitress—you owe me for that ice cream, by the way—and rode my bike home. No harm, no foul."

"Damn it. Now I'm a dead man once Monday rolls around."

"I don't think he'll fight you in school. He's not that stupid."

"You also said he wouldn't remember the first Melanie incident, and now look where I am!"

"I know, and I'm sorry. I honestly thought that he would forget. But hey!" Aidan abruptly changes the subject. "Was it just me, or was Melanie totally flirting with you in Wally's?"

Oh yeah. The one who started it all.

I glare at the phone, hoping he can feel my displeasure on his end. "Was she? I was so busy being terrified of getting caught with her that I didn't notice."

"Okay, so Dunstan caught you and you probably have to avoid him for the rest of your life. It was so worth it to find out Melanie's into you. She was completely flirting with you."

I sigh. It's useless to tell him any crush I had for Melanie is fading. He'll think I'm either crazy or playing a joke, he's that infatuated with her. She didn't even get his name right at the diner. Wouldn't that annoy anyone? It annoyed me, and I'm the innocent bystander.

"Is Nadia back home yet?"

"Nope. I honestly thought she'd get bored and come home early, but I guess not." I hear him pacing. "It's just so weird, her being friends with girls."

"Maybe she needs some girl friends. There's stuff she can't talk about with us since we're guys, you know."

"I still think she's doing all this to get some guy's attention. Maybe I should grill her about it so the poor dude knows what he's getting into."

"Do that and you'll never find anything out," I tell him. I wonder if I should tell him that it might be me she's interested in. It's just a suspicion, but I know I'm sensing more than friendship coming from her at times. This can only prove it. But what if it's all in my head?

"An excellent point," Aidan decides. "How about I ask her about it if something even fishier happens?"

"Like if she buys a skirt?"

"That'd never happen in a million years, but something like that."

"Sounds solid to me."

"Okay, that's a—" Aidan instantly stops talking. I hear shouting in the background.

"Hello? Anyone there?" What's going on over there?

"Hey man." Aidan's back. "Sorry about that."

"What happened?"

"Mom happened. Apparently I'm slacking on my chores and Mom just told me to get off the phone and do them."

"Then I better go. I don't want her mad at you."

"Eh, I'm used to it. But thanks, man. See you soon?"

"You know it. Bye."

"Bye."

I press END and flop back on my bed. The beginning pains of a headache are encroaching on my brain. Rubbing my fingers along my forehead, I sigh, both relieved and worried. Aidan didn't get hurt, but now it's more than possible his sister may have a crush on me. Yet another thing to add to the knotted disorder that is surviving school, living with the world's most emotionless man, worrying about the swamp's welfare, memories of Mom, the alligator accident, and keeping my ass out of Dunstan's sight. But Ivy…she's not among the tangle. Though she's my biggest secret, I feel no burden by being her friend. If anything, the relationship I have with her is the balloon that's keeping my messy life up in the air.

Thank God for Ivy.

There's a knock at my door. "Rylan? You in there?"

Babette. "Yeah, I'm here. Come in."

She does. The slight smile on Babette's face fades like fog in the sun the moment she sees me on my bed. "You okay, hon?"

"No." I tell her about Melanie, Dunstan, and my great escape and top it all off with the fight with Dad. I refuse to tell her my newfound Nadia theory.

Babette's eyebrows scrunch together. She knows what happened between the two of us, and she thinks it's disappointing how Dunstan's turning into his old man. "Just because he's the mayor's son, he thinks he can do whatever. Do you want me to—?"

"No." I already know what she was going to ask. "I don't want you calling anyone about it. I'll handle Dunstan on my own."

"All right. But if you come home one day a bloody mess, expect me to take drastic measures."

"Deal."

She shifts in my desk chair as she crosses her arms. "Did you really have to talk to your father like that, though?"

"Yes, I did," I answer. "It finally got him acting like a normal human being again, if only for a little while."

Babette's lips are a thin line. "Getting your father mad for the sake of getting him to feel isn't good, Rylan."

"It was *for* him," I retort. "He's been so emotionless and two-dimensional for so long, and I'm sick of it!"

Babette doesn't look away and stays quiet.

"He needs to show his feelings," I continue. My voice dips into a whisper. "If he shows his feelings...it proves to me he's still alive. And I...I just want him to live again."

Silence stretches between us, the uncomfortably thick type of silence that's an invisible fog that you just want to cut yourself out of. Finally, Babette starts talking, but the first thing she asks surprises me.

"Did the attack bring up memories for you, too?"

I stiffen, knowing what she's talking about. She's talking about the memory flashes that seem to cut right into the stream of time. The memory flashes I kept having for years after Mom's death. The memory flashes doctors claimed were all part of post-traumatic stress and would go away eventually. They haven't.

"Only a few," I admit. "The last one was in the hospital when I was recovering. They're not as bad as they were when I was a kid, Babette, but haven't you already asked me that?"

Babette gives a direct answer. "Your father told me he's been having a lot of flashbacks since the gator attacked you. And since his main mechanism with coping with anything having to do with your mom is emotional detachment, it's getting rather hard for him to keep that up."

My throat dries. "I didn't know…"

"Well, now you do."

Babette rises from my chair and leaves. She does make one last comment from the doorway.

"I want to see him recover from this as much as you do, Rylan. But forcing feelings on him isn't the answer, especially when these flashbacks are conflicting with that recovery. He could have a horrible breakdown if we're not careful. So…be careful."

I can't speak, so I nod. Babette leaves, and the moment she's gone I collapse back on my bed again. Another kink has been added to the snarl of my life. And even with Ivy as the balloon, everything is starting to go under.

How long is this going to hold?

Chapter 14

Tonight's a first. I get to use the front door. I know that doesn't sound like much, but it's a giant relief to me that I don't have to scoot my butt over hard shingles with pointy corners and scurry down a trellis that could collapse at any moment.

Just for the hell of it, I run around the driveway once before sprinting down to the dock. I stop and wait for Ivy. She's going to be so ecstatic when she sees that the cast is off. Just to check that I brought it, I feel the sides of my backpack and rub my fingers over the distinct lump.

"Rylan?"

I beam as I turn to see Ivy standing there. "Hey, Ivy."

She notices instantly. *"Your leg!"*

"Yep. Got the cast taken off this morning. It's all better now, and it's all thanks to you."

"May I see?"

Before I answer, Ivy squats down and begins to pull up my pants leg. I stare away at some random tree as my face ignites, trying to ignore Ivy's hand while she examines my leg.

Ivy straightens back up. *"It is completely healed."* I can see the corners of a smile popping up over the leaf mask. *"I am so…happy for you."* Stepping forward, Ivy gives me one of her gentle hugs.

"Like I said, it was all thanks to you."

"Come." Ivy weaves her hand through mine and pulls me to the water. It leaks into both my sneakers as we walk over the water. I wiggle my toes. It's cold and feels fantastic.

Eventually we reach her tree and sit down. She eyes my backpack.

"Your bag is rather lumpy…tonight."

That reminds me. "I got you something."

I open my bag. Her present is lying right on top. Ivy's eyes transform into dinner plates as I pull it out.

"The cast…"

"Yep." I hand the dirty-white, scribbled-on fiberglass monstrosity to Ivy. She takes it and holds it as if it would break at any second.

"You are giving this to me?"

I nod. "Yeah. I don't need it anymore, and it would make a good piece to add to your collection."

"It will. Thank you." Ivy leans over and gives me another hug. I accept it and hug her tightly, wanting so badly to absorb everything good that's in this one embrace.

"Rylan?" She sounds stifled.

"Yeah?"

"I am having…trouble breathing."

I let go and fall back, watching as Ivy takes in deep breaths. "Sorry, Ivy. I didn't—"

"It is fine," she somewhat rasps while massaging her neck. *"It is perfectly all right."*

"Good."

"But now I must ask you the same thing." Ivy gazes at me, her eyes as inspective as magnifying glasses. *"Are you okay?"*

"What do you mean?"

"I sense something is…off about you. You seem more tired than usual and your face…is a mask of exhaustion, though you try…to hide it. Is everything okay?

She's caught me. There's no way I can ever lie to Ivy about something that's so big, it's written all over my face.

"If you do not want to tell me…I understand." Ivy looks away and across the clearing. *"Everyone has the need for privacy."*

"But you're my friend. And friends tell each other everything. Even about the past, no matter how painful…" I stop and put my head in my hands, trying to control the sudden stress attack.

"Rylan?"

"It's nothing. I…I just got into a couple of fights today."

Her reaction is what I expected it'd be. Ivy leans forward, hands outstretched, worry etched upon her face. *"A fight? Why? Are you hurt?"*

I take one of her hands in my own and rub it. "I'm fine, Ivy. The fights weren't like you imagine fights. They were more like screaming matches. *Two* screaming matches."

"Two of the screaming matches?"

Taking a deep breath, I tell her what happened with Melanie and Dunstan, and then with my dad. Ivy stays mostly quiet as I speak, asking questions only when she doesn't understand.

"Why would you purposely upset your father?" Ivy asks after I finish. *"I thought that children…loved their parents."*

"We do," I explain. "But sometimes the relationships can get strained and end up falling apart."

"Like with your father?"

I sigh. "The thing with my dad is…he doesn't show any emotion. He hasn't for a long time. Sometimes I catch him scowling or smiling a little. But most of the time, he walks around in this emotionless haze. And during the fight…" I pause as my eyes wander over to the surrounding foliage,

178

to our hands, and finally to Ivy's eyes, ever patient and trusting. I swallow.

"In our fight today, I intentionally got him mad just to see him get mad. To see some type of feeling on his face because he's been acting dead to the world for so long."

Ivy stops stroking my hand. She pulls away and for a moment I feel dejected, like she doesn't want to be around me because of my freakish father. But a second later she's embracing me again, and I silently chastise myself for being stupid.

"I am so sorry for him. And for you." Ivy leans back, keeping her hands on my shoulders. *"To live without feeling anything...I cannot begin to imagine what that would be like."*

"Me, neither," I agree. "It'd be nice to block out sadness or anger or fear. But what about joy, or happiness, or love? What about the good things?"

"When you hide away from one...you end up hiding from them all," Ivy concludes. *"So it is best that you live...with all of them. Because the good helps us deal with the bad. You just have to...allow it to work. For in the end...that is the only way to live."*

I smile at Ivy's wise words. "That's pretty smart," I tell her. "Is this something you learned over your lifetime?"

"This was not something I learned. It was something I was told."

"By who?" I'm confused. Didn't Ivy say I was the first person she'd ever talked to?

"Yes. I was told this," Ivy restates, and I get the uneasy feeling she's reading my mind. I try asking who told her, but my mouth freezes in an open pout, no doubt making me look dumb. However, she gets the gist of my question.

"I was told," she gazes up at the sky, *"by my sisters."*

"You mean other swamp angels?"

Ivy glances back at me. Something like ageless wisdom creases her features, making her look even more calm than usual. I sense a story coming.

She releases my hands as she begins. *"There is one important event I remember…. It is the oldest of all my memories. It was the day…I was born."*

My heart skips a beat.

"At first, all I saw was this aura of light. And then…faces. The faces of all my sisters surrounding me, all of us nearly full-grown. One sister—the chosen leader—told us of instructions…that we were to stay together. And that was how we lived for a while, in a big colony. I do not know where it was…but I remember gathering food, practicing magic, and dancing under the sky.

"But then…a flood came. The leader sister had seen that much water was coming from the north. So we made a journey to high ground…and watched as the world drowned below.

"When it was done…the light came to us again. The light was pleased at our quick thinking and resourcefulness, and wished to give us…a gift for it. So it did; then, it separated us to our own swamps to carry out that gift."

It takes me some time after Ivy finishes to find my voice. "Who's the light, and what's the present?" I ask, my voice hoarse. But I feel I already know the answer to the first one.

Ivy smiles gently and looks up at the sky.

"I do not know. The light is the light…it is simple as that. But I know it is a good light. After all, it gave us the chance…at having a soul."

And that's when the shock arrives and sinks in.

"I…um…er…" I've been reduced to a babbling idiot. Would this be what everyone would sound like in the presence of something so divine?

"Rylan? Are you all right?" Ivy asks. She's leaning over, and is so close I can feel her breath leaking through her mask. If it were gone…

"I just—I—this needs to sink in. I'm fine."

Ivy sighs as she leans back against the tree. *"This is what I meant when I said there were things…you could not begin to comprehend about me. Maybe I should not have told you. This was what I feared…"*

She gazes at me, waiting for what will come next. I sort through multiple replies and can only come up with one.

"Soul…"

She straightens up a little, eyes wide. It's the action you see people do when they confront some crazy person.

"What?"

"Soul," I repeat.

She swallows hard. Ivy smiles at me, but it's uneasy, clearly questioning the meaning of what I said. *"You ask me about my soul?"*

"Yeah. You said your gift from this…light…was a chance for a soul." I reach for her hand, and gently take hold when she doesn't pull it away. Now it seems *she's* the one who needs comforting.

She nods, looking down at our fingers. Like me, she seems to get courage from the contact.

"Yes. That was our gift. For my people…have no souls."

"No souls? How? You talk and think like a normal person."

"But that is just it, Rylan. We…are not human. We are intelligent animals. And animals have no souls," Ivy explains. *"And when they die, they just cease…to exist. They're gone. But with a soul…one can live on forever."*

"So it gave you a chance at existence after death." I rub my thumbs in small circles over the skin of her knuckles.

"Yes. Because that is one…of the best presents of all." Her eyes drift off as she recalls what was said numerous years ago. *"So as a reward for surviving…the light gave us the opportunity to earn what we do not have."*

"But why just an opportunity and not a soul?"

"It is better earned. All things…are better earned. We need to know for ourselves how much we as swamp angels want…this and if we even deserve it at all."

"I think you do." My thumb stops as I look at her. "Not everything can live a billion years. To do that and protect important land; you definitely deserve a soul."

Ivy blushes, a forest green color staining her cheeks. For some minutes, we just stare at each other. In the background, crickets chirp and night birds squawk like an orchestra of animals. All I have to do is close my eyes and the rest of the world will join in.

"So…" I break the silence. "What do you need to do to get a soul?"

Ivy looks me straight in the eye. *"To receive my spirit, I need to do something for someone…I love."*

Now my own face is changing color. How Ivy's speaking with such an alluring expression…it's like she's directing this all to me. Like she likes me more than as a friend. I surprise myself when I decide it's not a bad thing if she does.

"Well, um, I hope that happens someday," I stutter, cursing myself for tripping over my words.

Ivy doesn't notice. *"Thank you. I…hope so, too."*

There's a rustle as she stands. Her dress billows out and reveals her bare, webbed, and clawed feet.

"Come." Ivy leans down, her hand outstretched.

I take it. "What's going on?"

With a small grunt, Ivy helps me up. She begins leading me across the clearing in a different direction than from our night walks. *"I wish to show you something."*

I don't question her as we push asides branches and shrubs. It's so dark I can barely see my own hand in front of my face. It doesn't help that the trees block out the moonlight either.

"Where are we going?"

"You will see. It is one of my favorite places…here in the swamp."

"What's it look like?"

"As I have said, you will see."

I hear water move around. It seems we're out of the trees and walking over a canal. We make our way across, and soon we resume weaving through the woods. The crickets seem to fade, the gurgling water mutes, and everything falls silent as we leave it all behind. Because everything looks the same in the dark, I can't help but feel we're going in circles. But I guess we end up getting somewhere, because Ivy pushes back another branch, points, and announces, *"Here."*

I look. In front of us is another clearing, but instead of a tree, there's a perfectly round lake in the middle. In the middle of said lake is a tiny, grassy island. A large mossy boulder is sunk in the island's center. Moonlight bounces off the shiny surface.

"What do you think?" Ivy asks.

"Wow." I stare, dumbstruck, at the scene before me. "How many of these clearings exist that we humans don't know about?"

"Very few. I found this one a long time ago. This is my second favorite spot…in the swamp…besides my tree."

"I don't blame you. It's pretty cool."

"Yes, it is." Ivy tugs my hand and we step towards the water. *"Shall we?"*

With the spell in place, we cross the lake. Around us, the noise of the swamp comes back. It echoes and swells as its instruments play louder and louder. When we reach the island, the first thing that Ivy does is touch her forehead to the stone. Seeing my raised eyebrows, she confesses, *"It feels so soft. Try it."*

I do. And she's right. The moss is surprisingly warm and it reminds me of my pillow back home.

Ivy straightens up. She gestures to a patch of grass next to the boulder.

"Please sit," she tells me.

"Why?"

"I wish for you to see something, but you cannot do so until you... sit down."

Sensing she won't tell me anything else, I sit. "Okay. Now what happens?"

Ivy moves until she's standing right in front of me. Water from the lake laps at her heels. *"Watch."*

At first Ivy doesn't do anything. She stands there with her eyes closed, a look of concentration on her face. Curiosity demands I question what she's doing, but common sense, telling me not to disturb her, wins over.

Seconds later, I'm glad I didn't. The animal sounds increase. Weaving wind and bubbling swamp water is mixed in, creating a natural melody. It's the sound of the earth—something I haven't heard in a while, but it's something I can never easily forget. I can hear everything.

And to it, under the diamond sky and pale moon, Ivy dances.

There's no pattern, no sense of direction. She moves to the fluctuating beat, arms swinging, legs bending. The water under her feet ripples every time she takes a step. When she lifts a foot, water trails behind it like the path of a shooting star. Her hair sways, a silk scarf caught in the breeze. Her bony wings flex and extend in time with her movements.

She keeps her eyes shut, so she doesn't notice when she leaves land and fully stands over water. As she leaps and twirls across the lake, the water rises up in spirals and lines. She waves her arms in one direction, and there the waves flow. She spins around with her leg outstretched, and the water streams after her.

It's enchanting. It's gorgeous. It's thrilling. Out there she's making a work of art.

And here I am, stunned silly at the sight in front of me. I thought she was beautiful before. But as I watch her move, I truly know how bewitching she is.

She's an angel. Not a swamp angel, but a bona-fide, beautiful, saintly angel.

I want the dance to go on. I don't want it to stop. But eventually Ivy leaps back to shore. She does one final turn and finishes with a bow so low that her horns touch the ground.

"Amazing," I whisper as she straightens up. "That was freakin' amazing."

"I am glad you liked it." Stretching out her arm, Ivy gives me her hand. *"But it is even better with someone else. Please, join me."*

"Wh-what? I'm not a good dancer. I'll end up tripping over my own two feet."

Ivy laughs. *"It is fine. I am not a good dancer either."*

I drop her hand. "Are you kidding? You're incredible!"

"If I can dance, you can dance, too. Anybody can." Ivy again gives me her hand. *"At least try it for me. Please?"*

It's so damn hard to tell Ivy no when she's giving me her version of the puppy dog pout. Human or swamp angel, any girl who uses it has control of one deadly weapon that always wins.

"Fine," I mumble.

I take her hand, and we both move to stand on the shore. Lapping wavelets brush my feet and let small amounts of moisture slip in to resoak my socks. Ivy starts to dance again, but stays on the ground this time. She beckons with a finger. *"Come."*

I nod creakily, my stomach full of nervous butterflies. My eyes close and I concentrate on finding the earth's song. Slowly I pick up the melody.

And I begin to dance.

With limbs flailing, I jump around, randomly spinning and gliding. Over my shoulders I see Ivy do the same, twirling and lifting her legs. She catches me looking and smiles. I smile back.

It's primal and harsh. It's refined and elegant. It's soft and light, yet heavy and down to earth. It's full of movement and emotion: anger, sadness, hope, joy, peace. I feel all my feelings leak out with each motion. They make me fly across the grass, twist my limbs, and give me comfort with their escape. Everything that was so pent up inside is running free, leaving me feeling a hundred times better.

I feel a hand rush down my back. I turn back around, meeting Ivy's eyes. A silent message is conveyed between us. Grabbing her hands, we dance together. Our movements are irregular and have no pattern, yet they still fit with each other like puzzle pieces. Above us the moon shines, a single spotlight to the stage we're performing on.

On and on we go, jumping and flapping and spinning, letting everything out until we're tired. In unspoken agreement, we each grasp the other's shoulders with both hands and spin around in a giant circle, arms locked, looking at nothing else but our partner's eyes.

We spin and spin, a tornado of a finale, before we stop. The song slinks away into the night as Ivy leans back against the boulder. I follow her, standing about an inch away. Hands still clasped, we breathe in and out, gazing at the other.

"Rylan." Her voice has gone faintly husky, sending pleasant shivers up my spine.

"Ivy."

We stand, gazing at each other, until Ivy moves again, pulling me into another super hug. But this time as my arms touch her waist, it somehow feels softer than before. I wish I could hold on forever.

"You were right," I murmur into her ear. "I can dance, and that was fun. I feel so much better now."

"So you felt it, too? The release of your emotions?"

"Yep."

Ivy rests her head on my shoulder. *"Good. I wanted you to feel that. That is why...I brought you here."*

"Huh?"

"Before, I could sense that you were still troubled...even after you told me what was wrong. So I took you here so you could dance and feel better. It is never good to keep emotions ...to yourself all the time. I was so happy that you shared your problems with me...I wanted to show you my thanks for letting me know your troubles." Her eyes glisten as she glances at me again. *"I hope that you will continue telling me in the future."*

I look at her and smile. "If it means getting to dance with my friend again, then most definitely."

Ivy hugs me tighter. *"Wonderful, Rylan. This is good to know. And thank you for calling me...your friend. I love being called that."*

Love. My cheeks catch fire and my heart races as we continue holding each other. That word has become so foreign in my house, ever since my dad started distancing himself. But here's my best friend using it in a way that makes me feel like everything's okay and that I'm whole again.

It's the same one word—the only word—that could describe what I'm feeling for Ivy.

Chapter 15

"No. I can't be feeling this."

What's wrong with liking her like that? Who could blame you?

"It's all wrong! It's all too quick! I promised not to get my heart stomped all over again."

You made that promise when you were six and at your mom's funeral. I can't believe you remembered it after all these years.

"Well, I did."

Come on. That's not the reason why you won't admit you're in—

"I'm not!"

Some hours later, after I've said goodbye to Ivy, I'm still not sleeping. I'm up and pacing around my room debating with myself. Every newly discovered feeling is laid out in front of me, and I think I can get through this quickly. But as I'm discovering, they're hard to straighten out.

It's rude to interrupt, dude.

"I know. I'm sorry." Now I'm apologizing to myself. Might as well get the padded room ready. "I just—I don't know."

Don't say you can't like someone. What about Melanie and that incredible crush you've always had on her?

"Had. I had a crush on her. And that was totally different! Every guy likes her."

And you felt the need to join in. You jumped on the bandwagon without even knowing her. How can you like someone you don't know? You can't.

"I guess so. And Dunstan kicks my butt every time she gets close to me, or tries to."

Exactly. Why risk getting your butt kicked over a girl? It's not worth it. Now, Ivy—she's up for grabs.

"Of course she's up for grabs. No one else knows she exists!"

And why is that?

"She isn't even human, dammit!"

My inner turmoil falls silent after that final outburst, most likely because I've finally admitted the main problem. It's not old crushes or ancient promises made to Mom that are holding me back.

She isn't even *human*.

Growling and sighing at the same time, I plop down on my bed and bury my face into the pillow. I can't be with her. I can't be with someone who isn't my species. It would be so hard to date and kiss and...

And what if Ivy was human? I roll over and face the ceiling. If she was human, she could meet all of my friends. If she was human, she wouldn't have to stay in the swamp the whole time. If she was human, she'd be that beautiful girl from my dreams.

If Ivy was human, we could be together.

Groaning, I roll over again. Damn it. I'm right. As easier as everything would be, as simpler as everything would be, I'm wishing for something stupid. I can't go back now.

I'm falling in love with Ivy. Simple—or complicated—as that.

My head feels like it's packed with cotton. Staring at light hurts my eyes. The faucet that is my nose keeps gushing goo no matter how many tissues I use. I'm ready to upchuck at any breathing moment.

I'm sick. And if I were the mushy type, I'd think I'm heartsick over Ivy.

"It must be the flu," Babette concludes as she examines the thermometer. "A hundred and one. That's it. You're not going to school today."

"I'm not complaining," I sniff.

"You stay in bed and try to sleep," Babette tells me. "I'll go make some chicken soup and grab the ibuprofen."

Babette leaves. I call Nadia, asking if she can bring me all my homework. She says yes and as we're about to hang up…

"DUDE! Is that Rylan?" I suddenly hear Aidan loudly interrupt in the background. "Let me talk to him!"

"Aidan, use the—no, give that back!" I hear shuffling and scuffling as they wrestle over her cell phone.

"Aha!" Aidan shouts, apparently winning the squabble. Nadia huffs as Aidan starts speaking. "Hey, dude. What's up?"

"I'm sick. That's what's up."

"Jeez, dude. With what?"

"The flu."

"Damn. Hope you feel better."

"Thanks, man."

"Do you want us to come over after school with your homework and junk?"

"Yeah. That's what I was asking Nadia about."

"Before you so rudely barged in," Nadia snaps. "Now hurry up. We're going to be late for school."

"With the speed you drive? Quite true, sister dear."

Now it's my turn to cut in. "Hold on. You're driving? I thought we only drove because of my busted leg."

"Nadia can't ride a bike with what she's wearing," Aidan tells me. He sounds like he can't believe what he's actually saying.

"What do you mean?"

"Aidan, now!"

"I'll tell you later, dude. I gotta go before Kitty here sinks her claws into me."

"AIDAN!"

"Dude!"

But it's too late. Aidan's hung up. I drop my cell phone and grab a handful of tissues just in time to catch a sneeze.

By the afternoon, I'm feeling a whole lot better, despite the drippy faucet nose. I've just snatched yet another fistful of tissues—I'm going to single-handedly keep the Puffs Plus factories in business—when I hear the front door open, Babette greeting somebody, and two sets of feet thudding up the stairs. With a bang, Aidan throws my door open. Like my dad, he's programmed not to knock on people's doors.

"Dude! You'll never guess what happened at school today!"

"Aidan, you jerk! Knock before entering," Nadia scolds her brother, closing my door as she follows her brother in.

"Yeah, listen to your…" I drift off as my eyes bug. I can't believe what I'm seeing.

Nadia's wearing a skirt.

It's just a plain denim mini, but the fact it's there at all is absolutely shocking. Has Hell frozen over? Nadia never wears skirts! She hasn't worn one since the fourth grade,

Colleen Boyd

not even for formal occasions. This must be what Aidan meant when he said she couldn't ride her bike.

Nadia sees me staring. "What?"

"Skirt...you're wearing a skirt."

Nadia looks down like she forgot it was there. "You noticed? It was one of the pieces I bought with Lizzie at the mall yesterday." Like a ballerina, she does a slow twirl on her toes. "What do you think?"

"It...looks good." And it does. I've never noticed how long her legs were before. "But I thought you didn't like skirts."

Nadia's smile falters and turns exasperated. "Rylan, don't tell you're going to have a fit like Aidan did."

"I didn't have a fit," complains Aidan. "I was just surprised. Like Rylan said, you don't like skirts."

"I never said that!"

"Yeah, you did. Remember that one time in fourth grade when we had to get our school pictures taken and your mom made you wear a skirt?" I remind her. "You made this big speech that you were never going to wear another skirt as long as you lived."

Nadia crosses her arms. "That was years ago. I decided to try again, and it's not as bad as I thought it would be."

"A number of guys were checking her out," Aidan states, looking nauseated at the thought. "I nearly went cross-eyed, I was glaring at them so much."

"You weirdo." Nadia playfully hits her brother's arm. "You didn't need to do that. I'm not interested in any of them."

"I'm your brother. Scaring off guys who want to date you comes with the job." Aidan shrugs. "Just like you're supposed to be overcritical of any girl I wish to date."

"Any girl, or just the all-powerful Melanie?" Nadia snorts.

At the mere mention of Melanie's name, Aidan switches into hyperactive mode. "Oh, oh, oh!" He waves wild arms and points at his sister. "She just reminded me. You'll never guess what happened at school today!"

"I'll save my breath," I say. "What happened?"

Aidan is literally jumping with joy. "Dunstan and Melanie broke up!"

If it could, my jaw would be lying on the ground, like one big stretched-out rubber band. The king and queen broke up? Hell really must've frozen over, and it's a frosty winter wonderland out there now.

Aidan nods at my shocked expression. "It's amazing, right? And here we were thinking they'd be together forever."

"Fat chance now," Nadia scoffs.

"How in the world did that happen?" I ask.

"Lucky for you it was a public thing," remarks Aidan. He pulls my desk chair next to my bed and sits down. Nadia takes a seat on my bed end.

"They did it right in the cafeteria. Nadia and I were just sitting there eating lunch and talking when someone slammed a tray really loudly. I turned and saw Dunstan and Melanie yelling at each other. Melanie said that she was tired of him and his being a jerk, like at the resteraunt and whatever, and said she wanted to see other people. Dunstan, the big oaf that he is, didn't understand her and kept going on and on about how could she do this to him when there's no one else worth seeing. Melanie said that she had an idea. At that point, Dunstan just gave up, shouted that they were over, and stormed away."

"And here comes the worst part," Nadia adds, looking one step away from livid.

"Or the best part," Aidan corrects her. "As soon as everything calmed down, Melanie came over to our table

and asked where *you* were." Aidan's smile is too big for his face. "I think you're her idea for a new boyfriend, dude. Melanie likes you!"

It takes a minute before I can start digesting what Aidan just said. Melanie, the goddess of the eleventh grade, dumped Dunstan the god and now seems to be going after me, Rylan Forester: tall, average, and nowhere near the top of the pack. I should be jumping out of my bed, dancing with happiness that the object of every boy's affection wants me. But I'm not, because this breakup and discovery has come a little too late.

"I don't like her anymore."

Hearing that sentence, Aidan goes from bright and beaming to gaping-jaw horror like I just said the worst thing ever. Nadia's no better. Out of snarling hate comes badly hidden hope, which makes me feel guilty just watching her.

"What!?" Aidan shouts, leaping out of my chair so fast it flies back and hits the wall. "How? Why? When did this happen!?"

"It's been happening for a while now," I admit, raising an eyebrow at Aidan's overreaction. "My feelings for her have been fading."

"How long has this been going on?"

"Ever since the alligator attack."

"Then no wonder." Aidan rubs his chin like a detective who just had an "Aha!" moment. "The attack must have given you brain trauma that the doctors didn't find. It's been slowly corroding your mind ever since and now you don't know what to think!"

"Cut it out," Nadia growls, hitting him in the back of the head. "And don't be such a dork. Rylan doesn't have brain trauma."

"But what else could explain the sudden change of interest?" Aidan asks. He really can't understand this. "All the guys in Roland have been head-over-heels for Melanie ever since she got pretty in middle school. Even the computer geeks who have even less of a chance than we do want to date her! And instead of running off to another jock jerk, she's flirting with my best friend, who is nowhere close to high school royalty. No offense."

"None taken," I mutter.

Aidan shrugs. "Melanie's totally into you, and here you are deciding you don't like her anymore. It's just weird for this to happen when you've been crushing on her for so long."

Nadia nods. "Aidan's right for once. As much as I can't stand her," her hands clench into fists, "you've been infatuated with her too long for your feelings to just suddenly die. There has to be some good reason."

There is a reason. Ivy. And I obviously can't tell them that. But from the intense look in their eyes, I have to give them something. Otherwise they won't leave me alone about it and they'll both go into rants—or maybe just Aidan—about how friends are supposed to tell each other everything or you're not a true friend otherwise and that they tell me everything so why can't I return the favor?

So to save Aidan from himself and save myself the drama and the headache, I give them the half-baked version.

"I'm seeing someone."

It gets quiet enough to hear our breathing.

"You're dating someone?" Aidan asks, sitting back down in my chair. Nadia retakes her spot on my mattress.

I glance down at my hands, feeling my cheeks redden. "Not dating, really. It's more like I have feelings I haven't told her about yet."

"Do we know her?"

I shake my head.

"Who is she?" Nadia inquires. I glance up and instantly hate the look of rejection on her face.

The lies flow out of me too easily. "Her name's Ivy. She lives over in Harraway with her parents."

"Is she our age?"

"Yeah. She's only a year older."

Try a lot older. I'm answering myself again.

"An older woman? Awesome! What does she look like?"

I close my eyes as I remember her human form from my dreams. "She's about my height, has long white-blonde hair, and green eyes. Ivy's very beautiful."

Beautiful? More like drop-dead gorgeous.

"She sounds like it." Aidan leans back, putting his hands behind his head. "So where'd you meet her?"

"At the hospital in Harraway. Ivy does her service hours there."

"How come we never saw her?"

"You missed each other. She came there at different hours than you guys did."

Nadia sticks her hands up and stretches. "What did you two do?"

"Talk. Just what we do now. Ivy gave me her phone number and email before I left."

"Have you talked with her since?"

"Practically every day. She's a wonderful person. You guys would like her."

That, or you would run away in terror.

"So let me get this straight." Aidan scrunches up his face as he thinks everything over. "The reason that you're not gaga over Melanie anymore is because of some older chick you met in the hospital?"

"Yep."

Aidan lets out a long, low whistle. "Damn. If she's good enough to kick Melanie off the love pedestal, she has to be worth going after."

I nod. "Yeah. Ivy is. I...I think I like her."

If this were a cartoon, Nadia would have a rain cloud over her head—she looks that bashed from my news. But quick as she is, she hides her disappointment with a crooked smile and a question: "Are you going to tell her?"

I rub the back of my head. "Maybe. I want to see where this goes first. I still need to tell her some things."

Some flicker of happiness returns to Nadia. I can sense it. It's small, but it's strong. She thinks she still has a chance.

Too bad she doesn't.

I tell myself to shove it as Aidan asks, "What do you mean you still have to tell her things? What's there to tell?"

"How about my mom, for starters?"

That instantly shuts him up. He looks like he wants to shove his entire leg into his mouth. Nadia glares at her brother for his lack of tact. I stare over at the window. Outside, the wind is making the leaves dance.

"Rylan?" It's Nadia. "You okay?"

I don't look at her. "Yeah. I'm fine. I just...I know I have to tell her about the whole thing. But...it's hard, you know?"

I don't see it, but I know they're nodding.

"It's been ten friggin' years," I mutter. "Ten friggin' years, and I'm just like my father. I'm no closer to getting over it than he is."

"Rylan, you were only six and the only one to witness the entire incident. You could've come out a lot worse," Nadia says. "And I actually think you're recovering better than your dad."

"Thanks. But I just want to get over it. I'm sick of feeling like crap every time I think about it. I want to get better."

"Then maybe telling her—Ivy, I mean—maybe that can help you."

Finally looking away from the window, I give Nadia a solemn gaze. "I had to tell you guys about it. I had to tell numerous psychiatrists about it. I had to tell the press, the police, and the doctors in the ambulance about it. I had to tell Dad and Babette—" I momentarily falter, then take a deep breath, "—I had to tell them how an innocent little six year old watched his mother die right in front of him. It's all had the same results. Nothing. It does nothing to help me."

Nadia looks down at the ground, her cheeks red in embarrassment and shame, and I feel bad for making *her* feel bad. Aidan breaks the silence before it gets too awkward.

"Maybe this time it'll be different." Instantly his eyes go to the floor as I glance at him. But he doesn't stop talking. "Maybe since you love her, it'll be different from all the other times you told people."

"I never said I loved her," I mumble. "And I love Dad and Babette and you guys. I've told you all, but it didn't work. What would the difference be?"

"Maybe because you love us and your family in another way." Aidan meets my eyes, his voice so serious it's scaring me. "You lo-like Ivy in a different way. Maybe that's the key."

Both Nadia and I gape at him like he's an escaped animal from the zoo. It's rare enough that Aidan's truly serious at any given moment. But what he just said? That's the first time he's said something not only serious, but also sincere. I guess Aidan can't be a ridiculous goofball all the time.

"Okay. Who are you and what have you done with my brother?" Nadia asks in complete disbelief. "If you need a description, he looks just like you but can't take anything seriously to save his life."

"Hey." Aidan sticks out his tongue, and he's quickly back to his old self. "I can be plenty serious when I want. You obviously weren't going to give him the girly advice he needed, so I had to fill in."

"It's really good advice." I give him a tight smile. "But even if it doesn't work, I still have to tell her about it. This isn't something you can keep from someone important to you. I'm just nervous about how she'll react. What if she can't handle it?"

"Then she's not worth it," says Nadia.

Aidan nods, but he looks perplexed. "Yeah. But why couldn't she handle it? All you have to say is that when you were a kid, your mom died in the swamp, with you as the only eyewitness."

"Yeah." I nod, but in reality I barely hear any of his advice. My eyes go back to the window. The gears in my head are turning and I need to concentrate.

Aidan said I was the only person to see my mom's death. Yet Ivy said she's never left the swamp and is "always watching." So doesn't that mean Ivy was there? Was Ivy there watching us as we rode the boat through the swamp?

Did she watch my mother die?

I want to slap myself. I can't believe I didn't think of this sooner. I mean, if she was off in some other part of the swamp, she couldn't have known. But if she was there...she could've saved her. Ivy could have saved my mom like she saved me.

Anger sinks its claws into me. My hands ball into fists and I feel the need to scream. I'm getting mad over just a mere possibility, but I can't help it. I've always said there was a chance that Mom could've lived, even when everyone else said differently. And now I'm sure there might have been a chance. But it wasn't taken. It slipped through Ivy's fingers like grains of sand. And now my mom's gone.

"Rylan?"

I sense a hand on my shoulder. My head snaps around and I snort like a bull ready to charge.

Nadia yanks her hand back, scared to be burned by the raging flames around me. "Rylan? Are you okay? You look like you're mad at something."

I tell myself to calm down. I need to. I can't freak out in front of my friends. Closing my eyes, I take deep breaths. With each inhale, I suck the fury back inside me, locking it away somewhere. I can't get mad at my friends. They didn't do anything wrong. I open my eyes and see their concern. "I'm fine," I tell them with a small fake grin. "I just realized...I missed another day of school."

The twins look at me, then at each other, then back at me. I nearly jump in my seat when they bust out laughing.

"Man? That's all?" Aidan wipes imaginary tears from his eyes. "You really know how to make a guy laugh at the most random subjects, dude."

"Speaking of which, your stuff's right here." Nadia gets up, grabs the backpack that she'd dumped on the floor when she first came in, and brings it over to my bedside.

"Here." She pulls out some textbooks and worksheets. "This is all the stuff we got assigned. I made some photocopies of all the notes I took today, too."

"Thanks, Nadia. I really appreciate this. I'm guessing you did this all by yourself?"

"I would've given you my own notes," Aidan tells me, throwing his hands up in a "don't shoot me" pose. "But knowing you, you might actually want the ability to read said notes."

"Which he cannot give," Nadia adds.

"Thanks for bringing all this," I thank them, feeling the smooth textbook in my hand. "I'm feeling better already."

"You are one twisted person if something as nasty as homework can make you feel better," Aidan declares.

"Yep, that's me," I shoot right back, forcing a smile. "I'm one twisted individual."

Hours later, I'm almost done with my English homework when Dad comes in, his tradition of not knocking still intact. I don't bother looking up and showing my annoyance since Dad's never going to learn.

"Rylan?" He stays away from me like if he gets too close, he'll catch what I have. "How are you?"

I keep staring at my pen gliding across the paper, its inky trail leaving an answer behind. "Better. Babette says I can go back to school tomorrow."

"Good…that's good."

Silence comes after this. I can hear him nervously shift around over the scratching of my pen. Writing the final words in, I cap it and finally look up at my dad. He's currently finding my carpet rather interesting to stare at.

"Is something wrong?" I ask.

Dad glances back up. Some of the anger I locked away earlier resurfaces as his eyes fall on my shoulder. He sighs. "Yes, I'm fine. Just had a tiring day at the office."

"How so?"

He waves his hand as if to bat the question away. "I don't need to bore you with it. So did Nadia and Aidan come over?"

"Yeah, they did. They brought me my homework and talked with me like normal human beings."

My sarcasm either falls flat or Dad ignores it, because he just answers with, "Good. Very good. We don't want you falling behind on your schoolwork."

He hasn't given a damn about how I do in school in forever, so why is he starting now? Is he finally trying to move on? I have to test this in the most accurate way possible.

Shifting around, I lower and bend my head until, instead of staring at my shoulder, Dad's staring into my eyes. Even though I'd braced myself for it, disappointment surfaces when Dad shudders and turns away to look at anything else besides his own son. He's not getting better. He's just trying to fill in the missing role of a father, and he's doing a horrible job at it.

He needs to leave. "Don't you have work to do?" I ask, my words biting as I peer out the window like I did hours ago.

Dad's gaze returns to my upper arm. "Sorry?"

"Don't you have work to do?" I repeat. Out of the corner of my eye, I see Dad frown at my tone.

"Yes, I do," he says. "Thanks for reminding me."

"Whatever," I grumble, pulling out another textbook and some of my other homework to do. I'm done talking. Dad manages to see that, and soon I hear my door close as I stare down at the swirling vortex that is suddenly the worksheet.

I want to throw the book against the wall. I want to stomp into his study and smash all of Mom's pictures.

I want to scream. I've had enough of these weak conversations, and I'm so close to boiling over.

But I don't. Breathing deeply, I again suppress all my anger. Not now. Don't waste this on mere thoughts. I'll keep the fury inside.

And tomorrow I'll see if it needs to be used.

Chapter 16

I don't go and see Ivy. I don't dream at all. The next morning I wake before my alarm rings, but I keep my eyes closed.

Today is going to suck.

You know when you wake up and you can sometimes sense how your day is going to pan out? Somehow, I know I'm going to end up wishing I'd never gotten out of bed.

However, I'm no longer sick, so I can't stay home. Groaning, I get up, wander around the house getting ready for school, and wait out on the porch for the twins. They come soon enough, riding their bikes up the driveway as they laugh and joke. That ceases as soon as they see me.

"Rylan?" Aidan gapes at me as I descend the front porch steps. "Is that you? What happened, man?"

"Nothing." I unlock my bike lock. "I'm okay."

"You don't look okay," says Nadia, full of concern.

"I'm getting over the flu. Did you expect me to look like Prince Charming the next morning?" I nearly snap.

Nadia takes a step back, surprised by my sudden meanness. "No, I didn't. I just—" She doesn't finish and drifts off. I sigh heavily.

"I'm sorry," I mumble. "I'm just extremely grumpy right now, and I also have this bad feeling today's going to suck. You know what I mean?"

Aidan nods as I straddle my bike. "Yeah. I have those morning feelings, too. They strangely end up being ninety-nine percent right."

Nadia rolls her eyes. "Is that supposed to make him feel better? I don't think it's working." We start pedaling down the driveway.

"Good attempt, though," I murmur. I'm barely riding straight, my legs are so lethargic.

"Thank you, dude. At least someone appreciates my efforts."

"What are you talking about? There was no help in that at all!"

Tuning out the twins, I focus on riding my bike without crashing. The sooner I get to school, the sooner it will end and I can go home.

Nothing bad happens at first. Aidan and Nadia bicker as always and I go to all my classes. I have to check every hallway before going down it for signs of Dunstan or Melanie, but other than getting scolded for sleeping in class, everything's okay.

Until lunch. Or more precisely, when I'm at my locker before lunch.

"Hi, Rylan!"

I flinch when I hear Melanie behind me. I've never noticed how squeaky her voice can get.

"Um, hey Melanie," I mumble a greeting over my shoulder, continuing to put my books away.

"So, like, how are you? You weren't at school yesterday. I asked those Marce twins you always hang out with. Adrian said you had the flu."

Again she gets my friend's name wrong. I look around for more books, but I'm out. Bracing myself, I turn around. Melanie's right there, and to any other guy here she'd look sexy in the tight T-shirt and miniskirt she's wearing.

"It's Aidan," I tell her, trying not to sound annoyed. As much as I want to avoid her, I still don't want to look like a jerk. "His name is Aidan. And look, there's Aidan and his sister right now."

I'm not lying. I point down the crowded hall to where they're coming from. Both wear their usual "we see Melanie" expressions—Aidan happy, Nadia pissed.

"You're going to eat lunch with them, right?" Melanie asks. "You can always eat with me at my table."

"As nice as that sounds, I can't. I like sitting with Aidan and Nadia. But thanks for the offer." I shut my locker door and prepare to leave.

But something suddenly grabs the hood of my sweatshirt and yanks hard. Completely caught off guard, I go veering back and land on my butt. The hallway goes eerily silent as I glare up at Melanie for being so pushy.

It's not Melanie. It's a scowling, furious Dunstan.

"Dunstan." I'm trying to keep calm, and in turn calm the raging bull above me. "Listen, Dunstan, I didn't tell her yes. I wasn't going to—"

I never finish. Dunstan drags me up by the sleeve of my shirt and flings me against the row of lockers. The students gasp, someone calls out, "Fight!" and over the sudden rumble I hear Nadia scream, "Rylan!"

"I'm not going to fight you, Dunstan." I'm shaking on the inside, but I manage to look him right in the eye like I'm not scared of him. He's never gone after me like this before, having made an effort to ignore me after our friendship fell apart. Now I know how his regular victims feel.

"Don't try to talk your way out of this," Dunstan snarls in my face. Outwardly, I try not to gag on his breath; he honestly needs a mint. "I saw everything. You were flirting with Melanie!"

I hold my hands up. "No, I wasn't. *She* was the one talking to *me*."

He's not even listening as he slams me against the lockers again. "What'd she ask you, anyway? To sit with her? To buy her lunch? To be her boyfriend?"

"She asked me to sit with her, but that's it! I swear!"

"And you said yes," Dunstan accuses, pulling a fist back.

"No! I said no!" I look into the crowd for Aidan and Nadia, but I can't see them. "Ask Aidan and Nadia! They'll tell you."

"You're not getting out of this, Forester," Dunstan leers. "Don't try using your friends for a distraction." Again he cocks a fist.

I frantically try to find another person to help. "Melanie!" I lock eyes with her. "Melanie will tell you everything! Melanie!"

I secretly thank God when she steps forward. "Dunstan, leave him alone. Can't you just accept I've dumped you and move on?"

"You didn't dump me!" Dunstan roars. "We're taking a break is all. And yet you're here playing with him—of all people!"

In one swift movement, Dunstan lands a clean punch to the side of my face. I fall and land on the linoleum floor, holding my left cheek in pain. But I have no time to recover or stand up as he kicks me in the ribs. I curl into the fetal position, placing my hands over my face for protection as

punches and kicks rain down on me. All around, I hear students cheering.

"Get up!" Dunstan kicks my unprotected back so hard, it's possible I have a broken spine. "Get up and fight!"

"No!" I shout. I'm not a pacifist, but I know better than to pick a fight with an opponent I know I'm going to lose to.

"What? You're a wimp, Forester! Get up and fight!" Another kick lands on my backside and I bite my lip to keep from whimpering.

"You're saying this to the guy who survived a vicious alligator attack with all his limbs intact." I open one eye and glare up at Dunstan. "An alligator attack *you* caused when you pushed me in!"

"Shut up!" Dunstan yells, and he lifts his foot again. I clamp my eyes shut.

But then it all comes to a screeching halt as a harsh voice rings through the hallway.

"Stop this immediately!"

The cheering crowd falls silent. There's shuffling and stomping feet. A hand brushes my back, and I flinch.

"Rylan?"

I relax. Opening my eyes, I see Nadia squatting next to me. Aidan's standing right next to her, and some feet away I can see the school principal, Mr. White. He looks completely pissed and has a heavy hand on Dunstan's shoulder.

"So that's where you guys went," I croak out. "I thought for a minute there you abandoned me."

"We'd never do that." Aidan looks horrified at the thought. "We just went to find some teacher before the fight got worse and you were smashed to a pulp."

"Although I did tell him to stay behind and try to help you," Nadia grumbles, giving Aidan a withering glare.

Before anything else happens, Mr. White interrupts in his booming voice. "All right, people. Show's over! Get to your next class."

The crowd disintegrates as they all fly off to their next period. Soon the only people left in the hall with me are Aidan, Nadia, Dunstan, and Mr. White.

"Mr. Forester?" Mr. White comes over and stands above me. "Are you okay?"

I squirm where I lie, feeling around to see if anything's broken. "I think so. Nothing's cracked, at least."

"Can you stand?"

I nod. Nadia grasps my forearm and with her help, I pull myself up. Once everyone sees I'm fine, Mr. White turns his attention to Dunstan. He instantly goes from concerned to mad.

"What were you thinking!?" he roars with enough power to shake the entire hall. "Attacking a student like that? You know fighting in my school gets you an automatic suspension, and yet you do it anyway!"

Dunstan reddens, turning into a mini version of his angry dad. "Suspension!? You can't do that! My dad—"

"I don't care that your father's the mayor," declares Mr. White, crossing his arms. "Fighting's fighting, and there's no exception."

"But what about Forester?" Dunstan points at me. "What about his suspension? He was fighting, too!"

"Not according to Mr. and Ms. Marce, he wasn't. They said you deliberately attacked Mr. Forester and he didn't fight back. And don't think of insisting he did, Mr. Lebelle, because how else would he be on the ground?"

"He could be making himself look innocent?" Dunstan tries. No one's buying it.

"My office. Now!" Mr. White shouts. He grabs Dunstan's shoulder again and leads him away, but not before Dunstan shoots me one last "you're so dead" glare.

"You okay, dude?" Aidan asks.

Considering I just got beaten up and my stomach kicked in, no. I'm not. But instead of admitting that, I put on a giant fake grin. "I'm fine, guys. I mean, I've had worse injuries, right?"

Both their answers are instantaneous. "Yep."

"Pretty much."

We share a little laugh over their quick replies as we head off to lunch. But it's all a mask for me. I'm really not okay: I'm hurt, I'm tired, and I'm close to lashing out at anyone who just looks at me funny. I almost did with my friends.

Oh, please let this rotten day end soon.

The rest of school drags on at its stupid snail pace. Everyone has heard about the fight, so all the students refuse to look me in the eye and all the teachers keep asking if I'm okay. I don't spot Dunstan in the halls, so I guess he did get suspended. Now I'm double dead if he ever catches me outside of school. Could this get any worse?

Stupid question. Of course it could. I tell the twins goodbye and bike home, only to find a half-concerned, half-angry Babette waiting for me in the foyer.

"Rylan Jacob Forester! How could you get into a fight at school!?" Babette rants. "Didn't I bring you up better than this!? How could you?"

"I didn't," I protest, trying extremely hard not to set free the frustration that's been inside me all day. "Didn't Mr. White tell you I didn't fight back?"

This makes Babette momentarily pause. "How did you know it was Mr. White who told me?"

I shrug. "He's the guy who broke the fight up and he's the school principal. I figure he has to report stuff like this. But he seemed to forget one important detail; I didn't fight back."

"He never said that. All your principal told me was that you had gotten into a fight with Dunstan Lebelle and you weren't hurt."

"Which I'm not. I got a bruised stomach, but otherwise I'm fine. Although I think any injury I get from now on is going to look pathetic compared to having a leg nearly bitten off."

Despite herself, Babette chuckles at my lame joke. "I guess it would." Quickly she becomes serious again. "So you didn't fight."

"No." I slip my shoes off. "A couple days ago, Dunstan got dumped by his girlfriend, Melanie, for exact reasons unknown. Today, Melanie was, um, flirting with me, Dunstan saw it, and he beat me up. I curled up on the floor to protect myself."

It's amazing how fast my grandma's emotions can change as she becomes livid all over again. "All because of that? That's it. I'm calling Mr. Lebelle and giving him a piece of my mind!"

"No!" I blurt out. "Babette, for all that is good and decent, please don't call Mr. Lebelle! It's only gonna give Dunstan yet another reason to hit me!"

"Which he shouldn't be doing in the first place. Didn't we have a deal that I could take drastic measures if you ever came home like this?"

"That was if I ever came home a bloody mess!"

"Frankly, Rylan, you *are* a mess. Now go and relax in your room while I make a few calls."

"But—"

"NOW, Rylan." Babette leaves before I can say another word.

I take my anger out on the stairs as I stomp up them. Getting sent to my room like this again; what happened? Did I regress to a six year old? As I storm down the hallway, I half-expect Dad to pop out of nowhere and order me to quiet down so he can finish whatever work he brought home from his job.

Dad.

I freeze mid-step. Where's Dad? If Mr. White called Babette, then surely he would've called Dad. Or Babette would have called him, telling him that his only son got into a fight and might be terribly hurt. Any other father would've rushed home right away and checked to see that everything's fine. But my father didn't. He couldn't. My nails digging into my hands, I swallow the urge to punch a hole in the wall.

I skip out on dinner, shouting down to Babette I'm not hungry. She most likely thinks it's because of the fight. But the truth is, I don't want to sit at the same table as the woman who sealed my fate as a permanent human punching bag and the distant man who doesn't care about the bruises now residing on my chest and cheek. They're traitors, both of them.

Minutes slowly tick by as I wait for them to fall asleep so I can slip out the door. To pass the time, I sit and stew there in all the crap that's happened today, getting madder and madder. It's unhealthy, sure, but I'm only a few hours away from the possible answer to the question that's been haunting me all these years.

Finally, when they're asleep, I slip out of the house and let the swamp swallow me up.

It's like the crickets can feel the tension in the air as I sit on the dock, overlooking the water. I just got here a few minutes ago, but they already seem to know something bad might happen tonight. I can hear it in their singing. It's not the usual happy chirping, but more like scared, random squeaks, terrified if they make too much noise it'll be the end of them.

The dock moans behind me. "Rylan?"

It begins.

I don't look back. "Hey, Ivy."

"Hello, Rylan. I am ready to go. But…are you all right? You… did not come down yesterday."

"Homework," I lie. "Had so much of it I had to skip to do it all. I actually fell asleep at my desk."

"Oh. That is fine."

"Thanks for not sending a dream, by the way."

"I did not wish…to scare you again. I have better…control over it now."

"I see."

"Well, I am ready to…go if you are."

I'm not. I pat the spot next to me. "Sit here, Ivy."

She doesn't question me. Her feet stroll down the dock. There's a flash of green in the corner of my eye as she sits down at my side.

"Is everything good?"

I continue staring out at the swamp. "I don't know. It depends…"

"Pardon?"

I glance over at Ivy. For once, I'm too preoccupied to think her perplexed expression is cute. "I have something very important to ask you, but I think I need to tell you something first so you understand why I'm asking."

I pause to rub the back of my neck. "It isn't something I like to talk about, but it's something you need to know. So please don't stop me."

Ivy looks even more puzzled, but she nods her head. *"Very well. I am, as you say, all ears."*

I simply begin.

"What have I told you about my family?"

Ivy rubs her forehead as she thinks. *"Enough to have a general idea. Your grandmother's name is Babette…and she is also a good friend. Your father cannot look you…in the eye, and is cold to you."*

"Have I ever mentioned why he's like that?"

"No."

I sigh. What I'm going to say next is like painfully peeling off a Band-Aid, but it has to be done.

"He's like that…because I look too much like his wife. My mom. She died when I was six."

I order myself to stare down at the murky swamp water, because I know if I see the sorrowful face I know Ivy has on I won't be able to continue.

"Her name was Dahlia Daniau, but everyone called her DD, which she hated. She had black hair and blue eyes, and was born and raised in a city called Tallahassee by her mom, my grandma Babette. Her father died when she was very little. When she was old enough, she went to the college there. It was there she met my dad.

"Dad was born right here in Roland, in the same house where I live now. They were two different people; he was a small-town boy, she was a city girl. But that obviously didn't matter, because they fell in love and were married as soon as they were done with college.

"It was around the same time that my dad's dad died of a stroke. Everyone was really sad, especially my other grandma. Less then a year later, she died, too. Everyone said it was old age, but I've got a feeling it was because of a broken heart.

"Once her will was sorted out, the house became his. Mom and Dad moved in. Since there was plenty of room, Babette was invited to live with them. A few weeks later, Dahlia figured out there was to be a new family member— me.

"Nine months later, I was born in the hospital over in Harraway. Everyone was so happy, especially my parents, because I was their first-born kid. They took me home and for the first years, I was happy and had a normal life. But then…then I learned the hard way that nothing lasts forever."

My hands are badly shaking as I try not to let my sadness overtake me. Ivy's green hand moves to rest on mine. It helps, but it does nothing to stop the memory flashes.

Splash, roar, scream, tears—

"It was in the summer." I find the strength to talk again. "I was six years old. Dad was at work, and Babette was doing errands. It was just my mom and me, and I was bored. So Mom suggested we take the boat out and explore the swamp. I remember gaping at all the plants and animals we saw. We'd turned the engine off and were drifting along. I was looking over the edge and saw a turtle swimming by. Being the stupid curious six year old that I was, I leaned over the side to get a closer look. Unfortunately, I bent over too far…I fell in, basically."

Splash, roar, scream, tears—

"I didn't know how to swim yet, so I was floundering in the water. Screaming my name, Mom dived in and pulled me out. Somehow, she put me back in the boat. Took a bit of a struggle…then she was holding onto the side, catching her breath. She asked me…she asked me if I was okay."

Splash, roar, scream, tears—

"Before we knew it was happening…something pulled her under. I stared at the swamp's surface…I was so confused. I didn't have a clue what was going on, or if this was another game or something. I kept saying 'Mommy?' and paddling at the water, trying to see her.

"I did see her a few minutes later. Mom came floating up, face down, and I was so relieved. But she wouldn't reply when I said her name. She wasn't moving. And when I touched her to try and help her out, she was so cold. But everything clicked when I grabbed her hair and pulled her face up. Open mouth, pale cheeks, empty eyes…and a watery pool of blood from around the slashes on her lower torso. She'd been dragged under by an alligator and drowned. She…she was dead."

The splash of a body—

The terrifying roar of a monster—

Me screaming over and over, "Mommy! MOMMY!"

A waterfall of hot tears falling down my face—

My hands fly to the side of my head and I clench everything shut. The flashes are so strong, they're nearly overtaking me.

"Rylan?" I can barely hear Ivy's concerned voice over the memories.

Lying there, so cold in that boat, holding her floating body—

The tears had no end in sight, the harsh sobs—

Holding on to a corpse's hand—

"HELP! PLEASE, HELP!"—

So alone; no one was there—

"Go away. Just please go away," I whimper, rocking back and forth. I can't stop them this time. They're too strong. I'm drowning in them….

"Rylan! RYLAN!"—

"Oh my God!"—

"Somebody call an ambulance!"—

"It's too late…she's gone…"—

A bright, white, healing light—

Wait…what?

My eyes peel open only to see a green healing hand on my forehead. I glance at Ivy out of the corner of my eye. Her own eyes are glowing as she concentrates on whatever magic she's doing on me. I feel all the horrid memories slip away, back into the corner of my mind where I keep them locked up. I'm no longer drowning. I can breathe again. Slowly, my hands fall back to the wooden dock boards as my muscles ease, my jaw relaxes, and my hurried mind slows.

"Is everything better?" Ivy removes her hand. I practically cry out for her to put it back. It's the only thing keeping all the scary thoughts away. *"Those thoughts should not bother you now."*

She's right. Nothing's resurfacing. They're gone for now.

"Yeah…yeah, I feel better." I give her a small but utterly grateful smile. "Thanks."

"What happened, Rylan? What was plaguing you?"

Said smile quickly disappears. I look back down at the swamp water. "It's what I call memory flashes. They're flashbacks to the day Mom died. I have them whenever I think or talk about what happened to her."

"I am sorry."

I shrug. "It's just one of the things from the aftermath I have to deal with."

"The aftermath?"

I nod and continue where I left off.

"For a long time, I sat there, holding onto my dead mom, crying over and over and scaring off any animal that came too close and wishing someone would come and help. But we were too deep in the swamp for anyone to hear me, and I couldn't drive the boat because I didn't know how to." I shiver. "Those were probably the worst hours in my entire life.

"It was late afternoon when Babette and Dad found me. When Babette had gotten home from errands and saw we weren't there, she assumed we were out having fun and didn't think of it. But by the time Dad came home from work, hours had passed and Babette was getting worried. So they went out to investigate. When they came down here and saw the boat was missing, they started looking for us.

"They first saw me…and then they saw Mom. Babette started screaming and Dad actually jumped right into the swamp, grabbed the boat, and pulled it back to the shore, yelling like a madman about calling 911. But it was too late. Babette said…she said Mom was gone. And the three of us just stood there crying."

I rub my hands together, taking a deep sigh.

"Everything that happened afterwards is kinda foggy. There were police cruisers, an ambulance, and lots of sobbing. The police asked me a lot of questions I don't remember, but I guess they were about what happened. Hell, I don't even remember if I even answered them, I was so freaked out. The one thing that's stayed with me all this time, though, is the cause-of-death report the medics gave us. The alligator had snapped her spine, and she had indeed drowned."

My head turns and I gaze up at the night sky like I've done with Ivy plenty of times. I smile sadly.

"There are times when I wonder what it would be like if it'd never happened. If Mom was still alive. Would my family be any happier? Would my dad actually be a normal functioning human being, instead of the mess he is now? So many things would be different if someone had saved her. Like how, years later, when I was in the same life-threatening situation, you came and rescued me."

Breaking away from the stars, I look at Ivy. She's peering over at the other side of the swamp, so I can't see her face all too well. But I can see her hands fine. They're trembling. My heart starts to drop.

"You said you are always watching, Ivy. Because of that, you saved my life. But I have to ask. Ivy, all those years ago…did…did you see my mom die?"

Ivy freezes. Everything freezes. Time has hit the pause button. It's teasing me. My guarded fury, the feelings I've been carrying around all day, prepare to ignite with her reply. Everything's ready to implode. Everything's ready to change.

The play button is hit and Ivy's head falls forward, her hair cutting her off from the world as she responds.

"Yes."

The news sinks right in. I lose the ability to breathe as everything starts coming out in short puffs. Rage zooms through my body, making every single cell alive and furious. I want to scream, shout, grab her by the shoulders and shake her. But all I can manage is a disbelieving, nearly silent, "Why?"

"I was scared," Ivy admits. *"I was watching you and your mother with interest…it had been a long time since I had seen someone so young. But then you fell in, and your mother jumped in after you… and I saw the alligator swimming towards her. I kept hoping she would climb out, but…I saw her get dragged under, and I knew it was too late. All I could do was watch you…and the rescue and how everyone cried."*

She lifts her head and moves her hair curtain out of the way. I see the tears coming down her cheeks. *"I am so sorry, Rylan. I could have saved her…but I did not. I…I'm sorry."*

I can't take this anymore. Jumping up from my seat, I go over to one of the dock posts and rest my hands on it, trying to calm myself down. It's not working.

"Rylan?" Boards creaks as Ivy stands up as well. *"Did you—"*

"Yeah, I heard you," I mutter between my teeth. My fingernails bite into the wood as I squeeze it. "But why? Why couldn't you save her?"

"You would have seen me," Ivy whimpers. *"You would have seen me, and you would have told people and they would have come looking for me, and the gator was not supposed to do—"*

"But it did. And I was six. No one ever believes what a six year old says. They wouldn't have listened."

"But your mother—"

"No one would have believed her either. And what do you mean someone would have seen you?" I swerve around, glaring back at Ivy as my hands ball into fists. My voice grows louder. "You could've told the gator to stop. You could've even fought it off and dragged her onto shore like you did with me. None of that could've involved you being seen. Any of that would've saved her!"

"I know, and I am sorry. But I was—"

"YEAH, YOU WERE TOO SCARED. SO WHAT!? YOU WERE STILL THERE. YOU STILL SAW EVERYTHING. YOU STILL COULD'VE SAVED HER! THERE ARE PEOPLE ALL AROUND THE WORLD WHOSE JOB IS TO SAVE PEOPLE'S LIVES ON A DAILY BASIS. THEY'RE SCARED, TOO, BUT YOU KNOW WHAT? THEY DO IT ANYWAY!"

All my rage, all my frustration, not only from everything that happened today but also from the last ten years, comes

pouring out all at once. Ivy's cowering before me, and I take a twisted delight in it.

"DO YOU KNOW THE HELL I WENT THROUGH THE FIRST FEW YEARS AFTERWARDS? VISIT AFTER VISIT TO STUPID SHRINKS, HEARING PEOPLE TALK ABOUT ME BEHIND THEIR BACKS—I THOUGHT MY FATHER BLAMED THE WHOLE THING ON ME! THAT WAS HOW HE ACTED! EVEN TODAY I HAVE TO DEAL WITH THE CONSEQUENCES OF WHAT HAPPENED WITH THESE STUPID MEMORY FLASHES AND DAD ACTING LIKE AN EMOTIONLESS ROBOT!"

We're both shaking—me with wrath, her with sobbing guilt. The waterfall of tears coming down her face is heavier than the time she cried over the movie. She looks so beautifully disastrous, I should be feeling guilty. But there's no room for pity when you're so damn upset.

"I'm sorry," Ivy whispers. Her whole body shakes with her weeping. *"I'm so incredibly sorry. What I did…it has been haunting me for years. I wish I could fix it—"*

"Well, you can't." I'm no longer yelling, but the anger in my voice is still enough to make her cringe. "There's no way we can, so there's no reason to keep on wishing for it!"

"But…I did. I kept wishing that I could have a chance to redeem myself. And it came." Ivy dares to look me in the eye, tears cascading down to her chin. *"It was you. Your rescue. Seeing you go down…I knew what I had to do this time."*

"'This time?' Why couldn't you figure it out the first time!? If you had, Mom would be here and my life wouldn't be the crappy, screwed-up mess it is now!"

"I know—"

"No, you don't! You know nothing! You don't know anything!"

221

"I'm so-sorry." It's hard to make her words out now. *"Please...for-forgive me. I-I—"*

It's too much. She falls down on her knees, hands over her eyes, trying to stem the tears crashing down her face. I've never seen someone so miserable since Dad and Babette at Mom's funeral. It's enough to make me feel sorry for her. But as I turn and stomp away, I feel none of that.

I leave her in a crumpled, crying heap.

Chapter 17

It's been three days since I last saw Ivy.

Three friggin' days, and one of them was the one-month anniversary of our meeting.

I'd noticed it long before the fight. If Ivy hadn't noticed herself, I was all ready to tell her and plan some celebration. I could have smuggled food out of the house, and we could have feasted and danced the night away to the music pouring from my portable iPod speakers.

But no. That didn't happen. And even though I don't want to, even though I should stay angry with her for the rest of my life, I'm starting to miss her.

"Rylan?"

"Huh?" I look up and see Mrs. Karcy standing in front of my desk. I'm in first hour, English, and already I'm spacing out.

"Sorry. Um, could you repeat that?" The class giggles, but Mrs. Karcy smiles kindly.

"I asked you if you could tell us what this scene means in your own words." She points down to my open copy of *Romeo and Juliet* on my desk.

"Uh, sure." I quickly scan the page. "Well, it looks like the Nurse just told Juliet the guy that killed her cousin was

Romeo. And instead of getting all mad and stuff, Juliet forgives him because he had to do it in order to survive."

Wait. I pause and reread the section. Of all the things to be studying right now…I wish I could find a way to get out of class, but I've missed too much time in the last few weeks, so I take a deep breath and prepare for the worst.

Mrs. Karcy nods. "Now tell me, class, what do you think of Juliet's decision to forgive so easily? Was she wrong to do so?"

"Of course she was," Vivian Reese calls out from the very back.

"You wish to start, Vivian?" Mrs. Karcy asks.

"Yeah. I think it was stupid for Juliet to forgive Romeo for killing Tybalt. He was family, even if he was a jerk. I know if someone I loved killed a family member of mine, I'd never forgive them. I just don't know why you continue to love someone who's caused you so much pain."

Neither do I.

"Because it's drama." It's Nadia from her seat up front. She glances back, speaking to Vivian but looking at me, worried. "Juliet loves Romeo regardless of her cousin's death, and that's a dramatic element."

"Yes," Junior Small joins in. "Not to mention this is a fictional play in which highly improbable events occur. If, for instance, this were to happen in the real world today, most likely Juliet would be angry and divorce Romeo right away."

Or yell at him and run away, leaving him bawling his eyes out.

"While you've made a point, Junior and Nadia, I wish to know your opinion on the idea." Mrs. Karcy moves to the front of the room, her eyes scanning over us all. "Tell me, class—is it right to love a killer?"

Students burst into conversation, but my mouth's a tight line.

"You okay, Rylan?"

I look up from the computer screen. Me, Nadia, Aidan, and a few other students from biology class are sitting in the library. We've turned in our swamp presentations, but Ms. Stern already has us working on a small paper about evolution. The work just doesn't let up, which helps keep me distracted.

"Huh?"

Nadia, who is using the computer right next to mine, turns in her seat to face me, her arms crossed. "I asked if you were okay."

My fingers dance on the keys as information writes itself on the screen. "Yeah, I'm fine. Why'd you ask?"

"Dude. You're not fine." Aidan looks over from the squashy chair he's currently procrastinating in. "You've been acting funny all day."

I sigh. They caught me, not that I've been trying to hide. "I know. I'm sorry. We were talking about the theme of betrayal in English, and it just…"

"It reminded you of your mom?"

It's weird how Nadia can be so perceptive. I nod, because she's somewhat right. "It makes me think of the situation Dad was in. Here's his wife, dead, and his son just sat there and let her die. It made me start wondering if he hates me or not."

Aidan frowns. "He doesn't, dude. It wasn't your fault. You didn't kill her. You know what the doctors said."

"Yeah. I know. The bastard gator snapped her spine. If it didn't outright kill her, it paralyzed her, which led to her

drowning faster." I rub the bridge of my nose. I'm taking a risk asking this, but I can't keep wondering. "But…what if someone else besides me was watching, and they didn't do a thing to stop it? What would you do?"

Nadia's eyebrows knit together. "Why are you asking something like that?" Realization dawns. "*Did* someone watch the whole thing?"

"No." I shake my head furiously. "It's just a theoretical question that's been stuck in my head for a while."

Nadia still doesn't look convinced, but thankfully Aidan saves the day as he rises out of his chair and stretches. "I'd probably be angry at that person for a little while, but after I'd cool off we'd be friends again."

I turn to face him, surprised with his answer. "You mean you'd forgive this person?"

Aidan shrugs. "It would take a long time most likely. I'd have to think over whatever they told me. Try to see their side of the story, and if I didn't like what I saw, then I'd leave them. But more than likely I would see where they came from. Yeah, this fake guy didn't do anything, but he's still not the murderer." He rubs the back of his head as he stares down at his sneakers. "You're the one who's always wishing your dad would get over it. But how could you get over it if you had all that anger for someone who's only barely involved in it?"

Nadia snorts, turning back to her computer screen. "Since when have you been an expert on maturity?"

"Hey! I have my moments. Like right now," says Aidan like it's something to be proud of.

"One-time exception. And shouldn't you be working on your paper?"

"I should, but I'm not." Aidan smirks as he sits back down. "But don't worry about it. I'll finish it before it's due."

"You mean like five minutes before class starts?"

"No!"

"Rylan!"

Out of nowhere, Melanie comes strolling up in her usual shorts and tank top.

"Hi Melanie," I answer, wishing I could turn invisible and sneak away.

"Hi, Melanie!" Of course, Aidan greets her delightedly. Nadia shushes him, barely hiding her utter contempt.

Melanie ignores both of them as she asks a little too cheerfully, "How are you, Rylan? Are you feeling better since Dunstan beat you up? Let me guess. You've been avoiding him ever since he came back from suspension?"

Dunstan got three days of suspension for bruising me up. They ended yesterday, so I'd been spending a lot of time dodging him and his death glares in the hallway.

"Sort of—"

"That's reasonable. Anyway, I'm here to tell you I'm having a party this Sunday at my house, and I'm inviting you."

"Sunday? Why Sunday?"

"Because, silly, we have a teacher in-service day on Monday," Melanie reminds me. "That means no school, so we can party all we want with no guilt!" she adds, as if I don't know what that means.

One of her nail-polished claws comes and grabs my sleeve. I visibly wince, but Melanie takes no notice as she goes on and on about the dancing, the music, and—in a whisper—the free beer.

"So it's going to be really awesome," Melanie concludes. She tops it off with one of her supposedly cute puppy-dog pouts, which in reality makes her look like a monkey with a fat lip. "You have to come."

A month ago, I would've jumped at a chance like this. Melanie's parties are legendary among the students of

Roland Roux High. It's said they can last for three nights straight, the beer tap never runs out, and there's always a handful of girls ready to make out with. Basically it's a paradise to all guys.

Funny how quickly a person can change in a month.

"As fun as that sounds, no thanks." I pull my arm out of her iron grip.

"Aw! Why not?" Again with the monkey face.

"Because drinking myself to death doesn't sound too inviting," I deadpan. "And isn't Dunstan going to be there? He won't think twice about pounding me into mush."

"Oh yes, he would." For once Melanie looks stern. "He'll be there—it's not a party without Dunstan, after all—but I'll tell him if he even thinks about throwing a punch, he'll be kicked out faster than he can blink."

"Why are you inviting him? He's your *ex*-boyfriend, for God's sake."

"To show no hard feelings. And half the people I've invited won't show if Dunstan isn't there."

I glance back at my friends, who stand there frozen like statues. Even their faces remain unchanged. Looking back at Melanie, I gesture to them. "What about Aidan and Nadia? I never go anywhere without them."

Melanie finally notices they're standing behind me. "Oh, hi. I didn't see you there."

"Sure you didn't," Nadia mutters under her breath. Aidan jabs her with his elbow, but predictably Melanie doesn't notice.

"I guess your friends can come. More the merrier, as they say." She clasps her hands together hopefully. "But asking if they can come…that's a yes? You'll come, right?"

I temporarily freeze. I don't want Melanie to hang all over me the entire time and risk getting hit by Dunstan. On the other hand, she said Aidan and Nadia could come, and

Aidan's going to be incredibly pissed if he can't go because I refused. Maybe this can even be a good chance to tell Melanie that I don't like her, once and for all, so she can stop attaching herself to me like Velcro.

"So? Will you be there?" Melanie shakes my arm.

"Yes," I mumble.

"What did you say? I didn't hear you."

"I said yes." With my other hand, I firmly remove Melanie's hand off my upper arm. "We'll come, but we don't want any trouble. If anyone gives any one of us a hard time, we're gone."

Melanie nods vigorously. "Good. I'm glad you're coming." Suddenly, Melanie's hand is on my cheek. Someone hisses behind me, and it's an easy guess who did it.

"I have to go, Rylan, but I'll see you there." With a final caress, she removes her hand and sashays out of the library, only stopping once to wave goodbye. All the other guys in here with us watch her leave, then give me thumbs up and the biggest "you're the man" grins before returning to work. Right now I'm their hero.

I don't feel like a hero.

"Dude!" Aidan suddenly wraps me in a giant guy hug, cutting off my supply of oxygen. "Thank you, thank you, thank you!"

"Knock it off, Aidan." Nadia tugs the back of her brother's hoodie. "You're not going to be able to go if he's dead."

Aidan lets go. "Sorry, dude. Didn't mean to kill you."

I gulp in big breaths of air and shake it off. "No problem."

"I just can't believe it! We're all going to Melanie's party! A Melanie party! You're my friggin' hero, man!"

"I'm not a hero."

Aidan snickers. "Try telling that to all the guys in here. Right now they're probably wishing they were you just so they could go to a party hosted by the girl who loves you."

"Melanie doesn't love him!" Nadia snaps. Her balled-up hands are shaking, she's so mad.

Aidan the fool doesn't see this and continues pressing buttons. "Not from what I see, sis. Quit denying it. Melanie so wants Rylan to be her boyfriend."

"Rylan? Why'd you say yes?" Ever the smart one, Nadia changes the subject before acting on her anger and punching her brother's lights out.

"Because I knew Aidan wouldn't let me live it down if I'd said no. Besides, I shouldn't pass up a chance to tell Melanie off. I don't like her."

"Oh." Nadia visibly calms down, unclenching her fists. "I guess…that's a good reason." She stares down at her feet with redness clinging to her face, most likely embarrassed because of her accusing outburst. I see this, but unfortunately so does Aidan.

"Wait a second." A teasing smirk slowly emerges from his lips. "You like Rylan!"

"What!? No, I don't!" Nadia hisses. Nothing's stopping the completely noticeable stop-sign-red blush creeping across her face, though. I feel my own cheeks heating up.

"Aha! You're blushing!" Aidan declares with a pointed finger. "Don't bother lying! You like him! You like Rylan!"

"No, I don't! Shut up!"

"Yeah, you do!"

"Stop it!"

"Enough!" All three of us freeze as Ms. Hilton, our lemon-faced librarian, comes striding up, her arms crossed and her usual scowl on her face.

"If the three of you don't start speaking quietly, I will be forced to ask you to leave," she whispers in irritation. "Now shush!"

"Rylan?"

I'm lying on my bed, staring up at the ceiling. I've been doing this since school ended an hour and a half ago. But apparently gazing at a bumpy, cracked, off-white surface for a long period of time can do nothing to calm all the ideas that've been running rampant inside my head for the last three days.

"Rylan?"

"Huh?" I look up and see Babette standing in my doorway. "Oh. Hey."

"Hey." Her arms are crossed and her face shows nothing but concern. "You came home and went right to your room. You didn't eat your afternoon snack and you didn't tell me how your day was." She raises an eyebrow. "Are you okay?"

Damn. She caught me.

"No," I grunt as I sit up. "I'm not okay."

Babette doesn't move from her spot. "Want to tell me what's wrong?"

"It's not more or less what's wrong," I confess. "It's more like I'm having trouble finding answers. You know how my English class is reading *Romeo and Juliet*, right?"

Babette nods, and I tell her about today's discussion.

I bring up my hands to rub my face as I finish. "I just want to know if it's possible to forgive someone who kills your own family like that. What you do in that position."

Babette doesn't answer right away. But when she does, she's right on target.

"Is this about Dahlia?"

"Yeah."

"If you're saying what I think you are, it wasn't your fault," Babette states. "Your father may not have ever told you, but he never blamed you for her death."

"I know. And I'm not blaming myself. I just...what would you do if someone else besides me had witnessed Mom's death and they didn't do anything about it?"

Babette curiously regards me. "Is this a hypothetical question?"

I nod.

Babette smiles, the corners of her mouth turning up inch by inch. "Simple, hon. I'd forgive them."

She says it so simply, it's astonishing.

"Now don't give me that look," Babette tells my surprised frown. "Is saying I would forgive them that hard to believe?"

"Sort of," I admit. "Wouldn't you be...you know, angry at him?"

Babette closes her eyes and thinks it over. "I might be," she concedes. "I'd be so upset with the death that I'd pin blame on someone, and this person who was watching and did nothing seems like the perfect scapegoat. But," she opens her eyes, "once I calmed down and reviewed the situation, I would know whose fault it really was that Dahlia died. It wouldn't be the innocent bystander. It would be, and still is, the alligator's fault. It was that beast that killed your mother, and it always will be."

This is not the answer I was expecting. To think my grandma and best friend are on the same page for once... not something I expected to happen. I fall back on my bed with a sigh as I rub my face, trying to rid myself of this confusing tiredness.

"Let me guess." I remove my hands to see Babette's small, knowing smile. "You personally would hate the guy who watched and did nothing until the day you died."

I don't speak. I just turn my head and look out the window. That's enough of an answer for her.

"I'm not going to tell you you're wrong," Babette murmurs. "For all I know, you may be right and I'm wrong. But one thing I'm sure about is that you can't hold onto blame or force it on someone forever. Doing that can ruin a person. Your grandfather, God bless him—when he died, I had a lot of hate inside. It was a heart attack no one saw coming, but I blamed myself for it. I blamed the hospital staff for not saving him. And I blamed him for leaving me behind and dying in the first place. All that anger stayed in me for a long time, even with Dahlia and eventually your father and baby you in my life."

She sighs. "I didn't realize that until your mother died. Seeing you crying, and the way your father started avoiding you, I realized what I had become. I saw myself in Olivier: cold, brittle, putting on a mask around the people I loved to hide the pain. I hated myself. So I just let all the blame go. It was easier than I thought. For the first time in forever, I felt free. For those who forgive know a happiness and freedom that stays with them like misery stays with those who resent. Because if you're the latter, you end up having to carry these burdens for your whole life and be miserable because of your own stubbornness."

Babette pats my hand. "I trust you to make the right choices, but sometimes even old ladies like me need help seeing what's in front of us. When you feel pain like this, don't become me, Rylan. It could ruin you for good." The door quietly shuts behind her as she leaves, leaving me overwhelmed with my newfound discoveries.

The sun is shining; it's early afternoon, I'm guessing. Above I hear swamp birds twittering. The water gargles like a plug's been pulled. Leaves and flowers wave around in the breeze. Somewhere nearby, thick mud makes a hacking, sucking sound. It's a beautiful day, and the dock is nowhere in sight.

How did I get here? The last thing I remember was falling asleep on my bed in exhaustion. Babette's speech, the incident in the library, the *Romeo and Juliet* discussion—it was all too much for my reeling mind.

A sudden roar that sounds like someone killing a motor surprises me. For some odd reason, I'm scared that someone will see me, and I duck behind a thick tree. Curious, I peek around the trunk.

From around the corner appears the *Dahlia*. What's it doing all the way out here? Did it somehow get loose from the dock? But if that's the case, the motor wouldn't have been on. I squint at the two figures sitting in the boat. It's a little boy and a woman, and neither of them are Babette. Boat stealers! Those thieves aren't getting away with it! I prepare to shout—

"Rylan, be careful!"

Rylan!?

My blood freezes in my veins as I watch six-year-old me clamber around. My mother moves next to him, her long hair swaying as she tries to keep the boat from rocking.

It's official. I'm dreaming. Is this Ivy's doing, making me relive the worst day of my life? How could she? I look around to try and find her, but she isn't there. She isn't anywhere.

"Rylan, look out!"

I look back just in time to see me fall overboard. Six-year-old me splashes around, not knowing how to swim yet. Sixteen-year-old me just stands there behind the tree with leaden feet.

With the commotion going on, only I hear the sound of something swimming through water. Out of the corner of my eye, I spot a dark shape moving towards the floundering me. It's the alligator.

It's beginning.

I open my mouth to scream, but nothing comes out. Instead, the sense of fear comes back to me. I can't be seen. So I stand there, watching helplessly as the beast approaches the dark-haired woman now floating by the side of the boat.

"Rylan, are you okay?"

Before little me can reply, Mom's pulled down with a sudden shriek and a big growl. And all the way over here, I hear it, even though it's underwater—the snap of the woman's spine.

Woman? That's my mom! Why am I referring to her like that?

"Mommy?"

The young boy stares at the water with big round eyes. He sticks his hand out and bats the surface, as if trying to unbury Mom. In mere seconds, I know what'll happen. I turn away.

"Mommy!"

There it is. The joyous cry. Mom's floated back up to the surface and for a minute, everything's okay.

"Mommy?"

I close my eyes. I can't see it again. I can't witness it again. Because any second now—

"MOMMY! NO!"

There it is. Against my will I open my eyes and peer over. The little boy is holding his dead mother's hand with one

of his one, and has her face turned up with his other. She's soaking wet with watery blood, and even from here I can visualize what her eyes must look like: empty, glazed over, and creepy.

Six-year-old me is flat-out bawling, whimpering away about how he wants her back and how she can't die. Tears slide down his little, scrunched-up face.

Something wet skims down my face. I raise a hand to wipe my eyes.

And I stop.

Because my hand is green, webbed, and clawed.

It's Ivy's hand.

I'm Ivy.

"NO!"

I spring awake, the shock sending me back into the real world. Taking giant gulps of air as if I'm a drowning man, I take in my surroundings. My room, black with night and moon shadows. Piles of laundry still needing to be put away. My bedside clock, the green numbers reading 3:05.

Groaning, my head flops down into my hands. Out of all the crazy dreams I've had, this one has to be the most extreme. I was in Ivy's place, seeing through her eyes and feeling what she was feeling. Like this incredible sadness. A sense of hopelessness. Self-loathing anger. Fear at being discovered.

And guilt. Lots and lots of guilt.

Is this everything she felt when she saw me cry over Mom? Is this everything she felt when I yelled that this was all her fault? Is this everything she's feeling right now?

The answers hit me like slaps to the face. Yes, yes, and yes.

I pull my hair as I bite my lip to keep from screaming at myself. I'm an idiot. I'm the world's stupidest, most immature idiot. How could I ever blame Ivy for anything? Seeing it from her view, witnessing it like she did—it showed me that my family and I weren't the only ones who've been suffering. Ivy's been hurting, too.

I leap up from bed and run around my room, yanking clothes and shoes on. Everyone is right: Aidan, Babette, even Mrs. Karcy. They're all right. Staying angry with someone forever for something that wasn't their fault is stupid. *I'm* stupid. I had the answers to everything lying right in front of me and I didn't realize it.

Nearly tripping as I tie my shoelaces, I dash to the window. I don't care if I end up waking everyone. It'll be worth it if I can fix what I've done.

Crashing through branches and undergrowth, I push leaves out of my way as I run to the dock. Will Ivy be there? If she is, what am I going to say? How I was a complete jackass for yelling at her like that? How I've had some time to think and recognized I was wrong? How I really miss her and want to be friends again?

"Ivy!" I call out as I reach the dock. I'm disappointed to see it's empty. There's no beautiful swamp angel standing at the end. Just the boat bobbing next to it.

She's not here, but that doesn't mean I'm giving up. Determined to set things right, I walk to the dock's end.

"Ivy?" I shout. "Are you there?"

No reply.

"Ivy, I know you're there somewhere," I continue. I take a breath before beginning. "Listen. I…I'm sorry. I'm really, truly sorry for yelling at you. I've been doing a lot of

thinking these past three days, and I…I understand now. It wasn't your fault my mom died. It was never your fault. It was the stupid alligator's. He's the reason why she's not here. So stop feeling bad now. I know you've felt guilty about the whole thing ever since. I had a dream…I watched the accident from your perspective and saw what you saw, and felt what you felt. It made me see how much of a jerk I was. It was stupid and immature of me to pin the blame on you. I'm…I'm really sorry, Ivy—"

I trail off. Not only am I a jerk, I'm a complete moron. I don't know if she heard that. If she did, she probably ignored me. She doesn't want to see me. I can't blame her.

There's a creak of wood behind me. I spin around.

It's Ivy.

For what seems like an eternity, the two of us stand there, gazing at each other. I don't know how she feels; her face is a blank slate as she looks me over. But my eyes stay glued to hers, waiting for any reaction to what I've said.

"It's not my fault."

She finally speaks. I'd be relieved if I wasn't confused by what she said.

"Huh?"

"The dream you had…I did not send it. It was not my fault… even in my distressed state."

I nod vigorously. "I know. Even if you had, I wouldn't be mad. Like I said, it helped me think stuff over."

Nervous, I dare to take a step forward. Ivy doesn't retreat, but she also doesn't approach, so I slowly walk to her until we're face to face. She still doesn't move.

"It helped me see I was being stupid," I say. "I *am* stupid. Blaming something on you that wasn't your fault to begin with."

"It would have been surprising if your reaction…had not been like that. It was expected for you to be upset."

"Even so, what I did was unacceptable. The way I treated you was completely out of line, and I was a jerk. Ivy…I'm sorry." I glance at my feet. "I'm really sorry for screaming at you, blaming you for Mom's death, and for being a bad friend. I don't know if I should call you my friend anymore. I'd understand if you don't want to see me—"

Ivy pulls me into a hug before I finish, draping her arms around my shoulders and pulling me to her. I pause for a second, unsure where this is going. But when nothing happens, I relax and return the embrace, feeling the material of her dress under my palms. Something wet trickles down my neck. Ivy pulls back and I see she's crying, but with happy tears.

"I could never stay mad at you, Rylan," she tells me. *"I was never mad anyway. You are my friend, and friends stay together no matter what."*

I smile. "So I'm forgiven?"

"You were forgiven the moment you came down here."

We hug again. My hands can't help but trail up to her neck and touch her cool skin. Ivy shivers but doesn't tell me to stop. I thumb away her tears. Her eyes close as something that sounds like contentment purrs from her throat.

"Ivy," I whisper. Her eyes open and we stare right into each other. My heart's a snare drum that's beating wildly.

"Ivy, I—"

Suddenly, gravel crunches. There's a turn of tires and an almost silent squeal of brakes. We seize up, and my head spins in the direction of the driveway. I see headlights. Someone's at the house.

"Shit." Crap, crap, crap. What the hell's going on?

"Ivy, hide." I step back and push her towards the water. Her eyes dart around, terrified. *"Rylan, what is—"*

"I don't know, but you have to go. You can't be seen." I hear feet approaching. We're running out of time.

She looks back at me. *"Rylan—"*

"Go!"

Without another hesitation, she steps off and quickly but silently sinks into the water. The moment she's gone, I run down the dock and hide in the trees. Peeking over, I vigilantly watch the dock. The footsteps grow louder and closer, and then their owner steps out into the open.

Chapter 18

It's Mr. Lebelle.

I fight the urge to jump him as he scans the clearing. Seeing no one around, he smirks his evil little smirk and whispers over his shoulder, "It's clear."

Out of the bushes step two other men. I recognize them as members of the town council. They're carrying some rather plump trash bags between them.

They're poisoning the swamp. I knew it! It's been Mr. Lebelle all along.

I come very close to declaring how I was right before I slap my hand over my mouth. Mentally scolding myself, I eavesdrop on their conversation.

"Do we have everything?" Mr. Lebelle asks his lackeys.

"I have the bags," one man replies.

There's shuffling as the other guy sets his bags down. Opening one of them, he pulls out rope and bricks. "And I got everything else."

"Excellent," Mr. Lebelle purrs. "Start weighing that garbage down. We need to make it heavy enough so it doesn't float away when we throw it in."

"Why are we trying again so soon?" Bad Guy One asks Mr. Lebelle, looking up from his work. "Don't you think we

should wait a couple months before trying again?" "Yeah," mumbles his partner.

"I'm not paying you to ask questions," Mr. Lebelle snaps. "I'm paying you to poison it. This land *will* be mine and nothing's going to stop me!"

"The Forester kid seemed to do that the last time," Bad Guy One points out.

Mr. Lebelle glares at him. "I don't know how the Forester brat managed to find the last drop-off, but he won't find this one. It's going to be in the middle of the waterway, where it can only be found if you're swimming, and I highly doubt that, after two gator attacks, he's going to do that anytime soon."

"You must really hate that kid," says Bad Guy Two.

"How can I not? Not only has he ruined my attempts to gain this land, he stole my son's girlfriend and got him suspended for three days. He's nothing but a troublemaker."

My hands clench so hard, my nails almost cut into my palms. It figures Dunstan would lie to his dad and make me look like the bad guy. That, I can deal with. But I'm not gonna put up with this bastard hurting the swamp anymore.

My hand brushes my jeans pocket, outlining the sleek rectangle stuck inside. A grin creeps onto my face.

I know exactly what to do.

I whip out my cell phone. You can't get any reception down here, but that does nothing to stop the built-in camera. Flipping it open, I carefully aim so that the three won't see the glowing screen. I tape it all, from when one lackey accidentally clacks the weights together to Mr. Lebelle continuously growling at them to keep quiet.

"How long does it take to tie weights to trash bags?" Mr. Lebelle barks. "Hurry up!"

I have enough. Time to take my leave. I turn to walk away.

And I step on a twig.

Like a gunshot, the snap ricochets through the area. Mr. Lebelle and his cronies shoot up straight. I freeze, my limbs stuck, my lungs refusing to take in air.

"What was that?" Mr. Lebelle asks.

"Sounded like a twig breaking, sir."

"I know what it was, moron. I'm just asking who did it."

"Probably just an animal."

Silence falls on us all. There's no grumbling, no footsteps, and no weights clanking together. Can I escape now? Or should I wait? It's completely nerve-wracking, but I might as well try. My brain finally warms back up and I move my legs forward.

"Is that a light!?"

Terror grips me. I can sense its claws passing through my skin. But even with my bodily systems going crazy, my mind simply thinks one thing: shit. Shit, shit, shit.

I've been caught.

"I see it, too!"

With that one last comment, the fight or flight reflex assumes control, and I bolt.

Running as fast as I can towards the house, I don't care about the noise I'm making as I stampede over shrubs and through branches. Behind me I hear heavy grunts and footsteps as they chase after me.

"Get the spy!" snarls Mr. Lebelle. He sounds so close and yet so far away. It's scary, and all it makes me think about is running to safety.

Just when I think the swamp is never going to end, I see the outline of my house appear. Putting on an extra burst of speed, I jump over a log, push vines out of my face, and there they are—the driveway and the house.

"I see him!"

Remembering what I'm running from, I sprint to the house, clamber up the steps, and grab the door handle.

Nothing happens.

I try giving it a hard yank. The door still won't open.

What the—? Why won't it open!? Wasn't it unlocked when I left? No, it wasn't. I used the window this time out of habit. Idiot.

"Aha!"

Loud crunching gravel tells me it's no use wrestling with the door anymore. I turn around. Mr. Lebelle and one of his partners in crime are standing behind me on the driveway. The other is by the car, sticking the trash bags and weights in it.

"No use going in that house there, unless you want to be charged with breaking and entering, too?" Mr. Lebelle growls.

"Fat chance. It's my own house," I retort, stepping out of the verandah's shadow.

The expression Mr. Lebelle makes is comical; it looks like he just got kneed in the gonads. But that instantly changes as his eyebrows knit together into his trademark sneer.

"You!" he growls through clenched teeth.

"Yeah. It's me," I snap back. "The Forester brat who likes to steal girlfriends and got Dunstan suspended. Except that's not what happened."

If my repeating his own words affects him, Mr. Lebelle doesn't show it. "What the hell are you doing?"

"I could ask you the same thing. But that'd be stupid since I already know. You were trashing the swamp again, weren't you?"

"You said 'again,' boy. What makes you think I was behind all the other times?" Mr. Lebelle scoffs.

I put a finger to my chin, faking deep thinking. "Well, let's see. You've been hassling my grandma forever about our land, insisting on buying it. But she denies you every single time. So to make things easier and have some payback, you poison the swamp to try and show everyone that it's dangerous and would be better with a mini-mall on it. In the end, Babette would be forced to sell. It also helps I just caught you in the act. You really should be more quiet unless you want to attract attention to yourself."

His lackeys do nothing but stare down at their feet. Mr. Lebelle swears some nasty stuff under his breath.

"So you saw us. Big deal." Mr. Lebelle smirks, thinking he's got me trapped in a corner. "No one's going to listen to you, boy. Once we pick up everything, it'll be like we were never here. You have no proof."

"First off, my name isn't 'boy.'" I jab a finger at him. "My name's Rylan. Drill that into that thick skull of yours." Mr. Lebelle turns crimson with rage. "And second, I do have proof. I hold up my phone. "God bless video phones," I announce. "No one can ignore this, not even the town council you've got wrapped around your finger."

His henchmen pale, but Mr. Lebelle only becomes redder. He takes a menacing step towards the stairs, but I stand my ground.

"Give me that phone." His voice is barely a whisper, but there's enough venom behind it to kill a person.

"You really think I'm gonna say yes and pass up a chance to get you off our backs once and for all? I don't think so." I stick my phone in my pocket and wave the men off like the roaches they are. "Now I suggest you grab all your crap and be on your way."

Mr. Lebelle only takes another step. "Give me the phone."

"No."

"Give it to me!"

"NO!"

"What's going on here!?"

The front door suddenly slams open and light pools outside. Like vampires, we flinch at the sudden brightness. But as my eyes become used to it, I see who it is.

It's Babette and Dad. Both are clad in robes, but only one wears the same furious expression as me.

Babette scans the porch and spots me first. "Rylan?"

I wave sheepishly. "Hey, Babette."

"What are you—Jules?" She now sees him and his buddies. "What are you doing here? And is that…Mr. Kiligan? Mr. Weatherby?"

"What on earth is going on?" Dad finally speaks. He looks tired. I guess getting awakened in the middle of the night doesn't agree with him.

"It's them," I say. "Mr. Lebelle's behind the whole swamp poisoning. I mean, we all knew it was him beforehand—"

"No, you didn't," Mr. Lebelle interrupts. He gives Babette one giant reptilian smile. "Ms. Daniau, there's been a misunderstanding. The boys and I here were just returning from a night on the town and we thought we'd stop by and admire the swamp."

"Admire my ass," I growl, ignoring Babette's patronizing glare. "I saw them, Babette. The car woke me up and I saw them sneaking down to the dock, so I followed—"

"You went down there in the middle of the night?" Now Dad's mad, but not at the people standing before us.

"They were going to trash the swamp again, Dad. I—"

"Trash the swamp? My dear boy, you're delusional. We've done nothing wrong." As an added bonus, Mr. Lebelle's smile gets even more disgusting, becoming some sickly sweet thing that makes me want to puke.

"Oh yeah? How come—"

"Do *not* call my grandson delusional," Babette growls, baring a bit of her teeth like a mother wolf protecting her pup. "If Rylan said he saw you, he saw you."

"But he didn't. He—"

"ENOUGH!" I roar, making every adult jump. "I'm not crazy! Babette, Mr. Lebelle was going to trash the swamp, and I have proof!"

I hand her my phone. "Check my videos. It's all there. And if you went and looked in the backseat of their car you'd find the trash bags and the weights they were going to use."

"Trash? Weights?" Mr. Lebelle chuckles. "You have quite the imagination."

"Please, Babette, it's all there. It's him. It really is," I beg. Please let her believe me.

Babette only stares down at the slick surface. I grow nervous with each second that quietly passes, and I can only imagine how big Mr. Lebelle's sneer would be if he could show it without giving himself away.

"Well," the jerk claps his hands together, "we're sorry about waking you all up. Next time we'll come around in the day and be less of a disturbance." He turns and gently leads his friends to their car. "We'll just be on our way."

"Yes." Everyone stops as Babette finally speaks. Her face is hard as rock. "Be on your way. Drive back home, Jules, and never come by here again."

I silently cheer as Mr. Lebelle's jaw drops. He can't believe what he just heard. "Excuse me?"

"You heard me. Do you honestly think I would believe you over my own grandson? He'd never lie about something so important."

Mr. Lebelle is starting to lose his fabricated cool and is turning red again.

"Now I ask again, please leave. And you'd better have yourself a good lawyer, other than my son-in-law, as soon as I see this video."

With that, Babette steps back inside the house. Dad follows her and I bring up the rear, but not before giving Mr. Lebelle the most evil/gleeful grin ever. His face darkens; he mutters something under his breath that probably shouldn't be repeated in polite company, and stomps off to his car. The doors slam, the engine squeals, and the car darts off. I watch until the lights turn around the bend and disappear.

Doing the happy dance in my head, I turn around and enter the house to be met by Babette and Dad in the foyer. Babette's attempting to watch the video, but she looks up and gives me a pleased smile. She's proud of me. Dad... on instinct, I take a step back towards the door. You can practically drown in the angry vibes Dad's giving out.

"So...how'd you wake up?" I try to defuse the situation with a question.

"I was already awake," Babette confirms. "I had the oddest dream about you getting chased by a horde of big black things. Woke me right up."

I can barely hide my smile. Ivy. Had to be.

"I was going to the kitchen for a glass of milk when I heard shouting on the porch. I thought it was robbers, so I woke your father and rushed down here. Imagine our surprise to see you, Jules, and his friends standing there. You had me real scared, kiddo."

"Sorry," I apologize.

"It's okay," Babette tells me, grinning. "After all, we can now finally prove that Jules Lebelle is behind the swamp poisoning. He's going to need to leave town by the time I'm done with him." Babette squeezes me into a hug, looking back at Dad. "I'm so proud of you. Aren't you, Olivier?"

"WHAT WERE YOU THINKING!?"

Dad explodes, his shouting echoing through the entire house. Babette leaps back, and my hands fly up to cover my ears. Dad's shouting.

Dad's *shouting*.

"Don't you know how dangerous it is to go down to the swamp in the middle of the night!? You could've been killed!"

"But Dad—"

"Don't 'but Dad' me. Shooting a little video isn't worth putting your life in danger!"

Oh God. Is he mad at me all because he thought I was going to die down there?

"Reality check, Dad. The swamp isn't dangerous!" The good mood I had before, from reconciling with Ivy and catching Mr. Lebelle, is quickly evaporating, leaving me empty enough for anger to fill in. I don't care if Dad's finally showing some emotion; no one likes getting yelled at.

"Yes, it is! You nearly died down there!"

"'Nearly' being the main word! I'm still here, Dad. That's all that matters!"

"I've already lost one family member to that goddamn swamp, and I'm not going to lose another!"

"You're not going to lose me! Get over it!" I bellow.

"You know what? That does it!" Dad shouts back. "As soon as Mr. Lebelle's free, I'm selling the swamp to him so he can stop harassing your grandmother!"

Babette gasps. I swallow, my throat suddenly very scratchy.

"You wouldn't," I whisper. "It's too important to everything living in it. And after everything she's done to keep it; you know he goes after her 'cause he thinks Babette's weak and will cave in under pressure and start bugging you to sell it. You can't prove him right—"

Dad's eyes are dark. "Watch me. The only reason I kept the land rights after your mother's death was because she loved it so much, as you and Babette do now. But after all this with you, I'd rather have a shopping mall over a swamp killing everyone who walks into—"

"SHUT UP!

Everyone's looking at me like I've lost my mind. I don't care.

"YOU KNOW WHY YOU'RE SUDDENLY LIKE THIS? ALL THESE YEARS HAVE GONE BY AND YOU HAVEN'T HAD A CHANCE TO YELL AT ME FOR WHAT HAPPENED TO MOM, SO YOU'RE USING THIS AS AN EXCUSE TO DO IT!"

There it is. The taboo subject. Babette gasps, and Dad glares at me.

"Go to your room," Dad hisses, for the umpteenth time not looking me in the eye. "We'll talk about this in the morning."

I don't move. "No."

Dad gets the same expression that Mr. Lebelle had when Babette told him off. "Excuse me?"

"No. I'm not going," I repeat. My hands shake, but my voice is flat. "Not until I'm done talking."

"There's nothing to—"

"YES, THERE IS!" They both flinch under my words. Dad looks down at the floor. "THERE'S BEEN PLENTY TO SAY THAT'S NEEDED TO BE SAID FOR A WHILE, AND I'M SAYING IT! LIKE THE FACT YOU NEVER LOOK AT ME!"

"I do—"

"LOOK ME IN THE EYES, DAMMIT!"

Shaking in fear or sorrow—I can't tell—Dad raises his head inch by inch. After the longest time, his eyes meet mine for the first time in years. His head twitches; I can tell he wants to look away.

"Look at me, Dad. Is it *that* hard to do?" My voice softens, but the anger doesn't leave as it hardens into a firm ball in the pit of my stomach. "I'm sorry I don't look more like you. I'm sorry I look too much like Mom."

Dad winces. Again with the M word.

"And don't bother denying it, either. I know that's the reason why you won't look at me. I'm a living reminder of what you lost. But Dad…it's been ten years. I know it still hurts for you. At times it hurts for me and Babette, too." I gesture to my grandma, who is busying herself with my cell phone but occasionally looking over at me with approval. "But we've tried to get over it. The question is—why can't you?"

I glance away this time, a small, sad smile on my face. This feels good, but I'm not enjoying this at all. "When I was little, I thought you hated me because you never looked directly at me. That you hated me and blamed Mom's death on me. I've been wrestling with that idea all these years. Sometimes I wonder if you really think that. You've never told me otherwise. All I want is an answer. Only one little word. It shouldn't be that hard." I stare straight at Dad. I've waited for this moment for a long time. Now it's here.

"Is it my fault that Mom's dead?"

I hear nothing except Dad's breathing and see nothing except my father standing in front of me. The world has shrunk to only him and me, and it's up to him to let it expand with an answer.

But there's no answer. Without a word or a backwards glance, Dad turns away, walks up the stairs, and disappears into his room, firmly shutting his door.

I feel a hand rest on my shoulder as Babette offers the most sympathetic look ever. "It's not your fault."

"I know," I tell her loudly so Dad can hear. "I know." I want to keep talking, but I yawn. I need sleep.

"I'm going to bed. You coming up?"

"In a minute." She gives me back my phone before walking towards the kitchen. "I've got some *very* important calls to make."

"Babette, it's nearly four in the morning. Don't you think this should wait?"

"No," Babette says, blunt as ever. "Now go to bed."

I peer down at my cell as I go upstairs.

That reminds me—I've got some calls to make as well.

"WHAT!?"

Ten minutes later, I'm sitting on my bed with both Nadia and Aidan on the line. Neither was very happy to be woken up—I guess I should've waited to call them later—but now they're wide-awake and listening intently.

"Yep. I just busted Mr. Lebelle trying to stick more crap into the swamp!"

"Wahoo! You go, dude!" I can perfectly see in my head Aidan cheering in his room. "That bastard's goin' down!"

Nadia shushes him before congratulating me. "Good job, Rylan. Lebelle's finally going to get what's coming to him."

"You should have seen the look on his face," I chuckle. "Completely priceless. I would've taken a picture if Babette wasn't already looking through my phone."

"Ooooooh, Mr. Lebelle's in so much trouble!" Aidan sounds positively delighted. "He's gonna go to jail for this!"

"And lose his position as mayor," adds Nadia. "It kills two birds with one stone."

"You're gonna be so popular at Melanie's party!"

"Is that all you are thinking about?" asks Nadia in disgust. "Sorry, Rylan. Ever since Melanie's invite, Aidan's been going on and on about how he's going to 'score big' at this thing."

"You've heard the rumors about Melanie Sweet's parties!" Aidan defends himself. "Nothing but booze, music—"

"—and girls. I know; that's like the fifth time you said that!" Nadia finishes for him. She groans into the phone. "Please help me. I don't know how much longer I can handle this!"

I chuckle. "Someone's really excited about it."

"Of course, I'm excited!" Aidan shouts, earning another shush from Nadia so he doesn't wake their parents. "I can finally show off my moves to Melanie and she'll totally want me. As long as I have your permission, dude."

"I think you're being delusional, but go ahead," I tell him. "You guys know who I'm interested in, anyway."

"Right. That Ivy chick from the hospital. How's she doing?"

"Uh, she's good. We been talking."

"But are we ever going to meet her?" asks Aidan. "I mean, if she ends up being your girlfriend, I want to know her."

"Me, too," agrees Nadia.

My hands grow clammy. How am I going to get out of this one?

"Ivy's, uh, very busy," I manage to spit out. "With her hospital job, and, um, getting ready for college and all that stuff. She doesn't have much time for fun."

"How about you invite her to Melanie's party?"

Of all the things Aidan had to suggest, he had to suggest that. I mean, can you see it? Waltzing into that party with a swamp angel on my arm? Yeah, that'll be a night to remember.

"Ivy doesn't like parties."

"How do you know that?"

"I just do."

"Are you nervous about us meeting her?" asks Nadia. "I'll make sure Aidan's on his best behavior."

"Gee, thanks sis."

"I…I don't know what I am," I confess, sighing into the phone.

"Here's what you do," Nadia instructs, sounding a bit hesitant. "Just tell her about it. If she says no, fine. And if she says yes, let her come. It won't hurt anyone, we'll get to meet her, and both of you will have fun on your first date."

Inwardly, I groan. I can't follow through with that idea, but once again Nadia's made a good point. I know I have to tell Ivy why I won't be coming down to the swamp Sunday night, but under no circumstances can I invite her.

Unless—

"Rylan?"

"Huh?"

"Dude, you spaced out on us. What's up?"

I shake the blankness off. "Nothing. I was thinking. Nadia's right. I'll…I'll ask Ivy if she can come. But I'm not making any promises."

"Okay." Nadia sounds pleased, but also slightly disappointed. "It's all set, then."

"Can't wait to meet—" Aidan breaks off as he yawns. It's long and loud. "Man, I'm tired. I think I'm gonna go back to bed."

"But I haven't told you guys what happened after Mr. Lebelle left."

"It can wait," says Nadia as she yawns, too. "I really need some more pillow time. See you tomorrow? Hear about it then?"

"Yeah, okay. See ya."

"Bye, Rylan."

"Bye, dude."

The twins click off. I set my phone on my bedside table and stare up at the ceiling. The wonky flower gazes back, its wobbly petals going every which way. That crack needed to be patched up years ago, but I'm actually glad it hasn't been. Looking at it helps me think.

I was only half-lying to my friends. I'm only going to tell Ivy about the party, not invite her. She still can't go, except if she wants to be locked up in a government-owned aquarium with tests done on her daily and people gawking at her like a freak.

Unless—

Unless she can somehow disguise herself. I call to mind the first dream and Ivy's appearance in it. A tall, elegant blonde…if she can somehow pull it off in the real world, I'd be thrilled to take her. Pleased with the possibility, I roll over to fall asleep.

No matter how it turns out, it's going to be one night I'll never forget.

Chapter 19

Because of my little late-night adventure, I sleep in way late; it's nearly 10:30 by the time I wake up, and only because someone's pounding on the front door. With a moan, I pull myself out of bed, go over to the window, and open it.

"Hey, dude!"

"Hi, Rylan." Nadia waves up at me while Aidan smiles goofily.

"Okay. Major sense of déjà vu," I mumble to myself, recalling the morning of my alligator attack. "What are you doing?"

"Dude, we're driving to the mall in Harraway. We gotta get some new clothes if we're going to Melanie's party," Aidan explains. "Plus, Nadia ran out of concealer."

I raise an eyebrow. "Can't you go to the Dollar General for that?"

"It's a specialty brand," Nadia mutters, stuffing her hands in the pockets of her hoodie.

"So get your butt down here, man. We've got some driving to do!"

I nod and shut my window. Quickly I change, go to the bathroom, splash some water on my face, brush my teeth, and rush back to my room to grab my wallet. I open the door…and nearly run into Dad.

"Sorry," I mutter, looking away. Last night's fight is still fresh in my head. I didn't think I'd be facing him so soon—I thought that he'd be trying to avoid me—but already we've crashed into each other. Silence reigns for who knows how long before I decide to talk.

"Um, Aidan and Nadia are waiting outside. They want me to drive up with them to the mall." I gesture weakly to the stairs. "Do you know where Babette is, so I can ask permission to go?"

"Your grandma's off doing errands," Dad informs me. He surprises me with the smallest of smiles. "But I'll let you go."

"Dad…" I thought he'd want to stay as far from me as possible, but instead he smiles at me?

There's a blaring honk from the driveway.

"Um, I gotta go. Aidan is getting impatient." I turn to leave, but not before noticing the cardboard box Dad's been holding the whole time. "What's in the box?"

Dad holds it out, and I look in. My heart skips a beat. It's all the pictures of Mom that Dad's been keeping in his office. What are they doing out of there?

"I'm keeping one in my office, of course," says Dad like he's reading my mind. "But I figured it's time to put these back where they belong. As soon as I'm done with these, I'm going to re-hang the family portrait. I'm thinking of putting it on the mantle over the fireplace. A work of art like that doesn't deserve to be kept away."

I numbly nod. Okay, Dad isn't acting like himself. He's looking at me, he's *smiling* at me, and he's usually so possessive with those pictures. Is the end of the world happening? Or was last night's fight actually a good thing?

The horn honks again.

"I, er, gotta go, Dad. Later…I guess."

I'm at the top of the stairs when Dad blurts out, "It's not your fault."

I look back at him. "Huh?"

"Last night, you asked if I blamed you for your mother's death." Dad looks pained due to the subject matter, but he doesn't shut up. "And no. I don't blame you at all."

He's gone before I can reply.

On the way to Harraway, we grab some breakfast and I retell last night's events.

Aidan pounds his armrest, he's laughing so hard. "Ha ha! Wish I was there to see his face when Babette said that!"

"It was pretty hilarious," I agree from the backseat, sipping my coffee. "Looked like he swallowed a lemon and got kneed in the balls at the same time. But that's not even the best part."

Nadia takes a delicate bite of her bagel, careful to keep both hands on the wheel as much as possible. "Then what is?"

"When everyone was back inside, Babette was praising me and talking about how proud she was that I caught them. Dad…he basically blew up."

As if their mouths got Super-Glued shut, Aidan and Nadia fall silent. They know how emotionless my dad is from the numerous times I've told them and the times they've been over at my place. So for him to lash out like that? It's completely illogical.

"That is probably how I looked, too." I gesture to their faces. "Dad ranted on about how dangerous it was going down to the swamp at night and that it wasn't worth catching Mr. Lebelle. That's when I started yelling that the

only reason he was yelling at me was because this was the perfect excuse for letting out the anger he's been storing over the years."

There's a collective sharp intake of breath. They've never heard me act like this with my dad. Ever.

"I kept shouting about how I needed to say things that needed to be said awhile ago. Like how Dad never looks at me." I chuckle, but it's a sinister sort. "I yelled at him to do it, to look at me. He did, and I just told him that I was sorry, but he needed to get over it. It ended with me asking if he'd thought all along it was my fault Mom died."

"It wasn't," Nadia declares. "It was never your fault." Aidan nods his agreement.

I shrug. "Dad's never told me otherwise, and it's a question that's been in my head for a while. But that's not the point. The point is my dad's reaction."

"What happened?"

"Nothing at first. He simply went to his room and didn't answer. However, when I was coming down to your car, I ran into him carrying out all of Mom's pictures he'd stored in his office. He said he was gonna put them back in their original places. And he said he doesn't blame me at all."

Aidan whistles, licking the icing from his bear claw from his fingers. "Wow. All that happened last night, and here he is with the speedy recovery."

"Do you think he's trying too hard?" asks Nadia.

"It doesn't seem like it. If he was, I think I would've sensed it. He never said it, but he seemed grateful I'd finally talked some sense into him. As far as I know, I'm just happy he's having a breakthrough."

"Good for you, dude." Aidan nods. "About time something good happened to you."

"Cheers to that."

Aidan pounds on the door again. "Nadia! You've been in there for like an hour! You're taking too long!"

"It's been fifteen minutes, thank you very much!" Nadia yells back. "And hold your horses! I'm having trouble choosing!"

Aidan throws up his hands in exasperation as I roll my eyes. It's been a few hours since we reached the Harraway mall. Right now we're stuck in Pac Sun while Nadia tries to find something for the party. She's been taking forever in every store we've gone in while she makes the hard decision of what T-shirt looks best on her or whatever. Nadia was never like this the other times we came to the mall. She knew what she wanted and got it in record time. What happened?

The changing room door squeaks open as Nadia emerges carrying two shirts, her purse and shopping bags swinging from her arms like pendulums.

"Finally! I'd thought you'd disappeared in there," Aidan whines.

"Sorry, but I couldn't choose which shirt to buy. In fact, I still can't choose." She holds the hangers out to us. "Which one looks cuter?"

They both look like fancy purple long-sleeve shirts to me, and I'm not the only one who thinks so.

"They look the same!" Aidan complains. "Just pick one already! I wanna go to GameStop and see what new stuff they have."

"I thought we came here for clothes, but fine," Nadia sniffs. "However, I blame you if this ends up looking bad on me."

Aidan about screams in frustration as Nadia prances over to the cash register. I pat his back.

"You okay?"

"Ah! Be thankful you don't have a sister! I swear sometimes she thinks I'm just an annoying idiot!"

"Calm down. You know she loves you; it's the whole love-to-hate-you type of thing siblings—" I immediately shut up when I spy someone through the store window. "Crap!"

"What?"

"I was never here," I mutter. Before Aidan can ask what's going on, I slip into the empty changing room, lock the door, and clamber up onto the bench, making sure my feet are off the floor just as the front door dings open.

From in here I can hear the small, "Ahheh!" Aidan makes when he spots the person I spotted. Unfortunately, it seems that he's also seen Aidan, because I hear heavy footsteps approach the stalls.

"He-hey, Dunstan." I overhear Aidan's nervous chatter. "Wha-what are you doing here?"

"None of your business, Marce. I'm just wondering if your boy Forester's with you."

Aidan gulps loudly. "Why'd you want to know that?"

"I just want to have a little talk is all."

I cover my mouth to muffle the snort I make. "Little talk" my ass. He probably wants to *kick* my ass because he thinks it's my fault his dad's waist-deep in trouble.

"Come on, Marce. I know you know where he is. Mind helping a guy out?"

"No-nope. Haven't seen him. Nadia and I are just here doing some shopping."

"You're a really bad liar, Marce. Where is he?"

"Probably at home, since he's not with us. You can even ask Nadia. There she is now! Hi, Nadia!"

"What's going on?"

Now Nadia's in the fray.

Dunstan wastes no time. "Where's Forester? I saw him in here, and I want to talk to him."

Nadia catches on instantly. "You must be seeing things, because he's not with us," she tells him. Unlike her brother, Nadia's an excellent liar when she wants to be. "We're here picking up some clothes for Melanie's party. That's all."

Dunstan laughs his mean little laugh. "You losers are actually going? Did Hell freeze over or something to let Melanie invite you?"

"If you really want to know, Melanie invited Rylan." Nadia tells him this nonchalantly, but there's no mistaking the hidden barb meant to hurt Dunstan's billboard-sized ego.

"What?"

"Yeah. Rylan's a good friend, so he managed to wrangle some invites for us as well," Nadia continues. "Aidan and I are here for some new clothes. We stopped by Rylan's house before to see if he wanted to come, but he said he already had something to wear and he had homework that needed finishing."

"All right, I get it!"

I release the breath I haven't realized I've been holding as he takes the bait.

"He isn't here. Fine. But tell him…" Dunstan pauses, and I imagine him leaning over the two menacingly, "…I want to talk with him."

Those same heavy footsteps stomp away. There's a soft knock on the door a minute later.

"Rylan? You can come out now. He's gone."

"Thank God I saw him in time," I say as I exit. "Otherwise I don't think Pac Sun would be too happy about hiring cleaners to get my blood out of the carpet."

"You okay, dude?" Aidan asks. He's looking a little frazzled, but he's quickly getting over it.

I nod. "I'm fine. But I think I better stay low the rest of the day if Dunstan's still hanging around here."

"You can go hide in Barnes & Noble. Dunstan never goes in there!" Aidan suggests as we walk pass the checkout line.

I chuckle. "That might be what I'll do."

As we all laugh, I spot a stack of free Pac Sun catalogs stacked on top of the glass counter. A sudden idea hits me, and I swiftly snatch one.

I know someone who could put this to good use.

After spending the rest of the day hiding in Barnes & Noble—yes, I actually did listen to Aidan for once—I go home. Dinner is the best I've had in a while, conversation-wise. Dad talks only a little more than usual, but he sounds more human than robot, and also joins in sometimes when Babette and I discuss the article about Mr. Lebelle getting caught that's in today's newspaper. My grandmother is all smiles, happy for the good change, and I can admire the family portrait's new spot above the fireplace.

It gets even better when I sneak out to see Ivy.

"Hello Rylan," Ivy greets me as she steps out of the shadows. *"How have you been? Are you...all right after last night?"*

"Yeah. I am. Thanks for sending that dream to Babette, by the way. Really saved my life."

"What happened?"

I give here a quick rundown of everything that went on as we head for her clearing. Ivy's eyes swell with each word until they look like they're about to pop out of her head.

"It seems I miss much when...I stay down here," she states as we stand under her tree.

"It was entertaining to watch, I'll give you that," I tell her. "But the jerk's been caught. You'll never have to worry about him hurting the swamp ever again."

Ivy bows deeply. *"Yes. Thank you so very much, Rylan.... This couldn't have happened without you."*

"It was nothing," I mumble, embarrassed from the bow. "I can't believe I didn't think of this sooner. A midnight stake-out! If I'd done that months ago, Mr. Lebelle would've already been caught and it would've saved us a lot of grief."

"True. But it does not matter now. That evil man has been caught, thanks to you...and that is what is important here."

"Yeah. You're right."

"And not only that, it is pleasing to hear about your father," Ivy continues. *"And that he is back to acting, how you said, normal."*

"It's awesome. The yelling and fighting part wasn't fun, but in the end, I finally got some sense into Dad's head." I sigh, contented.

I swear I see a happy tear in Ivy's eyes. *"Yes. I am happy he is...recovering. He has my blessing."*

"Your blessing is welcomed."

For some minutes, Ivy and I stand there, grinning at each other like fools while I try to remember what I wanted to ask her. What was it again?

"Party."

"Party?" Ivy stares at me confused.

"Sorry. I had something important to tell you and it all just came back to me. Ivy, tomorrow night I won't be coming down to the swamp."

"Why?"

"My friends and I are going to a party," I tell her.

"Party? What is this 'party'?"

I knew she was gonna ask that. "A party is basically when a bunch of people get together and hang out. In this case it's a bunch of teenagers going crazy at the house of the host—the person throwing it."

"That is all?"

"No. There's also food and dancing at these things. And beer, but you don't want to know about that."

Ivy tilts her head, curious. *"This sounds intriguing. Who is the host?"*

"Melanie."

"Melanie?" Ivy's eyebrows knit together. *"Isn't she the girl who likes you…but you don't like her? Then why are you going?"*

"Because I want to tell Melanie once and for all I don't like her the way she likes me. She just doesn't get it, so I need to make it clear, even if that means messing up her party. And if I didn't go, Aidan and Nadia wouldn't be allowed to go, and Aidan wouldn't like me for that."

Ivy laughs, amused. *"You are a good friend, not wanting to anger your friend. This Aidan character…ha! He makes me laugh every time you talk about him."*

"He has that ability," I chuckle. "Would you like a chance to meet him?"

Ivy goes from happy to fearful in about half a millisecond. It even seems the mood of the swamp does an instant u-turn.

"Wh-what?" Ivy can't believe what she's hearing, and it's written all over her face. *"Why do you… I cannot leave this place—ever. I cannot leave this place…to itself. It is my responsibility. Something could happen while I'm…gone."*

"Do you remember the old dreams you used to send me before we met?"

"Yes." I inwardly smile when I see comprehension beginning to dawn on her.

"You came to me as a human, right?"

"Yes. I didn't want to frighten you right away…so I used my magic to don a disguise." Looks like she's catching on.

"Yeah. Ivy, I'm thinking if you can do the disguise thing in the real world, I can take you to the party."

She nervously taps her fingers together. *"Why would you want to take me?"*

"Why wouldn't I? You're my friend. I want you to meet my other friends. And don't you want to see what the world is like outside the swamp?"

"Yes, but…I am nervous…"

"Scared of being caught?" She nods. "Don't worry. I'll never leave your side; you'll be safe with me." I reach out and pat her shoulder. "You've been watching over me all this time. Now it's my turn to do the same for you."

The little doubt she's showing fades away. *"All right. I would very much like to go with you. But first…we must see if the spell I used works in reality."*

Determined, she strides off back the way we came. I trot after her.

"Where are we going?" I ask as we reach the trees.

Ivy pushes a large branch out of the way, allowing me to pass. *"To the water. We need water if this is to work."*

"How come?"

She starts explaining. *"Whenever I sent you a dream, I went into this…this half-asleep state…and while like this I constructed the dream before sending it to you. I put all the elements together, from the greeting to the warning, and made myself act more foreward to get your…attention. But before I sent the dream on its way…I made my dream self submerge herself in the swamp water while chanting the spell I use. When she came out…she looked like you saw her."*

"So you need water to pull the whole thing off?"

"Yes."

Ivy steps past one last bush. *"We're here."*

I look up; we're back at the shoreline.

Ivy rolls up her a sleeve. In the moonlight, her pale green arm almost seems like ivory. *"Let's see if this works."*

Kneeling down, Ivy dips her arm into the dark water. Her hair falls over her face, hiding it from view as she concentrates hard. I hear her whisper words so quietly I barely hear them; what I do hear sounds like complete gibberish.

She completes the chant. Raising her free hand she brushes her hair out of her face as she stares down into the water's depths. We wait.

Nothing happens.

"Was there a flash of light under the water?" She suddenly asks me. *"I had my eyes closed."*

"Nope." I shake my head. "I didn't see any—hold on!"

It's so fast I nearly miss it, but I just make out the white outline of a hand at the swamp bottom before it's swiftly gone. Did it work, or am I seeing things?

"Ivy, pull your arm out," I tell her. She does.

We're greeted with a regular-looking limb. If the moon made it white before, now it's pretty much the same as snow. Ivy giggles with joy.

"It works! It really works!" Ivy claps her hands, her sleeve falling back over the creamy skin. *"This means I can come to the party."*

"Yeah it does." I'm just as delighted as she is. "You do know what this means, right?"

"What?"

"We've got a lot of work to do if you're going to fool everyone. But don't worry," I say, pulling a folded magazine out of my back pocket, "I've got everything we need."

It's here. Party day.

I should be so nervous, I can't sleep in or do anything right. But I manage to sleep way in; training Ivy to be human

was fun, although somewhat exhausting. I taught Ivy what to talk about in conversations, like the weather and the books we've read. I also taught her what NOT to do, like drink beer, use magical powers, and talk to animals, along with what people to avoid, mainly Dunstan and Melanie. We discussed what would be appropriate to wear—Ivy said she could alter some of the human clothes she collected over the years—and how she would be getting there.

"I will meet you there," she told me before I left.

I had asked why, and she'd said, *"It will take much time for me to completely disguise myself...since it seemed to take some time just for my arm to change. And I don't want to make you late."*

"But how will you know where it is?"

"Because I can follow the disturbance in the earth song."

Ivy then explained to me that incredibly loud noises, like deafening music from a party, can disrupt the natural "sounds" of the earth—like the swamp song she introduced to me—and ruin it. Ivy has discovered these disruptions can be traced, so when Ivy's done with her disguise, she'll follow the music to the house. It sounds fishy, but Ivy assures me it will work.

So everything's ready. I guess all we can do now is wait.

The theme song from the *Mario* games cuts through the air. I reach over to my phone and answer. "Hello, Aidan."

"Hey dude! Did I wake you up? You sound kinda sleepy."

"Nah, I'm just lying on my bed thinking. What's up?"

"What's up? The party, that's what's up! It's tonight, man, and I can't wait!"

"I know. I can't wait, either."

"I'm calling to see if you need a ride over and stuff."

"I'll be driving, of course." Like that, Nadia enters the conversation. We've been having a lot of these over the phone lately, which goes to show I can't live without my cell.

"Of course," Aidan scoffs.

"Real mature, bro. You're obviously growing up fast."

"Why yes, Aidan," I interrupt before he can snark anything back. "Thanks for calling. I would appreciate a ride over. What time?"

"Well, I'm thinking the party starts at 7:30…so how about 7:45?"

"But we'll be fifteen minutes *late*. And Melanie's house is twenty minutes away from mine."

"Dude, no one shows up for a party at the time it starts. Fashionably late, remember?"

"Nope. Never got that memo."

"It doesn't make much sense to me either, Rylan," says Nadia.

"It's not like it doesn't make sense as much as Ivy's going to wonder where I am if I'm late."

I have to yank the phone away from my ear as Aidan shouts, "Dude! No way! You got your girlfriend to say yes!? Awesome!"

"She's not my girlfriend!"

"Not yet, anyway," Aidan replies. "It's so clear you like her. You have to tell her tonight. If you don't, I will."

"No you will not!" Nadia jumps to my defense. "It's up to Rylan if he wants to tell this girl how he feels! And if you utter one word before he does, I'll stick your head in the booze barrel that's surely going to be there!"

"Okay! Okay! Jeez, PMS much?"

Before we can stop her, Nadia's ranting. "Why is it that whenever I'm upset you immediately assume it's PMS!? Have you ever stopped and considered maybe I'm mad

because of something else!? No, you don't! I can't believe you said that, Aidan! You can be such a…such a…guy!"

I flinch at each word that comes pouring out. If it's this bad for me, I can only imagine how much worse it is for Aidan.

Over the speaker I can hear thundering, stomping, and a slam that could only be a door.

"Phew. I thought for a moment she was coming after me."

"I couldn't blame her if she did," I scold him. "Man, you *never* suggest the PMS thing. If anything it's just going to make a girl madder than she already is! Didn't you know that?"

"Nope. Never got that memo."

I roll my eyes as I hear him repeat my own words. "Whatever. But if I didn't agree to it before, 7:45 sounds good. Pick me up then."

"Roger that. And Ivy?"

"She said she'll meet me there."

"You give her directions? If this is her first time in Roland, she's gonna get lost."

"How you can get lost in a town you can go around in fifteen minutes with a bike is beyond me," I mutter. "But yeah, I gave her directions. And if those don't work, I told her to find the stereo disguised as a house and the million and one couples making out on the lawn. That shouldn't be too hard to miss."

Aidan laughs. "Yeah, you'd have to be pretty stupid to miss…what's that sound?"

"Huh?"

"I just heard some sound like a growling dog. There it is again!"

"What are you talking—" I hear it now. I look down at my stomach.

"I think I know what it is, dude."

"Hmm?"

"It's my stomach. I just realized how hungry I am."

"Then you probably should go have some breakfast, bro. See ya."

"Bye."

I enter the kitchen whistling.

"You seem cheerful this morning."

I practically jump at Babette's voice. She's sitting over at the dinner table with an open book and cards laid out before her.

"Sorry for scaring you, hon." She looks up from the tabletop and smiles. "How are you?"

"I'm fine," I say, taking the milk out of the fridge and pouring myself a glass. "I've worked out the pickup time with Aidan for the party. I'll be leaving at 7:45."

"And you know your curfew?"

"11:00. I also know that unless I want to be disinherited, I should stay away from the beer, if there's any."

I chuckle at my own joke, but Babette doesn't laugh as she returns to gazing at the cards with a frown.

"Babette?" I put the half-empty cup down and approach her. "Something wrong?"

She sighs, not looking up. "Nothing's wrong. I'm just thinking over what all this means."

"*What* means what?"

"Tarot cards, hon."

"Oh." I'm close enough I can see the little pictures on the surface of the nine cards in front of her. It's another one of Babette's odd hobbies.

"I did a three-card spread for me, your father, and you. While I was able to interpret all of them, your row is very interesting."

"Why?" I pull out a chair and sit across from her.

Babette answers by holding up the first card. It shows a building being struck by lightning.

"Your past is the Tower," Babette begins. "Failure, ruin, and catastrophe."

"It could be referring to my own little catastrophe with the alligator."

"That's what I thought, too." Putting the first card down she picks up the second one. This card depicts a bright yellow sun.

"Your present is the Sun. Life is good for you now. Everything is sunny and bright. Love, friendships, and relationships of all sorts will be shown." Babette smiles at me. "Mind telling me what has you in such a good mood?"

"No," I tell her, but inside I'm cheering. Coincidence or not, that card's pretty much right about my present life with busting Mr. Lebelle, doing well in school, my awesome friends, and Ivy.

"Finally, there's the future." Babette places that card down and picks up the last one. An angel is blowing some type of trumpet. "Judgment."

"Judgment?"

"Yes. Impending judgment is coming your way, Rylan. Important change is close at hand, along with a choice that will alter your life and the lives of others."

A shiver traverses down my spine. From Babette's tone, she makes it sound like a bad thing. I tell her so.

She shrugs. "It can be either good or bad; the cards can't tell you that. But I know it is important; it must be for all three cards to be Major Arcana…"

I rise out of my seat. "Don't tell me you believe this?" I mean, I'm willing to believe anything after finding out Ivy was real, but still? Tarot cards?

Babette doesn't answer; she just looks out the back door. I'm starting to think she didn't hear me when she answers.

"Remember when you asked if I believed in swamp angels? I believe in these cards like I believe in them."

So you're saying you don't believe it?

"You really didn't answer that when I asked, Babette."

"Exactly."

"Huh?"

Instead of replying to my caveman grunt, Babette stands and stretches. "I'm off to patrol the swamp. Make sure the house stays in one piece while I'm gone."

And *poof,* she vanishes.

I scratch my head. What did she mean by that? It's not like there's an answer you can use to avoid the question entirely. You either believe in something or you don't. At least, that's what I thought before Ivy came along.

My eyes fall on the cards she left on the table, particularly on one. Judgment. That angel looks so serious, like it knows what's coming. Like it knows what's going to happen if I take Ivy to this party.

Impending judgment…important change…a choice…

The shiver from before is back, dancing along my spine.

This is insane! What am I doing letting a piece of paper scare me like this? Nothing bad will happen, I tell myself as I exit the kitchen. I'm going to take Ivy, I'm going to have fun, and everything's going to go well.

I hope.

Chapter 20

Finally.

For once, when I want time to fly by, it actually does. Before I know it, the whole day has passed. It's now twilight. The sky is a myriad of colors, and the few wispy clouds left are a deep plum.

I would appreciate its beauty more if I wasn't so nervous. I'm trying not to pace in the foyer as I wait to be picked up. Anxious, I yank at my T-shirt collar. I wish I wasn't so jumpy; it's a good thing Dad's in his study and Babette is reading in the den and they can't see me like this.

"HONK!" That stupid horn makes me jump ten feet in the air.

I'm out the door and down the steps in a single bound after telling Babette goodbye. The twins are patiently waiting—or at least Nadia is—in the Jeep.

"You know, you really scare people with that horn," I tell them while I clamber into the back seat.

Nadia smiles apologetically. "Sorry, Rylan. I tried my best to keep this idiot's hands away from it, but he's as slippery as an octopus."

Aidan doesn't even realize he's been insulted. "Enough chit-chat, people! Let's go already!"

"You might want to listen to him," I tell Nadia as she starts backing up. "Otherwise he'll pee in his pants from over-stimulation."

"Hey!"

You can hear Melanie's house before you can see it. Like most houses down here, Melanie's is a big old Victorian; it's supposedly been in her family for generations. But when we finally find a parking spot and get out of the car, it doesn't seem like a house with all the people outside. Half are standing around talking, and the other half are making out on the lawn like the place is some seedy club.

"Good grief." Nadia rolls her eyes as one of the couples on the lawn falls down and writhes around. "You'd think they'd get a room. Goodness knows there are enough of them in that house."

"Once beer hits the system, any idea of thinking goes right out the window," Aidan muses, looking around like he's standing in front of the White House. We head inside.

There's practically a hundred kids squished into the living room, the stairs above, and the kitchen beyond. Some of them I don't even recognize from school. The music's pumping like I've suddenly entered an earsplitting rock concert. There's movement everywhere as people run around with foamy drinks, dance wildly, make out, and play various card/kissing games. This party is everything it's been rumored to be.

I yell over my shoulder, "I'm thirsty! Want something to drink?"

They nod. Staying close to each other, the three of us weave through the tightly packed crowd towards the

kitchen. Random bowls of junk food, some already empty, litter the counter along with a variety of beer cans.

"Do you think they have any Coke?" Nadia bellows as we approach the cooler.

"I hope so!" I shout back.

I'm sinking my hand into the icy water when a girly voice screeches, "Rylan! You're here!"

Oh no.

Before I know it, Melanie's forcing me into one of her gridlock hugs. Aidan gives me a thumbs-up, Nadia gives Melanie the evil eye, and the majority of the people surrounding us smirk, half-drunk.

Melanie lets go just before my lungs pop and deflate like balloons. "Omigod! I'm, like, so glad to see you, Rylan! I'm so glad you could come!"

She leans forward, probably trying to show off the extra-tight tank top and skirt she's wearing. "Anyway, there's food in here, though by the looks of things it's not going to last long. Dancing's in the den, the pool table's downstairs, and the pool's out back."

I've only recently spotted the blue rectangle of water through the windows facing the backyard. Unlike the inside of the house, only ten or so people are wandering around out there.

"You should've told us you had a pool; I would've brought my swimsuit," I say.

"That's okay," purrs Melanie seductively, pushing her arms together so her...um, chest pops up. "We don't really need—"

"Rylan, didn't you mention you wanted to dance?" Nadia interrupts. Her face beet red, she grabs my hand and pulls me out of the kitchen. I throw one last glance behind me: Aidan's grinning like he won the lottery, and Melanie... she's not as pretty as usual when she's seething.

"Thanks for that," I mutter to Nadia as we step through the minefield of dancing people. I notice she hasn't let go of my hand yet.

She nods. "No problem. But my God, of all the stupid moves she could pull? What a skank!"

"Um, Nadia—"

"I don't understand what people see in her! I mean, look at her."

"Nadia—"

"She's nothing but a life-size Barbie with no brains and no—"

"NADIA!"

"Hmm?"

I gesture to our hands. Nadia's face gets even redder, and as fast as lightning she lets me go like I've got the plague.

"Sorry," she mumbles, staring down at her shoes.

"It's okay," I murmur. We stand still, looking at anything other than ourselves, surrounded by blaring music, dancing people, and drunks who have yet to puke. A change in the song rouses Nadia out of her discomfort.

"So…do you want to live up to what I said and dance?"

Dancing *does* sound good, but I've realized something I have to do first. "Okay, but in a minute. Wait here."

Leaving Nadia, I head to the front door. Tim Powers is standing by, watching people enter like he's some type of bouncer. I figure if he's going to be staying there the whole night, he'd be the best person to ask.

"Hey, Tim."

He acknowledges me with a nod, his floppy bangs falling into his eyes. "Hey, Rylan. Whatcha doing here? Haven't seen you at a party of Melanie's before."

"She invited me."

"Ah. Your shadows here, too?"

"You mean Aidan and Nadia? Yeah. They're here somewhere."

Tim nods again. "Cool."

"That's good. Do you mind if I ask you something?"

"Shoot."

"Can you do me a favor?"

"Depends on the favor."

"The Marces aren't the only ones coming with me. I invited someone else as well. You wouldn't know her; her name is Ivy, and she lives in Harraway. I met her when I was in the hospital."

Tim raises his eyebrows. "Potential girlfriend?"

"Most likely. In any case I invited her here, she said yes, and I'm just asking if you can come find me when she arrives."

"What does she look like?"

I think again of her dream disguise. "Tall, pale, long hair. She's easy to pick out of a crowd."

"Okay, I'll keep a lookout."

"Thanks."

Turning around, I head back to the dance floor to find Nadia. When I do, she's spinning around and shaking it with another guy. With nothing else to do, I grab a vacant spot on the couch before any kissing couple can move in on it, open my can of Coke, and take a sip.

It's still icy cold.

Thus begins the period of couch sitting. I don't know how long it lasts, but for what seems like forever I just sit and watch the world move around me. Occasionally, I spot Nadia flitting through the crowd, wiggling with the beat and having a good time.

Two things do happen in this timeless equinox. First, I watch as Aidan flirts with Vivian Reese. It seems like she's found her latest victim. But Aidan doesn't mind; he looks

278

cheerful, and so does Vivian. Eventually she takes his wrist and pulls him towards the stairs and the dark, *empty* rooms at the top.

The second and much more terrifying event is Dunstan's arrival. Flanked by two of his cronies—like father, like son—he comes through the door, ready to greet his subjects. But because everyone knows by now what his dad did, few people bother to take notice. The rest give him passing glances and a few disapproving scowls. Dunstan only gets angrier when he sees me.

A furious scowl grows on his face faster than a garden weed and he starts heading over, ready to painfully interview me on why the hell I'm here. Out of nowhere Melanie intervenes, pulling Dunstan away from me and towards the kitchen. Even over the music, I can hear them arguing. Whatever it's about—although I have a pretty good idea what—Melanie wins, for when Dunstan emerges he gives me the nastiest sneer ever but doesn't approach me.

Other than that, nothing really happens. Ivy doesn't arrive. And so I sit there, a now-empty Coke can in my hand, watching and waiting, waiting and watching…

"Rylan?"

I jerk up, my eyes springing open. Looking around wildly, I find myself still on the couch, with classmates still dancing around me. The only difference is the smell of alcohol coming off the majority of them.

"Rylan? You okay?"

I turn to my left, and there sits Nadia, red-faced and sweaty.

I put a hand to my forehead. "I think so. What happened?"

"You fell asleep."

"With all this noise?"

"I know, right? Surprised me too when I saw you."

My hand slides down over my eyes. "Crap. It's been a rough couple days. I must've looked so stupid."

Nadia waves it off. "Don't worry. Everyone's too busy to notice, and if they did, they'd probably thought you were passed-out drunk."

As my mind clears, one important issue comes to mind, and I propel out of my seat. "Ivy!"

"What?"

"Ivy. I asked Tim Powers to come find me if Ivy arrived. Is she here?"

Nadia shakes her head. "I haven't been paying that much attention, but I haven't seen Powers at all, so I don't think she's here."

Defeated, I slump back down on the couch as I check my watch. 9:30! I've been out for a long time and Ivy still hasn't shown up.

"She said she'd be here," I murmur, throwing my head back with a sigh. "I wonder what's taking so long. I hope she's okay."

"You must really like her."

I turn my head. "Huh?"

Nadia tilts her head back, staring at the ceiling. "Whenever we talk about Ivy, you just seem…happier. Like you're on top of the world."

Despite it being insensitive to Nadia, I smile. "I don't know about the top of the world, but yeah. I like her. And I hope you like her."

We're silent for a minute.

"Remember when we first met?" Nadia suddenly asks.

"You mean the first day of third grade? I remember."

"The teacher—Mrs. Gettern—she introduced me and Aidan right in front of the entire class. We both said, 'Hi!' and waved our hands around like they were on fire."

"Then Mrs. Gettern assigned you your seats and as you were walking over…"

"I was so distracted and happy to be here, I didn't see where I was going."

"And you tripped. Right over your own feet." I laugh to myself at the image of an eight-year-old Nadia falling down, her arms flailing.

Nadia nods. "Yep. Everyone burst out laughing, and I didn't get up because I was so embarrassed. Aidan came over to help, but I just wanted to stay down."

Nadia then smiles dreamily. "But then…I heard a voice asking me if I was okay. I looked up, and standing there was a boy with shaggy black hair, holding his hand out to me. I took it, he helped me up…"

"And we've been friends ever since. All three of us." I sigh. Maybe it's weird to be evoking memories on a saggy couch in the middle of a party, but I like this little trip down memory lane.

"You were my hero, you know."

"Huh?" I stare over at Nadia. I heard what she said perfectly, but the way she said it… I can't help but feel there's a second meaning to those words.

"You were my hero," Nadia repeats so quietly, the pounding music almost swallows up her words. "Anyone else could have come and helped me up off the floor, but it was you. Only you."

"Well…it looked like you needed help. And Babette always told me to help with small things, no matter how insignificant they seem," I mumble, playing with my Coke pull-tab as I wiggle it around.

If Nadia sees my sudden discomfort, she doesn't stop. "I know, but it wasn't just a tiny good deed to me back then. It was the bravest thing I'd ever seen anyone do."

The tab clicks back and forth furiously.

"As we got older, I saw you do more good deeds," Nadia goes on. A faint blush can be made out on her cheeks, even in the bad lighting. "Helping my brother when he procrastinates, occasionally standing up for Junior Small and his friends, the swamp…the way you love that place is so admirable."

Are those tears in her eyes?

"It was only like two months ago when I finally realized why you did all those things." Nadia turns to me, her eyes glistening. "It's because you're so nice. And I'm not just saying that. You…you really are a good person, Rylan."

Nadia's face is getting closer, coming right towards me. I want to lean back, but there's no room to go. And if there was, it'd be no help. I can't move; I'm frozen as Nadia comes toward me. By accident, I look at her lips, shiny with gloss, pushed together like she wants to kiss me…

No! No no no no no no! Nadia can't kiss me! It'd be a disaster! I don't feel the same way about her! Someone stop this!

"Rylan!"

Nadia and I turn our heads simultaneously towards the entrance to the living room as Tim Powers appears.

"Yeah?" I yell across the room.

That's when I notice the expression on Powers' face. A mixture of awe, amazement, appreciation, and a bit of jealously.

"Your girlfriend's here," Tim informs me.

He steps aside, and a goddess enters the room.

It's been forever since I first had those dreams Ivy sent me with her in her disguise. But I still remember how she

looks. Pale skin, long hair, bright-green eyes, and a model's figure. A perfect dream girl, who's now in reality.

Ivy smiles shyly as she steps into the room. Her skin is porcelain, unflawed and shiny. White-blonde hair, straight and flowing, falls down her back and ends a little bit past her waist. She's not wearing her woven grass robe, but instead a dress most likely altered from a piece of clothing from her clothes sack. It probably reached the floor at one point, with long sleeves, but the sleeves are gone and the skirt's been snipped away, leaving behind a green dress that shows off mile-long legs.

But her face…all that pales in comparison to her face. Heart-shaped, with high cheekbones, an elegant nose, a well-shaped chin, and her lips—she's not covering them anymore—are smooth and inviting. Her eyes are captivating—two shimmering, bright green pools I would be happy to drown in or go through. People believe the eyes are windows to the soul, and Ivy's soul is beautiful.

Ivy turns to Tim and tells him something so quietly I can't hear her, and Tim has to lean over to catch her words. But whatever she says causes his whole face to light up. Silently she walks over to me. Practically everyone in the room has noticed her by now; all the guys and even some of the girls stare at her, their mouths hanging open as they wonder who this mystery girl is, who invited her, and, in the case of the guys, does she have a boyfriend? All that is answered the moment Ivy stops in front of me.

"Hello, Rylan," Ivy greets me. Even with her transformation, her voice still has that magical quality about it. Her white arms wrap me in a hug, which I return. Throughout the room, I can hear disappointed sighs; the crazy-hot babe is taken.

"Hey." My reply is scratchy, and I clear my throat. "Hi, Ivy. It's good to see you."

"It is good to see you, too." Ivy steps back, her beaming smile still in place. "The boy at the door said you told him to watch for me?"

"Yeah. I didn't want you to arrive here and have to look around for me in a crowd of strangers."

"Oh. I see. Well, thank you. It was very convenient."

"Rylan?"

In all the excitement of Ivy arriving, I forgot about Nadia and the kiss that nearly happened. Suddenly nervous, I look back at my friend, ignoring the hurt behind the curiosity she's showing.

"Nadia. Um…I'd like you to meet Ivy." Like a salesman with a new car, I present Ivy in the same fashion. "Ivy, this is Nadia."

Nadia flinches, but Ivy doesn't notice as she sticks out her hand and gives Nadia her most charming smile. "Hello, Nadia. Rylan has told me such wonderful things about you and Aidan. It is wonderful to finally meet you. How do you do?"

At a snail's pace Nadia extends her own arm and grasps Ivy's hand, pumping it up and down. "It's, er, very nice to meet you, too. I'm fine, thank you." Liar. Nadia's not okay. The stuttering, the flinching, the badly hidden unhappiness and jealousy, the way her eyes flicker around looking for escape, and the fact her teeth were slightly gritted when she greeted Ivy; she's anything but okay. I feel like shit.

Letting go of her hand, Ivy asks Nadia, "So where is your brother? I wish to meet him. Rylan has told me he is quite the comedian."

"Um, I don't know where Aidan is." Nadia glances around the room. "He isn't in here. I think I'm gonna go find him."

Like I said. Looking for a way to escape.

Ivy being Ivy doesn't notice any weird behavior and just grins. "Okay."

Nadia disappears.

I sigh—there's nothing I can do for now—and motion to the couch. "Wanna sit down?"

Ivy nods, so we squeeze into the available space left. The room by now has reverted back to its normal self with people dancing like crazy, but once in a while someone's eyes flicker over to the unknown beauty who just walked in.

"Thought for a second you weren't going to show up," I confess.

For the first time since she showed up, Ivy's grin falters. "I know. I'm sorry."

"You don't have to apologize."

"Yes I do. You said so yourself the party started at 7:30…and here I am, arriving hours late."

"It's fine. I'm not mad. But is everything okay? Did you get lost on the way here or something?"

Ivy shakes her head. "No. I found this house fine. I could sense the vibrations of the music…a mile away. It was the spell I had complications with."

"The spell? What about the spell?"

"First off, it took longer to cast than I originally thought," Ivy explains. "By the time I was finished, I knew I was late so I tried to rush over here as quickly as I could. But then I ran into another problem…literally."

"Huh?"

"I was wading through swamp water to get here most of the time. And when I climbed out…any part of me touched by water had reverted back to its original form, my original body. I had to recast the spell all over again."

"Touching water breaks the spell?"

"Yes. But it makes sense, does it not? Water makes the spell work—should it not also be the breaker as well?" She

shrugs. "I don't know about you, but it makes good sense to me."

"Yeah, it makes sense," I agree. "And hey. Your speaking is excellent. There are barely any pauses now."

Ivy's cheeks turn a pleasantly pale pink. "I was practicing all day. I…I did not want to give people a reason to stare."

I nod, internally deciding not to tell her it's a little too late for wandering eyes.

The song ends and a new one starts. I stand up, stretching my arms over my head. "You know something? I've been bumming on this couch the whole time." Turning to Ivy, I stick my hand out. "Wanna dance with me?"

Ivy thinks it over, nods, and clasps my hand, pulling herself up. Still holding on, I lead her onto the dance floor and claim the last little bit of empty space available. I take note of the many pairs of eyes still examining the new girl and probably if she dances as well as she looks.

At first it's just me dancing as Ivy merely stands there, staring around as she tries to pick up the beat. Eventually she does and starts to move, shaking and gyrating in time to the music. It's like the notes have entered her brain and taken over, telling her how to dance to the unfamiliar song.

Our eyes catch. Grinning, Ivy comes forward and grabs my hands. Together we start to move, ending up doing the craziest, oddest, yet totally awesome dance ever. Out of the corner of my eye, I see every guy and most of the girls watching us. But they aren't mocking our weird movements; they're trying to copy them.

The song flows into the next one, then the next one, and we continue dancing. I don't feel tired at all. Instead, I'm energized, ready to keep going all night. Therefore it doesn't surprise me when I happen to look at my watch to see a whole hour has passed since we started. It's also when I notice how dry my throat is.

"I'm thirsty!" I shout. "Let's take a break."

Ivy nods. I grab her hand and we leave the living room. Upon entering the kitchen, everyone who hasn't seen Ivy yet stares. It's sorta distracting, but since Ivy isn't noticing, I guess I can keep ignoring them.

Ivy examines the colorful bottles as I take some water from the partly full cooler. "What is Coke?" she asks as I unscrew the plastic cap.

"It's a type of soda," I explain, taking a sip. "And soda is this sugary drink."

"Am I to assume the other cans are other sodas?"

"Yep."

"Dude!"

We turn around and there stands Aidan, looking like he just won a million dollars. He can't keep his eyes off Ivy.

"Hey, Aidan," I greet. "I'd like you to meet Ivy."

"I am quite pleased to make your acquaintance." Ivy gently shakes his hand.

Finally getting a grip, Aidan returns the shake, his goofy grin reappearing on his face. "Yeah. I'm Aidan. Good to meet you, too."

"Rylan has told me so much about you."

Aidan rubs his chin, a comically sly glint in his eyes. "Oh really? Did he say how dashing, brilliant, and incredibly handsome I am?"

"No." Ivy shakes, completely unaware it's all a joke. "Rylan said you were loud and that if it was not for him, you'd still be stuck in the third grade."

I snort into my water as Aidan scowls.

"But he also says you're a good brother, a trustworthy friend, and very funny." She breaks off giggling. "And I see what he means. You should see the look on your face!"

"Oh, ya like this?" Aidan puts his hands up and wiggles his fingers as his expression contorts into something even

crazier. Ivy continues giggling; even I let out a chuckle, feeling my nerves disappear. No more worrying with the whole "meet my friends" situation. Aidan clearly likes her, and though Nadia didn't show it, I'm pretty sure she likes her, too.

This night's been going well.

"Hello there."

I speak too soon.

Dunstan enters, his two cronies behind him. Everyone standing around goes quiet. I flinch, but not for me; he's gazing at Ivy like a lion at a piece of meat. Ivy just keeps grinning.

"And may I say you are the prettiest girl I've seen all night," Dunstan says, not noticing the fact Ivy's already taken.

Ivy stares down at her feet, a pale blush the color of pink roses brushed across her cheeks. "You don't mean that," she whispers, not knowing she's accidentally flirting.

"I really do," Dunstan continues in his oily, supposedly charming voice, and I roll my eyes. I want to pull Ivy away, but if I do, Dunstan will notice me. And without Melanie breathing down his neck, who knows what he'll try to pull?

"So what's your name, beautiful?"

Ivy's blush deepens and I feel my nails dig into my skin. *I'm* the one whose supposed to tell her she's pretty, not this jerk.

"My name is Ivy," Ivy replies.

"Ivy. I like it. It suits you."

I feel an arm on my shoulder and turning around, I see Aidan holding me back. Unconsciously, I've stepped forward, ready to challenge him.

"So what is your name?" Ivy asks, still shyly peering down at her shoeless feet.

Acting all surprised he got asked this, Dunstan runs a hand through his hair. "My name is Dunstan."

Ivy's flush instantly vanishes, the corners of her mouth turn down, and her eyebrows knit together.

"Dunstan? That is your name?" Quiet as she's being, I know there's anger there. I'd hate to be the recipient of this tone.

But Dunstan the egotistical baboon butt isn't aware of the change. "Yep, that's me."

"What is your last name?" I feel someone shaking. Aidan's still hanging on to me, and he's nervous, too.

Dunstan still doesn't detect her malice. "Why, my last name's Lebelle. Dunstan Lebelle." He chuckles. "Perhaps you've heard of me?"

"Oh yes," Ivy hisses, suddenly radiating ferocious fury. "I've heard much about the boy who nearly got Rylan Forester killed."

Even with blaring music in the next room, you can hear a pin drop throughout the kitchen as everyone goes quiet, having lost all ability to talk due to flapping jaws. Someone whistles.

"Excuse me?" Dunstan sounds like he can't believe what he's hearing.

"You heard me." Ivy glares, knowing she has him caught. "You pushed Rylan into the swamp where the alligator attacked him. Sure, you can blame the alligator, but when you really think about, if you had not pushed him in, Rylan wouldn't have nearly died. Who, by the way," Ivy steps back, clasping my free hand in hers, "happens to be my friend and my date."

Everyone bursts into titters—no one has ever spoken to Dunstan Lebelle like that—as Dunstan stares at me wide-eyed, finally taking in my existence. But before he can do anything, Ivy pulls my hand.

Colleen Boyd

"We're leaving," she declares, giving Dunstan one last stink eye. And with her nose in the air and me following, Ivy boldly walks right out the back door.

The roaring music instantly deadens the moment we step outside. It's still loud, but now we actually have a chance to retain some of our hearing. Ivy attracts attention from the few people who've stayed outside the whole time, but again Ivy doesn't notice and I ignore them.

I have to admit I like Melanie's backyard. The whole setup looks like something out of a fairy tale. There's a wooden gazebo decorated with vines and strung with lights that make the concrete deck glow. The pool sits at the edge of the deck, filled with sky-blue water that's shiny with pool lights. Deck chairs dot the sides, and beyond it, thick wild vegetation shows the swamp's beginning. No matter where you go, the swamp is in everyone's backyard.

"To think I actually talked to the boy who nearly got you killed," Ivy mutters, shuddering with disgust. "I'm so sorry I did."

"It's okay. You didn't know," I reassure her as we take a seat on some pool chairs.

"But you told me before what his appearance was. I should have recognized him!"

"It's fine, Ivy. Even if you did your best to avoid him, he would've found a way to hit on you eventually."

Ivy wrinkles her nose at the unfamiliar language. "'Hit on'? What does that mean?"

"Flirting. Or, for Dunstan, more like a procedure. He's been hitting on any pretty girl he sees ever since he and Melanie broke up. I don't know if he's doing this to make her jealous or what, but it's real annoying."

I look back up to see Ivy go rigid. For some reason she looks classically surprised; her hand is over her mouth, and the rosy blush is back with a vengeance.

290

"Ivy? You okay?"

Ivy removes her hand, muttering something so quietly I can't hear it.

"Sorry?"

"You called me pretty." The moment those words are said, Ivy stares down at her feet as her face gets brighter.

"Well, yeah," I murmur, my face hot. "You really are beautiful tonight, Ivy."

The following silence is awkward. Both of us are shades of crimson and admiring our feet as if they're the most interesting objects in the world. Luckily this doesn't last long, because eventually Ivy's brave enough to resume talking and soon we're discussing random things and occasionally laughing like two good friends.

But you don't want to be just friends, do you?

I shake my head, dismissing the idea, as the sound of groans meets my ear. The loud strains of a slow song drift outside along with complaints to change the music.

I couldn't ask for a better setup.

I stand, and like with the couch an hour ago, I turn to Ivy and offer my hand. "Let's dance."

Ivy stands without hesitation, and hand in hand we walk under the gazebo. Ivy prepares to let go, but I don't. Taking her hands, I place them on my neck. In an instant, Ivy stiffens, looking about ready to faint.

"R-Rylan?" She's stuttering. I hope I'm doing this right.

Ever so slowly I put my thankfully non-sweaty palms on Ivy's waist. A tiny gasp escapes her and I ask if I should move my hands. She shakes her head. "It's fine."

For some seconds we only stand there, getting used to this weird but oddly comforting position. My heart is going a million miles a minute and I feel like both screaming with joy and hurling at the same time.

"So…" Ivy meets my gaze; we're close in height and I don't have to look down like I do with nearly everyone else. "What do we do now?"

"Now…" I clear my throat, getting rid of the sudden huskiness in my voice. "Now we move."

I shift my weight to the right, my foot barely coming off the deck. Ivy follows me. Her hands are soft against my neck, making it extremely hard to concentrate on where I'm going. But we do move and sway, in our own little circle, in our own little part of the gazebo. Few people can see us in here, so it's like we're in our own world.

At one point there's a distant rumbling, as though someone's moving furniture in the house. But there's another roll, and I realize it's thunder. I hope it doesn't start raining. I mean, that'd be good for the swamp because it's been uncharacteristically dry lately, but it wouldn't be good for Ivy's disguise.

I feel something on my chest. Ivy's resting her head on me. In fact, she's pulled herself so close that we're touching everywhere. My heart picks up speed again, but I'm surprisingly calm, seeing her beautiful face close to mine, her eyes closed in an expression of contented bliss, and—the best part—feeling her own heart pound in time with mine. She's feeling what I'm feeling.

That is when I know for sure.

"Ivy?" I know what I have to do.

"Mm?" Her songbird voice is a calm purr.

"I think…no. I really, really like you."

Like moving through molasses, Ivy raises her head. Her eyes are enormous with bewilderment. But there's no fright, no dislike, no anything that discourages me. With that in mind, I don't hesitate as I move my face to her face and my lips to her lips.

Ivy's lips are cool like water but delicate and velvety and smooth like round pebbles. She smells like wildflowers, wet earth, and freshly cut grass, which only makes me want her more. I press my lips harder against hers, and a shiver of delight snakes through me when I feel her press back. Daring myself, I open my mouth. So does she, and the kiss deepens. My hand slides upward to caress her satin cheek, and the back of my neck tingles as her fingers play with my hair.

This is it. Ivy's and my first kiss. I wouldn't have it any other way.

Unhurriedly we pull our faces away, though we leave our foreheads touching.

"Ivy?" I peer into her eyes. She doesn't look upset, but more calm and curious.

She meets my eyes and asks, "What was that?"

"A kiss. You do it with people you like."

To my amazement Ivy leans forward and kisses me again. It's as incredible as the first time.

"That is my feeling towards you," she tells me as she leans back. She meets my eyes, her face flushed but determined. "I...am...really liking you, too."

I smile and pull her to me, and we grasp each other like we never want to let go.

She likes me. I like her.

This can't get any better.

There's a loud slam as the back door swings open, hitting the wall with a loud smack and causing everyone in the backyard to jump. Melanie comes out, and she doesn't look too happy. If she has to be compared to something, she's like a pissed off cat who just lost her favorite catnip toy.

Catching sight of me, Melanie walks over. She's smiling tightly, keeping her eyes solely trained on me. An array of shadows suddenly darkens the deck as people press up

against the windows and come out the door, wanting to see what going on.

"Rylan!" Melanie squeals, high-pitched enough to break glass. "I'm, like, so sorry I haven't talked to you all night. Being a hostess is hard work." She dramatically wipes imaginary sweat off her forehead. "Anyway, I finally have some free time. So why don't we go dance, hmm?"

Gripping my wrist a little too tightly for my taste, she tries to pull me back to the house. I stand strong, jerking Melanie back when I don't move.

"No thanks, Melanie." My free arm tightens around Ivy's waist. "I already *am* dancing with someone."

Melanie's sight flickers to Ivy, and for a moment contempt skews her big grin. But it's gone in an instant as Melanie stretches her fake smile to the point she's showing gums and asks, through gritted teeth, "Hi. What's your name?"

Ivy can tell there's something off with the girl in front of her, but she still gives her a polite greeting. "Hello. My name is Ivy. How do you do?"

Melanie completely ignores the question and turns back to me. "You never told me you invited someone else, Rylan." Melanie's smile goes harsh. "I'm sorry, but unless I give the okay, no one outside of school is invited." She glares at Ivy. "I'll have to ask you to leave."

Ivy tilts her head, befuddled at the sudden hostility. "You want me to go?"

Melanie rolls her eyes. "Uh, yeah. I just said that."

Ivy stares down at her feet, ashamed and no doubt feeling guilty for the wrong reason. She nods. "Okay."

She begins to leave but I grab her wrist and pull her back against me. I glare at Melanie. "What if I don't want her to go?" I growl.

"Yeah, Melanie!"

To my relief, I see Aidan and Nadia wiggle through the crowd. Neither of them looks very happy; Nadia's downright fuming. Despite the whole "my liking Ivy" case, she's still there for me.

"Don't go telling people they can't be here," Nadia growls, her eyes flashing dangerously. "Who died and made you think you can boss everybody around?"

"Last time I checked, this is my party, and therefore I choose who I invite or not," declares Melanie with an obvious edge in her voice.

"That's no excuse! The only reason you want her gone is so you can make Rylan your new boy toy, which he doesn't want!"

"Oh, like you know him so well?"

"I'm his best friend, bitch!"

"*Excuse* me!?"

"ENOUGH!"

With one word, I bring the argument to an end and all attention back on me.

"Nadia's right," I state, glowering at Melanie. "Nadia's always been right. You know one of the reasons I came, other than to show Ivy a good time? It was to tell you to leave me alone, okay? I. Don't. Like. You. So leave me alone!"

It's like I announced I farted. Everyone starts whispering with disbelief. No one has ever turned down the advances of Melanie Sweet—until now. It's turning into a night of firsts for them.

Melanie obviously isn't used to this, as her face reddens like a tomato, her beautifully manicured hands clench into fists, and her usually angelic face morphs into a full-blown snarl.

How sweet.

I gently pull on Ivy's hand. "Let's go," I tell Ivy, who, despite it all, still looks calm and poised. She nods and we walk away towards the back door, skirting around people and the rim of the pool.

I realize how stupid it is when it's too late.

"You WHORE!"

Melanie is a blur of motion. I feel Ivy's hand leave mine as she shrieks. I spin around and watch as she falls back.

Right in the direction of the pool.

Chapter 21

"IVY!"

I move to catch her, but with a splash Ivy falls into the pool and immediately sinks to the bottom.

Any part of me touched by water had reverted back to its original form.

Crap. Shit. Damn, and all other swear words. What's going to happen now!?

"You BITCH!" There's a slap and a collective gasp as Nadia hits Melanie full across the face.

"Oh, you did not just hit me!" Melanie snarls, ready to charge into an all-out catfight.

Surprisingly, Aidan steps in the way. "Aren't any of you concerned that she hasn't surfaced yet?"

It's true. Ivy should've come up by now, but she hasn't. I can still somewhat make her out, rolled up into a ball at the bottom. And I say "somewhat" because the crystal-clear pool water is quickly growing as thick as pea soup, like there's a dense cloud of fog developing underwater. I'm not the only one who's noticed.

"Dude, look at the water!"

"You think the sewage is backing up or somethin'?"

"Ew!"

To my horror, about half the party guests are all crammed around me, looking for Ivy.

"I don't see her, do you?"

"Naw, I don't. Shouldn't she have, you know, floated up or something by now?"

"Maybe she hit her head on the bottom!"

"But that means she's drowning!"

"You see what you did!?" Nadia yells at a panic-stricken Melanie. "She's drowning, she might die, and it's all your fault!" Melanie doesn't speak as she stands there, no doubt thinking of all the various lawsuits to come. A part of me is actually quite pleased to see her freaking out.

As I struggle with my laces, cursing myself for knotting my Converses too tight, something extraordinarily cool but bad happens—the deck starts to shake.

"Earthquake!"

"In Florida!? It's not possible!"

"Run for your lives!"

But before anyone can move, there's the hissing sound of pressurized water, followed by a giant boom as the pool's surface explodes, as if an underwater mine had gone off. Flying straight up, water sloshes everywhere, and people scream as they get soaked.

"What the hell!?" Dunstan yells, finally making an appearance.

Before anyone can answer, there's another explosion. This time, the water turns into a fine mist partly obscuring everything outside. Everyone's freaking out, and I finally see what people mean about running around like beheaded chickens. Me? I'm trying to remain as calm as possible, telling myself that, in the end, everything's going to be okay.

"Look!"

Nadia points over to the opposite side of the pool, the one closest to the swamp. Through the mist, I can see Ivy pulling herself out of the water—slowly, like she doesn't want to get caught. She doubles over, clutching her waist like she has a stomachache. Her skin shifts to pale green. I want to close my eyes and pretend nothing's happening, but I can't.

There's no ignoring the transformation.

A bird screech escapes Ivy, and with the sound of tearing cloth her bony wings slowly sprout out of her back. Despite the thing in front of them, no one is screaming "What the hell!" or running off in fear. They only stand there, jaws slack, wondering what on earth is going on.

I stand there wondering why my world had to fall apart.

The change ends and Ivy straightens up. For a long minute, no one moves. Not the crowd, not Ivy, and not me. I stare at her back. Finally, she turns her head to face me with a look of complete sadness in her eyes and a frown on her mouth.

Her uncovered mouth, which is filled with rows of teeth like shards of broken glass.

At that climactic moment, the sky thunders again and the clouds burst open, letting torrents of rain fall. With a flap of her wings, Ivy flies off into the trees.

"Ivy!" I shout after her, leaping up, ready to take off after her.

"R-Rylan?"

The nervous stutter stops me dead in my tracks. Turning back, I see Nadia, Aidan, Dunstan, Melanie, and everyone else staring, unnerved and alarmed, right at me.

My heart cracks to see Nadia refuse to meet my eye. "Wh-what was that? Who…" Her voice fades. The truth of the matter has yet to sink in. She doesn't know what to think, and I don't know what to tell her.

But hearing Ivy being referred to as "that" hits me like a handful of stones and my face hardens. "She's Ivy," I declare, "and I like her."

I turn and run into the brush.

The rain pounds down, soaking every inch of the swamp and turning the ground to mush under my feet. But I take no notice of the howling wind and erupting sky as I leap over stumps and push past low branches, searching wildly for Ivy. She's nowhere to be seen. But I keep looking, and keep asking the same question over and over as I do.

Why?

Why did water have to break the spell? Why did Ivy have to be pushed into the pool? Why did Melanie have to push her in? Why did Melanie choose me to be her new boyfriend? Why did everything have to go wrong at the end?

"IVY!" I cry out in frustration and despair. Only the wind and thunder answer me. But over all the racket, I hear the unmistakable sound of sobbing.

"Ivy?" Peering around the tiny clearing I'm standing in, I try to track the source. Despite all the noise, I zero in on it immediately—to my left and nearly hidden by bushes is a tall stump. Perfect for someone to hide in, if it's hollow.

Carefully I go over, push the leaves out of the way, and peek through a hole in the front. She's curled up into a ball with her arms wrapped around her legs, sobbing into her knees.

"Ivy?"

She jolts, and our eyes meet. I can see how hard she's been crying; it's like she just lost everything she ever had. Silently we stare at each, the rain temporarily filling in for our voices.

300

"They saw me."

Her voice is back to normal as her mouth moves and the rows of teeth dance.

"They all saw me. They know…they know I exist…" Ivy murmurs, sounding frantic. I can only crouch there and listen.

"They saw me…and now they will tell everyone, and they will come looking for me. They will cut down trees and kill my animal friends. I can keep hiding, but they will find me eventually and take me away from my tree, my treasures, my swamp. And you…I cannot lose you." I open my mouth to speak, but her words keep pouring out. *"And they will take me to a horrible place, where I will be stuck with needles and tested on…like in your books you shared with me, and I'll be put out for all to see and be laughed at, and all my sisters around the world will be in danger as well, and…and…"*

Ivy doesn't finish as a new wave of tears overtakes her, making her body shake as if with a bad cough. I can't think of anything to say right now that would comfort her. The one thing I manage to do is stick my hand in and grasp hers, squeezing tightly and hoping she finds some comfort in it.

Gradually, Ivy's sobs grow quieter as she calms down. She uses her free hand and wipes her leftover tears away, silently thanking me.

"What do we do now?"

It's the question I've been dreading, since I don't have an answer. We can't stay out here in the swamp during a bad storm; God knows what will happen to us. Ivy's probably too nervous about going back to her tree, and I can't leave her…

"Come to my house."

Ivy isn't the only one completely surprised by what I suggested. *"What?"*

"I said…you can come to my house," I repeat, the plan coming to me as I talk. "You can hide out in my room until you feel it's safe to return to your tree."

"But your family—"

"They're no problem. If they come into my room, you can hide in my closet. They're most likely asleep right now, anyway." I sigh. "I know it sounds scary and everything, but it's the only plan I've got. Just know…you can trust me and I'm not gonna let you get hurt. Okay?"

There's a pause, and then Ivy nods.

Flying is friggin' awesome.

By the time Ivy climbs out of the tree stump, I realize I have no idea where we are or what direction my house is. Luckily Ivy, the one with the better sense of direction, picks up our location quickly and points out which way we need to go.

Before I know what's going on, Ivy hugs me tightly to her chest and takes off. We soar through the trees, up and over branches and around vines. It's incredible, like I've transformed into a bird with my own set of wings and just discovered the joys of flying. Granted, it would be more fun if thunder and lightning weren't crashing around us— maybe flying wasn't the smartest choice after all—or I could've kept my eyes open longer than five seconds to see where we were going—stupid raindrops in my eyes. But it's something that's gonna stay with me until the day I die.

Much too soon, Ivy asks, *"Is that it?"*

Squinting through the rain, I see a familiar structure appear on my left. "Yup. That's it. You think you can land on the roof?"

"Yes, I'll try."

Slowing down, Ivy swoops up and with a small shake of her wings lands right on the roof for a perfect touchdown.

"My room's this way. Follow me."

Carefully, we creep along the wooden slats, making sure to watch where we put our feet so we don't slip and fall. Reaching my window, I get it open. I crawl inside and help Ivy through.

"We're safe for now."

Ivy nods, but her attention isn't all on me. She's gazing around my room, taking in everything from my desk to my bed to the numerous piles of dirty laundry on the floor. She's never seen so many human objects before. This must be like a museum for her.

"This is your room." It comes out like a statement instead of a question.

"Yeah. Sorry about the mess."

"It's fine," says Ivy, sitting on my futon mattress and stroking my pillow.

Ivy sneezes, followed by a shiver. She has to be freezing after flying around in the rain; I know I am. I wonder if swamp angels can get colds.

"I'm going to get something hot to drink to warm us up," I announce as I head to the door. "There's some blankets lying around here somewhere you can wrap up in. I'll be back as soon as I can. Don't move."

"Okay."

I shut the door behind me and creep down the stairs, taking extra care to avoid the squeaky steps. Dad's definitely asleep by now, but Babette may still be awake as she waits for me to come back home.

I breathe a sigh of relief as I enter the kitchen to see Babette asleep at the kitchen table, a cup of something sitting next to her hands. That makes everything easier.

Discovering the cup is filled with tea, I also find a kettle filled with the stuff, still warm. Grabbing some mugs, I turn to go. Silently I tiptoe out of the kitchen and up the stairs. Reaching my door, I tap on it and whisper, "It's me. Open up."

There are near-silent footsteps and Ivy lets me in. Gently shutting the door with my foot, I clear my bedside table of my alarm clock, set the tea down, sit on my futon, and pour. My mattress squeaks as Ivy joins me, rewrapping herself in the blanket she found to keep warm.

"Here." I pass her a cup. "I don't know how hot this is, so be careful."

"Thank you." Ivy takes a sip. I do the same, letting the bitter but homey taste spread across my tongue and down my throat.

And that's how we sit there for a while, just sipping tea like we're two normal people in a coffee shop. But how far from the truth that is with Ivy being what she is, and me… I've been abnormal since the day I first met Ivy. Maybe even before that.

Like the day she saved me. Or the day Mom died.

Death can really change a person.

I'm about to pour myself another cup when I feel a weight on my shoulder as Ivy rests her head, careful with her horns so she doesn't poke me as she snuggles. My cheeks heat up, but it feels really marvelous.

"Rylan?"

"Yeah?"

Ivy gives me her empty cup. *"What is going to happen now?"*

I sigh deeply as I set our mugs aside. "Most likely, it took about ten seconds for the truth of the matter to sink in after we both left. Then everyone started freaking out, going 'Oh my God' and all that. Some probably called the police or their parents."

304

Ivy winces.

"But," I continue, "no one's going to believe them. The police and everyone are going to think the callers are drunk and delusional. All high and stuff. No one's going to listen to a word of it, and there's going to be a lot of guys arrested. At least, we can hope that's what happens."

"For what?"

"Underage drinking and drug use. You have to be twenty-one or older to drink that stuff that was in the keg." I shake my head. "The point is, no one's going to come looking for you, Ivy. Half are going to refuse to believe what they saw, and the half who do believe probably won't be able to convince anyone else that they aren't crazy. You're safe."

"But what about Aidan? Nadia? Dunstan and Melanie?"

"Dunstan and Melanie are in shock, but they're probably going to leave us alone. We don't have to worry about them." I sigh. "Aidan and Nadia…they're going to come to me with questions. I'm going to have to lie to them."

"Lie to your friends?"

"I don't like it, either. But if it keeps you safe, then I'll do it. I'll tell them I don't know what they're talking about and they got caught up in the moment. If that doesn't throw them off the trail—and it probably won't—I still won't talk."

Ivy leans back onto the bed with a moan. *"I am starting to feel bad. I'm a dirty little secret that is tangling up your life."*

I frown at her. "Don't be like that. You're not doing anything wrong. Nothing's your fault."

"But what about tonight? I am still scared that I will be hunted. I cannot abandon my swamp…and it would be so hard to leave you behind."

Heaving yet another sigh, I lie down next to Ivy and join her in ceiling-staring. "Ivy…whatever happens after tonight, everything's going to be okay. I mean, everything

ends up okay in the end, one way or another. We can hope that happens, right?"

It's a perfectly stupid question to ask when I know the answer is a definite no, but it seems to calm Ivy down some as she looks at me.

"*I would like to think so,*" she whispers.

"Me, too," I whisper back.

Silently we lie there, staring at each other. Eventually Ivy moves; to my delight she rolls closer to me, snuggling her head into the crook of my shoulder and placing a hand on my chest. Carefully I drape my arm around her waist and comb my fingers through her long hair while my other hand pulls the forgotten blanket over us.

"*Rylan?*" Ivy murmurs a minute later.

"Yeah?"

"*Tell me again the words you told me when we were dancing.*"

I grin into her scalp. "I like you."

"*I...like you, too.*"

Her fingers dance across my heart.

This bliss can't last forever.

"*Rylan? What's that?*" Ivy asks sometime later.

I don't have to wonder what she means because I see it, too—yellow light streaming through my window.

Car headlights.

Swallowing the fountain of curses bubbling up, I whisper, "Stay here," get down on my stomach, and crawl over to the window. I look out and nearly bite my tongue off; through the rain, there's a whole line of cars pulling into the driveway.

Mr. Lebelle's Lexus leads the way.

"They're here." Ivy scoots next to me and peers out the window.

Car doors slam as everyone emerges. I instantly recognize Mr. Lebelle and Dunstan's golden white heads of hair. The others are members of the town council, friends of Mr. Lebelle, and other men who I'd never associated with our corrupt, crazy mayor. They all hold weapons—sticks, nets, rope, and stun guns.

My stomach takes a dive. They mean business.

There's a crunch of gravel as something else appears out of the pouring rain. But it's not a car—it's two bikes. Aidan and Nadia's bikes. What are they doing here?

"What are they doing here?" Ivy asks, echoing my thoughts. I can only shrug and watch as they both stand to the side and watch the scene unfolding.

Other than a death glare from Dunstan, no one cares about the two teenagers that have arrived, as they're too busy listening to Mr. Lebelle. I strain my ears, but I can't hear anything over the thunder and wind. With how Mr. Lebelle is flinging his arms around and opening his giant mouth, you'd think that the rumbling thunder was his actual voice.

Done with whatever he was telling the crowd, he nods at Dunstan. Stepping forward he yells something at the house. I can't hear it because of the storm.

"Damn it! We can't hear a thing," I mutter.

"Oh yes we can," says Ivy, firmly taking my hand in her own.

I feel the spell she's casting before it kicks in, like a gentle trickle of water falling on my skin. There's a whoosh like a vacuum cleaning out my ear canal, and suddenly I can hear everything.

"Oy! Forester! Get out here," Dunstan shouts at the house. I snort—like I'm obviously going to obey that.

Cupping his hands around his mouth, Dunstan calls out. "Come on, Forester! We just wanna talk about the party! No need to hide! You can just stick your head out the window and we'll talk like that! Yo! You even listening—"

He's abruptly cut off by the creak of the front door opening. Out comes Babette, looking completely bewildered and totally angry.

"Ah! Ms. Daniau. What a pleasant surprise," says Mr. Lebelle in his usual oily voice.

From up here, I can imagine Babette's eyes narrowing. "What in heaven's name is going on, Jules? It's nearly midnight and here you are leading a mob about ready to break down my front door. Aren't you in enough trouble already?

Mr. Lebelle ignores that last jab. "Good evening to you, too," he continues in that fake cheery tone, his smile stretching too wide for his face. "And don't worry; I'm not here for the swamp. I only want to talk to your grandson."

Babette glares at Mr. Lebelle. "Why do you want to see Rylan?"

Mr. Lebelle moves forward. "We need his help with something gravely important."

"What is so important you come to my home and harass me and my family?"

"Well you see, Ms. Daniau, Dunstan just came home from a party, the same one your grandson went to, and the first thing he told me about was your son's girlfriend. A beautiful girl—my son even used 'unearthly' to describe her."

I didn't even know Dunstan could be descriptive.

"And while it was interesting, do you know what caught my attention? Your grandson's dream girl fell into the pool… and a monster came crawling out." He smiles menacingly, all cheery traces gone. "Rylan's been dating a swamp angel right under your nose."

"Rylan," Ivy whispers, gently tugging my sleeve. *"Someone is in the hallway; I can hear them."*

I hear it, too, soft feet quietly but quickly marching down the hall. Panic arises in me—did Mr. Lebelle send someone in the back door?—but as the footsteps reach the stairs, I notice they're walking in the other direction.

"You've been drinking, Jules," Babette tells him, her voice scornful. "You're drunk, and your friends are drunk, and you're angry about the upcoming trial. This is why you're making trouble for us."

"Am I? Did you ever think I could be telling the truth?"

"I would be surprised if you were, considering how you've done nothing but lie since you took office."

The front door creaks open.

"Ah! Olivier!" Mr. Lebelle shouts with glee as Dad joins Babette's side wearing his tattered bathrobe and rubbing his eyes.

"What's going on? Why's everyone shouting?" Dad asks through a yawn, still half-asleep as he stares at all the gathered people.

"It's nothing." Babette tries to push him back into the house. "Dunstan Lebelle just told his father something crazy, and now everyone's over—"

"My son is not crazy!" All pretense of politeness vanishes in a flash. "He knows he saw a swamp angel, he knows Rylan has something to do with it, and we need him if we want to catch that thing. So give us the boy!"

At the mention of me, Dad snaps awake and into full-on father/lawyer mode. "I have no clue as to why you're here or what in the world this 'swamp angel' is, but I do know this—you will not lay a hand on my son," he declares, crossing his arms. "Now leave before I sue your ass off."

I resist cheering Dad on. But his blatant threat does nothing.

"Impressive," Mr. Lebelle chuckles. "You're finally stepping up and being the father you never were. As an award, I'll show you this."

Out of his back pocket Mr. Lebelle whips out a piece of paper. Dad narrows his eyes. But Babette only asks, "What's that a photo of, Jules?"

"You don't see it?" Mr. Lebelle hisses. "This is the swamp angel I saw on one of your boat tours twenty years ago!"

I hear Ivy gasp beside me.

"So all these years you were after this land…" Babette mumbles. "You weren't seeking to turn it into a mall complex…"

"And as soon as that thing was caught, that's what I most likely would've done." Mr. Lebelle takes a step forward. "But they are real, Olivier. This is no hoax. To catch a swamp angel and prove such a creature exists? The fame, the money to be made…it's too good to pass up. And best of all, that monster would be gone and this town would be protected." Mr. Lebelle snarls, an ugly primal sneer that shakes me to the core. "And I will not be denied it anymore!"

"He's lost it," I sigh. "This isn't working." Shifting around, I unlock the window. Ivy grabs my wrist.

"What are you doing!?"

"Defending my home," I reply. "If I don't step in now, someone's going to get hurt, and I can't let that happen."

With a tiny creak, the window opens and we're hit with an onslaught of wind and rain.

"Stay here," I order Ivy. She nods, though I can tell she wants to go with me.

Carefully, I crawl out the window and onto the roof. Down below, the fight is getting more heated between my family and Mr. Lebelle's crowd as they keep throwing insults at each other. Aidan and Nadia are still standing where they arrived, wanting to do something but not knowing what. Everything is set to explode.

And I am the spark.

I leap up off my stomach just as Mr. Lebelle takes a swing at Dad.

"LEAVE HIM ALONE!" I roar. Rather appropriately, lightning streaks across the sky, lighting up the faces of everyone below as they all look at me. My family and friends look at me like I'm suicidal. Mr. Lebelle's group all glare with knife-like sharpness, and the leader and his son smirk with sadistic triumph.

"Well, look who finally decided to show," exclaims Mr. Lebelle, poison lacing his voice. "The man of the hour!"

"Cut the crap," I growl. "And leave my dad and grandma alone. It's me you want."

"Yes, but if you get technical, it's your friend I want to talk to."

I bare my teeth. "You're insane," I declare. "Listening to Dunstan and thinking that swamp angels exist. He's lying."

"Don't call me a liar!" Dunstan roars, hate in his eyes. "I know what I saw, Forester. Your little girlfriend turned into a freak right in front of me and everyone else at that party!"

"You saw nothing," I continue denying. "You and everyone else were so drunk you were seeing things."

"There was beer!?" Babette interrupts. "Rylan Jacob Forester, you better not have taken a single sip—"

"Not now, Babette!"

"So what if I had something to drink?" Dunstan hollers. "I saw everything!"

"You're just as crazy as your dad!"

"Yeah, Lebelle! Shut your big mouth up!" The twins run forward and stand alongside Dad and Babette. It's about time they said something.

It takes Mr. Lebelle some time to identify the two soaked teenagers standing there. "Are those the Marce kids?"

"Yeah, you big jerk. It's us," Aiden exclaims. "Rylan's friends."

"Who were at the party," Nadia joins in.

"And didn't have any beer."

"And saw the whole incident, too."

"And we can happily report Dunstan was seeing things," concludes Aidan, glaring at said guy, who snarls back. "We didn't see any girl transform into some kind of freak. Ivy just crawled out of the pool and ran away, and Rylan ran after her."

"Ivy?" Mr. Lebelle sneers. "What's that? Your little pet name for her? Frankly, I think you could've done better."

"Aren't you listening to us!?" Nadia barks. "We just said nothing happened—"

And that's when Mr. Lebelle pulls a handgun from his back pocket and points it straight at Nadia. This situation has just gotten much more dangerous.

Among the stunned cries of protest from Dad, Babette, me, and some of the mob members—guess they aren't as loyal as I thought—Aidan steps in front of her, acting like a shield. Mr. Lebelle only smirks.

"How precious," he hisses. "But do please shut up. Both of you."

With unnatural calm, he turns back to me, aiming right at my head. "Now, Rylan, I really didn't want to do this, but now I have no choice. You *will* tell me where the monster is, and you'll do it now. And don't think about calling the police, Olivier," he adds to my dad, who tries to sneak back inside. "I've got nothing else to lose. Now tell me where she is."

Staring down that barrel, I feel no fear. Mr. Lebelle could be threatening me with a bazooka and I still wouldn't spill. I tell him so in two words.

"Hell no."

There's a flash of light; for an alarming second, I think he's pulled the trigger. But no, it's more lightning, streaking down from overhead. It strikes a clump of trees far from our house. They burst into flames that, despite the rain, begin to spread. For an instant we all freeze as we watch the fire lick upwards. It ends when a single voice cries out.

"MY SWAMP!"

Before I can move, before I can shut the window, before I can make up any more excuses, there's a flash of green and Ivy's standing on the roof edge, gazing in complete horror at the fire eating her beloved home, not caring at all that she just showed herself to everyone.

I try to get her back inside, pushing at her hard. She won't move. Down below, everyone stares up, surprised scared, still.

Dunstan shouts, "That's her!", setting off a chain reaction in the mob.

"She's real!"

"The swamp angel!"

"Get that monster!"

They move forward, ready to swarm the house and capture her, but Ivy takes no notice. She looks back at me, determination overcoming her. Without speaking, she mouths three little words to me. And she leaps, spreads her wings, and flies off.

I'm not gonna leave her.

By the time she hits the trees, I've jumped off the roof and hit the ground. I ignore the painful tremors that snake up my thighs and start running, knowing full well what's chasing us.

"They're getting away!"

"After them!"

"Follow the boy!"

Like a herd of elephants, they stampede after me. I don't look back; I just keep running, hoping I'll lose them in the swamp. Glancing up, I see I've already lost track of Ivy. I can't make her out through all the branches. The darkness, the wind, the rain, and the long shadows caused by the distant fire aren't helping either. But I know where she's heading.

Now I'm at the dock. The *Dahlia* is straining on its tether, nearly being pulled away in the crashing waves. Even if I *had* the boat key, there's no way I'd be able to pilot it now. So enters Plan B.

With an Olympic dive I charge right into the water. No hesitations, no second thoughts about any lurking alligators—just splash and go. Arms flailing, feet churning, stinky water stinging my eyes—I'm no swimmer, but I reach the other side in record time and duck behind a tree just as the crazy people show up.

"Which way did he go!?"

"I don't know! I can't see in this storm!"

"You idiots!" That was Mr. Lebelle talking.

"Wait! I saw something move! I think he went this way!"

Away they charge, thankfully in the opposite direction of where I want to go. I wait a few minutes to make sure they're gone before I stagger up and run away again.

I'm half-blind, I've got multiple stitches in my side, I'm wet, I'm muddy, and I definitely look deranged. But I keep moving towards Ivy's tree, wondering why the hell she had to leave the house. Why did she have to expose herself?

And what did she mean by the words she mouthed to me?

I press on, trying to disguise the feeling that everything is ending.

This is what Hell must look like.

I reach the edge of the flames and that's all I can think. Fire engulfs whole trees, turning soft brown into harsh yellow. Super-dry shrubs and bushes, devastated by the drought, are blazing like campfires. What's already been burnt is just as unpleasant. Large, blackened blobs distort the once-familiar swamp and morph it into some fantasy world of misshapen creatures.

Quickly yet carefully I make my way around the burning bits and sprint past the skeletal remains, kicking piles of wet ash out of the way. I cough, choking on cinders still floating in the air, but I'm almost there. Just a little more...

I burst out of the trees and into my destination: Ivy's clearing. My heart falls into my stomach.

This can't be it. Where's the long grass that tickled through my pants leg? Where's the night sky, and the stars I could see so clearly? And where's Ivy's tree? Now there's only hardened dirt, gray smog spiraling upwards against the rain, and a giant upright flaming log.

This was the place the lightning bolt struck that started the whole fire. Her home is gone.

"IVY!"

There's a grunt. Out of the smoke Ivy appears, dragging her sacks of treasures with her. She looks up, her face wary and tired and streaked with dust, and yet she's still able to smile when she sees me.

Her bags slip from her hands as she straightens up and I come running over.

"Ivy." I hug her tightly, pulling her farther away from the fire. "Are you okay? Please tell me you're okay!"

She squeezes back, nuzzling into my chest. *"I'm fine, Rylan. I am okay."*

Quietly, in the pouring rain and the surrounding inferno, I lift her chin and kiss her, even though her jagged teeth are on display. She responds with her lips opening like a flower to greet the morning.

"I wish you hadn't run off like that," I murmur against her mouth. "You said so yourself; if touched by fire, you'll burn to a crisp."

"I know." Ivy rests her chin on my shoulder. *"But I had to save these, make sure all the animals were safe, and see if I could put the fire out. But now…I see it is best if I just let it burn itself out."*

"They saw you, you know."

Ivy winces.

"Now they know for sure you really exist and that it wasn't a bunch of drunk kids making something up."

"I know."

"What are you going to do now?"

She sighs. *"I do not know. Maybe find a new encampment, perhaps by the hidden lake; I surely can't stay here anymore. Then I'll just wait out there…and pray those men give up and leave me alone."*

"You think they will?

"I hope so." She caresses my cheek. *"They'll come after you, too. They will bother and threaten you and your family…trying to get information on my whereabouts."*

"I guess they will."

"Are you going to tell them?"

"No. I won't. I never will."

"But the danger that it will put you in…"

"It'll be worth it to keep you safe."

Ivy smiles at me, and I know I can put up with any future torture.

"Come on." I lean down and grab one of the sacks. "It's time to take you home."

Ivy grabs the other bag and we turn to go, hands clasped so tightly.

Nadia and Aidan are standing there.

Automatically, I push Ivy behind me, where she cowers out of view as the three of us stare at each other. For a time, the only sound is the falling rain and crackling and pop of fire.

"How…I thought I wasn't being followed…" I whisper.

"Truth be told, we nearly lost you," Nadia answers, talking to my shoulder like Dad used to do. "We were trailing behind Mr. Lebelle's mob and we were about to follow them, but Aidan saw you running in the opposite direction, so we snuck off the other way…and yeah," she finishes with a shrug.

"You went after them? Didn't you once think how dangerous that could be?"

"It was your grandma's order." I swivel towards Aidan, who stares at his shuffling feet. "She and your dad rushed inside to call 911, and she told us to go find you and make sure nothing got out of hand."

The police? I swear under my breath.

"Then we don't have a lot of time." I tighten my grip on the sack. "I gotta get Ivy to her new home before we're found."

For the first time, the twins look at Ivy. She peeks at them from behind me like a scared child.

"Do you need help?"

I'm so scatterbrained and worried I don't hear Nadia's question. "Huh?"

"I asked if you needed help."

I can't believe it. There's a mythical creature standing right in front of them, and yet they're offering to help carry her luggage. I guess they *are* my true friends after all—and Ivy's, too.

"Actually, I need you guys to go make a distraction," I tell them. "One that can keep Jackass Senior, Jackass Junior, and their gang occupied long enough to make sure Ivy's safe."

"Where're you taking her?"

"A place only we know of and where no one else can find her. She'll stay there until they stop searching for her."

"Okay." Aidan give an army-grade salute. "You got it, dude. One distraction coming up!"

"A little late for that, I'm afraid."

With an echoing click, a gun cocks as Mr. Lebelle steps out from the trees to the right of the twins. Dunstan and their insane posse follow, waving their weapons and sneering victoriously. Ivy starts to shake.

"You almost had us fooled," says Mr. Lebelle, all high and mighty. "If my son hadn't caught your little friends going the other way, who knows where we'd be loping off to?" He winks cheekily at the two.

"You said no one was following you," I snap at Aidan and Nadia. "You said…"

"What those dorks think and what really happened are completely different," mocks Dunstan. "Thanks for the help, by the way."

"You little…" Aidan steps forward, red with anger and ready to fight, but Nadia stops him with a hand on the shoulder as Mr. Lebelle raises his gun.

"Enough chitchat," he growls. He aims at Ivy, who's trembling behind me like a leaf about to fall, clutching at the back of my shirt like a security blanket. "Now I'm going to ask this only once, boy. Move."

Everything inside me is set to die as I eye the barrel.

"You wouldn't dare shoot," I say, thankful my voice isn't shaking. "You want Ivy alive, and a gun isn't the weapon of choice for that."

He snorts. "That beast behind you is immortal, sonny. A bullet's only going to weaken it enough for capture."

"Don't call her a—"

He shoots. He actually shoots. I close my eyes.

I bite my tongue and choke on my scream of pain as the bullet grazes my shoulder before flying back into the burning remains of Ivy's tree with a dull *thunk*. I turn instinctively and see the red smear pooling on my left shoulder. I suddenly feel faint.

"RYLAN!" Nadia screams.

"Now look what you made me do." Mr. Lebelle's tone is hollow, completely void of emotion; he doesn't care at all if I die. "I will repeat it one more time. Move."

Everything goes unnaturally quiet; even the fire and rain are silent. No one moves. I meet Mr. Lebelle's eyes. There's no doubt in me that he'll shoot again, maybe fatally this time. A voice in me screams that I want to live, so is it worth dying like this?

Something shudders. Turning my head, I see Ivy nestled behind me, scared out of her mind. She lifts her beautiful wet face to glance at me.

Important change is close at hand, and a choice that will alter your life and others will be made... Babette and her tarot cards weren't talking about the choice to take Ivy to the party.

She meant this choice, which I make now.

"You'll get Ivy over my dead body," I snarl.

Something flashes across Mr. Lebelle's dangerous face, and he slowly raises his gun. Aidan shouts "No!," and Nadia starts crying. They both rush to stop him, but they aren't running fast enough. Ivy whimpers, but I stay silent. I'm ready for whatever comes.

Crack!

It echoes through the clearing like the snap of a whip, making everyone jump. I close my eyes and wait for the pain and darkness to come over me.

Nothing happens. Mr. Lebelle never fired his gun.

I peel open my eyes. Everyone is looking at something behind me with dreadful apprehension. *CRRRAACCK!*

There it is again, but after hearing this noise twice I realize it doesn't sound like gunfire. It's more like cracking, snapping wood.

I whip around.

As if the bullet had hit glass, numerous cracks split across the surface of the trunk of Ivy's tree. Large chunks of burning bark fall off in handfuls as the groaning gets louder. Ever so slowly, the tree leans over our way.

It starts to fall.

Even after all the time I've hung around it, I still haven't fully understood its full size. It's huge. The shadow creeps along the ground as it gains momentum, blacking out my world and swallowing half of Mr. Lebelle's mob.

"Run!"

No one knows who yells it, but immediately people scatter, dashing in all directions. Aidan and Nadia turn around and yell at me to move as they run away. But I don't. My feet are cinderblocks, my mind is fried. I can only stand there with Ivy as certain death rushes to us.

A month ago, I nearly died. Drowned by an alligator, choking on filthy swamp water, my body slowly accepting the lack of life, I'd been all ready to leave. To go wherever Mom went. But I had a vision at that moment. A gorgeous vision that swooped in, beat the gator, and saved me from doom.

Just like she does now.

"RYLAN!"

I feel Ivy's palm on my chest and, with a powerful shove, she pushes me back, away from fire, danger, and death.

In that moment after the tree plunges, I see Ivy for a single second as I fall. In those emerald eyes is a look of complete calm, undying gratitude, and powerful, protective love.

The tree crashes down, the sound echoing in my head.

For an eternal moment, I sit there on my butt, staring at the spot where Ivy was standing. I'm numb, only registering the slightest changes; the wind dying down, the rain lessening.

What just happened?

Desperately, I look side to side, praying that Ivy jumped to the side and what I saw was just an illusion made up by my panicked mind.

But Ivy's nowhere. And there's an arm sticking out from under the trunk.

"IVY!"

I sprint to the fallen tree. The smoldering wood stings my hand when I grab the trunk, but I grit my teeth and bear it. Pulling with all my might, I throw the remains of the tree aside.

Ivy's lying there, her eyes closed and her lower half on fire.

"No…" I fall to my knees and yank off my sweatshirt to try and smother the flames, but they burn strong, and soon the fabric's on fire. I toss it away, not knowing where it lands as I'm unable to tear my eyes off the most gut-wrenching sight of my life. My hands go to my head and my shouting grows even louder. "No, no, no!"

This can't be happening. She can't be—

"Ry—Rylan?"

Ivy's voice is faint. I crawl over to her side, my eyes never once straying from hers.

"Rylan?"

"I'm here," I whisper, stroking her forehead with tenderness. "I'm here, and I'm not leaving you."

She grins weakly. The light in her eyes is starting to slowly fade. *"Thank you. I wish I could say the same…for me."*

"Don't say that," I beg. "You're not going to die. I'll get some water, put the fire out, and everything will be fine—"

Ivy places her hand on mine. *"Water will not stop it. Once it starts, the fire will keep going. See how it spreads?"*

She's right. In these few moments the flames have spread up to her waist, licking her body with searing tongues.

Something glows. Glancing down, I see Ivy healing my burned palms. Once she's done, she places her hand on my bloody shoulder and heals that, too.

"There," she murmurs, letting her hand drop. *"You are all healed. My last gift to you."*

"You can't leave," I whisper, more to myself than anyone else. Tears prick my eyes. "You *can't* leave."

"We all have to leave sometime," Ivy muses, so calm in the face of death. *"Even swamp angels. But at least in my death…I achieve life."*

"Huh?"

"Look."

I don't know what she's talking about. But soon I do.

Ivy's glowing, and not in the white healing sense. Vivid yellow radiance is completely surrounding every part of her body, even the flames. As I watch, the light becomes more dazzling until it hurts my eyes. I have to look away.

"Rylan…"

I swivel my head back. The brightness is gone, but Ivy's happier than I've ever seen her.

"Ivy?" I squeeze her hand. The flames are up to her chest. "What was that?"

Ivy's smile is so beautiful it hurts. *"That was me…gaining my soul."*

I feel a jolt of joy. "Your soul? You got it?"

Ivy barely nods. *"Yes. I can go to the light now, and see my other sisters…and, I hope, your mother."*

Hot tears run down my face. "Ivy, that's…that's fantastic. But how?"

"Do you remember…what I told you…when we first talked about this?"

I do. The memory is quite clear.

Ivy bites her lip, suddenly appearing guilty. *"Truth be told, I never went into exact detail about how I could obtain my soul."* She peers at me dead in the eye. *"Rylan…the way we swamp angels gain our souls…is to sacrifice our lives for the people we love."*

I feel like I've been kicked in the stomach. Because now the words she mouthed to me before she jumped off the roof are all clear.

Don't hate me…

In some twisted way, I've been used.

"I don't hate you," I tell her. And I honestly don't. Because love can't be faked when magic's involved. Ivy didn't push me out of the way just to gain a soul. She didn't force anything. It was all her choice to save and love me.

From her wide eyes, she can't believe what I've said. *"Rea-really?"*

"Yeah." I grin despite the waterworks. "Because I know you love me. Just like I love you."

"I do," whispers Ivy. A single tear escapes her eye. *"I love you, Rylan. And thank you for letting me hear that…once in my lifetime."*

The end is near. The fire's up to her neck. The moment it hits her face, Ivy's gone.

"Does it hurt?"

"My magic…takes away most of the pain. I feel nothing. But Rylan?"

"Yeah?"

"Kiss me. Please. One last feeling."

Heat tickles my chin as I lean down and grant Ivy her final request. I kiss her like I don't want to let her go, hard and soft

and urgent and slow until we both need air. The sound of us breaking apart echoes too loudly.

Ivy sighs, tilting her head back, her eyes closing. *"They are crying."*

I furrow my eyebrows. The only one crying here is me. But Ivy must know what I'm thinking, for she smiles serenely.

"My sisters know I am dying. They...feel my pain. They are sad to see me go. But they also rejoice...in my passing. For I have gained what we all seek."

"How did it feel? Getting your soul?"

"Like...coming home." She lets out a wisp of a gasp. *"I can see it, Rylan. I can see it."*

I stroke her forehead one last time and remove my hand. She's almost there. "What's it like, Ivy?"

"Light...so much light. And this gorgeous music and everything's so soft and... It's...so beautiful over here..."

"Well, don't let me keep you. I guess...this is goodbye, Ivy."

"I...love you...Rylan. But do not fear...I'll be seeing you... again... I am...forever watching..."

She breathes her last. The fire races across her face and through her hair.

I watch as she is lifted up with the rising smoke.

Epilogue

Song birds twittered above my head. A soft breeze blew through the trees. Wispy, barely-there clouds hung in the powder-blue sky, and the peaty, warm scent of mud and moss had hovered, like a cloud of perfume, all the way up from the swamp banks.

It was a beautiful day that I opened my eyes to, as the smoke disappeared, the thick fires faded, the rain fell away, and the long flashback ended.

It's been a month since Ivy's death.

I can't remember what immediately happened after Ivy died. Whenever I try, I'm never able to get anything straight. I only see a bunch of discombobulated shards—running feet, numerous tears, firemen, policemen, my family appearing, Aidan, Nadia, and the mob reappearing, flames, shouts, screams, and someone gently pulling me away from the spot where Ivy had been and the barren clearing that was once her home and back to my house.

I ended up staying in bed for who knows how long. Curled up under the covers, crying softly as I tried to get my head around the shock of what happened, I regressed back to my six-year-old self in the days after Mom's death. Everyone mostly left me alone, with only Babette coming in

to drop off meals and homework left by the twins. I felt so sick when I was awake, but sleep was no escape. My dreams were filled with lots of fire and raging storms. Though I saw Ivy in most of them, she was always dead or burning, and I never felt her wonderful presence like in the dreams she sent me.

But in the end, maybe it *was* the nightmares that saved me. Somewhere in my head, I began to think. When Mom died I'd gone into mourning, but not for this long. Dad… Dad had stayed out of sight, mostly in his bedroom. In fact, he never really left his room until it was time for the funeral. And even after that, he was so tired, so vacant, turning into the sad little man I've known for most of my life.

As years went by, I've told myself over and over I wasn't going to be like my father, staying stuck in the past, all gray and mopey. Yet here I was, starting to become just like him. Would I turn into the one person I'd promised myself never to be?

It scared me.

It was hard, telling myself to get out of bed every morning, to go around like everything was fine and whatever. Part of my brain screamed that I couldn't do this, it was too hard, and what was the point anyway? Yet an even louder part of my head bellowed that the point was to live my life, that Ivy wouldn't want this for me. That one thought has kept me going, and as of now I feel somewhat better than I felt weeks ago. Yeah, I'm still incredibly sad. Yeah, the process is going at a snail's pace and it will continue to be slow for some time.

But it's been worth it.

I fingered the stems of the daisy bouquet I was holding as I sat on the front steps, staring at the bracelet—I'll *never* take it off—Ivy gave me so long ago. Today, for the first time, I'm going back to Ivy's clearing. I'm going to make

some type of grave marker, put these flowers there, and talk to her. I'm not going alone. Aidan and Nadia are also coming.

They've been very helpful, but everyone really has been in their own ways. Dad's been surprisingly good, as if my own tragedy has made him slowly start getting over his. Being him, he has no clue as to what exactly happened that night, who that person standing on our roof was, or what Mr. Lebelle was blabbering on and on about. So, true to form, he's chalked the whole situation up to a combination of hallucinations, the storm, and people going crazy. I'm going to let him keep thinking that; since he's finally starting to get over Mom, he doesn't need anything more to deal with. I don't think he'd believe me if I told him the truth anyway.

Babette's been supportive and helpful as ever. But unlike Dad, she has a general gist of what happened a month ago. Whenever the subject's brought up, she gets this little, almost invisible smile like she already knows everything there is to know, including the fact that Ivy was real. Not today, but someday, I'll tell her everything.

As for Aidan and Nadia, I didn't see them until I finally got back to school. Like Babette, they haven't said anything about Ivy, but I can tell that they know she was real. But they've quietly accepted it. They've been at my side ever since, comforting me, trying to get me to laugh, and just being the best friends they are. When I told them what I was planning to do today, they said they were coming, too.

"If she was a friend of yours, than she was a friend of ours," Aidan explained when I'd asked him why. "Besides, you might want some company when you go." Nadia had nodded in agreement.

I don't think I'll ever love those two more than I did then.

My ears picked up the crunch of gravel. Calmly, I watched as Aidan and Nadia biked up the driveway. In the wire basket on Nadia's bike was a small bouquet of purple flowers. Heaving a sigh, I stood up and walked down the steps as they kicked out the kickstands of their bikes.

"Hey," I greeted them.

"Hey."

"Hi, Rylan. You okay?"

I shrugged. "I guess. Today's been a good day. Let's hope it stays that way." I gestured with a lift of my chin. "What are the flowers?"

"Lavender. From Mom's garden," said Nadia. "I meant to go to the flower shop and buy something, but I forgot until this morning."

"It's fine," I replied, but I was only half-listening as I noticed Aidan's expression. He seemed troubled.

"Dude? What's wrong?"

Aidan nervously bit his lip, but he didn't look away. "We…kinda ran into Melanie on the way here."

Oh.

"She saw us, but she pretended like we weren't there," Aidan continued, his voice growing soft. "She got this upset and distant expression on her face. Made me wonder if she regretted what she did…"

I looked off into the trees. Aidan's news didn't affect me that much—I'd seen the very look he was talking about whenever I ran into Melanie at school. The moment she spots me, she gets spooked and veers in the other direction, avoiding and ignoring me when she can. After what went down at the party and the rumors that started after the fire, most of the student body doesn't know what exactly to make of me anymore. But I don't care about the quiet ignorance, as long as I have all the people important to me.

It's quiet partly because Dunstan's gone. While I was stuck in bed, Mr. Lebelle finally got called out for the swamp poisoning and they had the trial. It went by quickly. Dad, of course, stood for our side. Other than nailing Mr. Lebelle with numerous bits of evidence of what he'd been doing, including the video footage I had, Dad also hit him with his antics on the night of Ivy's death. In the end, Mr. Lebelle was found guilty of land damage, corruption, threatening my family, attempted murder, and a bunch of environmental charges. Mr. Lebelle's in the process of being shipped off to prison somewhere, and town hall is currently trying to find a new mayor and a less corrupt council. With his dad staying in jail for a long time, Dunstan moved out to Miami to stay with his mom. From what I've heard, he hates it there and isn't really all that popular anymore.

At last, justice has been served to the both of them. I just wished it could've happened earlier.

I sighed again as I turned back to my friends. "It's okay. I guess if I was to look on the bright side, I finally got Melanie to leave me alone."

We all chuckled. It was weak, but none of it was fake.

Earlier, I'd gotten permission from Babette to take the boat out. None of us said anything as we went down the trail, got into the *Dahlia*, and drove to the drop-off point. But as Aidan tethered the boat to a nearby stump and I got ready to climb out, Nadia reached over and gently brushed my arm, breaking the silence. "Rylan?"

"Yeah?"

"Listen…can I, um, talk to you?"

"Sure."

"Alone?"

I peeked over at Aidan, who went on like he hadn't heard anything. Straightening up after he finished tying the knot,

he said, "I'm gonna go ahead. I just need to go straight, right?"

"Yeah."

"Okay." He nodded to us, his face calm and respectful, and silently walked away.

We were quiet again, lapsing back into the strange silence we were in on the way here. It was odd and uncomfortable, not at all like those quiet times I had with Ivy when we could stay quiet and still feel like we were doing something.

"How've you been?"

Nadia's question was so simple, but the answer was so complicated. I could've said a million and one replies.

"I've been better," I admitted, watching the shore with feigned interest.

"You okay with what we're doing?"

"Even if I wasn't, it's still something that needs to be done."

Nadia nodded, accepting that as an answer. Thinking she was done, I got ready to stand, but Nadia stopped me again.

"Rylan…about that night…"

I visibly winced. I wasn't ready to talk about that just yet.

"I mean…before Ivy came…I was going to tell you something. Something real important."

I closed my eyes.

"A-and I know I shouldn't being telling y-you this at this time," Nadia stuttered, her face turning red as she peered down at her twitching fingers. "But if I don't te-tell you now, I don't think I ever will." With a deep breath, she stared at me straight in the eye and blurted, "Rylan, Ireallyreallylikeyou!"

Her confession echoed in the corners of my brain. I'd been so caught up with trying to get my life back to something resembling normality, I'd completely forgotten about Nadia's crush on me.

I nodded. "I know."

Nadia's cheeks got even redder. "You-you knew?"

"The signs were there," I said, my eyes never leaving Nadia's. "The makeup, the skirt, always staying by my side—there were others, but the point is, I've known for a while."

Nadia quickly looked away, her hand over her mouth as she struggled not to cry. "You knew...and all this time I thought I was being discreet. I'm such a moron!"

"Hey now." I scooted over and gave her a hug. "You're not a moron."

"But I am! Here you are in the middle of mourning, and I just told you about my feelings," she cried into my chest. I felt water leaking through my shirt. "Why didn't you say anything?"

I sigh. "Because if something went wrong, I didn't want to lose your friendship. I've already lost too much. But if I've learned anything from my dad, it's that hiding from your problems never works. I hid from you. I'm sorry."

She only continued to cry, and rightly so. I felt like a jerk.

"It's okay. It's all okay," I murmured, rubbing her back as she silently wept. In my arms, Nadia felt so different from Ivy—smaller, skinnier, but no less warm. It'd been a while since I let someone hug me, so I drank it all in, liking being close to someone again after so long.

Nadia eventually calmed down and she pulled back, her face shiny with tears that she quickly wiped away. She whispered, "Please...give me an answer. Anything at all."

I gave her a little smile.

"Nadia...first, I'm flattered you like me. You're a wonderful girl, and I'm lucky that I met you. You're one of my best friends, my only friends. And since that night with Ivy, you've been amazing. You and your brother have truly been there when I needed you to be."

I sighed. "Maybe if things had stayed normal—if I never got attacked, if I never met Ivy—I may have been able to return your feelings. But now…right now, I need a friend more than a girlfriend to help me get over this."

Nadia didn't look very happy, but she nodded; she understood. "You really liked her, didn't you?"

There was no doubt about my answer.

"Yeah. I did. I still do. And I will for the rest of my life."

Nadia moved back but left a hand on my arm. "We'll be there for you, you know. Aidan and I."

"I know." Reaching up, I placed my hand over hers. "And who knows? Maybe once I'm over this, we'll see where this can go."

Nadia instantly cheered up, her smile as bright as the sun. "Really?"

Before the conversation could continue, there was a loud crash. With an "oomph!" Aidan fell through the trees and landed flat on his face.

"Ow…"

Quickly, the both of us clambered out of the boat and over to him. Nadia shook her head as we stooped over and grabbed Aidan's shoulders, helping him up. "You goof. Why'd you come running back here? You'd better not have been eavesdropping on us!"

Aidan's face said otherwise. He was as pale as a sheet, despite breathing as heavily as if he'd run a million miles.

"Aidan?" Nadia realized that he looked like he was about to puke. "Aidan, what's wrong?"

"I…it…God…" Aidan couldn't get a single sentence out, he was that winded—or scared.

"Words, man. Use words," I told him, worried anticipation jittering under my skin.

Aidan took in a big breath of air and started over, still gasping but managing to spit out coherent bits of sentences.

"I was walking...straight like you said, and...and then I pushed the brush away...and..."

"And what?"

"Everything's new." Aidan's face, which had been regaining some color, went back to the shade of bleached bone as the statement left his mouth. "The grass, the tree... everything looks like it never got burnt. It's all there."

There were a few seconds before this all came together in my head. When it did, I exploded forward.

Nadia calling after me barely registered. My feet hitting the ground, I ran around ashy bushes and burnt logs. Even a month later, new greenery had yet to pop up over the black and gray.

There's no way what Aidan said was true. Life doesn't return to the dead. Something burnt isn't suddenly healed. It's all gone, and the clearing is never going to be the same, even when new grass starts to grow.

So why was I still running?

Up ahead was the clearing; all I had to do was take a few more steps and I'd be there. From where I stood, it seemed like nothing had changed, and the field was still a barren wasteland. The baby buds of new leaves weren't registering.

But Aidan wouldn't lie. So maybe, just maybe...

I pushed the plants away, and entered a world of green.

Ivy's clearing looked as if not a single ember had ever touched it. The grass was back, long, wild, and waving in the breeze as if glad to see me. Scattered across the turf were bright wildflowers in every imaginable color. Fallen logs were coated with fuzzy moss and dotted with ghost orchids. Everything was even brighter and clearer than before, like all the gunk in my eyes had been washed away.

It was beautiful.

"Rylan!" Nadia's shout broke through the tree behind me, but I didn't glance back as the branches shuffled away. "Rylan, what—oh my God…"

Nadia came up next to me, her mouth gaping like a fish. Aidan stood on my other side, exclaiming, "See? It's all normal again!"

He was right. Everything *was* normal again—in a month, the clearing had been restored, something that normally should've taken years to do. To be like this now? It could only be a miracle. Or magic.

"God…" Aidan started pulling on my sleeve. I glanced at him, and he pointed to the tree.

The tree. In all my bewilderment over the clearing, I had forgotten about the tree…that wasn't lying on the ground anymore.

The black gum stood erect and proud, with no sign it had once toppled over. The bark was its healthy light brown with a green mottle, and a curtain of leaves surrounded each fruit-laden branch.

The three of us staggered over, my eyes never leaving the trunk and the overarching branches. I felt my foot hit something soft, and I looked down. The corners of my mouth curled up; it was one of Ivy's treasure sacks. The other was lying not too far away. Both seemed to be untouched and in good condition. I made a mental note to take both home when we left.

"Rylan…"

Hearing Nadia's voice, I straightened up and jogged over to the twins, who were standing in the shadow of the tree. I saw them staring at the green growing on the trunk. As I came closer, it took shape: long, slender, and curling, with numerous heart-shaped leaves. I felt my soul leap inside me.

For Ivy's tree was now hung with her namesake. Jade-green ivy clutched the bark with such strength that, no matter how hard you pulled, it would never let go.

I know I started crying then.

My friends came to my side at once, patting my back and telling me that everything was going to be okay. And though the tears kept coming, I knew they were right. Everything *was* really going to be fine now.

Because here, in front of me, was something I'd been hoping and praying for. I'd been searching for a sign, a signal to give me comfort in Ivy's passing and to tell me she was okay. And at last, here it was, growing all around me.

I'll never see Ivy alive again.

But she's still everywhere. In every drop of bubbling swamp water. In every leaf hanging from every tree. In every speck of swamp mud. In every blade of grass. In every gift she left behind for me: two sacks of miscellaneous objects, a grass bracelet, her home, her love, and my life.

A swamp angel named Ivy lived in my backyard. And now she doesn't.

But wherever she is, I know she's watching me.

Just like the angel she's always been.

Acknowledgements

I never realized how much work actually goes into making a book, and how many people are actually part of the process. And I'm not just talking about the professionals. Both those with "book smarts" and those without all had a helping hand in getting this work done, and now it's time to thank them all.

To my editors, Rich Storrs, Marie Romero, and Kate Kaynak. Your help was invaluable since the very beginning, and I know *Swamp Angel* wouldn't be what it is without all of your help. There'd be a whole lot more grammar mistakes if it wasn't for you. You're amazing people, and I wish you well!

To Lisa Amowitz, who created *Swamp Angel's* beautiful cover. As an artist myself, I know a good piece of cover art when I see it, and you have made a masterpiece.

To everyone at the wonderful Spencer Hill Press. Who would know where this book would be if you all hadn't taken a chance on it? I shiver at the thought. Either way, thank you so much for helping my dream come true.

To my agent, Leticia Gomez, bright as she is bubbly. Thank you for taking an interest in my work, and I hope we can work together for a long time.

To Paul Marasa, Trio Program Writing Coordinator. See what my independent study has become? I couldn't have gotten through editing it the first time without you, and you have my greatest appreciation for all you've done and the skills you've taught me.

For my family: my mom Kathy, my dad Bob, my sisters Allison and Maggie, the Lyons, the Walshs, and Grandma Mulcahy. I could not have done this without each and every one of you by my side and supporting me every step of the way. I love each one of you more than you know, and I'm blessed that you've encouraged me ever since the beginning of this. I love you all!

Finally, to all those who picked up this book and read it. I hope you liked it, and I hope it's touched you in some way, just as all good writing should.

forest
of
whispers

JENNIFER MURGIA

About the Author

Photo by Seth Schwieterman

Colleen Boyd was born in Burwyn, Illinois, and can't always remember that fact. When she's not attending Knox College in Galesburg, Illinois to earn an English degree for Creative Writing, she lives in Overland Park, Kansas, with her mother, father, two sisters (she's the eldest), and Mollie the Schnoodle. This is her first (but definitely not her last) book. You can visit her blog at colleeneboyd.blogspot.com or her Facebook page.